GROSSE POINTE INFERNO

Also by Mark Steel:

Grosse Pointe Pimp

Read where it all began!

GROSSE POINTE INFERNO

Mark Steel

Riveting Publishing
marksteelbooks.com

Copyright ©2005 by Mark Steel

All rights reserved. No part of this book may be reproduced in any form or by any electronic or mechanical means, including information storage and retrieval systems, without permission in writing from the publisher, except by a reviewer who may quote brief passages in a review.

The characters and events in this book are fictitious.
Any similarity to real persons, living or dead,
is coincidental and not intended by the author.
Any name usage is entirely coincidental as well.

ISBN 978-0-974-5806-16

Riveting Publishing
marksteelbooks.com

Cover design by Bruce Worden

Printed in the United States of America

Acknowledgments

I am extremely grateful:

To Erin—You saved the last from disaster and took this one to a higher plane.

To Cyd—For arguing with me and belittling me when I needed it.

To Susan—For your dedication to this project, your sharp eyes, and your willingness to nit-pick until I saw the light.

To Rose—For being so hot.

To Al Fleming—The master photographer.

And to all of you who contacted me with info and insights.

Just because you're paranoid doesn't mean
they're not out to get you.

1

I HAVE ALWAYS REACTED badly when somebody tries to kill me. Revenge, although satisfying, is very time consuming.

~~~~~~~~~~~~~~~~~~~~~~~~~~~

Cocooned inside the black interior of the sleek, dark blue sports car, I rocketed along the Davison Freeway. The freeway sliced through a dilapidated Detroit neighborhood where nobody ventured outside to watch the sun set. In the dimming light my headlights were already on. The Datsun's radio was off. Inside the two-seater's cabin, a throaty exhaust provided the background noise. A low hum and erratic beat added more decibels as hard rubber tires met a pockmarked road. A lunar landscape of concrete passed under my field of vision as I slid between slower moving cars to pick open lanes.

It was 1983 and debris punctuated the crumbling freeway as its grassy, weedy, sloping walls gave up some of their accumulated waste. White paper fast food bags marked every quarter mile—some with their contents spewing like red and yellow intestines—others still bunched up tight and round, rocking gently in the backwash when trucks hurtled past. Cardboard, dried balls of weeds and chunks of truck tire retreads were constantly assessed by each driver as they negotiated the ugly stretch of road at 70 miles an hour. The unending mess was either avoided or carefully passed over as each car and truck bobbed and weaved along the crumbling connector between the Southfield Freeway and I-75.

Vying for attention on the list of noises that accompanied my drive was the 75-mile-per-hour wind that whistled through the window trim of the 280Z. A slight tapping of the overhead cam on the valve stem rockers and the faint whine of meshing gears emitted from beneath the 5-speed's transmission hump, completing the mechanical accompaniment of my solo journey.

Unfortunately for many of the bugs on this warm summer evening, the last thing to go through their mind as they hit my windshield was their intestines. Their remnants dried instantly and I knew from experience that a good soaking from my washer fluid was useless until I stopped moving.

Warm red lights glowed reassuringly from multiple instrument pods embedded in the stolen car's curvaceous dash. I glanced up ahead to an overpass. Two figures stood at the railing in the fading light. As he stood on the walkway of the bridge, the taller of the disadvantaged locals was wearing a white T-shirt and dark wraparound sunglasses—he reminded me of a ghetto Lone Ranger. His Tonto was wearing an orange warm-up jacket and a black bandana.

As I tapped on the brake with my right foot to avoid a slowing semi-truck, my left leg tensed in case it needed to hit the clutch. The muscles in each leg felt hard and ready for another series of runs tonight. At 6-foot and 185-pounds, I had been training my 26-year-old physique as though it belonged to a cruiserweight boxer. Weightlifting, push-ups and chin-ups by day filled a chunk of my afternoons. Windsprints, ab work and long sessions on both the heavy and speed bag occupied three of my evenings every week. Until recently, a hellacious work schedule had precluded setting aside more than two or three hours a week for any Rocky Balboa-type of activities. A recent business development, however, had now afforded me the luxury of moving away from Detroit to the suburbs and gave me plenty of time for hours of intense, boot-camp-like physical training.

Although I had never allowed myself to lapse far from the

muscular condition of my late teenage years, my body responded with the exuberance of an artillery shell, exploding with energy after years of lying ready. Seldom did I pause to dissect what it was that fueled this training passion. The underlying impetus was most certainly frustration, of course. The workouts were an outlet for the frustration and impatience that a young man feels when his career has gone awry and his marriage is on the rocks. It was also possible that the motivation came from a deeper source, drawn from the youth of a shy and skinny boy whose only defense against the taunts and jousts of schoolyard bullies had been a sense of humor or outright avoidance. Every workout of late had become a test. Every test was to ascertain if the body could be pushed yet again past a limit. But the muscles, lungs and heart showed a willingness—even an enthusiasm—to goad themselves through ever more taxing performances. The bodyfat, sparse even at the onset, continued to vanish until tanned skin stretched over conditioned sinew. The pre-ulcerous stomach was a distant memory…the haggard, trance-like state of mind from months of sleep deprivation replaced once again by crisp signals from the brain to the muscles.

 A quick glance in the passenger door mirror revealed a 30-foot gap in the next lane. With a slight twitch of the muscles in my right arm, the steering responded and the car leaped over the dividing line to claim the gap. As the vehicle accelerated to 80, the engine roared slightly and the sports car began to find its element.

 While the Datsun rushed horizontally across the concrete, a cantaloupe-sized object began its vertical descent. Its initial release wasn't observed by anyone—at first.

 The Lone Ranger's breath smelled of alcohol and PCP still controlled large sections of his brain. A quarter of a second later, his laughing companion witnessed the concrete meteor's send-off and a felonious smile began to distort his bottom jaw. Falling slowly in the beginning, its velocity grew as gravity sucked it down to earth. The irregularly shaped 10-pound block of hardened gravel and limestone reached 40 mph by the time it smashed into the hood of the 280Z. Aided by a latent springiness in the now massively dented sheet of metal, the object bounced up to smash itself into the windshield of the speeding blue car.

Sprawled across two blocks of prime lakefront real estate in prim and proper Grosse Pointe, the War Memorial is frequently the social center of the monied neighborhood. It is a former estate that used to epitomize the symbols of wealth and extravagance that could be obtained near the epicenter of Detroit's lucrative automobile industry. Donated by the Alger family after World War II, the Grosse Pointe War Memorial is a sprawling collection of stone and marble buildings. The buildings are set sufficiently far back from Lake St. Clair to provide enough acreage for carefully manicured landscaping and a spotless concrete promenade.

The complex is closely watched over by a board of trustees that give selflessly of their time and talents to ensure that long standing traditions, decorum, and rules are met in the leasing of the various ballrooms and anterooms. Much more than just a self-sustaining entity, the War Memorial is the cultural center of the Pointes as it hosts 2,000 events per year. Theatre, dance, music and science are all nurtured through its many scheduled events.

Although not supported by community tax dollars, the War Memorial breathes life and social function into a sometimes aloof community.

2

My world inside the cocoon exploded as shards of safety glass showered my arms and face. The car shuddered involuntarily at the unexpected violation of its space on the freeway.

Instinctively my foot came off of the accelerator pedal but only hovered over the brake as I strove to see ahead through the overlapping spider webs that blurred my forward vision. Peripherally it was a different story. The weeds and garbage of the grassy slope maintained a steady distance through the unblemished passenger side window as my right hand froze the steering wheel—and the car—in a straight line.

I should have been in shock but I was not. Fear would have been an understandable byproduct of the moment…but I felt none. What I did feel was anger. The anger began to permeate my gut until it spread up into my chest and head. With the anger came an old familiar tunnel vision that started to blur the weeds rushing by the corner of my right eye, but by then I was in the far right lane and braking slowly. Cars rode up to my rear bumper briefly, but then careened into gaps in the traffic on our left and roared around my stricken sports car.

Adrenaline propelled my blood pressure upward as my racing heart clued me in on what I was about to do. I knew I would need some luck. A building rage inside me blocked out most reason as I twisted my body to peer through the rear glass hatch at the bridge one-half mile back. The Lone Ranger and Tonto could not resist viewing the results of their handiwork. They had watched their projectile find a mark and, like hungry coyotes drawn to a sick animal, had crossed to the other side of the bridge to view the carnage. Even though I was stopped one-half mile away, they had crossed to my side and now stood transfixed. Their mistake would improve my chances to 25/75. Now I would know which side of the freeway they would choose to flee to. With my jaw clenched nearly hard enough to crack a molar, I slammed the clutch down and wrenched the stick shift into reverse. The engine revved and howled and the rear tires protested as I dumped the clutch and smashed down on the gas pedal. Like a wounded animal in full retreat, the Datsun charged backwards toward the abutment. The top speed of the car in reverse was probably 40 miles an hour and together the disfigured beast and I found every bit of those 40. Shoulder debris clunked and thumped on the floorpan of the low slung car as it clawed its way back to the scene of impact. I *should* only have been looking at the shoulder behind me—but I needed to keep one eye on the bridge as well.

Pitching violently as we ran over refuse, the stolen car and I closed the gap. One hundred feet at first, then five hundred, we soon covered a quarter mile, with my quarry still in my sights and gawking—before realization struck them. There would be no crash to witness…they were *not going* to watch the pointy snout of the sports car jam itself into the sloped side of the road. Nor would they witness an unconscious or panicking driver veer the car up the steep embankment—only to have it flip and roll back down to the roadway. There would be no sound of ambulances in the distance…yet.

The drug-addled pair then made their second mistake. In full escape mode, but without a single complete thought between the both of them, they darted off of the bridge. They ran to my side of the freeway. My chances had now increased to 50/50.

In another eight seconds the Datsun was within 100 yards of the bridge and I had to make a choice of my own. I needed to guess whether the pair had run toward my car and into the surrounding neighborhood…or away. If the former were the case I needed to stop immediately. Through storm clouds of anger I decided that they wouldn't linger along the service drive unless they were armed. If they *were* carrying guns, my trump card lie in the fact that they didn't know anything about me and didn't even know if their random murder attempt was against a lone victim. Their rapid bridge exit said that they were bound for the sanctity of the surrounding slums—undoubtedly laughing hard enough to slow down their progress in spite of the thrill of a possible chase.

    Calculating that the most direct route was the surest bet, I slammed down on the brakes and the car ground to a halt nearly under the bridge. Without even shifting back to neutral, I snatched the keys from the ignition and, in one continuous motion, bolted out of the car and slammed the door. Darting around the front of the stricken car, my tennis shoes scrabbled for traction on the gravel-strewn shoulder as I built up speed before lunging at the weedy slope. My initial thrust brought me halfway up before I needed to hunch over and further assist my ascent by grabbing the thicker weeds in my hands. After not running for two days, the quads in my legs felt very strong, surging with a reserve of power that seemed deep and inexhaustible.

    Carefully glancing down so as not to mistake the tails of any large rats for a weed stalk, I reached the top of the slope in one more bound and placed a hand on the low fence. With a leap I was up and over…loose in the territory of my prey.

    Luck shined on me early and brightly as I paused to peer into the neighborhood. The Lone Ranger, with his dirty white T-shirt in need of a seamstress and his black shades now slightly askew, was being chased down the driveway of the first house that I saw. A huge woman, young enough to still be agile—but with torpedo-like mammaries and tree trunk-like legs stretching out her purple elastic pants—was yelling at top volume. She was swinging an iron rake as though trying out for the Yankees as she stampeded after the Ranger. He had foolishly tried to hide in her backyard or garage only to have incited the now enraged buffalo into protecting her herd.

    Every muscle was tense as I waited for the strange scene to play out. No other neighbors were outside to gawk. I was the only one that could even be remotely identified as a passerby. I was about 100 yards away. My nighttime sprints had yielded a "40-yard dash" time of slightly under five seconds on smooth asphalt. For a young man of average weight, the Ranger didn't seem to move very quickly. Although the terrain involved one corner lawn and a curb or two, I determined that I could be on him in about 11 seconds. Unfortunately, that meant that the buffalo would to be a witness to any mayhem. With his tormenter still yelling behind him but steadily losing ground, the Ranger jogged slowly down the street. A decision needed to be made. I couldn't be this close and lose sight of him now. I waited. Lowering her rake, the buffalo turned around to amble back up her driveway, presumably to return to foraging off a barbecue grill. I began to jog toward her, on tiptoes at first and then picking up the pace as she filled the gap between two houses. She never turned around as I came up on my toes again to break into a full sprint and flashed past her. My target was eight small houses down. I flew past the eight houses and had closed the gap to two more. My arms pumped and my shoulders felt tight and ready. I caught up to my target as he stopped jogging and began to walk past a telephone pole between the sidewalk and the street. Angling out to his right slightly, I suddenly cut in at full speed, both arms ready. He never saw it coming. My left hand grasped at the fabric of his left sleeve as I got my hand around his upper arm. My right hand found the back of his head as I crashed into my victim at top speed, my momentum propelling us into the coarse telephone pole. My own abrupt halt was cushioned by the Ranger's forehead and body as he impacted into the unyielding pole.

3

STORIES STILL ABOUND about the elitist social scene that swirled around the ballrooms of the War Memorial in the 1950s, '60s, and '70s. In an era bereft of cholesterol lowering medications and arterial stents, hard charging executives, entrepreneurs, and other barons of industry were dropping dead of heart attacks without warning. Stress and other diet-induced coronary problems, coupled with strokes and cancers, claimed husbands at an alarming rate. These overachievers were leaving sizeable estates to their widows…who had little prospect of a future mate of a comparable social status. Certain stigmas, while whispered but never voiced to one's face, were still attached to the widow that continued to venture unescorted. The same events and soirees that she had readily attended with her now-deceased husband in the past could be a source of discomfort if attempted after she was alone. In addition, the early demise of her loved one (once the shock and mourning were over), did not necessarily coincide with a sudden lack of sexual desire. If anything, the ritual of the children starting college—or families and households of their own—left the nouveau-widow with more free time than ever for herself. With no husband to dote on and serve while attending to every drycleaning and home beautification need, this still-desirable woman soon found herself shut out of his former company's gatherings as well as those of her sympathetic (but still wed) social acquaintances. To date men from a lower social caste was fraught with complications, however. Unless receptive to efforts made by the widow to school them in some of the rudimentary social graces, rubes from the bottom of the hierarchy stuck out at see-and-be-seen events like O.J. Simpson at a Parents Without Partners meeting.

Even today, one of the favorite topics is about Marina Buick's husband, Moe, the ex-carpenter. Much more that just another Grosse Pointe heiress, this capable and accomplished auto executive has shown an incredible knack for troubleshooting one division after another. After a division is painstakingly rehabilitated and placed once again on the road to productivity and profitability, Marina moves on to another.

Their eyes locked on each other years ago, while Moe was remodeling a section of her mansion. Their sometimes tumultuous marriage has produced offspring, though, and until recently boasted of a 24-hour security staff that protects the heiress/executive from dangers from both outside and inside her estate. She continues to receive well-deserved write-ups in the business section of *The Detroit News* as well as inter-company laudations.

But these inter-caste unions were discouraged in the aforementioned era, so thus arose a need in the Pointes for acceptable male escorts. Often well-schooled, always well-mannered but with an inherent aversion to any work that required arising from bed early, these well-groomed younger men filled pressing needs in more ways than one.

While they were often presented at gatherings as "a friend of the family" or a relative or business acquaintance of some sort, the truth was often supposed correctly but suppressed for reasons of propriety and respect. The Grosse Pointe gigolo's compensation for hanging on the widow's every word and trying his utmost to charm her social peers was, at the least, a free meal and the occasional gift of appreciation. At most, outright monetary compensation was rendered after a series of manipulations and negotiations. All the while, the ambitious gigolo pondered ways to turn his social and sexual offerings into permanent compensation through a gift of real estate or inclusion in the will. And the widow tried to convince herself and her closest friends that the relationship could work in perpetuity in spite of the difference in their years—because he really loved and adored her for the mature, stable woman that she was and for the lusting sexual being that she had recently rediscovered in herself.

~~~~~~~~~~~~~~~~~~~~~~~~~~

    I bounced back two feet and stood watching. The Ranger was in a coma before he hit the dirt. Blood gushed from a wound in his forehead as he lay crumpled on his side. I briefly considered whether to use my belt as a tourniquet around his neck to stem the flow from the cut—but decided against it.

    Feeling terrific from the warm up run as I loped off, I began to calculate how much time I had before the arrival of a Detroit Police Officer. In the fading light, with no immediate witnesses, it would take a resident at least five minutes to discover and report the Lone Ranger as he lie where I'd left him. The response time would be at least ten minutes. Although I'd be out of the immediate area in another 30 seconds, patrol cars may be in the vicinity within 15 minutes. To be safe, I had seven and a half minutes. While this was more than ample time to jog back down to my car and limp it away, it left me with very little time to find Tonto.

    Trying to feel past the adrenaline rush of revenge, I performed a quick physical evaluation. Since the Ranger never saw his retribution coming, I had no cuts, swellings or abrasions to deal with. The recovery period from my quick sprint involved ten deep breaths followed by 20 shallower ones that left me breathing normally. I casually walked away from the scene of the Ranger's mishap. The blood in my upper body coursed through my chest and shoulders and my arms felt thoroughly warmed up and ready. The leg, calf, and glute muscles that had been twitching for a workout felt warmed up, engorged, and ready for another hour of intense use if necessary.

4

I FIRST MET LEE PANTELY when his then-girlfriend, Mary, brought her MGB into a repair garage that I owned for some routine maintenance. Mary was 5-foot 9-inches tall with long dark hair and a model's perfect features and jawline. If Sophia Loren and Elizabeth Hurley (provided Liz were of Italian heritage) had somehow managed to meld the best features of their DNA, the result would have been Mary. She had a *Cosmopolitan* magazine physique sculpted by years of aerobics and resistance training that could not be obscured by the business outfit she wore that day. Mary was without question one of the five most beautiful women I had ever seen in person and while she was probably aware of it, her demeanor was nevertheless more unassuming than conceited. I would have been hard pressed to think of a male counterpart with the ability to rival her physical beauty until a black BMW pulled up behind her…and Lee stepped out.

Lee had jet black hair casually combed back in layers. Piercing blue eyes, set amongst his other amazingly symmetrical facial features, vied for attention with a dazzling white smile that showed rows of perfect teeth. His Greek heritage was evident not only in his dark good looks but in his confident, practiced swagger.

The son of a native Greek Grosse Pointe real estate businessman, Lee's carefully assembled, weight-trained physique and minuscule, 29-inch waist on a 5-foot 11½-inch frame would have looked spectacular in any business suit had he chosen to work for his father's company.

Lee had three passions in his life. The first was his music.

Besides having received more trips to the GQ gene pool than any one man should ever be allowed, Lee cultivated his prodigious musical talents in a band that commanded top fees for weddings and parties throughout the Detroit area. With a brother that had been assigned a chair in the Detroit Symphony Orchestra at a tender age, Lee's versatility on keyboards, guitar, trumpet and drums did not come as a great surprise. But Lee also sang like an angel, showing a far greater vocal range than the casual listener might have expected. He could belt out the high notes like a diva or croon like Dean Martin. While able to deftly mimic any song requested, Lee had written a substantial repertoire of original music as well.

Lee's second passion was his modeling career. Making it in the modeling business in Detroit is harder than signing up taxidermists for a PETA meeting because most of the print and TV ads are done out of New York or Los Angeles—where the competition to model was fierce. Local car dealerships or appliance stores that used a hometown celebrity in their ads required that you first become a celebrity. Some of the Detroit Tigers, Detroit Lions, and a couple of washed up newscasters made extra money this way. I once thought I saw a Detroit Red Wing doing a poly-grip commercial but I can't be sure. Tim Allen once did some ads for Big Boy restaurants long before national fame struck. Usually, however, the owner of the dealership, appliance store, or "upscale" furniture store would be loathe to pay homegrown talent when he could clear his throat and try it himself. The results usually made the viewer rather uncomfortable, as if watching Siamese twins do an ad for Doublemint Gum.

Lee persevered, however, and in the ensuing years after we met I would often open the front section of *The Detroit News* to a grinning Lee in a suit from Hudsons or a serious Lee with his movie star physique in a pair of Jockey underwear.

Our meeting at my repair garage occurred after I had finished writing up Mary for a tune-up and oil change. I smelled gasoline. Not wanting to appear on the eleven o'clock news as "Mark, The Human Torch," I prudently and cautiously circled around Mary's

MGB and peeked underneath. There were no puddles. I looked back to Lee's BMW, where he stood impatiently checking his Rolex and conferring with Mary. A thin stream of gasoline flowed out from under a rear tire. Assuming an "Allah is Great" position, I got down below the rear bumper of Lee's car. The stream emanated from a pinhole leak in the valley of a dent in the 318i's gas tank. I politely interrupted and pointed out the situation.

Lee responded, "You know, I felt a clunk on the freeway last week and ever since then I've been getting terrible gas mileage."

It immediately became obvious to me that this perfectly-groomed Adonis—and early-1980s prototype of the modern day metrosexual male—was also the most mechanically naïve man in the Motor City. The possibility also existed, however, that Lee knew deep down that his little BMW should be getting more than two miles to the gallon but had been too busy to have it checked. It may also have been that his overriding devotion to Mary and the well-being of her transportation was more important than his own car's gas economy.

For Lee's third passion in life was his Maria. To see them standing together in a live embodiment of what male and female perfection ought to be, was breathtaking. Watching them walking together in even an ordinary setting was to watch every happy ending in every romantic movie at one time. Although public displays of affection from the two were rare, watching Lee's intense blue eyes search out Mary's smoldering dark ones was all the evidence of their infatuation that was necessary.

I sometimes imagined their private discussions and even arguments as his hot Greek blood boiled and cooled and Mary's even hotter Italian lava seared and then soothed as her emotions bubbled to the surface. I often wondered whether Mary openly fumed at the waves of young ladies that fawned and gaped at Lee until finally throwing themselves bodily at him in panic and desperation. I also wondered if Mary ever observed and resented that even a smile or glance from Lee could tear a woman away from her partner and send her tripping across the room to bask in his aura and charisma.

Ultimately, however, Lee's devotion to his beautiful, haughty, raven-haired soul mate always prevailed. He even had a special way of calling out to his Maria, rolling the "r" in her name ever so slightly, emphasizing it just enough until it nearly sounded like the letter "d."

~~~~~~~~~~~~~~~~~~~~~~~~

I love Dobermans and have owned and trained several over the years as both pets and my personal bodyguards. In between them, however, I owned a German Shepherd named Alex. Alex was an 80-pound furball that divided his time between the kitchen floor and the fenced-in backyard of my house. Alex was as randy and adventurous as any two-year-old male dog on earth. Unfortunately, he was also the reincarnation of Harry Houdini. Alex's favorite exit strategy was to dig a hole under the back fence early in the morning while I still slept. With a quick squeeze and a little shimmy on the other side, Alex was free to roam the neighborhood. He would run off in search of a receptive female companion and reconnoiter her yard, looking for a way in…in more ways than one. One of the major flaws in Alex's romantic plan was that my next door neighbor's dog was a stoolie. The poodle would rat out the escape artist with a tirade of furious barking that eventually awoke me. Pulling on shorts and tennis shoes, I would stagger out of my back gate into the surrounding suburbia. I soon learned to track Alex's position by sound. I would listen for dogs barking, no matter how faintly, and head toward the noise. As I jogged past yard and gate, other wolf ancestors would lunge and snarl, offended at my intrusion of their area. A casual listener on my back porch also would have been thus able to track my movements in the early light as I searched for my unleashed lothario. But what should have been an hour or more of hunting for my dog was consequently reduced to an average of six minutes. I had Alex neutered two hours after his fifth escape.

5

STILL FURIOUS AT my near-death experience on the freeway, I slowed my pace to a tiptoe. A quick glance back at the slumped form of the Ranger showed him still taking a time out. The distant sound of the freeway's traffic echoed out of the grass and concrete ditch. I listened carefully, but not for cars or trucks. I wanted to apply the lesson that Alex had taught me two years ago. Then I heard it. Once, twice rapidly, then came a whole series with what sounded like a second joining in. The barking sounded close. It might be on the next block to the east. It might be two blocks at most. I brushed my fingers over the pant pocket that held my little .25 caliber Beretta. It was still snug and deep at the bottom of the pocket. It was time to hunt again. I homed in on a position and broke into a trot. The barking was off to my left and about ten houses ahead. I decided it was also in fact two blocks over. But hopping fences and cutting through yards might attract unwanted attention. I picked up the pace on the sidewalk and reached a cross street. Staying on the now undulating sidewalk, I wheeled left. Another canine chorus ahead indicated that I was still on the right track. The second barking salvo also hinted that my quarry might be moving farther away from the freeway. I wanted to be closer to the Ranger's accomplice before the shadows that had been crossing the street began to blend into twilight. I maintained a steady pace and focused on avoiding heaved portions of sidewalk in a neighborhood that looked ever more decrepit in the gloom. An older car coming from the other direction passed me without slowing down. As soon as the exhaust note subsided I arrived at the next junction. This was the second block. Nobody appeared on the streets or walks. A howling hound alerted somewhere to my right. I cut hard and darted across the street and down block number two. My baying guide sounded off again as I neared the end of the street. I was getting close. The fuss came from a backyard of the street to my left. I reached the end of my street and spun left. The two small yards went by quickly. I slowed a little as the sidewalk's end neared and looked to my left. Staring back at me was Tonto! He wasn't grinning the way he had on the bridge but the orange shirt and black bandana were undeniable. His reactions were quicker than his cohort's and he turned, ran across the street, and up the nearest remnant of a driveway. The houses on either side were abandoned and Tonto sped up to them while I kicked my pace up to three-quarters. Rapidly negotiating the rocky rubble of the driveway, I could see that I was gaining on Tonto and might have my first chance soon if he tried to climb the rickety wooden fence ahead. He scurried into the backyard and checked his options, concentrating on looking for a gap in the fence—finding none—he suddenly stopped and wheeled around, a shiny knife blade flashing in his right hand. *Dumbass brought a knife to a gunfight*, I thought, but decided against reaching into my jeans' pocket yet. Amongst the refuse strewn around the backyard was an old wooden milk crate. It was empty. I broke stride, scooped it up with my right hand, and holding it in both hands accelerated again toward Tonto. The aspiring murderer looked puzzled as he held the large blade out slightly from his side. Tonto was at least six feet tall with long arms. He might have tried to reason with me, but I probably was incapable of listening. He had pieced together where I had come from—and he knew why. I was eight feet away. I held the milk crate in my outstretched arms, took a deep breath, and gripped tightly as I lunged. Tonto attempted to stab around the milk crate at my wrist. I flicked the crate to the left and the knife clacked on the wood. Lowering my right shoulder, I drove into his chest and lifted him cleanly off his feet. I prepared for a stabbing pain to my left as we crashed into the back fence. It never came. Tonto grunted loudly as he cushioned me from hitting the fence. Still in full contact with each other, we both landed on our feet as I dropped the crate. He seemed wobbly and started to crouch defensively, I swung my right elbow up into his jaw and followed through until his head snapped to the right. He started to flail at me with bony fists and it almost felt good as one bounced off of my skull. The knife had disappeared and I began to crash my right fist through his pathetic defense. It took four tries to drop him. His arms encircled his head as he lay. I felt his ribs buckle with my kick. Exhaling with a whoosh, Tonto stopped moving.

Pausing to take a couple of deep breaths, I felt something wet and warm on my outer right hand. Puppy dog noses were probably rare in this neighborhood so my second best guess was blood. Tonto was lying in darkness so I was unable to determine if he had all of his blood. Prior to tracking down my assailants, the Gods of Luck had not been smiling on me much. It was probably my blood. I spun on my right foot and jogged out of the yard and down the driveway. I knew from past experience that I was a world-class clotter. There was a doctor at a walk-in industrial clinic near my home that did beautiful stitchwork. It would require a magnifying glass to critique some of his previous work around my right eye and I resolved to insist on being repaired only by him. I slowed my pace under a streetlight and glanced down at my hand. Already the dripping was minimal, and in that brief assessment I decided that I was only slated for six or seven stitches in total. I could open the hand completely as well, which was a positive sign regarding lack of tendon damage.

To a resident of this particular neighborhood, the probability of a person of my particular ethnicity being out for a casual jog was slight, but a sprint might attract even more eyes. In Detroit, "Neighborhood Watch" signs were sprouting up quickly in the absence of regular police patrols. So far, I hadn't felt any neighbors watching me and my overall impression was that this immediate neighborhood was too poor to even afford the sign. I arrived at the freeway retaining fence unchallenged and hopped over to scramble down the embankment toward my damaged sports car. I was mildly surprised to find that the AM/FM cassette could still be listed as one of the unlocked auto's accessories. During my mad rush for retribution, it had crossed my mind that the shiny aluminum wheels of the unattended car would serve as a beacon for every thug in a ghetto-cruiser that passed by. A believer in omens would make a case that my luck had shifted the moment I began to change the health status of the two men who had tried to kill me. A policeman would have maintained that I should have called the police from the nearest pay phone and let them handle it. A psychologist would have doubtlessly encouraged me to drive directly to his office to begin dealing with some possible anger management issues. Instead, I soon found myself explaining to a skeptical physician how dangerous opening a can of dog food could be.

~~~~~~~~~~~~~~~~~~~~~~~~~~~~

With his athletic reflexes and carefully-honed ability to assess traffic conditions, Lee Pantely was an excellent driver. Unfortunately, many traffic cops in the Detroit area did not agree. As a result, Lee's driver's license was in constant jeopardy of being taken away by the State of Michigan. With only 12 points allotted over a two-year period, the influx of special driving awards (and the points assigned to each) that Lee received —from the police officers that could catch him—were a continuing source of concern. Printouts of Lee's record were regularly mailed to his home and the month's current crisis could be quickly ascertained by the thickness of the envelope. Lee's yearly insurance premium would have made a nice down payment on a new Corvette—and his fines supported several local district courts.

After my mechanics successfully repaired Lee's gas tank, I became his repair facility of choice. His brake and clutch jobs alone paid my electric bills. Shortly after this relationship began, Lee hit on the idea of bringing his mechanic with him to traffic court as an expert witness. My role was to patiently explain to the judge that the wrong size replacement tires on Lee's car had thrown off his speedometer so that, try as he might to abide by the law, he was misled into breaking it. Occasionally the strategy worked. Just as often it did not.

On one beautiful July morning Lee and I were sitting in a packed Grosse Pointe courtroom. The sparkling complex of newer construction was situated right on Mack Avenue in Grosse Pointe Woods, the most populous of the five boroughs that comprised Grosse Pointe. Mack Avenue almost succeeded in dividing the Woods and the Farms from the insidiousness of the adjoining Detroit neighborhoods. The gleaming municipal complex stood as a bastion of lawfulness and community activism, and this bastion and the bastionards in it needed to generate some money that day.

Although this day was my first ever in any of The Pointes, it was certainly not my first in a courtroom. At my urging, we had arrived early and procured front row seats. Fifteen minutes later I looked around and the courtroom was packed, with defendants that had arrived in a *timely* manner standing along the walls.

The female judge looked as though she were not only suffering from PMS but had caught her husband cheating with her best friend the night before. The large room was warm, presumably because the air-conditioning hadn't been turned up yet. The warmth may have emanated, however, from the anteroom that, according to legend, housed the electric chair used to fry violators of local city ordinances in the strict community. A barking dog, it was rumored, was worth a $200.00 fine and a three-second jolt—while more serious offenders were allowed to meet with a priest before their sentence was imposed.

The good citizens twitched and fidgeted as they were called up one by one. The judge's wrath smote any and all. Those that pled guilty and threw themselves upon the mercy of the court, soon found that the court *had no mercy that day!* They were quickly sent off, trembling and quivering, to apply for loans to satisfy their fines.

The hanging judge had meted out justice to ten hapless drivers in a row—until Lee's glances to me were those of a condemned man. Since Lee's point total was at least 14 that day and his driving privileges were on the absolute verge of being revoked within hours, we stood fast. I mentally rehearsed my spiel. I knew it would be futile today but told myself that it would serve as a rehearsal for the next time. Lee's name was called. Confident on the outside, but with tails secretly tucked between our legs, we took our places at the defendants' table…*the table of the damned.*

Sneering, the judge looked down from her bench to ask Lee how he pled. In a clear voice, Lee said, "Not guilty, Your Honor."

As she grimaced to contain her annoyance, the judge was unexpectedly interrupted. It was the prosecutor. "Your Honor, this was written by Officer Fife and he is not able to be here today. His presence was required at a very serious traffic accident on Lochmoor last night. Due to the last minute notification The People would be willing to try this on the first available date next week."

The judge casually turned in her seat to face Lee. She looked down and raised her eyebrows slightly. She wasn't acting surprised at the development. She looked expectant…and she was overacting!

Lee's eyes widened. For possibly the first time in his life his confidence wavered. His dark eyebrows furrowed.

"Is next week okay with you, Mr. Pantely?"

The bright light of understanding illuminated every corner of my brain. The many hours I'd spent in courtrooms as "Defendant" now bore fruit. I was able to see right through the tango being performed by the judge and prosecutor. I could see right down to the dance floor. Lee had been doing 25 over. This ticket meant big revenue, and *this* Judge would make certain that my friend's driver's license was just a fond memory as well. The music however, had stopped playing and the Judge knew it, but I knew that Lee did *not* want to accept an invitation back to another dance!

I leaned over to Lee, "No!" I whisper/yelled, "You do *not* want a court date next week! The cop didn't show! He's the only witness! They have to dismiss it if you ask! They know that! Lee, you gotta ask!" Lee's eyes got wider. His eyebrows flew up. His panicked look said *you sonofabitch, you'd better be right.*

The judge glared down at me as I advised my friend. Spitting out the words, she demanded, "Mr. Pantely, who is this man with you?"

The courtroom was silent. The florescent lights stopped humming in order to listen. Other watching defendants paused in their sweating, lest the sound of droplets hitting the floor cause them to miss a single word.

Lee made his decision. His confidence came back in a rush as he squared his shoulders. With it he regained his "radio-voice" and all of the charisma and eloquence that had charmed 100,000 wedding guests.

"Your Honor, this man is my expert witness. He owns a repair garage and a used car lot. He is a state-certified master mechanic and he employs six other master mechanics. I took time off from work today and came at the date and time specified prepared for a trial. May we please try the case this morning?"

The only sound was that of the blood rushing to the Judge's face as she reddened. She began to swallow hard as bile from her stomach erupted into her throat. Air whistled through her nostrils. Her lack of choices was causing her great pain. The prosecutor's face was blank. The pause seemed interminable. Finally, with great effort, "Mr. Pantely, I strongly suggest that you pay a lot more attention to your driving. I am dismissing this case."

Pandemonium ensued as the spectators went ballistic. Sporadic applause broke out and rippled around the room. Quiet cheering punctuated by "Alright" and "Yes sir!" left lips parted by wide smiles.

Lee thanked the Judge and he and I battled to suppress grins as we realized what had just happened. Turning to go, we shook the outstretched hands proffered to us from the front row and along our exit path. I felt the joy and renewed hope of 110 people enter my soul in the 15 seconds it took to pick our way to the back door.

A casual observer in the parking lot would have seen two men in their mid-20s tuck briefcases under their arms and skip and prance to a black BMW. Once in the car, our whoops and hollers rattled the windows. The sheer joy and energy that rushed out of us almost started the car's engine. My career as a jailhouse lawyer had peaked 26 years after I was born.

6

IT WAS EARLY in the spring of 1942 and the surgeon was just returning from a four-month tour of 18-hour days at Pearl Harbor. He had seen trauma of this nature before—and recently—but never on a ten-year-old girl. After a marathon 12-hour procedure, the experienced army captain had repaired her uterus, her liver, one kidney, and stitched together her bowels before replacing them back into her abdominal cavity. Although her recovery, due to her young age, was quite rapid, there was an initial concern about lingering disfigurement. The young girl, however, had a very resilient epidermal layer and the youthful captain, who would go on to become one of California's pioneering plastic surgeons, felt as though his hands were guided by an angel that day. His fine stitching was evident for only a year as the rapidly-growing Annie healed. By her teenage years even the light pink streak from her mid stomach to well below her navel had nearly disappeared.

Her childhood "accident" would, of course, leave her barren. The horrible fact that it had occurred while Annie was in her drunken father's care prompted the police to take him into custody immediately. When the investigation revealed that Annie's mother had not been seen for two days, her father was denied bail.

An aunt was summoned to the hospital. Aunt Louise had three children of her own but quickly assured the court-appointed guardian that there was "always room for one more." The surgeon spoke at length with the good aunt about everything from post-op care to the unlikelihood of Annie ever bearing children.

During Annie's two-week hospital stay Aunt Louise was repeatedly assured by the surgeon that Annie, while still in possession of all of her original plumbing, had suffered far too much trauma to expect it to be in the proper working order in adulthood. It would thus come as a surprise eight years hence when Annie became pregnant.

Only then would Aunt Louise stop her gentle, continual reminders that for Annie, starting a family would be out of the question. But for eight years Aunt Louise provided a loving household for Annie, with her workaholic husband putting in long hours at his Los Angeles grocery business. Although the good-hearted aunt spread her time equally between her four charges, she felt the shame from what her drunken brother had done to her niece. Her heart ached for the girl as the years went by with still no communication from Annie's mother. Louise's resolve to protect the girl from her past deepened in the year preceding her brother's release from prison. But when Annie turned 12, her "rehabilitated" father repeatedly sought to visit the girl anyway—until an older neighbor man—an ex-Marine—intervened. The neighbor came quickly to the rescue each time that Annie's father, sotted and rampaging, banged at the front door of Louise's home while the woman and girls cowered inside. The old military man would gallantly and rapidly defuse the onslaught with submission holds and short chopping blows. The interventions often left Annie's father either holding an arm or bleeding from the nose and mouth as he staggered to his car before the police could arrive.

Three of these confrontations occurred over two weeks until one afternoon the ex-Marine went out to the hardware store—and never returned.

After an initial contact by the investigating detective, Annie's father pledged to come down to the police station the following morning to answer any and all questions. He never did. Years later one of Annie's "sisters" would claim that she had seen the father at a theme park in Florida. Annie herself never saw her father again other than to be inexplicably haunted by composite newspaper images projected nationwide in connection with a man in Louisiana that was wanted for a series of murders.

The pastor at Aunt Louise's church preached that no sinner was beyond redemption, but Louise found some comfort nonetheless in Annie's barrenness. Whether Annie's father was a bad seed or merely a misunderstood man given an unfair shake would be determined by a higher power in the afterlife. The important thing was that Louise's natural children did not seem to exhibit any sociopathic tendencies and that Annie's inability to further the strain of her father's mutated DNA was a blessing in disguise.

Annie's teenage years were quiet and routine in Southern California during the 1940s. At 16 her family moved to San Diego, where she was hired to work at a small pawnshop. Two uneventful years went by until Jack swaggered in. The plain, shy young woman was mesmerized by the tall, angular sailor in his slightly unkempt uniform. After pawning several watches and two gold rings, the naval man turned his attentions to a fawning Annie behind the counter. Regaling her with his exploits at sea, Jack neglected to mention that his enlistment had been strongly encouraged by a county judge back in Iowa. With his sailor's beret rakishly cocked to the right, Jack entranced the impressionable Annie with his lofty plans to make commander aboard his aircraft carrier, and after an early retirement, to captain a huge cruise ship through exotic locations. As he romanced Annie with dinner at a local restaurant, he failed to mention that the bill would be covered with ill-gotten funds. Shipmates had unknowingly supplied the watches and rings that Jack was using to finance this sudden courtship. Their first kiss, and the second and third, occurred as they were leaving that night. Because of Annie's condition and the fact that she had reached the age of 18, Aunt Louise no longer required updates on her whereabouts as often as in the past. On the night of conception, Annie's evening out culminated on a small cot in the back of the closed pawnshop. The bedazzled young woman, reassured by her aunt's constant reminders of an inability to bear offspring, was determined to make this dashing figure her future husband. Jack had never gazed down upon a woman as enticing as Annie that he did not have to pay first. In the dim light of the pawnshop's back room, she allowed the tall young sailor to slowly unbutton her blouse until, with a final shrug, it fell to the floor. Her milky white cleavage spilled over the top of her ill-fitted bra, and within minutes her pleated skirt joined its matching mate. In the dim light the pale pink scar was invisible. Jack, referring to his lack of protection, kept murmuring, *Is it all right? Are you sure it's all right?* As the moment rapidly drew near, Annie could only whisper that it had been taken care of.

Jack departed that night amid promises of spending his entire shore leave next week with his new paramour. Starry-eyed, she dreamed of nothing else over the next five days. Her first disappointment came on the Monday morning that he failed to show at the pawnshop. Two nights previous, a bunkmate of Jack's had narrowed down the circumstances of the disappearance of a gold wedding ring. His confrontation with Jack on the outer edge of the flight deck at midnight had resulted in a shouting match. The majority of the words were lost to the wailing winds but Jack clearly heard the words "evidence" and "your superior officer." With a quick blow from a metal flashlight and a hearty heave, the thief became a murderer as the unconscious bunkmate was pitched over the edge of the flight deck with his accusations.

The bloated body was found floating three days later by a harbor dockhand. A formal inquiry was launched post haste. By this time, however, Jack was a crewman on a tramp steamer to Indo-China, where rumor had it that an enterprising American could find business opportunities among the rice paddies.

Annie's second disappointment occurred six weeks later when the first bout of morning sickness came in a wave of nausea and vomiting. The influenza explanation satisfied Aunt Louise until the second day of the affliction when the suspicious woman noticed an absence of symptoms by early afternoon. The pawnshop provided a refuge from her aunt's increasingly more pointed questions, but its back stock room haunted Annie with its memories of that night. She could sense the little cot's presence but averted her eyes whenever a task took her near it. The aching of abandonment and of feeling victimized and seduced by the sailor's promises fed the dead spot that grew daily inside of her heart.

By the time a seasoned Navy Lieutenant's investigation brought a discarded pawnshop receipt full circle to Annie at work, Jack's flawed seed had taken hold in her womb. It had met with the dormant but distorted DNA of her father in the supposedly unimpregnable woman…and had thrived. Like a spike-leafed weed that found opportunity between a thin crack in a sea of concrete, the bad seed combined with one of the eggs that Annie's fallopian tubes did in fact produce…and created life. It was not to be the kind of life that God smiled benevolently upon nor wished on the rest of humankind, but its hardiness and tenaciousness made divine acceptance unimportant. Annie's cooperation with the Lieutenant during his investigation did little to assuage the growing horror she felt as the bad seed grew inside of her. An increasingly pious Aunt Louise could not accept the evolution of circumstances and banished Annie to a home where others of her ilk resided. The owner of the pawnshop was more understanding (provided that Annie agreed to wear a pawned wedding ring at work) and agreed to let her stay on.

The banishment from her home and adopted sisters caused less heartache each day as the tumor of dead emotional tissue grew in her chest cavity and metastasized to various centers of her brain. Annie's feelings of vulnerability and betrayal numbed as the being inside of her grew. She went back and forth to work each day on the bus in a trance, staring blankly out the window, yearning to trade existences with nearly every passerby.

The bad seed continued to grow and thrive. It seldom moved or shifted inside of her. It lay waiting, patiently—as though not wanting to draw attention to itself.

Forty weeks to the day after the cells combined and implanted themselves into the wall of Annie's placenta, the angel of death arrived. There were no plaintive wails as the creature's eyes were assaulted by the bright lights of the delivery room. There was no kicking—and no contortion of the features as they were wiped clean by attentive nurses. The dark eyes could focus as the small Anti-Christ examined its surroundings—and then lie still. An immediate examination revealed that all vital signs were normal and the quiet newborn was proffered to the owner of its place of gestation. Annie's expression remained blank and emotionless as she accepted the swaddled bundle and they both lie, unflinching and staring in opposite directions.

The quiet infant refused to suck on its mother for nourishment despite the exhortations of the nurses for Annie to keep trying. Cows milk was finally recommended and the pair sent home at week's end. Annie was in the communal living room with the other mothers when she heard the name Ricardo mentioned. Ricardo cut a dashing figure as his motorcycle prowled the neighborhood and was the object of several unwed mothers' fantasies. When Annie went back to work, the other mothers called the boy Rico and soon Annie began to do the same. Unsure of the ancestral heritage of the infant's father as well as that of her own missing mother, Annie eventually conceded that Ricardo might in fact cover several of the possibilities.

The infant would never complain if hungry but always accepted a bottle when it was offered. Rico seemed to take stoicism to a new level…never crying, he fell asleep quickly whenever placed on bedding, and woke only briefly in the middle of the night— as though to check his surroundings—before falling back asleep. Rico never cuddled, never cooed, and never smiled. Annie, for her part, made few attempts to get the child to respond to any stimuli. She would often sit, staring out the window for hours, as though waiting for Jack's return.

The other women in the home would remark that the pair could pass considerable time in the same room, each lost in their own world, never acknowledging the other. In a more current era the boy might have been diagnosed as autistic, but it was 1951 and he was not.

Rico began to crawl at six months and by seven was extremely proficient. Watching him propel himself was remarkable in that there was never any wasted movement as he practiced. Methodically, as though preparing each limb for a lifetime of doing exactly as commanded, Rico would pick out an object across the room and head for it in a perfectly straight, predetermined path. Upon arrival Rico would rest, scout out another destination, and repeat the process.

When Rico was eight months old, the six young women in the home asked for and were allowed to share the responsibility of a kitten. A black and white fluffball was donated by the local shelter and the women and their infants smiled and fussed at the new arrival. On its second night the group was gathered in the living room, distracted by a radio broadcast, and the kitten wandered into the kitchen. In an unusual burst of maternal awareness, Annie glanced up just as Rico crawled back into view from the kitchen. Twenty minutes later, cries came from the kitchen as a young mother discovered the lifeless corpse of the kitten in the middle of the floor.

The last piece of Annie's soul died that night. Her thoughts during the endless, vacant staring had often gone to worries about when and how the bad seed would manifest itself—after all, it was inevitable that it would. She speculated as to when the exact moment would come that the demon inside her son would feel emboldened enough to take over the earthly vessel that carried it. An inner voice had whispered to her since that first day of morning nausea. The voice had warned the young woman. It warned that the rapidly dividing cells inside did not belong to her. These cells reproduced for the sole purpose of destroying other groupings of cells. They were being given life only to destroy life. And now the prophecy was coming true. Whether these were actual voices or the premonitions of a profoundly depressed woman was not important—the child needed to be isolated from others at once. A quiet plea to her boss yielded help in finding a small ground floor apartment. Although dark and featureless, it boasted a minuscule backyard. The baby would go with her to work and spend his days in the windowless back room of his conception.

7

While I parked the Datsun in my garage, I rationalized that everyone in this life is given a cross to bear. As I began pulling together my suit and shoes for Lee's wedding the next day, it occurred to me that when God was dolling out crosses, I might have been given more than one.

Part of my business involved selling used cars to a public that was often economically disadvantaged. Atypically, these poor people, in spite of the cars being in a lower price range, were unable to pay cash for them. Once in possession of the car, these owners did not always meet their financial obligations to the credit union. When they did not, they usually stopped answering their phone or responding to their mail. The only solution was to retrieve the car and prepare it to be resold. Due to circumstances beyond my control, the only reliable option for retrieving these automobiles was me. At first, the excitement and nervousness I encountered while sneaking into a neighborhood to snatch back a car had been very unpleasant. In spite of taking many precautions, I had several close calls with the Angel of Death. After a year, my confiscation skills increased and I began to enjoy the excitement that I felt during a midnight mission. Soon after, I began looking *forward* to the surge of adrenaline that I would experience during these formerly stressful retrievals. Occasionally, I found myself sitting out a week in which everyone was paying, if not precisely on time, at least close enough not to warrant a retrieval of their car. But practice makes perfect and I had become very adept at taking cars away in the middle of the night. By the end of a week that saw everyone paying promptly, I felt stressed out from *not* having to drop down into a yard or break into a garage. For two years I had practiced my new craft…reluctantly at first, but with growing gusto. Over time, my techniques grew more sophisticated. If I had a key I still used it, but it only shaved a minute or so off of the process. I studied door locks, fabricating tools that hastened popping one open at 2 A.M. to the point where only using the actual key would have been faster. Ignition locks gave up defending the car 45 seconds after my specialized tools and I began our assault. I had become a sophisticated car thief and looked forward to every opportunity to snatch a car. On more than one occasion there were no cars slated to be repoed…but *I* was overdue for a fix. I developed a craving for the thrill of the grab. Sometimes I repossessed a car when all of the payments were current and I had never seen it before. A BMW may end up in my larcenous care when my only claim to it was that it sported a hood, fender, or grill that I could sell, trade, or barter. My beloved Datsun had met two of the criteria for the wedding that I intended to drive it to the next day. While neither old or new, it was most definitely something borrowed and something blue.

I undoubtedly had more than one cross to bear. At my then current rate of inventing new bad habits, a stand of trees was growing somewhere for the express purpose of providing me with new crosses. It would not be for another year that a unit of the Michigan State Police demanded I seek my adrenaline rushes elsewhere.

Mary came from a large family. She was the oldest of nine children. She had grandparents. There were aunts and uncles. There were cousins too. Her family had friends and neighbors, and Mary had many friends. They were mostly female, but Lee allowed her to speak to ex-boyfriends as long as he was within earshot. Mary's childhood friends had parents that had watched her grow up. Mary had co-workers as well. She split her working hours between three Detroit area modeling agencies and a firm that sold business owners advertising space on coupons mailed to area homes. Between all of the family and friends and models and agents and business owners on four miles of Mack and another four of Kercheval, Mary knew 2,000 people—all who would have gladly accepted an invitation to her wedding.

Lee had a close family as well. Although he only had two brothers, his extended Greek family ranged from the Pointes to outlying areas with names like Sterling Heights and Shelby Township. His modeling and music contacts numbered well into the hundreds. He made friends easily and ran into them often at "must attend" parties and "see and be seen" events. By the end of every wedding that he played and sang at, anywhere from 100 to 500 people felt as though they knew the talented and magnetic front man for *Lee Pantely and the Romantics* personally.

Lee and Mary's August wedding reception was to be held at the Grosse Pointe War Memorial's Grand Ballroom. By far the largest of the venues available at the complex, it had the advantage of being the most traditional as well.

Floor-to-ceiling windows overlooked Lake St. Clair and served as a stunning backdrop. A well positioned guest could view yachts and freighters creeping into and out of view as they watched the wedding band serenade the lucky couple.

Reserving the Grand Ballroom required that certain criteria be met. Mary's father was a veteran of World War II, so requirement number one had been addressed to the satisfaction of the Director of Events. There were several seating configurations to choose from based on whether or not a band—and thus the dance floor—would be utilized. The entire polished wooden floor would be required that evening. Given the nature of the miniature orchestra that was to play, the grand piano would remain in its place at the eastern end of the dance floor.

The catering would be provided by the Memorial's excellent in-house staff. The arrangement of the tables chosen by Mary allowed for the seating of a total of 250 guests. It would not be an exceptionally large wedding by current Pointer's standards, but it was to be a perfect one. If one were to believe that a storybook wedding could come to life in a pure, unspoiled form without the benefit of editing, special effects, or retakes, this would be it. Mary would be allotted 125 guests. Lee was allotted the same amount. And Mark Steel was the man who had saved the groom's driver's license from the depths of purgatory when all looked lost. Mark and his wife, Satan, would be catapulted from *Lee's possible guests* number 1,080 and 1,081 to guests number 124 and 5 respectively. My invitation to the "most perfect wedding not staged for the movies or television" came, surprisingly, not by special courier but in the U.S. Mail. Unaccustomed to being invited to an affair that required selecting the evening's fare in advance, I studied my menu choices carefully. I had ordered Soup du Jour in some decidedly upscale places before and, although each restaurant seemed to have a different recipe for it, had thoroughly enjoyed it each time. Unfortunately, Mary had not seen fit to offer it as a selection and I found only French onion, a tomato basil, and a portabella mushroom soup on the list.

The main entrée was a no-brainer. Portions of beef or veal or even fish may vary according to a chef's whim. An entire chicken, however, was guaranteed to sate my appetite. I ordered the Cornish Game Hen.

I sent my best sport jacket to the cleaners and applied *SPOT OFF* judiciously to my favorite tie. I gave Satan 200 dollars. She slunk off with Lucifer and Beelzebub (her mother and sister) to Sears to buy a new outfit for the occasion.

Until a few hours before, the Datsun had been my most presentable car. Without the parts or the time to repair it, I needed to act quickly to procure a suitable ride to the reception. A customer had left a stunning black Jaguar convertible at my facility over the weekend for repairs that were not scheduled to commence until Monday morning. After a millisecond or so of wrestling with my conscience, I located the keys, opened the gate of my back lot, and commandeered the car for the day.

The Jaguar's engine purred powerfully as Satan and I eased into the War Memorial's parking lot. Valets darted about, but I had developed a kinship with my new ride in the last 20 miles and I was reluctant to relinquish the keys. Already, I harbored the thought of making this new driving experience a permanent one but further research—such as whether the owner parked it in a locked garage at night—would be necessary. We parked on the outskirts of the War Memorial's lot and on the way in I looked wistfully back at the piece of British machinery that had ensured our regal arrival. My second foray into the Pointes was proceeding so smoothly that at first I failed to notice the properly pedigreed guests gliding toward the sign for the Grand Ballroom. Being a heterosexual male who is not widely known for his refined tastes in clothes, architecture, and culinary accoutrements, I am ill-qualified to describe the scene that Satan and I stepped into. But I do remember that if Oleg Cassini, Yves St. Laurent, and Queen Elizabeth's jeweler had joined forces to present their vision of what a wedding would entail, Lee and Mary's would have been the end result.

The seating was divided into two distinct sections. Section One had 125 seats reserved for relatives and close friends of the family. There were no children, as it was difficult for even an adult to make the "A" list for this event. A couple of teenage siblings of Mary's were the only ones in the room to represent their generation. Section One was grouped around and behind a dance floor that was soon filled with hugging, gregarious relatives—rehashing what must have been a memorable wedding ceremony. Occasionally, one of Mary's younger siblings would be isolated from the group by one of her older relatives. In these instances ritual dictated that the older person stand next to the younger with open hand outstretched—palm down and chest high. Custom then dictated an exclamation and a demonstration as to how tall the younger was when last encountered by the older.

Section Two was another 125 seats and farther from the dance floor. It was reserved for the most beautiful people in the United States. Lanky, wasp-waisted women, some with porcelain complexions and others with a tanned California look, filtered to their assigned seats. Shiny, Clairol-commercial hair caressed slim, perfect shoulders before cascading down lightly muscled bare backs. Women from the pages of *Cosmo* and *Vogue* sprang to life and floated across the room to greet their peers before wafting back to their table.

I have always been forthcoming in saying that I married Satan only for her looks. Still slim and eye-grabbing with her bleached blond hair and soft, delicate features, Satan was becoming visibly agitated minutes after we arrived. Whenever she and I entered a restaurant, I would quietly trail far behind her to count the number of men that placed down their forks and stopped eating to watch her walk past. An elbow jab from the man's wife was an added bonus point to my tally. The effects of a heavy smoking and drinking regimen would not become noticeable for another three years and Satan was still usually the most attractive woman in any venue…except for this one. In Section Two, she was dead last. Her lower lip quivered uncontrollably as she looked wild-eyed at the parade of Mary's beautiful acquaintances. Through teary eyes, Satan began to search for the placard that designated our seats in this sea of perfection. Before she could find it, she began looking at the men that accompanied these goddesses. Most of the men were prettier than her as well. Clean shaven and dressed in carefully tailored suits—in colors that complemented those of their dates—each confident, preening hunk strutted to the bar, greeting cohorts and eyeballing the nearest five women immediately to see if they were awestruck by him as well.

With her knees buckling beneath her Cheryl Tiegs sundress, Satan staggered to the bar to begin ordering and downing the first of many.

As a teetotaler, I was left with little to do but find our table and sit down. The ornate settings took a back seat to the eye-popping women that began to seat themselves across from and around me. A dead ringer for the exotic model Helena Christiansen paused directly across from me and looked down at the placard. Upon seeing her name, she glanced expectantly at the tall, rugged looking man standing next to her. His dark brown hair was slicked carelessly back and his black, deep-set eyes stared out from beneath heavy eyebrows. His face had the beginnings of a dark beard but this was the type of man that could shave early in the morning and have a three-day growth by evening. A heavily muscled neck stretched his shirt collar above squared-off shoulders. A deeply tanned face and squint lines from the corners of his eyes made determining the square-jawed man's age difficult, but I guessed him at 30.

Sensing his date's hesitation, the outdoorsman reached down with a large, rough-looking hand and pulled back her chair. The shadow of a smile passed across the model's face and she gathered her gown before sitting down. Although not ugly, this he-man was definitely the model's "and guest" and not in that profession himself. As he noticed me sitting across from him, he stared with a bored expression that seemed as though he were contemplating whether to send me up for their drinks.

Within two more minutes the table was filled. Satan found me while carrying three rum and Cokes and set them down without spilling a drop.

While the soup sat on wheeled serving tables the priest said a prayer. Sincere, heartfelt toasts were proffered after the soup and salad, but the hushed silence at some of the tables of Section Two made it clear that seats would be exchanged after the entrée as some of the young ladies smiled and waved to other tables.

I mistook the Cornish Game Hen for another appetizer until I noticed the vegetables alongside each morsel of a meal. A stunning but pitifully thin model who also sat at our table eschewed the entrée with an exclamation that *she was a vegetarian*. I could have eaten seven of the stunted little birds and watched longingly as they cleared her plates with her tiny foul untouched. My Navajo was rusty but I vaguely recalled that *vegetarian* meant "lousy hunter."

The only thing that the 5-foot 10-inch vegetarian/anorexic had ever hunted for was haute couture clothing at half off. Her high cheekboned, almost effeminate date was two inches taller and equally thin underneath his Armani suit. I considered coaxing my twiggy tablemate into raising his arm above his head so that the rest of us might observe whether his Rolex would slide down to his shoulder. At that moment, though, the band began playing and the dessert carts started to make their way across the room, drawing my attention elsewhere.

After 20 minutes the band ceased playing. It was time for the bride to take the traditional first dance with her new husband. As the bandleader began to make the announcement, Lee, resplendent and dashing in his tuxedo, jumped up and grabbed the microphone. Flashing his million dollar smile, he looked over at the bride. Mary, in a wedding gown that cost more than an entire VFW Hall wedding, raised her delicately arched Italian eyebrows in surprise.

Lee said, "Marrria, before we begin to dance, I have composed three songs for the love of my life. I would like to introduce them to you now."

With that statement, Lee walked over to his stunning bride and in one seamless motion scooped her up. Together, they wafted toward the grand piano where he seated her gently on top with a flourish. He pulled out the piano bench and slid onto it. Still smiling to the mesmerized guests, he began to play for his beloved Maria. Smiling, her gaze was transfixed on Lee and she seemed unaware of the other 250 people in the room. The notes of the first song circled the room before entering our ears. By the time that Lee began to sing, the sobbing in the room had become very distracting. Even some of the men had begun to dab at their eyes as surreptitiously as possible.

After Lee began to sing, a quick look around revealed that at least half of the female guests had forgotten about their makeup and were openly weeping. Of the eight at our table, only myself and Mr. Rugged, seated directly across, retained our composure. My hollow-legged wife, with ten drinks in her by this time, had the smeared-mascara look of a raccoon and continued muttering *I don't belong here, I don't belong here.*

8

AT ONE YEAR of age Rico could walk. In the tiny backyard, his gaze never focused for long on inanimate objects. His attention was drawn instead to the sparrow, starling, or pigeon that may be perched on any fence, wire, or roof. Rico would pause for minutes and stare at the little winged bundles of life—watching their every movement.

The toddler began to grow. His play was never without purpose. Grabbing an object, he would strike another. Little Rico would then get closer to the object that was struck, inspecting for damage. A wooden spoon became a club. A toy block became an anvil for crushing pieces of cereal or ants—or any other insect that moved around indoors or out. When Rico turned two, a regular customer at the shop suggested to Annie that their sons play together on a Saturday. Annie hoped the woman's three-year-old son could teach her son to play a game…or a song…or even to smile. She reasoned that Rico's unusual behavior came in part from their isolated situation…and that he sensed their abandonment.

Alone together in the living room with his new playmate, Rico stared, his head cocked curiously. The mothers spoke in the kitchen. Two minutes later, a wailing three-year-old staggered into the kitchen, blood streaming from a head wound. Rico soon followed, the fireplace poker still gripped tightly in both hands. As the wild-eyed mother attempted to extract information from her hysterical child, Rico stepped closer to inspect the gash as well. The boy screamed even louder, and Rico cocked the iron poker back for another attempt. In one motion Annie grabbed the poker and her son, throwing the weapon on the floor. She and Rico left without words. The play date was over.

After Rico turned four, his fascination with the fauna in the tiny backyard became an obsession. Whenever his mother allowed, Rico would hunt in the little yard from sun up to sun down. A piece of board could be propped up on one side by a stick. A string could be wrapped around the top of the stick. Cereal from breakfast snuck out in a pocket or bread crusts from lunch were sufficient as bait. Rico would patiently crouch for hours behind the yard's sole bush, watching for any living creature to approach the makeshift trap. Hungry sparrows and inquisitive squirrels were stunned by the board after a flick of the young killer's wrist on the string—as he perfected his timing. The sparrows' lives ceased as the board crashed down on them, but the squirrels were far more resilient. In their panicked state, the adult squirrels could scramble out easily from between the board and the earth. Juveniles, however, squirmed and fought for freedom from the crushing weight. Soon, Rico taught himself to rush forward at the first sign of a quarry in distress. With a focused rapidness, the young hunter would add his 40-pound bodyweight to that of the board. The tide would quickly turn and his victim would succumb. In time, Rico smuggled school glue and play blocks out into the yard. The young trapper had learned that gluing additional weight onto the "killing board" allowed him to detain increasingly older, stronger victims until he could rush over and deliver the coup-de-grace. Because of the limited size of Rico's hunting territory, and because his success had diminished the wildlife population in his neighborhood, Rico's chances to kill were limited. A 60-hour week might yield only two fresh corpses, and young Rico dreamed of expanding his territory.

Rico started school at the age of five. The school playground adjoined a large park. The public park was home to a variety of squirrels, chipmunks, rabbits, and carefree birds of all types. Rico's entire school day revolved around the two recess periods when he was allowed access to the playground and, more importantly, the outer edge of the park. Rico soon learned to maneuver into the classroom seat that afforded the best view of the playground and the park's edge. The park teemed with life, each organism going about its daily business of survival and procreation…unless another organism decided to intervene. Rico visualized what it would be like to be the one who controlled whether the animals in the park lived or died. For the first two weeks, Rico divided his time between studying the movements and habits of the park's fauna and determining which teachers monitored their playground charges the most lackadaisically.

Soon these guardians began to accept that fact that Rico did not enjoy playing with the other children. He wasn't aloof or shy. Their foolish games seemed pointless to him. They expended energy without purpose or resolve. Inversely, Rico's precious outdoor time was utilized judiciously, so that he may begin to have as much impact on the surrounding environment as soon as possible. In retrospect, a more callous summation of the young boy's drive would have been, *so many animals, so little time.*

Rico's obsession with the park and its contents became all consuming. He quickly learned to read once he became aware that a book in the library contained stories about hunters and fur trappers. At six years old Rico scavenged enough materials to lever up an end of a railroad tie that served as a parking block for automobiles. A sturdy stick propped the end as the young trapper crouched 20 feet away, watchful and patient but prepared to yank hard on a length of cord that connected the hunter to his trap. A small mangy dog eyed the bit of Rico's lunch that had been planted under the railroad tie that day. The school bell rang and officially ended the lunch period as the wary prey inched closer. The boy bided his time and waited behind a peeling park bench as the cautious mutt crept to within ten feet…and then five. A classroom headcount revealed that a student was missing, and a frantic teacher launched a young messenger to the principal's office to initiate the formation of a search party. The 15-pound dog was beginning to sniff the air downwind from the bread crust when a blood curdling yell from a matronly school teacher caused both hunter and prey to flinch. The searcher and the hunter were soon surrounded by other members of the horrified party. The trap was sprung and the mongrel sent into flight. Rico's mother was summoned from her duties at the pawnshop.

There were no self-proclaimed children's behavioral experts to consult about the staff's discovery on that California spring day in 1956. The school staff was evenly divided. The first group called the discovery a harmless childhood prank. The second group labeled it as something much more sinister. The second group saw the makeshift trap as a portent of things to come. They sought to earmark the quiet first grader as a young killer. His withdrawn single parent was deemed incapable of giving Rico the time and direction required to alter the budding miscreant's behavior. However, the entire staff agreed on one point. They were unanimous in their opinion that Rico needed a father figure to guide him through a civilized world, and strongly recommended that Annie take any immediate steps necessary to procure one.

Fortunately, Annie was still relatively young and had retained much of her beauty. The honor of her company was requested almost weekly by male suitors after they browsed the glass cases in the large pawnshop. One week after the incident at the edge of the park, a man and his two teenage sons entered Annie's place of employment. The man, recently widowed, was immediately taken with Annie, as many other prospective suitors before him had been and for once, mindful of her son's increasingly tenuous situation at school, Annie did not avert the conversation to strictly business matters when it became personal. She complimented the friendly customer on his two fine sons and on his own clear blue eyes. The small talk moved methodically from the man's farmland on the outskirts of the city to Annie's own young son and the long days he'd spent occupying himself in the postage-stamp-sized yard.

One of the man's sons interrupted politely to point out a .22 caliber rifle that would make a fine addition to those already at the farm. During his purchase, the man invited Annie and Rico out for a visit on the following Sunday. When Annie haltingly explained about her lack of transportation, the friendly widower assured her that for the price of her home address, a farmhand would be by on Sunday morning to pick up the two of them.

The working farm was 800 acres of lettuce, cabbage, tomatoes, beans…and rabbits. The man was not a farmer by trade. He sold real estate for a living and had invested in the parcel after hearing of a foreclosure from a friend at the bank. Two of the original farmhands were retained to plant, water and repair. The job of varmint control was turned over to the man's teenage sons and their .22 caliber rifles.

Annie and Rico arrived at the farm at noon that Sunday. By 12:10 P.M., a wide-eyed Rico had spotted his first rabbit in the flat fields and had begun to plot its demise. By one o'clock his new teenage friends were giving Rico shooting lessons in back of the barn and remarking among themselves how naturally their young guest held his weapon. By two o'clock the older boys were satisfied that their protégé could not only shoot straight, but competently reload the ten-round magazine. The three hunters ventured out, searching for signs of wild game among the heads of lettuce. Rico, with an eye already trained from years of searching for any flicker of animal movement, was the first to spot a rabbit. His two teachers exchanged knowing smiles as the novice prepared for his first shot at 100 yards. Guns at the ready, Rico's mentors prepared to pepper shots at the greedy animal after the first shot spooked it.

Methodically, young Rico trained the rifle sights on the unsuspecting trespasser. The rest of his team brought theirs up as well and three slim black barrels covered the hungry bunny. Instinctively, Rico held his breath and slowly squeezed the trigger. As the shot rang out, Rico's hand flew to the bolt on the side of the rifle to discharge the spent shell and load a second. His instructors scanned the surrounding area with practiced eyes, ready to fire upon the fleeing intruder. But there was no rabbit zigzagging between the lettuce rows. There was no need to console a crestfallen Rico—and encourage him to try again. The rabbit lay in a small brown heap on the ground with a piece of lettuce leaf still in his mouth. As the hunters approached the lifeless hump the older two kept their rifles raised, preparing to get a shot off should the victim suddenly jump up and run. Rico did so as well, but watched elsewhere. His cold young eyes were already scanning the landscape for signs of more quarry. The three hunters picked their way amongst the crop, finally arriving at the little furry mound. The two brothers stood together, looking down and murmuring to each other. There had been no need for a second shot—the back half of the rabbit's head was missing.

 The more experienced brothers began to turn to Rico to laud him for his lucky shot. As they did so the crack of a rifle shot two feet away caused both to tense and freeze. Rico had raised his rifle in the field for a second time and fired at something far to the group's left. His teachers mildly admonished the young hunter not to shoot wildly at anything that offered movement, but Rico crouched down to peer curiously at the dead rabbit. The two brothers had never known a child to be so quiet…with an intensity and seriousness that was belied by his small stature. A chill crept up their spines in spite of the warming day. Simultaneously, both older boys began to form the thought that perhaps the .22 should be temporarily removed from Rico's possession until some retraining could be provided. As the words to communicate this thought began to form, Rico suddenly stood up. Spinning on his heel, the young trainee began to lead his instructors in a new direction. With his short but confident stride, and a focus that began to unnerve the teenagers, the boy set a course for an unseen objective. Their curiosity rising with every step, the two brothers fell into line behind their young charge.

 Their trek lasted for 100 feet, then 200, and finally 50 more. Young Rico seemed oblivious to his two instructors, swiveling his head slightly to the left and right to cover a 180-degree arc of farmland.

The two brothers divided their time between trying to peer ahead of Rico and catching each other's attention with questioning glances. Just as the older brother cleared his throat to speak up, Rico stopped in his tracks. The teenagers caught up and stopped as well, flanking him. They followed his gaze to a head of cabbage on the ground. A small rabbit lie prone in the dirt, perpendicular to the cabbage, his mouth filled with an outer leaf. The young rabbit was not chewing on the leaf however. The portion of his brain that controlled his jaw muscles—and other vital functions—had been blown out the right side of his head by the .22 caliber bullet from Rico's rifle.

When one witnesses an automobile accident, the first emotion is the mind denying what the eyes have just seen. Metal and chrome that was smooth and shiny one second ago is now jagged and crumpled. Glass either explodes or forms intricate, web-like designs, obscuring the car's interior. Steam and smoke spew from under the compacted hood instead of the rear tailpipe. Confusion sets in quickly as the witness is prompted to act or to help somehow, but then realizes just as quickly that they don't know what to do.

There is a queasy feeling that can start around and up one's stomach lining until it feels like a weakness that spreads to the hips, legs, and knees. Public speaking causes it for some. Being pulled over by a police officer turns on the process for others. It is not fear that is being felt…at least not the kind where one's life, health, or safety is jeopardized. It is a dreaded anticipation that the unknown is suddenly upon you, must be dealt with, and cannot be put off.

Finally, there is a feeling of awe and rapture that one gets in the presence of great art or an unimaginable performance. As one witnesses a work that could only have been inspired by a divinity—even if it is an evil one—one is struck dumb and only able to stare and attempt to comprehend. The budding comprehension is interrupted only by the feeling of desire that wells up…the longing to achieve something of this nature as well. But the desire is just as quickly suppressed with the realization that the art or performance that has been witnessed could only have been rendered by someone already born with a great gift.

Staring down at the rabbit, the two brothers experienced all three of these feelings at once. Rico squatted down as he had at the last one, examining it with a cold curiosity.

A half dozen more were exterminated that afternoon, and Rico stopped hunting with great reluctance only as the sun began to set.

A month later Annie quit the pawnshop and moved into the farmhouse with her son, and the five of them existed as a family. Within two years the brothers discovered cars and girls, and Rico was left to patrol the fields around the farm by himself. On the days that the immediate fields were eradicated and devoid of life, the young hunter patrolled farther into the acreage and forests of other landowners.

9

Most of the automobiles of the '60s and prior could be started and driven without an ignition key. It was a simple process. It was called hotwiring and any backyard mechanic with minimal skills could do it. From under the hood, a wire needed to be placed from the positive terminal of the battery (or any other wire that was hot) to the positive terminal of the ignition coil. Then a screwdriver could be used to bridge the gap between two protruding terminals of the starter solenoid. "Jumping" the solenoid this way activated the starter and made the engine turn over. With the ignition already hot the engine would start. Before the advent of locking steering columns, a car that was built in the 1960s or before could be hotwired and driven away. Of course, if a car was hotwired, the accessories would not function. The driver would thus not be able to use the turn signals, windshield wipers, power windows or even the radio. To use these, more hotwiring would be required, and to a busy car thief this would be time unwisely spent.

In the late '60s and early '70s, automobile manufacturers began to provide every new car with a locking steering column. The ignition lock was relocated from the dashboard to the column and now performed two functions. The first was to provide power to start the car and operate the accessories—the second was to engage a long bar of metal with teeth cut into it with a half gear that turned the key. As the long bar was pushed deeper into the column, the steering wheel was released. Releasing the steering wheel was useful in case the driver wanted to steer the car as he drove through traffic.

Armed with this knowledge, it is very difficult for me to watch a movie in which the protagonist, antagonist, or any other character needs to commandeer a car. Some movie directors would have the viewer believe that if one needs a car in a hurry one has only to check above the visor of an unlocked car for the keys. I have never done a physical survey of this phenomenon, but apparently one out of every two drivers leaves their unlocked car in a parking garage or outside a bar with a full set of keys in the visor. A frequent moviegoer might well draw the conclusion that half of the dangerous chase scenes depicted in movies are preventable. If the automobile owners in these movies were alerted to act more responsibly and take their keys with them, half of the car chases would be foot chases. Foot chases would be far safer because people do not flip end over end and land on their backs while bursting into flames after hitting another person the way cars in movies always seem to do.

The other half of movie directors would have the viewer believe that on modern cars, the hero has only to duck underneath the dash, find the correct two wires, and pull them loose. These wires can then be touched together until they spark, whereupon the car will start up immediately. The director always neglects to explain how the hero managed to unlock the steering column—the one that is completely encased in tempered steel to prevent such a theft.

But in the '70s and '80s, steering columns were not manufactured with a host of impregnable safeguards. It would be a decade, still, before coded computer chips were imbedded into ignition keys and "kill switches" were controlled by a remote key fob.

As soon as locking steering columns were standard equipment on new automobiles, car thieves set about learning how to defeat them. It was a short learning curve. Standard car theft tools evolved from a screwdriver and a length of copper wire to a screwdriver and a hammer. The graduate car thief now needed only to position himself behind the wheel of a car and deliver one hard blow to the left side of the column. The cast aluminum housing would shatter, exposing the toothed bar. The screwdriver was used to lever the bar down, unlocking the steering wheel and starting the vehicle simultaneously. The entire process involved less than ten seconds. For several years the locking steering column proved to be a real time saver for the car thief in a hurry.

Sooner rather than later, the automobile makers began to receive feedback from the insurance industry that the locking steering columns had only temporarily deterred car theft. Word spread among inner city youths and professional car thieves alike that the columns were easily defeated with the hammer and screwdriver. In lieu of the actual door key, a brick or a piece of cinder block from a crumbling building was instantly effective at smashing either the driver or passenger side window. Of course, the more experienced ghetto resident would soon find that smashing a back passenger door window was nearly as expeditious in gaining entry—with the added benefit of not having to sit in shards of broken glass while transporting the stolen car.

As in many crafts, there was a technique to be learned even when smashing an automobile's window. If the brick or block was merely thrown, the invention of safety glass made the possibility of it bouncing off—without any shattering taking place—very real. To be effective on the first attempt, the brick could not be thrown. In accordance with Murphy's Law, the arc of its return trip would invariably end as it landed on top of the tennis-shoed foot of the individual who had done the throwing. This was especially undesirable if the noise created by the unsuccessful attempt awoke an armed homeowner and being fleet of foot became an instant requirement.

There was only one proper technique when one wished to gain access with a kiln-fired or limestone amalgamate product. As hazardous and reckless as it may first seem, the proper technique begins with the proper stance—and the proper stance begins with placing the left foot (assuming one is right handed) nearly beneath the undercarriage of the car… and perpendicular to the window being smashed. The key is now to propel the brick forward with the right arm but *not release it* as it makes contact with the glass. Instead, as contact is made, the brick should be grasped tightly and "punched" through the glass in the same "follow through" motion used when hitting a baseball, a tennis ball, or punching an opponent in the boxing ring. A boxer may, in fact, imagine himself as hitting an opponent who is standing *behind* his opponent when he finally commits to delivering a hard punch. This commitment applies equally to the ambitious car thief, and one cannot accomplish this while worrying about glass shards lacerating the hand and forearm upon follow-through. The aware car thief must bear in mind that the reason for the window being difficult to break in the first place lies inherent in its name. It is called *safety glass* and is manufactured to be this way. Once the pane does give way, however, it further lives up to its moniker by shattering into small irregularly shaped ovals that are not prone to easily cutting unprotected flesh.

If an aspiring car thief is slight of build, it is important to remember that the actual power to drive the brick through the glass comes from the proper twisting of the torso as one moves the arm and brick toward the pane that has been selected. As in the aforementioned sports, scrawny participants can excel in their field nearly as well as larger ones by utilizing as many muscle groups as possible when taking a swing at anything.

If one has scrutinized the last several pages carefully, they may be experiencing a growing sense of agitation. At first, the last few pages may seem like a virtual primer for the aspiring car thief. One may be concerned that if these pages fell into the wrong hands…or their content became widely known…a rash of motor vehicle thefts would erupt, both in economically disadvantaged areas and the rings of prosperity that form the outer suburbs.

While these pages may have laid a solid foundation for a handbook on car theft in the 1970s and 80s, thus making the very act of publishing them irresponsible, this is no longer the case. Other than illuminating the novice about breaking car windows with whatever miscellaneous objects are at hand, the entire treatise is now obsolete. Car manufacturers began to respond to the hue and cry about the vulnerability of their products to theft by increasing the strength of the steel around their steering columns tenfold. The manufacturers developed steering columns that were virtually impregnable unless one began with something messy like a welding torch or C-4 explosives. And in reality, if these or similar brutish methods *were* utilized, there would not be enough of the internal mechanism or wiring left to successfully start and drive the car. Some of the early Humvees in the second Iraqi War had less armor than these fully evolved columns.

Eventually, a computer chip was impregnated into the ignition key. Even if the key from another car of the same brand matched up to the ignition lock of a vehicle, the unique code implanted into the chip would prevent the vehicle's electronic brain from recognizing the key at all.

As an additional safeguard, anti-theft systems sprang up with kill switches that could only be disarmed by a unique remote control.

On television and in the movies, every time the hero needs to get inside a car quickly, there is never a brick laying around. Instead, he is always adept at using an elongated piece of flat flexible steel that he slips down the door between the glass and the outer skin. After a moment of probing, the door lock pops open and he is free to hotwire the car in spite of the realities involved. In real life, this piece of steel was mass produced and marketed everywhere in the 1970s and 1980s. It was commonly known as a slim-jim. One end of the slim-jim was notched for *pushing* on lock parts deep down in the door, and the other end had a tee for hooking and *pulling*. When bent at odd angles, the flat slim-jim would hold its shape and could be snuck in through small gaps to probe blindly but often effectively. Some car door locks were easily defeated, others took time and patience. With practice, I was able to open some types of doors as quickly as the people in the movies, but a car that I was unfamiliar with took time and perseverance. By the late '80s, the car manufacturers placed additional steel guards beneath the door skins and the heyday of the slim-jim was doomed to end.

With this and the invention of the high-tech ignition key, it looked as though the relatively low-tech profession of car theft would die, not of outsourcing, but as the result of clever American engineers.

But the car thieves did not give in to their displacement without protest. The better capitalized thieves turned increasingly to the use of tow trucks. The underfunded ones turned to an invention that was older than the automobile industry itself. They went out and bought guns. They had quickly realized that if technology had insured that only an authorized person could start and drive the automobile they needed to steal, they first must establish control over the authorized person. They found that a gun was the surest way to start up a car that did not belong to them, provided they could catch the owner when they were vulnerable. Gas stations, parking lots, and occasionally the residents' own driveways became prime opportunities to practice this latest advance in car theft—called car-jacking. The cleverness of the automotive engineers had now endangered the very public that it had intended to protect. While the main object was still to get the car and sell the parts, a host of ancillary crimes were born as well. In many cases, the victim of a car-jacking was forced at gunpoint to drive to various ATMs, withdrawing the maximum amount of money from each. Car owners were now being shot, raped, and terrorized during the theft of their car, and it took the police some time to put most of this new breed behind bars.

10

AT FIRST, HIS new school was nothing more than a mandatory and unwelcome impediment to his only passion: hunting. But, in Rico's teen years, any history classes that addressed war and conflict began to hold his interest and occupy some of his thoughts. By this time, he had added the use of sophisticated booby traps and decoys to his hunting methods, rigging elaborate pits and nooses that killed when Rico was absent. His marksmanship, already far beyond superior, improved even more as Rico learned to account for the effects of the wind on his bullet over hundreds of yards. He also became adept at anticipating the path that his quarry would take to flee—sending a bullet to a sure rendezvous with the unsuspecting animal.

For Rico's classmates, their senior year was a time for applying to colleges, football games, dating, and trips to the California coast. For Rico, it was a time for long hunting treks through rough terrain. It was a time to attune his 20/10 vision to look for every nuance and variation in soil and vegetation. A bent twig, a paw print, or a dozen blades of grass that curved in an illogical direction told Rico everything about a species—its size, and its destination. But Rico's fixation with hunting did not end with traversing the fields, valleys, and forests of the surrounding terrain. He devoured every word of the *Soldier of Fortune* magazine that arrived in the mailbox each month. He visualized hunting in far-off lands. More and more frequently he aspired to hunt for more than small game or coyotes or even elk. Rico's ideal new targets would be self-aware. They would fear that they only had a limited time on earth and that a bullet from his gun would end that time. His new targets may be armed as well, but would stand as much chance of avoiding their fate as the first thousand rabbits that he had killed. Rico formed a new goal. He wanted to hunt for man! The latest issue of *Soldier of Fortune* had an article about the snipers in the Vietnam conflict. After a brief history of the Garand sniper rifle that had been used since 1903, the article espoused the benefits of the latest model, the Remington 700. Unlike the Garand, the Remington was a bolt action rifle. Exhaust gages from expelling a spent cartridge would no longer influence the sniper's aim. With the Garand, a trained sniper could expect to kill effectively from as far away as 550 yards with a two and a half power scope mounted on the barrel. The Remington 700, however, could accurately deliver a bullet to 900 yards, and kills of over 1,000 yards were alluded to.

Something deep inside of Rico stirred at the prospect of being able to kill a man from half a mile away. That the man had a gun also and would willingly shoot Rico should the opportunity present itself made the scenario all the more savory. The thought of being the sole decider of when a human being's stay on earth should end began to intrigue Rico to the point of obsession.

There was a way to be able to make that decision again and again without fear of reprisal. Quite the opposite, each kill would be sanctioned…approved…by his government. Rico's 18th birthday was the following month. A week after reading about snipers in Vietnam, Rico sat in front of a Marine Recruiter in a small office. Hunting, trapping, and running for hours to track his quarry had left the 6-foot 1-inch Rico at 180 rock hard pounds. The doctors that administered his pre-induction physical only shook their heads at the contrast between the emotionless Marine recruit and the others they saw that day.

Boot camp at Camp Pendleton began one week later. To the

tough Drill Instructor, Rico had the conditioning and focused demeanor not of a raw recruit, but of a recent graduate. Rico quickly became his favorite. Rico, for his part, was already aware that to be accepted into sniper school he would be expected to excel in every portion of training camp. The D.I. could not help *but* observe the extra level of attentiveness from the young recruit during every facet of weaponry instruction. Within hours of being assigned one, Rico could disassemble and reassemble his M14 as quickly as the instructor himself. At the shooting range, the D.I. fought to hide his astonishment at the discipline and accuracy of the Marine recruit at any distance. By the end of boot camp, Rico was head and shoulders above the rest of the platoon—moving and thinking like a battle-tested, hardened Marine. Days before, the D.I. had approached his star pupil about the possibility of sniper school. For the first time he thought that he detected a hint of a smile on the normally implacable young man.

At the Marine sniper school at Camp Pendleton, it was known and accepted that fully 20 percent of those that began it would wash out. Although each new arrival had qualified as an expert marksman during basic training, some inevitably failed to master the advanced techniques that were introduced daily. The bullets fired from each rifle traveled at 2800 feet per second, but gravity affected them as though they had just dropped out of the barrel. Snipers needed to become adept at estimating distance for this reason. The farther away the target, the higher the rifle needed to be sighted above it. Each man had to learn how to sight in his rifle with an eight power (8x) scope affixed to the barrel. Wind speed and direction become important factors in the successful completion of a long distance shot and the men were instructed at length on estimating each.

In an era well before the invention of portable Ground Positioning Satellite units, map and compass reading could be as important to survival as a rifle. The subject was covered for an entire day at sniper school. Radio procedures were set forth and each student practiced on one until the instructor was satisfied.

Rico was being trained at Camp Pendleton to be part of a two-man team. Tales of a lone, Rambo-like Marine spending months in the jungle and living off of the land were to be greatly exaggerated in latter-day movies. In reality, the Marine brass intended that these smallest of units in the armed forces were to have dual roles. Officially known as a scout-sniper team, the men involved were not only trained to kill at a distance. They were also taught to move forward, slowly and undetected, to a position well in advance of an artillery unit. Using a radio while peering through binoculars or even their rifle scopes, they were charged with relaying enemy positions to the rear. Mortar and artillery fire could then be directed from the main unit to rain down on an unsuspecting enemy. As such, target detection and camouflage and concealment received a great deal of attention during the course. Although the best experience would not be attained until they were in the jungles of Vietnam, the teams were coached to anticipate and think like the enemy. Survival, evasion, and escape were stressed at length.

Every day, after the classroom activities were over, the entire squad moved to the fields to practice. They sighted and re-sighted their scopes. They shot thousands of rounds at impossible distances until they could place bullets in a small grouping that was not much bigger than a human heart. They fired one shot at a time or sped up the process to empty their five-round magazines within 15 seconds or less. At the end of each training school, those that made it could hunt humans in the jungle for days on little or no sleep. Their rifles were encased, protected, and viewed by some of them as an object to be worshipped. Soon after graduation, they were shipped off to the hellhole that was Vietnam.

It was spring of 1969, and Rico had boarded a military transport plane with 30 other Marines as it hopscotched across the Pacific. After a brief stop in Hawaii, the plane took off for Guam. Six hours later, the plane lifted off on another leg in Rico's journey. It landed in Okinawa, Japan the next day. From there it would take the young sniper two days to line up a flight to Da Nang in South Vietnam.

On the long airborne rides across the ocean, Rico, had he chosen to, would have had plenty of time to assess his fellow passengers one by one. Half showed visible, outward signs of nervousness but the other half, like Rico, seemed to show little emotion at all. Rico, of course, had always been distant, even in boot camp. He lacked either the ability or the desire to make friends...or both. He eschewed the camaraderie that began to permeate his unit at sniper school once the students began to feel united with a common purpose toward a common cause. None of the men in the school had been drafted. Some had enlisted for patriotic reasons, others for a career. A few had joined because they figured that they might be drafted anyway and wanted to have at least a modicum of control over their own destiny. But Rico felt none of the community. In fact, Rico felt no emotions at all...not at boot camp...not at sniper school, and not on this bare bones, overloaded cargo plane. Rico had joined the Marines for but one purpose...to be allowed to kill. The thought of killing men without concern of incarceration or reprisal while being paid a nominal sum to do so was very attractive indeed. Of course, there had been psychological testing and evaluations prior to his acceptance into sniper school. Those tests, as Rico quickly saw, were to determine if a young marksman had the mental toughness to site through his scope and gun down an unsuspecting combatant from hundreds of yards away. The psychologists were there to try to predetermine if the potential sniper was the type to be overcome with remorse, as remorse can be a fatal flaw in the chaos of war. The shrinks were well aware that even a hint of ambivalence about the last kill might affect the aim and determination of the next. Every evaluator that came into contact with the distant young man agreed...Rico would have no problem with killing again and again.

Now, on the Asian-bound plane, Rico finally stared at several of the more fidgety men with curiosity. None of the men were smokers, not by coincidence but because most smokers were weeded out during the acceptance process. The glow of a cigarette at night was a sure way to give away a team's position during their semi-solitary missions. In addition, the North Vietnamese Army was reputed to have scouts that were able to detect a waft of smoke lingering in the heavy, humid air from hundreds of feet away. Undesirable also were the aftereffects of nicotine withdrawal in a profession that depended on steady hands even more than the many other requirements.

Some of the men made weak attempts at humor while two or three attempted to occupy the time by reading. Rico flashed briefly on the letter in his duffel bag. Written by his stepbrother, it was a rambling and poorly worded attempt to break the news to Rico that Annie and his stepfather had just died. Four drunk teenagers had lurched into the couple's lane at 60 miles an hour and killed them head on. Two of the teenagers succumbed instantly as they were thrown through the windshield and one other lingered for two days before beginning his eternal rest. Miraculously, the driver survived with broken ribs and facial lacerations. Rico recognized the driver's name in the letter as a fellow classmate at his high school. The letter had been delivered to Rico at a critical juncture at sniper school. The class was scheduled to field test a Starlite night scope that evening. Leaving in time to make the funeral the next day was an impractical impossibility. Rico had refolded the letter after reading it—and avoided bringing up the subject to his commanding officer.

The propeller-driven C123 that ferried Rico to Da Nang was loaded with Marines and their gear. It took nearly eight hours to complete the last leg of his journey before touching down on a tarmac on South Vietnamese soil.

As the cargo door came down, blinding sunlight poured into the hold. The men blinked and squinted as they adjusted to this bombardment of the entire spectrum of light. After several blinks, the first heat wave rolled into the plane, engulfing them. Gathering their gear, the newly-landed Marines stepped single file through the hatch and down the stairway. By the bottom step, the oppressive humidity took hold, and each man began to bead with perspiration. In a land where temperatures at night may not fall below 80, the newcomers instantly found themselves taking deeper breaths as their lungs searched for oxygen. Rico smirked at the inconvenience. He had hunted in the desert before under blistering conditions, and knew that his goal now lie less than 100 miles to the east, just past the Marine base at An Hua.

Two days later, Rico left at dawn on board a chopper with seven of the cargo plane's other passengers. He used the ride as a mapping opportunity, closely inspecting and comparing the jungle terrain with all of the other areas that he had hunted in. His sharp eyes repeatedly picked out things that the others on board could only see through binoculars.

Eleven pairs of eyes looked out over the dense growth, clearings, rice paddies, and villages. Coming in low and fast to the Marine Base at An Hua, ten pairs of eyes watched for danger. They watched for saboteurs who would blow them out of the sky. They watched for the telltale puffs of smoke that indicated mortar rounds or heavy caliber bullets were on their way up.

One pair of eyes, however, saw only opportunity. This was the hunting land that Rico had envisioned. Although riddled with booby-traps, it was unfettered by fences, landowners, or city ordinances. Somewhere beneath that canopy—perhaps looking up at the overlapping layers right now as the chopper passed—crouched his first quarry. The chopper landed fast but with little jarring. Rico had been assigned to a 20-man recon unit and wasted no time in finding the lieutenant. He soon learned that one sniper/scout team had been assigned to the unit. Leaving on the same chopper that had just brought Rico in was half of the team. The corporal had just one day to go until his 13-month tour of duty was complete. Wounded twice, he had not opted for another tour. As a sniper, he had performed admirably with 12 confirmed kills and at least twice as many unconfirmed by senior officers. Rico was assigned as his replacement and quickly introduced to his new partner. PFC Miller had been in Vietnam four months longer than Rico and was six months older.

To the northeast of An Hua lay a no-man's-land dubbed Arizona Territory. Pockmarked by villages, rivers, and very violent tangles of jungle, Arizona Territory was thought to be harboring several units of the North Vietnamese Army at the moment. Almost nightly, sappers had been probing the defenses at the Marine Base, searching for weak spots in its perimeter. Sappers were bomb-laden, opium-fortified, half-crazed Viet Cong. A sapper's primary mission was to get as close as possible to a squad of Marines or an ammo dump and blow themselves up, inflicting maximum casualties. The base guards remained in a constant state of high alert, eradicating sappers with .50 caliber machine gun fire or by other means. In the past two weeks, the rate of sapper-attempted penetrations had been unusually high. They were being sent to die by somebody in Arizona Territory. The next day the recon team would be sent to ferret out the chain of command.

11

AFTER LEE AND MARY'S wedding, my blemished Datsun sports car was still in need of a hood and a windshield. A person of average intelligence may ask why I did not simply make an insurance claim. My answer would be that there were discrepancies in the title work. I was thus reluctant to leave the repair responsibilities in the hands of anyone other than myself...particularly anyone who might involve the police. A person of average intelligence *but* substandard moral character might then ask another question. If I claimed to know so much about car theft, why did I not just venture out in the night and procure another car? The answer to this is that I was making an attempt to reform. But I was also face to face with a conundrum. I could not force myself to spend the funds necessary to purchase the parts new at a Datsun dealership. I had no qualms, however, about purchasing them from an unauthorized redistribution facility, otherwise known as a chop shop. I made a phone call. My regular facilitator was out in the field procuring additional inventory. I made a second phone call. The regular procurement specialist was unavailable. His second in command was in the office, however, and would like to talk to me about a dozen previously owned car stereos. I thanked him and hung up.

My third phone call was answered by the procurement specialist himself on the second ring. I described the parts that I wanted. He had his entire inventory committed to memory. Unfortunately, he knew for certain that they did not currently have an automobile of my make—or the remainders of one—in the warehouse at the present time. To demonstrate his commitment to customer service, though, he would be happy to furnish me with another phone number. The owner of the number advertised deep discount pricing as well and had just approached him with an auto of my particular model two days prior. I thanked him and made a fourth call.

The phone rang eight times before a groggy voice answered. I explained what I wanted. I was assured that the parts that I sought would be removed from the vehicle by my arrival that evening. Further conversation revealed that I was dealing with a home-based business. It was in an area of Detroit City where the quality of the average home was often below the minimum standard. I received an address but was asked to park in the alley. I still owned a reliable tow truck and arrived in the alley by 9 P.M. A rat as big as a small child offered to valet my tow truck, but in economically disadvantaged neighborhoods I always prefer to self park. I waited for my salesman to appear. After several minutes, two salesmen stepped from behind a fence. I opened the door of my truck and identified myself. One of the salesmen greeted me and identified himself as the same customer service representative that I had spoken with over the phone.

In this particular neighborhood, most of the garages opened into the back alley. My salesman directed us to a nearby garage. It was of an older architectural style and had two wooden doors that swung out instead of up. My salesman's unfamiliarity with the latch led me to believe that perhaps the garage did not belong to him. A peek around the side of the garage told me that he probably did not reside in the home that I saw out front. The residence had a pronounced lean to it and all of the glass windows were missing. My salesman finally got one side of the doors opened. To my surprise, a dim light shone down from the ceiling when my salesman pulled on a string. As promised, a Datsun sports car was parked in the garage. But my shoulders sagged in disappointment. Regrettably, somebody had made the wrong entry on an inventory control sheet. The Datsun that sat in this garage had been manufactured in 1971. It was seven years older than mine. Because of my discovery, I was not particularly upset that the parts had not already been removed as promised. Although I did not see any other customers in the showroom waiting to be helped, I did not want to take up any more of the staff's time. I quickly told the salesman that I would not be making a purchase that evening. He looked crestfallen and asked me why. I explained that in spite of the car being close to mine in appearance, the parts were not interchangeable. What had been a pleasurable shopping experience thus far now began to turn tense. My salesman steadfastly maintained that in spite of the huge gap in the dates of manufacture, the parts would indeed work.

He broke several of the cardinal rules of a quality salesperson. He began to strongly disagree with his customer. He also began to raise his voice to his customer, although I will confess that his customer raised his own voice back. The salesman then began to insist that the customer complete the purchase regardless of whether the items met his needs. He said that if the merchandise was unsatisfactory it could be returned for a full refund. But the customer did not believe the salesman and shouted that he did not believe that he would honor the money back guarantee. Admittedly the customer did not word it as delicately as in the previous sentence but the general meaning was well understood.

Then my shopping experience turned very sour. My salesman committed the ultimate customer service faux pas. He began to pull a cheap chrome revolver out of his pants pocket and asked me, in a different tone altogether, "How much money do you got on you muthafucker?"

A Beretta .25 caliber Jetfire is a small gun. It can fit neatly into the front pocket of your jeans and no one ever suspects that it is there. It is a semi-automatic, which means that it can fire until empty as fast as you can aim and pull the trigger. The magazine only holds seven rounds but the one already in the chamber gave me eight. I looked like I was only fishing around for my car keys but I pulled out my tiny gun in a kind of ghetto quick-draw motion that I had practiced often both at home and at the gun range. Then I shot my salesman. I *had* been trying to keep his associate in my peripheral vision, but that became impossible after the shot rang out because he ran out of the garage.

My salesman stopped pulling the revolver out of his pocket and started screaming. He had his hand on his left hip and was leaning against the Datsun. My little gun was not very accurate and I had not had a great deal of time to aim. It did occur to me, though, that I had almost missed. My salesman was now yelling words at me that should never be said to a customer if the final sale is yet to be salvaged. I had seven more shots left, but I was concerned that my salesman may still think of firing back. In spite of the noise and hostility coming from my salesman, I took several quick steps forward and stuck my Beretta in his neck. He quieted down and stopped writhing long enough for me to grab the handle of the revolver still protruding from his pocket. It was a cheap Saturday Night Special, but it was loaded and the .38 caliber bullets looked real. My salesman resumed his diatribe toward me. If I were patronizing another establishment and the salesman behaved in this manner I would normally demand to speak to his supervisor and report him. Whether the employee was written up or fired from that point would be a decision that would be totally left up to management. I did not think that my salesman had an immediate supervisor…although 30 seconds ago he *did* have an associate. I hurried over to the door of the showroom and peaked outside. If anyone was lurking they were well hidden. I held both guns momentarily in my right hand while fishing out the keys to my truck. I stuffed the chrome revolver into the waistband of my pants and "palmed" the little Beretta. Ten seconds later I was in my truck starting the engine. Fifteen seconds after that I was out of the alley and onto a residential street, listening for police sirens. Not hearing any, I gradually found my way to a freeway and headed for home.

On the ride back, I tried to decide whether my salesman or his associate intended to involve the police after our misunderstanding in the showroom. My best guess was that they would choose not to. I decided that the salesman would be reluctant to summon the Detroit Police to a shooting scene where he kept a stolen car with his fingerprints on it. He obviously knew that I had confiscated his weapon. He had no way of knowing, however, whether the gun might still be connected back to him by prints on the handle, barrel, or even a bullet casing.

There had not been time to determine precisely where the salesman had been struck. He had been clutching his hip, however, and I calculated that if the little projectile had impacted on bone, it would have flattened or distorted. Tracing it back to my gun would have thus been difficult with a ballistics test, but it still would not do to surrender it should I be contacted by a law enforcement official. I resolved to retire it for a year or so and instead switch to my bulkier Glock. I made some other resolutions that evening as well. I would never again patronize any more of the unconventional automobile parts wholesalers, no matter how deep the discount. I would also continue a transition that I had already begun to the fitness industry, where disputes were rarely settled by gunfire.

12

MARINE SNIPER/SCOUT teams consisted of two men. One long-range sniper rifle was assigned to each team. Private First Class Miller, as the most senior man on the team, was to be in charge of it. Although Miller and Rico were both extraordinarily qualified marksmen as far as the Marines were concerned, it was customary for the most seasoned team member to do the actual shooting. Rico's duties included but were not limited to the care of the backup weapon, the radio, and as much food, water and equipment as he could carry. Should a target present itself, Rico would also be expected to supply input as far as estimating range and the target's value. In Vietnam, the sniper teams were unique in that they usually did not require clearance from the chain of command to fire.

    Miller and Rico crept through the jungle, well in advance of the rest of their unit. Their immediate objective was a heavily forested hilltop that would give them a protected but panoramic view of the surrounding countryside. They reached the hilltop by dusk and dug in for the night. They alternated with four-hour watches, with Rico insisting on taking the first and the last. As Miller slept, Rico used the Starlite scope to examine every tree, bush and vestige of a trail within a one-mile radius. Two hours into his watch, Rico's patience and persistence were rewarded. In the pitch-blackness—which became an eerie green in the lens of the scope—a low branch quivered in a half-second of movement. With experience and instinct born of years of hunting much smaller game, Rico calculated that the next branch that moved would be 20 yards to the left. Two minutes later, he proved correct. Waking Miller, Rico quickly advised him that one individual would be showing himself in eight to ten minutes as he crossed a ridge that led around their position. Miller was fully awake now and looked at his quiet new partner with some skepticism.

Somewhere in the night, a North Vietnamese Army scout was picking his way silently through thick foliage, listening intently, with his Russian AK47 pointed forward.

On the hilltop, a still doubtful Miller nevertheless handed the M40 sniper rifle back to Rico. He reminded Rico that he was a couple of hours shy of having a full day of experience in the field. Rico stared through the scope, unresponsive. But, Miller continued, if Rico was that sure that a target was going to appear at a precise location in just minutes, it wouldn't hurt to preset the scope for the 400-yard shot. Rico's nod of acknowledgment was barely perceptible as he made the adjustments and took up a firing position.

The NVA scout was the veteran of a thousand missions. Treading lightly in sandaled feet, the soldier paused every other step to listen, sifting through the few noises that a sleeping jungle made. His main unit was encamped in relative safety five miles to the north. For the past two weeks, he and another scout had been ferrying explosive laden patriots of the revolution to the huge base where the American bastards cowered behind minefields, walls, and barbed wire. Most of the patriots had committed indiscretions against the State and Chairman Ho and had "volunteered" to redeem themselves in this one final act of bravery. But building up their courage required a great deal of opium to be smoked first during their training period. The opium inevitably caused a drop in their appetites. Their weakened states thus made the journey to the American camp difficult and threatened the success of their gestures of repentance.

Tonight, the scout was to determine if a natural haven existed somewhere along the ridge, or if a cave or tunnel needed to be dug.

After a day of rest in a hidden position, a patriot would then be able to make the entire final thrust under cover of darkness. At 20 years of age, the scout's vast experience would also enable him to detect the presence of the enemy. They were sloppy, these foreigners, and even a small group of them trampled the ground like an entire herd of the villager's cattle.

Soon the rains would come, sometimes for days without stopping, and tunnels would be impractical. Enlisting the help of the local villagers to find a cave would be unwise as well. An elder might proclaim his commitment to the revolution on one day but fall victim to the absurd American "hearts and minds" campaign the next. The cave's location would be the first and easiest betrayal. The scout would have to continue the search on his own, he thought, as he stepped warily into a clearing on the ridge.

His search ended abruptly when what felt like a severe kick in his chest halted his forward motion. His right lung and part of his spinal cord exited through a gaping new hole in his back. His legs went numb and he crumpled to his knees, dropping his head to look down. An instant later, the back of the scout's head exploded, spraying brain tissue and bone across the clearing as the second high velocity round struck.

The scout's mission was over the moment round one found his sternum. The Marines had a term for it. The North Vietnamese Army scout was DRT (dead right there).

The second shot had been unnecessary for the kill but Rico enjoyed firing the rifle. The crack of the M40 had echoed quickly twice against the trees. Miller thought that his still-green partner was just trigger happy and was about to caution him about giving away their position. Wordlessly, Rico turned the rifle over to his partner and indicated the clearing with a slight twitch of his head. Miller sighted through the scope at the motionless figure, muttering under his breath, "I'll be damned, I'll *be* damned!"

Rico had killed at night before…and often. With the night-vision scope and the precision-made rifle, tonight's kill had been ridiculously easy. But the lack of challenge was more than offset by the prey. Rico had not experienced a feeling like this since that first day in the field with the .22 rifle. Not terminating any prey's existence since entering boot camp only intensified the thrill that Rico had just experienced. The hiatus from delivering death made tonight's event all the sweeter as the pent up need was suddenly released. Outwardly Rico was as emotionless as ever, but inside a form of euphoria spread through him, leaving an extremely pleasant afterglow.

An hour after the kill, Miller nodded off again. Rico spent the rest of the night combing his surroundings with the night scope, declining to wake Miller for a watch.

By morning some of the euphoria had tapered off, and Rico was able to catnap. At mid-afternoon the rest of the unit caught up with the sniper team. One hour before dusk, Rico continued his probe of the countryside with field glasses until once again a branch moved counter to the direction of the wind. A minute later Rico caught another movement and gestured to Miller. Ninety seconds later Rico, Miller, their sergeant and their lieutenant all lie with their field glasses riveted to a point on a hillside three-quarters of a mile away. Collectively, their best estimate was that a NVA unit of 30 men lie beneath the canopy, waiting for the cover of darkness before they continued. A strategy to neutralize the unit was quickly developed. The coordinates of the NVA unit's position were radioed to the rear. At eight miles from the artillery unit's position, the NVA were just out of range of a 105mm-howitzer shell. But a nine-mile shot was well within range for the 155mm-howitzer. The lieutenant called in the fire mission to the artillery battalion himself, encoding the coordinates as he supplied them. In several minutes, a 90-pound artillery shell would be on its way, hurtling to a distant location on the Arty Battalion's map. Its impact would be devastating. Highly explosive cyclonite would kill by blast effect while shrapnel sought out any living organism within a wide radius. After impact, the sniper team would be allowed to shoot at any survivors, although their success at hitting a moving target at three-quarters of a mile was unlikely. Rico cocked an eyebrow quizzically at Miller. With a bemused expression, Miller nodded toward the sniper rifle. Quickly, Rico was in firing position, making last-minute adjustments to the scope.

"Shot" was heard over the radio, meaning that the howitzer had fired its projectile. Soon, "ten seconds" was heard, meaning that the shell would impact and explode within that time. After exactly ten seconds, there was a flash on the hillside, followed by a rapidly expanding cloud of smoke.

Rico had decided that any survivors of the devastation would tumble downhill and to the right. The prevailing wind would blow the cloud of smoke to the left, giving him the possibility of a clear shot. As the four men watched, two shell-shocked North Vietnamese Army regulars staggered down into a clearing, away from the carnage. The lead soldier partially obscured the one that followed, but both seemed disoriented. Rico's rifle cracked sharply as he fired. The first soldier stopped in his tracks as his chest caved in and disintegrated. Immediately, he toppled backwards onto his companion. Rico instantly racked another round into the chamber, checking in at two more clearings through the sight.

Sergeant Michael Cholak had already seen one tour of duty and was on his second. As the last of the smoke continued to waft along the hillside he continued to monitor the impact zone. Nothing moved. The experienced non-com wasn't surprised. The two NVA survivors hadn't surprised him either. In battle, survival might depend on little more than being behind the right rock at the right time. However, Sergeant Cholak did have two immediate concerns. The first was why Rico, the sniper, was sweeping his scope across other areas instead of the impact zone. Sergeant Cholak had watched *two* men enter the clearing, one behind the other. Surely, Rico must have seen the same thing through his scope before he fired. Therein lie Cholak's second area of concern. What had happened to the second man? If he was playing possum, he would be risking a second artillery shell. If he had dived for cover when his buddy fell, he should have made a move by now. Out of the corner of his eye, Sergeant Cholak glanced at Miller. Miller's field glasses had been trained on the clearing as well. The Sergeant signaled to Lieutenant Peter Spina, who had now been in country for nearly three years. Lieutenant Spina had just signed off with the Arty Battery, thanking them for their accuracy. He stepped back to the group and brought his field glasses back up. The three men stared at the clearing. Sergeant Cholak was the first to speak. "Private Pagan?"

"Yes, Sergeant?" Rico replied.

"Can you give me a reason why you do not continue to monitor the clearing south of the impact zone for the second enemy soldier?"

"Because he's dead, Sergeant." Rico answered.

"How do you know he is dead, Private Pagan?"

"Because I shot him, Sergeant." Rico informed him.

Sergeant Cholak hesitated. It was Lieutenant Spina's turn. "Private Pagan?"

"Yes, Lieutenant?" Rico replied.

"Private Pagan, I think that all four of us were present when you fired your rifle. I also think that all four of us would agree that we witnessed one helluva good shot. My question to you, Private, is whether the Sergeant and myself somehow failed to hear or see you take a second shot?"

"I did not take a second shot, Lieutenant." Rico answered.

It was Sergeant Cholak's turn again. "Rico, if you didn't take a second shot, how the hell did you shoot him?"

"I shot both men with the same bullet, Sergeant."

Rico's teammate had never taken his eyes off the clearing. "I'll be damned," Miller said. "I'll *be* damned!"

The next morning, the patrol set out for the hillside. Cautiously, they approached the area that the howitzer had sent its shell to. There were torsos of North Vietnamese soldiers on the ground, around a crater, and stuck in the limbs of trees. Severed limbs, some with weapons still strapped around them, lie strewn about.

Lieutenant Spina ordered two men to count up the pieces and give him a total. When they finished, they arrived at a figure of 28, give or take one or two. Flies had already descended on the rotting carnage as it cooked in the intense morning heat.

Two hundred feet down the hill, PFC Miller and Sergeant Cholak stood in a clearing examining an enemy corpse. A small entrance wound at the sternum had initiated the soldier's untimely death. As they rolled him over, a gaping hole in his back marked the exit path of the bullet. The corpse underneath sported a slightly bigger entrance wound, caused no doubt by the bullet beginning to tumble after striking bone in its first victim. Corpse number two had been shot directly through the heart…death had been nearly instant. The Lieutenant joined them as Miller was damning himself once more.

After taking a moment to evaluate, the Lieutenant spoke. "Private Miller, under what circumstances did Private Pagan kill that scout two nights ago?"

"It was the damnedest thing, Lieutenant. It's like Rico became the guy. Rico said he saw some leaves moving…which *I* sure as hell can't see through the Starlite when *I* use it. From that he claims that he knew where the gook was gonna be and when. So then he gets off a shot and I'm guessing…that he missed with the first one, and got him with the second. But here's the thing, sir. When we got to that one this morning, we all saw that he'd been hit twice. Now if Rico had hit him in the head on the first one, the gook would have just fallen over dead. But then, that means that there couldn't have been a torso shot 'cause the guy would have been lyin' on the ground for Chrissake. So what happened is that Rico gets him in the chest first, like he had the round waitin' ready for the guy the minute he steps out of the bush. Then the guy's hit, see? So he goes down on his knees. It hasn't set in yet that it's fatal and he's gonna die in ten seconds anyway so he looks down to see how bad it is. When he looks down the back of his head is exposed like…see what I mean?" Miller got down on his knees, tilted his head forward, and demonstrated.

"Now I dunno what Rico had in mind. Maybe he didn't believe that one round would do enough to kill the guy, but I don't think so. Maybe he wanted to send two rounds in the guy's direction anyway in case the first one just winged him, but I don't think that's it either. Lieutenant, I think that Rico was just showin' off *to himself!* It was his first kill while in country and maybe he was just enjoyin' it. You know, makin' it last…like a good steak! I couldn't see jack shit that night without the Starlite and he knew it. He didn't know for sure if we'd ever go check the body, either. I don't think he even cared if we got over to verify anything. He didn't say a word after. He just kept huntin'. Now you see what he did to these two. One shot, two kills. I think he was just evening things up on purpose. When you average 'em all in, Lieutenant, Rico is still makin' one shot, one kill!"

Sergeant Cholak spoke up. "I might buy into your story, Miller, except for one thing. Rico took this shot at 1200 yards. That means he was aimin' maybe six feet above the heads of these guys to make up for the bullet dropping as it got there. There was a pretty stiff wind comin' from the east that he had to figure in, too. Now I don't doubt that one round killed both of these gooks but I've done some shootin' myself and I've never even heard of a hit from almost three-quarters of a mile. I'm thinkin' that Private Pagan was just damned lucky!"

Lieutenant Spina was quiet for a minute. Finally he spoke. "Well, I think we would all agree that Private Pagan gets credit for killing three enemy soldiers within a 24-hour period, no matter how he did it. My report will reflect that accordingly."

13

KAREN COLUMBUS WAS a very thin woman. At 5-feet 7-inches, she was tall in stiletto heels but topped out just above my chin when barefoot. Karen had to eat on a timetable to maintain her weight at 100 pounds. At 37 years old, she had never borne children. The ligaments that attached the two halves of her pelvic bones never had reason to respond to the presence of the hormones that signal them to soften and allow the pelvis to spread. In short, Karen's hips were extremely narrow. She and her stick-thin legs shopped for jeans on the slim rack in the teen boys department. Her pencil-like arms drew stares when she wore anything with a half-sleeve, so Karen wore only long sleeve blouses or sleeveless tank tops. Karen was of Russian heritage, with a very Russian sounding surname—until she married 40-year-old Dennis Columbus after her 22nd birthday. Karen's straight ash blond hair fell just past her shoulders and was cut to complement her thin but beautiful face. Huge brown eyes looked out over a long thin nose that allowed her to change her expression from regal to bitch with a half squint. Karen was blessed with a complexion that required little makeup. God also favored the woman with disproportionately large, uplifted breasts and they were a great source of pride for her. Unfortunately, the entire amount of ultra-thin Karen that the Lord allotted for the construction of her magnificent bosom left nothing to spare for the peaks. As I would discover later on when I became her co-worker, Karen had extremely small nipples.

14

BETWEEN MISSIONS, RICO declined to participate with the other men in the constant search for ways to alleviate the tedium. He also seemed to revel in the heat and humidity of the intolerable climate, as though his body responded best when subjected to conditions that paralleled those of Hell.

Early in the morning, Miller would open one eye to see his partner float back into his bunk after a run around the camp's perimeter. Several times, Miller stumbled upon Rico doing push-ups in a area behind the mess tent or chin-ups on the bar that supported a makeshift clothesline. Rico was not aloof from the other men…in fact he knew all of their names and would say them aloud in acknowledgment during passing. But Rico seemed more content when separated from the rest of his unit, reading the books on war and tactics that one of his stepbrothers had sent him from home. Almost daily, Rico could be found in the guard towers, sweeping the surrounding lands with field glasses for signs of enemy combatants that the men on duty might have missed.

But it wasn't until Rico and Miller went out on a mission that Miller saw his partner in his natural environment. Loaded with food, water and weapons, Miller by now had relinquished any deference that his seniority might have commanded, and merely settled in behind Rico. They covered ground in long strides at first, but as the relative safety of the camp fell away, their profiles changed.

Rico had a fluid, stalking way of gliding over the terrain that reminded Miller of a hunting cat. Miller spent much of his travel time checking and rechecking their flank.

With Rico handling the sniper rifle, the body count of Viet Cong continued to grow. His uncanny ability to seek out anything in the fields or jungle with a weapon amazed Miller almost weekly. After a time, Miller began to notice that Rico seemed to be alternating the way they stalked enemy soldiers. On one day they may be lying in wait as a small group or solitary enemy came to them. But on the very next day they may be the ones doing the overtaking, picking off a rear guard or the leader as opportunities presented themselves. Rico seemed to know where quarry could be found at any time. It became a given that Rico always took the longer shots and the multiple shots himself, but offered any short range chances to his partner.

In the Vietnam War, several legendary snipers were purported to have upwards of 90 or more kills confirmed by their commanding officers. By the time Rico's own count approached 50, he seemed to have lost all interest in any verification procedures. If he showed any inclination at all to document a kill, it was only to strip paperwork off of a dead enemy officer and turn it in.

As Rico's kills soared, the end of Miller's tour of duty drew near. He was now known as a short-timer, and looked forward to marrying a long-time girlfriend back in the States. Any soldier—whether a Marine "grunt" or an officer—with less than 30 days left in Vietnam before shipping home was labeled a short-timer.

Since the highly trained snipers always seemed to be in short supply, and Miller's record was exemplary, he expected an invitation from an officer soon to re-enlist. With less than three weeks to go, Miller's Sergeant delivered a message that Marine Captain James Klauza wanted to see him. Ten minutes later, Miller was sitting across the desk from Captain Klauza. Seated next to the private was Lieutenant Spina. The Captain spoke first. "Private Miller, first of all I'd like to say that you're being promoted to Corporal, effective immediately. I show you as having 15 confirmed kills on this tour, and I have no doubt that there were probably several more that did not get reported."

"Thank you, Captain," Miller replied.

"I'm also promoting your partner to Corporal, effective immediately, and I wanted you to be the second to know. Has he told you?"

"No, Captain. Believe it or not, we don't talk much."

"Yes, Lieutenant Spina here has apprised me of the fact that Corporal Pagan isn't much of a talker. I would also observe that with 70 confirmed kills he prefers the bush to the camaraderie of his fellow Marines. Corporal, that 70 number seems unusually high. Do you accept it as being accurate?"

"No sir, I don't."

"You don't?"

"No, Captain. I'm guessing that the actual number is maybe five times that. That doesn't include all the bastards that got fragged with all the different booby traps that Rico came up with."

"Corporal Miller, as you sit here, does *that* figure you just cited seem high? Would you like to reconsider your statement?"

"No, Captain. It's true. We got so many gooks so many different ways that there wasn't always time to count up what was left of 'em. I've never seen anything like this guy. It's like he's part Indian the way he gets us to sneak up on 'em. It's real strange workin' with him, Captain. The last two months, we never come up on an enemy by himself anymore. I don't think it's by coincidence. I think Rico just doesn't want to. When we come across 'em, they're always in small units. He never calls in arty support anymore, either. He'll kill two or three before they can drop or scatter. Then when the rest run…we'll spend two days straight huntin' 'em down until I'm so tired I can't stand up or pull a trigger. Then Rico will let me rest for a day and we do the whole thing again. The stranger thing is, Captain, that I feel safe while were doing this. I know safe and Nam don't go together but when I'm partnered with Rico that's kinda how I feel 'cause I know he wants someone to come within range. That's what he waits for when we're resting. 'Course, the other side of the coin is the way it feels when we're walkin' around out there. Like I said, he doesn't talk much and I've had a lot of time to think about this. Captain, when we're walkin' together it's like I'm walkin' around with Death. It's creepy, I'm tellin' ya. He's like somethin' that was sent down here just to collect these gooks up and send their godless souls straight to hell."

Lieutenant Spina spoke for the first time. "You talked about Rico making booby traps with hand grenades?"

Miller replied, "Don't get me started on that. I could go on 'til it's time for me to ship out. You know how the gooks dig those pits and then plant the spikes sharp side up at the bottom? I think Rico used to do that back in the States to catch animals. I told him that the gooks also smear crap and poison on the points so that even if the puncture doesn't get to ya the infection eventually will. Well, he got a real distant look after that and had me help him dig a few pits of our own on their routes. Now, our pits were only maybe waist deep on these short little bastards. And they were cone shaped…you know…they got real narrow at the bottom. So the gook falls into it for a second and nothing happens to him. But then he climbs up and out real easy except that he's stepped through a noose at the bottom of the pit. Now he's got a rope tight around his ankle when he gets out. At the other end of the rope is a fragmentation grenade. When the grenade follows the guy out of the pit the pin gets pulled and comes out just as the gook joins his buddies again. Then the grenade explodes and they're all f---ed! Rico used to put a bunch of these pits close together and then at night when they were on the move listen for the explosions. Then we'd go hunt down anybody that lived. He had about ten different traps but I think his favorite was the one that had the grenade up in a tree. When you tripped a thread on the ground the damn thing would swing down from the tree with the pin out. He had it figured to blow chest high as soon as it got to the place where the thread got broken. Lieutenant, I've seen eight, maybe ten bodies scattered around after one of those tore into a unit. This guy, its like he's always thinkin' of a new way to kill."

Miller had their full attention, so he continued. "Now remember the part I said about feelin' safe. I don't know if it's his eyes or if it's because you can't fool Death, but he knows where every booby trap they set is. It gives me the willies, like he helped them set 'em up and that's how he knows where they are. We might come to an area that looks okay and he'll stop me. You know how he likes to disarm the exploding ones? He'll take his knife and throw it… he's got an arm like Mickey Mantle… and he'll cut the wire like that before I've even seen it. That way it never goes off and the gooks don't realize that we're in the area until it's way too late for them."

Captain Klauza spoke again. "I'm sure I'm speaking for both the Lieutenant *and* myself when I say thank you for giving us that insight. But as you probably know, one of the reasons that I wanted to meet with you was to see how you felt about re-enlisting."

Corporal Miller cleared his throat. "Yeah, well, I've given that some thought too, Captain. See, the thing of it is that I've made it through the last nine months without a scratch. Now, I got a wound in my leg the first week that I was here with my other partner…the one Rico replaced. So maybe I re-enlist and I get a different partner eventually and he ain't like Rico and we get in a scrape the first time out and I die. Or maybe I re-enlist and I get to stay partnered with Rico but then I gotta put up with these creepy feelings he gives me. Like sometimes I feel safe…like I'm safe as long as I'm walking *with* Death. But then sometimes I catch him lookin' at me with his head cocked and I feel like my life ain't worth jack shit if I'm not able to help carry his precious grenades and supplies. Naw, Captain, I think that I've made it this far and that I'd better call it good. And honestly, I think I've helped this guy kill maybe 500 gooks so I *know* I've served my country enough already."

Captain Klauza sighed. Miller was going to fold 'em and walk away. He would not be dissuaded by anything that would be said in the Captain's office that day. It sounded like he had already seen more death and carnage in nine months than many career soldiers saw in a lifetime. The Captain thanked Corporal Miller and excused him, extending his hand to wish him the best of luck in civilian life. Lieutenant Spina stayed on to discuss Corporal Pagan's next partner. An experienced man may have conflicts with Rico, they agreed. A man just out of sniper school would be content to let Rico lead and would be as safe as possible as long as he could carry his fair share of water and weapons. Lieutenant Spina was very pensive as he left the Captain's office. He was also concerned. Men like Rico often had difficulty adjusting to civilian life after the horrors of war. The Lieutenant resolved to have a talk with him once his tour was over, counseling him as necessary.

Rico was assigned a new partner/spotter within a week. A typical hunter-kill mission might be two or three days. With Rico as the unquestioned team leader, his new spotter had to endure a week at a time or more. To the new man, it was a relief when their C-rations ran out because it meant a return to base camp within 24 hours.

Lieutenant Spina's reorientation talk with Rico was to be postponed indefinitely when the Corporal re-upped with two months remaining in his tour.

Rico's new spotter did not last. While the confirmed kills of Corporal Pagan remained steady at two or three per mission, the reality was much higher. His new spotter lasted one month before applying for a transfer. He began to drink heavily at every opportunity, and soon his drunken mutterings to his squad leader began to work their way up the chain of command. Lieutenant Spina soon began to hear bits and pieces of tales that described Corporal Pagan intentionally wounding a Viet Cong soldier and allowing another to remain whole. Rico and his spotter would then trail the unwounded soldier as he helped his stricken comrade back to a hidden base camp. Darkness would be spent booby trapping the camp perimeter and all paths leading to the sniper team's position. As the sun rose, Rico would begin picking off the main unit from 1000 yards away.

Lieutenant Spina downplayed the reports until the man's replacement hunted with Rico for a month before also applying for a transfer amid identical accusations. A third man lasted for two months and in spite of gentle admonitions from Lieutenant Spina about endangering his team members unnecessarily, Rico persisted. Reluctantly, the Captain took action the only way he could. Corporal Pagan was promoted to Sergeant and transferred to the Sniper Training and Refresher School at Da Nang as a Range Instructor.

Like a wild animal that's been lured into a life as a zoo exhibit, Rico chafed under his new assignment. Twelve months passed—during which Rico applied twelve times to be reassigned to the field. Sergeant Pagan was denied permission to transfer each time as the United States commitment began to wane in 1971. The handwriting was on the wall and Rico saw that soon no American would be paid to hunt for enemy soldiers in North Vietnam. His application for transfer to stateside was immediately granted. Within one week, Sergeant Pagan was pushing paperwork back at Camp Pendleton and using his accumulated leave time to hunt and kill four-legged game once again. By the spring of 1972, Sergeant Pagan was honorably discharged.

15

I HAD MY FIRST contact with Karen Columbus when she called into my fitness studio in late 1989. She spoke succinctly, in a carefully modulated voice that sounded like Glinda the Good Witch. Her voice also had an ethereal quality that increased when she wanted to make a point, as when she explained to me that she had always been not only thin but extremely weak. She wondered if weight training might help her build some of the strength that she'd always lacked. I explained that if we started gradually, increased slowly and prudently, and if her attendance was consistent, my fitness studio would be the answer. I opened the facility at noon the next day and Karen pulled up at 12:01. She drove a new, completely spotless bright red Olds Cutlass Supreme. In an inspired design move, the manufacturer had fitted the outer door handles into the window pillars, and the beautiful chrome-spoked wheel covers accentuated a carefully thought-out trim package. Karen stepped out, her white outfit in sharp contrast to her medium tan. Her nearly wraparound sunglasses gave her a sporty, yet classy look that blended perfectly with her expensive-looking gold jewelry. Psychologists speculate that the reason that bright red lipstick became popular was because it drew men's attention to the orifice of the mouth when women smile or spoke. Further speculation was that it reminded men of another orifice surrounded by red lips that society dictated be kept obscured from public view. Karen's lipstick was a *very* glossy shade of red. From our phone conversation I already knew that Karen had always been thin and self-conscious. Although she struggled somewhat with the glass front door of the studio, it was not an invalid that seated herself in front of me at the gym's desk that day.

Tuning out the rehash of her tale of a life without muscle and her fear of strong winds, I focused on the movement of her ruby-red lips and ample bosom. In spite of her waif-like structure and long nose, the woman exuded sex appeal. She spoke in a highly educated tone and demonstrated an extensive vocabulary. When her litany of the perils of being the weakest woman on the planet began to subside, I jumped in. I explained to her about muscle fiber recruitment and the fact that 95 percent of what was available to her lie fallow. I assured Karen that we would summon up that un-utilized portion to turn her into an Amazonian goddess if that was what she desired. She emitted an approving squeal of delight and we agreed to start that minute.

16

During the grinding routine at Camp Pendleton, the problem began as a fluttering at the bottom of Rico's stomach. At 6-feet tall, Rico was a hard, muscular 190-pound physical specimen. He could not recall being sick since childhood, but over a period of weeks the occasional fluttering turned into a dull discomfort that began unpredictably…and then subsided. His appetite and unusual strength remained a constant but soon the turmoil in his stomach became a nagging recurrence. Rico pushed it out of his mind but it came back like a jungle parasite.

A week prior to his discharge, Rico was walking from his living quarters to his desk when he stopped dead in his tracks. A matronly looking woman, clad in a flower-patterned dress and sensible shoes, was standing on tiptoe to kiss a Marine recruit on the cheek. Without warning, Rico's discomfort began again immediately. Rico cocked his head to stare. A mother was saying good-bye to her son, nothing more…but the act sent Rico's insides into a spasm of protest. The answer flashed to Rico an hour later. The day after his discharge, Rico stood in front of his mother's grave for the first time.

~~~~~~~~~~~~~~~~

At 22, Kelly Essman spent most of his waking hours drunk. It had been over three years now since the five people had died in the accident he had caused on that lonely California highway. By the time that the hospital staff had thought to draw his blood, he was just below the legal limit…and for that he was grateful. Fortunately, the traffic court judge and the prosecutor were close friends of Kelly's father. They agreed with Kelly's counsel that the young man had suffered enough with the loss of his three best friends. Added to that, the death of the couple in the other car would be a burden that Kelly would have to bear for the remainder of his days. Kelly received six months probation and a stern warning to never drive an automobile again after consuming alcohol. The pain from his injuries subsided soon after leaving the hospital and the scars continued to fade weekly, but inside Kelly still hurt—he really did. It seemed as though the only painkiller that helped was made by Jack Daniels. If Kelly slept until 11:30 A.M. he could begin medicating after noon, which assured him that he was not yet an alcoholic.

Several job attempts came and went until his father grew tired of arranging interviews. If Kelly stopped drinking by six or so, he found that he could clear his head enough to eat the dinner his mother prepared and drive to the bar by 9 P.M. By 2 A.M. it was time to start up the old Ford his mother had given him and drive cautiously home. He had learned a hard lesson during that careless night nearly four years ago and did not want to hurt anyone again. Once safely home, it was time to sleep it off until the next day, when the need for medication would arise again.

Kelly's father left promptly at 7 A.M. every weekday to begin an 80-mile drive to the law office. His mother drove off at 10 A.M. on Mondays and Thursdays to see a "close friend" two towns away. Neither ever noticed the driver in the dark blue '68 Impala as it passed their house sporadically. And on Mondays and Thursdays, neither Mr. nor Mrs. Essman would return until after six.

Rico knew this for a fact as he had cruised by the pleasant home in the quiet neighborhood at 5 P.M. one Monday and at 7 P.M. the next. His nondescript Chevy cruised the Essmans' street twice a day for three weeks until he had everyone's schedule down pat. The postman was always finished by noon. The neighbors on either side of the Essman family always left for work by 8 A.M.

The neighbor's house on the east side of the Essmans intrigued Rico the most. They had an in-ground pool.

Early Monday afternoon a white van from Clear Way Pool Service swung into a driveway on the quiet street. The man that regularly drove the van on the route wasn't driving at the moment. He was lying unconscious in the back amid pool skimmers and buckets of chlorine. Nor was this house a regular stop on the comatose man's route. The residents at this stop performed their own pool maintenance.

Rico, looking smart in his commandeered uniform, stepped out of the van while staring down at a clipboard. Still giving the board his full attention, he rang the front doorbell of the home. When the door failed to open—as he knew it would—Rico walked up the driveway to the rear of the house. *Still* consulting the clipboard when he reached the pool, he kept going…to the rear yard of the Essman residence.

A narrow walkway lead directly to the rear door of the neat brick ranch. Twelve hours ago, Kelly Essman had used this same door to stagger inside and then careen down the hallway to his bedroom. Kelly usually forgot to lock the door behind him when he came home drunk. Lately, he always came home drunk.

The knob turned easily in Rico's leather gloved hand. He opened the door and walked in as though invited, closing it quietly behind him. The sound of a television program at the front of the house drew Rico down a thickly carpeted hallway. Kelly was seated on the front living room sofa, his second glass of Jack Daniels half gone and resting in front of him on the coffee table. He startled as Rico entered the room and tried to focus up through bleary eyes.

"Oh! Hey buddy. Whadda ya, lost?" Kelly looked at the clipboard. "Oh, uh, I guess my mom let ya in." He looked back at the television. "I hate to break it to ya buddy, but we don't have a pool. Wish we did though, I could use a dip now and then to clear my head after too much of this, if ya know what I mean." Kelly raised his glass and took a sip. "Just havin' a little hair of the dog right now, if you get my drift. Geez, I met this broad last night and she musta had a hollow leg. I'd order one up and she'd be ready for one too. We went glass for glass 'til we closed the place. I think it took me three tries to get outta the parkin' lot. Hahaha!"

Kelly had amused himself and looked over at Rico to see if his joke was appreciated. It wasn't.

"Hey lighten up. I don't know if you guys can take a break when you're on duty or whatever you call it, but maybe I can get you a little refreshment or something?"

Rico's silence was starting to irritate Kelly. Kelly took a harder look at the uniformed poolman. "Hey, you look familiar. I've seen you before!"

Rico still offered no explanation. Instead, he selected a footstool from several feet away and moved it near the coffee table before seating himself.

"You are…you are Rico, Rico Pagan! I went to school with you!" Kelly announced triumphantly. "So when did you start fixin' pools? I didn't even know you still lived in this town. I swear!"

All at once, Kelly's face went pale. His hand trembled and it made the ice cubes clink on the sides of the glass. He set the glass down hard on the table. He missed the coaster by a foot.

"Oh, geez, Rico. It just hit me. That night. Geezus, Rico, your ma. Lissen, I wasn't trashed like the paper said. I mean, oh geezus, Rico. I'd had a few, but I was still okay to be out there. Y'see there were four of us in that car and the others, well, they were outta control. I was the only one that could see straight enough to get us home. And I *wasn't* drunk. I swear. I'm sorry about your ma. The other guys, they were yellin' and shovin' at me and shit. I told 'em to knock it off…one of 'em grabbed the wheel a mile before it happened but I got it back on the road okay. Oh, geezus, I feel like crap about it still. I ain't been handlin' it so well myself. I talked to a shrink about it. He says I got issues with guilt and shit."

Rico's silent presence was causing Kelly's heart to start pounding. Although the front drapes were drawn shut, the afternoon sun had driven the outside temperature to over 80 and normally the living room would heat up as well.

Kelly, however, found himself shivering. His dirty white T-shirt and worn jeans hid most of the goosebumps, but the dozens on his arms gave away his discomfort. There was a distinct chill in the room, as though it had suddenly been converted into a meat locker. Kelly spoke very nervously. "So, uh…how long ya been fixin' pools Rico? And…and why does a pool guy need leather gloves anyway? The chemicals bother your hands, huh? Say, let my ma bring ya somethin', okay. Ma! Hey Ma! Rico looks thirsty!" Mrs. Essman didn't answer. A tense 30 seconds passed. Kelly had begun sweating *and* shivering.

"Lissen Rico, I know we weren't close in high school or nothin'. So you're not here to talk about the old days. I know that. This has gotta be somethin' about your ma. I already told ya I'm sorry, I don't know where else ya want me to go with that. But I gotta give it to ya straight, here. You are really wiggin' me out by not sayin' anything. Is it money ya want? I got a few bucks in my room. It's yours. I'll get it!"

Kelly started to rock to his feet. In one fluid motion, Rico reached behind his back and his hand returned with a 10-inch Bowie knife. Kelly froze. Still seated on the footstool, Rico moved his thumb slowly around the handle, as though checking for rough spots. Kelly trembled uncontrollably. Then, in a quiet voice, he asked, "Rico, my ma ain't here, is she? *She* didn't let you in, right? I think maybe she's gone and I think maybe you know that. If you thought maybe you'd come over and scare me a little and see me sweat for what you think I've done, I can unnerstand that, okay? But geezus, Rico, I'm different now. And…and there's somethin' I never told nobody. That night…that night *they* came across the line, not me. Maybe your step-dad fell asleep…I dunno. I just didn't tell the police that 'cause I didn't wanna cause any more pain. So if you just go now I'll still keep it my secret, you know? Nobody will hafta know."

The figures on the television set stopped moving. No sound came from their mouths. Rico's square jaw remained motionless. His dark eyes were vacant, hollow, and not human. Kelly rocked forward, quicker this time, but the blade flashed in an arcing blur. The razor sharp steel blade entered at Kelly's carotid artery and sliced a deep furrow across the entire front of his neck. Skin, muscle, and trachea parted as blood poured out in a crimson waterfall down his neck. The tip of the blade then neatly bisected the jugular before Rico pulled the knife back. Kelly's eyes bulged as he reached up to his neck with both hands, but the skin was far too slippery to grasp. The middle of the wound gaped open two inches as air whistled out from the lungs. Kelly pitched over unconscious. His heart rhythm grew weak and stopped less than one minute later.

Despite the torrent of blood that soaked the T-shirt and pooled across the coffee table, the bottom legs of Kelly's jeans were dry. Rico's head cocked to one side for a moment as he examined the path of the blade's travel. He reached out with the knife once more—much slower this time—and wiped both sides across Kelly's left calf. As he stood up, he returned the huge blade to its sheath above the belt beneath his jacket.

Rico returned the footstool to its original position, lining it up carefully with the indentation in the carpeting. Moving quicker now, he glided down the hallway, glancing into the bedrooms. He found 40 dollars in a nightstand drawer in Kelly's room, and nearly 1,000 more between three more drawers in the master bedroom. After each currency find, he tossed the remaining contents of the drawer on the floor. All jewelry was placed into a small handbag that he would dispose of in a dumpster that evening. Four minutes after Kelly's blood first began leaving through his neck, Rico left through the back door.

Without ever looking up or around, he consulted his clipboard as he strode back to the van. It was hot inside and the regular driver was beginning to moan through his duct tape, but traffic was still light and Rico was soon back at his car. Rico blocked two cars in with the van. He left the windows down and the doors unlocked before pulling away in the Impala. His stomach felt fine.

17

THE BENCH PRESS has been a standard measure of strength for well over half of a century. As its name connotes, the exercise is performed by lying flat on a padded bench. A metal bar is grasped with both hands spread three feet apart and extended straight up over the chest. The bar is then lowered to the chest by the presser and pushed into the air again until the arms are straight or "locked out." The bench press uses many of the same muscles that a push-up does but the amount of resistance is easier to control. A beginner can start with a light bar for ten repetitions and switch to a heavier bar or gradually, over weeks and months, add weight to the ends. Young men who lift weights for looks, sports, to fend off bullies or to become one constantly ask each other, *"How much can you bench?"* The response is usually in terms of the maximum amount of weight that can be pressed into the air for one repetition. The reply, thus, may be, "I max out at 300." This is almost always a lie. Just as young men lie about the size of their penis, the ease of their sexual conquest, and about the speed of their car, they lie about their "bench." Occasionally, the answer will be to the effect of, *"I work out with 200."* This infers that the young man is able to bench press 200 pounds at least eight to ten times without stopping or cheating. In the 1950s, a man who could bench press his bodyweight one time was considered to be strong. Currently, one measure of a strong man is his ability to bench press his bodyweight ten times without resting. Hence, if a 185-pound man can bench press this amount of weight above his chest for a set of ten or more, he meets the criteria.

Very few men can bench press 200 pounds ten times. Fewer still can bench 300 one time. As an aside, a maximum bench of 400 is an extremely unusual feat of strength and power. Some football players, pro wrestlers, and a few other men who spend inordinately long amounts of time in gyms accomplish this prodigious feat of strength. Five hundred-pound benches have been measured but require years of preparation and often the injection of illegally obtained synthetic hormones and other black market drugs.

I began with an eager Karen that day on a series of warm-ups for her shoulder and chest muscles. Her grunting and gasping made it apparent that these warm-ups (which the average nursing home resident could sail through) were quite difficult. After the preliminaries, I settled her onto a bench. In the uprights over her head I placed a small solid bar weighing 14 pounds. A husky six year-old should have been able to press it using only one hand. Karen used both hands and could not. The bar crashed ignominiously to her chest. Fortunately, Karen had plenty of natural padding there and was not injured (other than her pride, which had already been in an ICU and was on its way to the mortuary). I had to move quickly to save face (and to stop a chagrined Karen from asking for her check back and slipping out the front door the next time that the wind blew it open). The woman had absolutely no chest muscles beneath her perfect breasts, and her shoulders sported even less. I improvised. A back closet in the little gym featured a push broom with a sturdy steel handle. I unscrewed the handle. It weighed about two pounds. We began bench pressing with the broomstick, being careful to keep it away from Karen's neck to thwart the possibility of her windpipe being crushed as she tired.

It took two weeks to master the broomstick. I found some short pieces of iron pipe and duct taped them in matching sets to the end of the broomstick to increase the total weight every week. Soon, the nation's frailest 37-year-old woman had improved in the ranks of the weak to number 100,000 or so. Karen continued to make three appointments per week and keep them. Her part-time job as an interior decorator occupied little time. She continued to eat a healthy amount, dining out nearly every night with either her husband Dennis or her boyfriend Andrew.

One month after our quest for strength began, I weighed the broomstick and its taped on pipe pieces. The entire affair weighed 12 pounds. Karen was able to bench press this enormous weight for three sets of 14 repetitions each. My student was also able to squat down 15 times with a staggering 20-pound bar placed across her slender shoulders. Her frail looking arms seemed to grow muscle daily as they increased in girth from the size of my thumb to the size of my wrist. Muscles began an ever-so-subtle punctuation of the straight line above her knees when she flexed her legs. The day for Karen to graduate from the broomstick had arrived. With great ceremony, I placed the 14-pound bar from that discouraging first day across the uprights of the bench. With the confidence of a long legacy of massive Russian weightlifters coursing through her blood, Karen grasped the bar. Tensing every upper body muscle available to the now 103-pound Amazon, she pounded out a set of 15 repetitions!

I recorded six months of workouts as I continued to make promising progress with my attractive, sensuous client. By the time she weighed 112 pounds Karen was able to bench press a 45-pound "Olympic" bar 12 times and squat the same bar with a 10-pound weight affixed to each end. As her strength and confidence grew every week, so did her trust in me. She confided that her 15-year marriage to Dennis was on the wane. The successful breadwinner traveled a great deal, and some months the couple only saw each other on weekends. The take-charge, up and coming 40-year-old ad executive that Karen had found so exciting 15 years ago seemed like a very old 55 to her now. Dennis' itinerary included trips to Chicago more often than all of the other cities combined. Karen suspected that her husband's travels also included frequent respites at an apartment tower near the downtown area. But Karen's face belied neither jealousy, anger, nor remorse when she spoke of this neglectful rotting of their union. They had little in common. Sex was infrequent, and when it did occur it was passionless and compulsory.

18

In the spring of 1973, Lieutenant Peter Spina USMC (Ret.) eased his gray Pontiac Catalina past the blocks of anonymous apartment buildings. Two festively wrapped red packages—complete with gold bows—occupied the rear seat. He passed a very plain two-story apartment house that was clearly marked Building 400. Building 500 was equally nondescript and came up quickly afterward. It wasn't until the Lieutenant turned right at the corner that Building 600 jumped into view. Several parking slots on the side were marked with a "visitor" sign and he parked the Pontiac in the one nearest the front door. Reaching around, the Lieutenant scooped up the packages, got out, and made his way across the lot. Once inside, he climbed the stairway to the second floor and turned left. He found apartment 210 quickly and stopped, taking a deep breath before he knocked. He could not hear anything inside and was on the verge of knocking again when the door opened several inches. When no face filled the gap for several moments, Lieutenant Spina spoke quickly.

"Rico! Sergeant Rico Pagan! How the hell are ya? You *must* remember me…your commanding officer. Stop being so shy and invite me in!"

Rico made his decision quickly—soon Lieutenant Spina was sitting in a modest recliner in a sparsely furnished living room. He hadn't expected a warm greeting, and none was offered. Pete Spina had an inkling that his presence would not be tolerated for an extended period of time. He would make the most of the time that he would be allowed. But first, he needed to ensure that he was protected.

"I hope you don't mind, Rico. I got your forwarding address from a good buddy in records at the base. He remembered you, too…I mean, with your record…and the rumors of your unofficial body count, who wouldn't? I told Diane where I was going too, although I didn't mention who I was going to see. I just said I was going to check on one of my men…see how he was doing after *his* war ended. My God, you look fit! You're going to need bigger T-shirts, soldier. All of that muscle won't fit into that one pretty soon! Anyway, Diane and I went over the map and I left a copy of the address with her in case I ever needed to look you up again someday!"

The Lieutenant eyed Rico. He had never been able to tell what the man was thinking when they were back in country. Nothing had changed. He still could not. But he had established that at least *two* people knew of his whereabouts today. It would afford him some measure of safety if his proposal was not well received.

"Rico, I know you've never been one to sit around and shoot the shit. I'm not here to waste your time and try to change that. You know that there must be something I want or I wouldn't be here. First of all, I want to say that both of those packages are for you. Now, I know that you couldn't give a rat's ass about what's in there, but I assure you that the bigger package is something that you had and that you miss…you just don't know it yet! You can keep them both even if you turn me down, all I'm asking is that you hear me out."

Rico was sitting upright in an armless wooden chair. He did not look uncomfortable. Compared to sitting on a log at the edge of a swamp, he probably wasn't. But his hard stare did not indicate any interest, either. Taking his second deep breath of the afternoon, Lieutenant Spina plunged ahead. "How did I know you were still in the area? I didn't. But I read a newspaper article and I figured that you had been in the area. You see, a fellow was killed during a burglary last month. His throat had been slit. Slit doesn't even cover it. His damn neck had been cut halfway through. It wasn't like he surprised the burglar, though. He was just sitting there, watching television…getting an early start on his Jack Daniels. No sign of forced entry either. Every door was locked—except in back. The burglar either had a key or just walked right in. Nobody else was home. The neighbors on either side weren't either. Nobody in the neighborhood heard anything. Nobody saw anything. Burglar didn't get much. Maybe a thousand bucks or so. I guess some jewelry turned up missing, too."

Rico's eyes had narrowed to slits. They opened when Pete paused. There was no turning back now. At this point, if he stopped talking and tried to go he probably wouldn't make it out of the chair alive.

"The dead guy was young, too. Just 22, no job, lived with his parents. I'm reading between the lines. The guy had nothing going for himself. Seems as though this human waste had some problems in the past, too. Got a snoot full, killed five people in a head-on collision. Three were in his car. The other two were a married couple that he had to cross the highway to hit. Never got any time for it. Killed five people and never did a day."

Pete was halfway through the forest now. He was still alive. Now he had to negotiate the other half before he got out safely.

"You want to know what I think, Rico? I think that this piece of garbage got what was coming to him. I think that the world is better off without him. I think it was his fate to be in the same house as that burglar. His life wasn't even worth the cash and jewels that the guy who did him in got. You know what else? I'll bet the burglar was smart. I'll bet he kept the cash but got rid of any jewels that same day. I don't think he sold them, though. I think he just threw them away. Didn't fence 'em. He's too smart to sell them and have the cops trace them back to him. The cops don't have anything to go on and this guy will never get caught. Just like they'll never figure out who thumped that pool guy and then took his van for a joy ride with him in it. Brought it back to the same spot, too. Broad daylight and nobody could help the cops with a description or a motive."

Rico didn't move a muscle. Pete noticed for the first time the chill that permeated the room. *What the hell am I doing here?* This guy had killed 1000...maybe 2000 men. The government told him to do it for his country. He did it for some other reason. But Lieutenant Peter Spina had faced death before. This would be just another time.

Pete leaned forward slowly to emphasize a point. "And Rico, nobody's ever gonna help the police with this one. You know why? Because somewhere, at any given moment, there's somebody walking around alive that deserves to die. Maybe they hurt somebody else. Maybe they've done a wrong that's so terrible that they should be stopped before they do one that's even worse. That drunken piece of shit deserved to die, Rico. Whoever did it should get a medal, not be investigated or judged. Whoever did it was doing his country a favor. Taking this guy out means that there won't be any more mothers in the future without their sons because of him. Husbands won't lose wives because of that asshole. And sons won't lose their mothers. The cops were never going to take care of him. The judges were just going to keep looking the other way. But Rico, it was something that had to be done. And I for one am damned proud that somebody stepped up and did it."

Pete took another deep breath. He had passed a critical juncture. He had revealed what he knew and was still alive to say his next piece. He could not read Rico's reaction. Nobody in the United States Military ever had. It was doubtful that Rico's own departed mother knew what made this guy tick. It could be, of course, that nobody ever wanted to know...to open the lid on *that* box of horrors for a peek inside.

"Now, Rico, I know you haven't been out long. Couple of months...maybe a little more. The war was winding down anyway. Our country lost its stomach for fighting...for a while maybe. But probably not forever. I don't want to get too personal, but my guess is that you haven't lined up a career yet. No hurry though, right? The Marines didn't pay us much and I don't think you spent any of yours while you were in country. You got yourself a car and enough left to carry you for a while. It's probably not enough to go out and start buying expensive toys though, which leads me up to the two packages here. The big one is like being reunited with an old friend. It's a Remington 700, just like you used over in 'Nam. Don't ask me where I got it because I already forgot, just like I'll forget where I left it the moment I walk out of here. The other package is a .22 caliber Smith & Wesson fitted with a new silencer. It's about as loud as a mouse fart, you know what I mean? I don't recall where I got that one either but I *do* know that no serial numbers were ever stamped onto the frame. How it left the factory that way nobody will ever know. I'm rapidly developing amnesia about where I left that one too."

Pete had not expected a warm rush of thanks and none was forthcoming. He did however, clearly observe Rico blink his eyes. Suddenly he realized that he had never seen Rico blink before. Was it a sign of trust or a sign that a decision to terminate this conversation had been made? Pete moved quickly to the next item on his agenda.

"Rico, I know a guy. He's a businessman. He imports things. I don't like what he imports but it's not up to me to decide what he does for a living. If he doesn't import it then somebody else will…somebody who might sell the product to school children. Now the businessman does in fact have a competitor. His competitor has done more than just compete. The guy *stole* from the businessman. He killed some of the businessman's employees, too. This competitor wants to put the businessman *out* of business. I admit the guy I know is never going to be elected Pope, but this competitor of his is about three rungs lower on the scum ladder. Rico, in the left inner pocket of my jacket is an envelope. It has $10,000 in cash. It has the address of a post office box that's not in my name but I have access to. It also has pictures of the businessman's competitor, his home address, and a half dozen of his favorite hangouts. Whoever killed that drunk back in your hometown was patient. He knew about people in the area. He knew when they were coming and going…waited until the guy was alone. Well, this competitor is never alone. He keeps two or three goons around him everywhere he goes. But sometimes he's more out in the open than others. If the big package looks too big for just the rifle, it is. I've got a night scope in there, too. And two extra barrels. If somebody were to take a shot at somebody else and the coroner recovered the bullet, it couldn't be traced back to that rifle if the barrel had been replaced."

Pete only had his continued existence on Earth to indicate how well his proposal was going over. He was still breathing.

"Rico, you have got to be thinking…what's in it for Lieutenant Spina? The price tag for this job is $30,000. I was paid half up front." He removed the envelope and set it on the arm of the chair. "I'm giving you ten right now. When the job is finished I get the other half, and you get another $10,000. This is the last time we ever see each other. After the job, I need you to get a P.O. box under another name. You send the info on your P.O. box to mine and check back a week later. Your other $10,000 will be in it. Don't go in yourself. Give some kid a hundred bucks and the key. That's it though. My cut is one-third of every job. I do okay because I've got more than one guy doing your end of it. I don't live flashy, but I've already got a nest egg that I *didn't* have when I got out. I can't see you spending much, but a guy has to make a living. Still, I don't think that what you saw and did over in Nam left you with the desire to work a nine to five."

Lieutenant Spina stood up. He had survived yet another brush with death. He would go home one more time. His wife thought that he was a camping gear salesman. He intended to leave it that way. As he reached the door, Pete turned back with a last thought. "You know, Rico, in a way we're still fighting for our country. Citizens are being hurt every day. A goddamn heroin dealer is trying to kill people in this country from within our borders. He doesn't give a crap about America. So what if they're gonna pay *us* to take *themselves* out! As patriots, we would probably do it for free!"

19

Over several confidential weeks Karen fed me parts of her life, piece by piece, and would carefully gauge my reaction to each morsel. The origin and consequent slow demise of her marriage was only the first course. It was a course that I'd already seen on other clients' menus dozens of times by then, and except for the larger than normal age gap, offered no unusual ingredients. The second round of revelations varied more from the norm but was presented and received—although matter-of-factly—with a garnish of sadness. Karen was fully aware that Dennis kept a paramour in the Chicago apartment tower. He made no great effort to conceal it. Some cursory credit card detective work in regards to last month's business trip had revealed dual entrees at dinnertime—and shoe purchases from Fantastic Fashion. Travel invitations to San Francisco, Los Angeles, and New York had admittedly grown more infrequent from Dennis over the past five years. Requests for companionship to Chicago, however, had become non-existent in the past two years and Karen was loathe to press the issue. Much of her reluctance to delve deeper into her husband's infidelity stemmed from a relationship of her own that Karen was pursuing.

20

JORGÉ SIGHED. ALREADY the heat was making him sweat like a virgin on the night of her marriage. He mopped his swarthy face yet again with the small white towel. His face now included a larger part of his forehead where ten years ago it had not, he mused to himself. But if those were his only two complaints, that he was losing his hair and it was already 80 degrees here in Miami, then he was a lucky man, indeed. Not just one, but both of his boats had made it in last night. Both trucks had been waiting not 500 yards from the boats' final position on the beach. With the four men from each truck and the two from each boat, the entire load of marijuana and cocaine had been transferred in less than three minutes. The events of the night had meshed together like the gears of the clock, and Jorgé Consuelo was a satisfied man. In Miami, many men dreamed to be such a man as Jorgé, but few could combine his business sense with his ability to demand loyalty and respect. Jorgé was a man who did not hesitate to order his men to do whatever it was that had to be done. Jorgé was a man of his word until he was crossed. And lately, Jorgé had maybe been too much of a ladies man. He knew how this upset his Lorita and now—as he sat poolside at noon—he regretted striking her pretty face when they had argued. He had explained that the chica was just a whore for the coke but that he was a man and a man could not be expected to push away one so young and insistent all night long. Perhaps if Lorita had more of the friends of her own then she would not whine and complain so. Jorgé was only doing what a rich and powerful man was entitled to do. After all, he may have accumulated great wealth these last five years because of his sense of business…but before that he had won the heart of his Lorita because he was a *man*!

By the late 1980s the drug running techniques that Jorgé had perfected could gross him a million dollars in a good week. His fleet of fast offshore boats now stood at ten. At least two of them were always being rotated out for repairs and refittings to make them faster still.

After the demise of his Jefé in 1985, Jorgé had branched out on his own, pooling his money to purchase a 30-foot Scarab. He spent his 33rd birthday hollowing out the cabin area, removing the head and any other creature comforts to make room for product. With its two big engines roaring in back, the deep-vee offshore boat could make its run from the drop-off point in the Bahamas to a Miami marina in less than four hours. Although Jorgé had spent $100,000 on the boat, his first run alone had netted him nearly that much. It was after that first successful transaction that his business savvy came bubbling to the surface. He worked to improve his supply chain, extracting promises that—as he committed to purchasing more—the cost of his product would diminish. In the temporary vacuum left by the death of his Jefé, this calculating man of business secured the most important guarantees of distribution as well.

But the competition had fast offshore boats also, and after another profitable run Jorgé bought a newer 40-footer, nearly doubling the payload of each run. The vans and trucks he used were always rented, and it would not be long before he would learn to obscure each rental with layers of shell corporations. Soon Jorgé had a small but reliable workforce, and only the most senior had ever seen his face.

If Jorgé had a special edge, it lie not in his ruthlessness, but in his ability to be able to find any advantage that would keep his business healthy and prosperous.

The U.S. Coast Guard knew all about the fast boats that added to the flow of drugs pouring across the country's borders. Their own intercepting gunboats had been embarrassed hundreds of times by successful traffickers—catapulting across the waves until they were out of sight. Jorgé's growing fleet of 40-foot drug runners had a maximum speed of 50 miles an hour. As the Coast Guard began to order boats that were often from the same shipyard and had similar speed capabilities, his operation was becoming more vulnerable.

Jorgé recognized early on that losing a boat to the authorities every now and then was just a cost of doing business, but new innovations could help keep costs down. The Coast Guard's boats were getting faster, so in his second year of business he had all five of his retrofitted with superchargers. At wide-open throttle, the belt driven add-ons would accompany the roar of the exhaust with a steady whine as they shoveled torrents of air down through the huge carburetors. Soon each of Jorgé's boats topped out at 75 miles an hour as they screamed across the South Atlantic Ocean.

Crime prevention measures were also tightening at every port and harbor. A suspicious boat at night was almost as likely to be challenged as not, and a valuable shipment could easily be lost at the dock before it could be unloaded.

Jorgé had developed a novel but simple technique to avoid disasters like this after reading about a whale that had beached itself along the Carolina coast. Frantic beachgoers had gathered and pushed and heaved until the confused animal was once again afloat.

Jorgé directed his men to find a stretch of sandy beach that was accessible with a truck. He instructed them to purchase battery operated strobes and beacons that could be placed atop the cargo compartment of the truck. On a clear night, the approaching boat could be guided in without the use—or the risk—of a marine radio. In the wee hours of the night, an experienced captain could cut his engines and pull up his drives while still well offshore and glide the heavily laden boat into a landing. With enough men to assist, the boat could be unloaded in minutes, and with some assistance from the propellers that now were barely immersed in the water, the men would heave at the boat until the water became deeper. From there it was back to the marina to be gassed up and prepared for a future run.

21

If course number one had been a recital of Karen and Dennis' salad days, and number two an explanation for the marriage falling into a soup of discontent, the third course was still only the appetizer for what she really wanted to tell me.

At first, Andrew was mentioned only as a luncheon companion. She had met him after he requested a quote from her fledgling interior design business. Andrew, at 35, was two years Karen's junior. At 5-foot 10-inches, he carried his 165-pounds with the ease of a thrice-weekly runner. His curly brown hair was kept short as befitted the rapidly rising supervisor of a multi-branched bank's consumer loan division. Andrew's sixth floor bachelor apartment was situated near downtown Birmingham, Michigan in such a way that it afforded a view of busy Woodward Avenue and still overlooked the small park near the library. At work, many loan applicants that met the requisite standards never came into contact with Andrew. His loan officers merely checked the information and approved or rejected the loan. By the time the paperwork arrived in Andrew's office, his secretary needed only a rubber signature stamp to finalize the application and initiate the creation of a check.

Twenty percent of the loan applicants, however, were lacking in one area or another. Party store owners—with 200,000 in cash to put down on their 400,000 dollar dream home—could only produce tax returns that alluded to an income of $5,000 a year. Auto execs making $300,000 a year had nothing to put down after their divorce settlements and attorney fees. Young couples with entry level jobs tried to explain their need for a top-of-the-line Mercedes Benz on paper. The bank had rules, and it was ultimately Andrew's job to make sure that their rules were followed. It helped that Andrew—with his Masters Degree in Finance—had recommended many of the policies and procedures adopted by the rapidly growing bank eight years ago. Since that time, Andrew had been the manager of the department. He controlled the battalion of loan officers employed by the bank. He approved the interest rates set by his division. Andrew was in charge, primarily because he was never wrong. He had the final say over the hopes and dreams of hundreds of people daily for the burgeoning Bank Corporation. Andrew controlled lives. Although the bank had rules, it was also in the business of lending money. Sometimes the rules needed to be bent a little to accommodate a customer—and thus lend out more money. Occasionally, an ironclad requirement needed to be reinterpreted to complete a deal. For instance, a million dollar home might not be located in a neighborhood of other million dollar homes. For this reason and others, the appraisal might come in too low, and the man who wrote the rules would be asked to use his power to adjust them ever so slightly. With Andrew in charge, the division's profits doubled almost yearly.

This pleased his father—at once the parent company's President, CEO and largest stockholder—greatly. From 8 A.M. to 6 P.M. Monday through Friday, Andrew wielded his power like a benevolent dictator, loaning and denying, hiring and firing, but always in control. By week's end Andrew had usually made a thousand decisions and was weighing a thousand more.

It was after just such a week that Karen arrived at Andrew's apartment. It was 9 A.M. Saturday morning and Andrew had postponed deciding on breakfast fare due to the presence of both granola *and* bagels in the pantry. Karen, awake since 6 A.M., was vibrating with ideas and bombarded her decision-weary client with a myriad of color and texture possibilities. The living room's furniture necessitated the use of pastels and neutral colors like taupe…unless, of course, her client wished to consider changing the carpet and sofas as well. Andrew was more concerned with the ample bosom that swelled out of the enthusiastic designer's white linen top. The display was not entirely by accident. A plunging neckline had been carefully selected at 8 A.M. after a confirming phone call had determined that Andrew required her services due to a lack of input from either wife or girlfriend. Karen suggested earth tones in the master bedroom. Andrew shrugged his shoulders, distracted. Karen raved about Corian countertops in the kitchen. Andrew inhaled her perfume deeply, tilted his head, and responded with a goofy smile. Karen reached up on tiptoe in the living room to indicate the height of a border while Andrew gazed at her long, thin legs. After two hours of energetic suggestions about the apartment's possibilities, an excited Karen invited a hungry, enamored Andrew out to brunch.

And after three weeks of taking her trainer into her confidence, Karen was at last ready to serve him the entrée.

22

Jorgé sighed again. Sweat now ran down his face in rivulets. His little towel was soaked and he signaled to Paco to get another one from the pool boy. Members of his security staff were seated at various tables around the hotel pool. With their dark hair slicked back, and their eyes covered by even darker sunglasses, Jorgé's soldiers halfheartedly tried to blend in with the other guests. Some of their flowing flowered shirts bulged at odd angles with the Mac 10s underneath. Out of the six, four were wearing earpieces, but were not tapping their feet to any music.

These annual meetings with the Columbian cartel representatives always made Jorgé take extra precautions. His security was well paid, vicious when necessary, and loyal. But the Columbians could be unpredictable...with sudden territorial changes and outrageous advance payment demands—that sometimes had to be dealt with harshly.

Yes, Jorgé thought, *I will be glad when meetings like this are a thing of the past.* His planned retirement on his fortieth birthday two years hence could not come soon enough. To stay alive for seven years in this business was not an easy feat. He had invested much of his money in warehouses about the city, hoping for this to provide a substantial retirement income for himself and perhaps his Lorita... if she could learn to control her outbursts. Jorgé thought back again with some regret. This time he had cut her on the cheekbone when he had struck her, and he hoped for her sake that it would not leave a scar. If she could not learn to accept his infidelities as the years passed, he would be forced to set her free. She would need every bit of her remaining beauty to secure another patron, but already there were areas of her that showed wear and tear from their disagreements.

Jorgé thought of what he had seen when he looked in the mirror that morning. The worry and the pressures of this business were exacting a heavy toll on the features of one who had once been a dashing and handsome man. His once jet black hair was not only falling out, but what was left was sprinkled with gray. Creases in his forehead and 80 pounds of extra weight made him appear at least ten years older, of that he had no illusions. Still, when he did venture off of the grounds of his walled-in mansion at night, the chicas continued to flock to him like thirsty swans to a lake.

As he sat at the best tables, ordering the finest wines, everything from the gold around his neck and his wrists to the way that he carried himself spoke of a man of wealth and power. How could they not be attracted to such a man as this? Afterwards, once they had discovered the passion that lie within him—and the staying power when things became sexual—they were reduced to tears when told to leave him to sleep.

Jorgé considered carefully his net worth. The emergency account in Switzerland held five million, give or take. His accounts in the Caymans combined would yield nearly 25 if he so chose to remove it. His warehouses and the lands around them were worth at least five or more. Already they brought him half a million a year in rents, and that figure would multiply many times as he added to their number. The warehouses had other value as well, providing Jorgé with a plausible means of support should he fall under the scrutiny of the authorities. His sweating increased as he performed the mental calculations. When he had 50 in the Cayman accounts he was going to walk away, which should be on or about the fortieth year of his birth. On the radio, a man sang this advice as well. He sang that you got to know when to hold them…and when to fold them. The man said also, of course, that you can count your money later but this seemed foolish to Jorgé. He would walk away at 40 years old or at 50 million dollars…whichever came first. He would perhaps still keep Paco on, but he could not pay him so much.

Jorgé looked around. His security was still alert, but he did not see Paco. The man was valuable because he worried about everything. One minute the men and the situation here at the pool. The next about the men guarding the rooms and the cars. Still, the cars could be checked for bombs later. Right now, Paco's place was here, at the side of his Jefé.

A man in a white suit opened a gate in the fence that surrounded the entire pool area. Behind him, another man in a white suit stood waiting to be escorted through. The man behind the boss was also dressed in white, eyes no doubt darting everywhere from behind the black wraparound shades. As the three men from the cartel approached the table where Jorgé sat waiting, he gave an involuntary snort. *All three with the white suits, they look like pissed off vendors of the ice cream.* But he knew that beneath the suit jackets at least two of the men had more firepower than the police force of a small town in his native land. He thought of his mama who still lived there. Here in Miami, he was a rich man among many rich men. But back in the old country, he would be known as a man who could buy the entire land with the stroke of a pen.

The men were almost here and still Paco was nowhere to be seen. Jorgé himself signaled to a passing pool boy, indicating for the umbrella at his table to be raised. It would not do for the men who spoke for his suppliers to confuse the sweat caused by the sun with that of the sweat caused by the fear. As always, the men had faces that looked like they had just been told that their wives had all taken lovers. *They must practice this look of seriousness in the mirrors of their hotel,* Jorgé thought.

The pool boy finished with the umbrella as the spokesman for the little group sat down. Even in the shade, the skin of the spokesman's face looked like it had been borrowed from a bumpy road. Out of the three serious looking men, this one must have practiced the most, because he looked very grave indeed. Of one thing Jorgé could be sure: If the man looked like he was glad to see him and treated him as one would an old friend, then Jorgé was paying too much for his product. The man had the grimmest look of someone with something to say who could not wait a minute longer. He leaned forward to emphasize his opening words. The men's eyes locked.

The noises of the outside world faded into the background. Neither heard the pre-teen children splashing in the pool. Neither heard the sounds of the musica on the boombox at the end of the pool. Certainly neither could spare any of their attentions to admire the heavily landscaped beauty of the grounds that surrounded the hotel. Even Jorgé's soldiers had not paused to admire the architectural orderliness of the monolithic hotels nearby with their rows of jutting balconies racing up and down the facades. If for some reason they had thought to, they would still have missed the furtive movement of a drapery behind one of the balconies. The doorwall of the fifth floor balcony was cracked open, but even with binoculars it would have been difficult to see the tip of black metal. This balcony of the Tropicana looked to the observer like every other. It was 500 yards away. No one's suspicions would be aroused until it was too late.

Jorgé leaned forward to glare at his ugly opponent. Suddenly he felt a sledgehammer blow to his chest as he was pushed back hard in his chair. He could not take a breath and his eyes grew wide in shock and panic. His opponent stared now in surprise at Jorgé.

23

It was a Monday. Her husband had been out of town for nearly a week and Karen had been spending long nights at Andrew's apartment. Her usually abundant energy was missing, but like a trooper she had kept her one o'clock appointment at my studio. Lacking her typical gusto, Karen had faked her way through a half hour of upper body exercises. She walked slowly to the squat rack to work on her slim, tanned legs. After a halfhearted set of warm-ups, she approached the bar in the rack with obvious reluctance. Reaching up and out to grasp the thick bar in each delicate hand, Karen turned to me and said, "On days like this I feel like I need somebody to stand here with a whip and swat me until I do these."

Jokingly, I replied, "We don't have time for fun right now, we have to do a set of 12 of these!"

Deep from within Karen's tired brown eyes, a spark ignited. It grew into a flame and her eyelids flew open from the heat. The smooth skin on her face glowed with a smile and my attention was drawn to two rows of brilliant, white teeth and a flashing red tongue. "Ooooh," she squealed, "I'm intrigued as to why you said that. But there is something I'd like to share with you after I do this set."

The aftereffects of her sleep-shorted night fell away instantly. Her intensity and spirit returned in a rush as she grinned her way through 15 repetitions. Quickly completing her set, she set the bar back and turned abruptly to face me. I had somehow given her the opening she needed to get something off of her substantial chest. In her cultured, measured voice she began, "I know I've alluded to the time I've spent with Andrew as being very passionate and very liberating for me. I think I have even mentioned the term soul-mate in our conversations about my relationship with him. I don't know why, but I've felt an urge to discuss this with you for some time now."

I indicated my continuing interest with raised eyebrows and an encouraging smile.

"You see, not only has Andrew rekindled my interest in a sexual relationship as his lover, he has introduced me to something else as well."

We were alone in the studio. If the phone had rung I would have ignored it completely. She had my full attention.

Karen went on in carefully modulated tones, "As I got to know Andrew better, he slowly began to confide in me about some of *his* wants and needs. After 15 years of marriage to Dennis, I was surprised to find a man who would take a chance and tell me about his most secret fantasies. Just the thought of having a conversation like that with Dennis is not possible."

So, I thought, *Mr. Hotshot Banker has some secrets he doesn't want anybody to know about.* I was all ears.

Karen lowered her sophisticated speaking voice and went on. "This took place over several long nights, mind you, but Andrew finally explained to me that all day long he has to be in control. His employees are always looking up to him to make the hard decisions. On the outside, he must maintain a certain façade. No matter how he feels on the inside that day, once he makes a decision, he can never flinch or waver lest someone sense weakness or the possibility of him changing his mind. His success at his position has thus far been based on him exhibiting strong leadership for ten hours a day, five days a week."

Karen's cultured way of speaking reminded me of an over-educated schoolmarm patiently explaining a curriculum to a student.

"Andrew indicated to me that after the stress of being in total command at his job the last thing he wanted to do upon arriving home was to have to make decisions. He would often have the same thing for dinner several nights in a row merely to avoid having to decide what to heat up. He said he has not had a complete week's vacation in several years simply because he did not care to be burdened with having to determine a destination. As far as dating went, the circumstances are quite similar. He often cannot bear to decide where to dine or what movie to see. He has been looking for a woman who is willing to take charge of the evening or even the whole weekend. He assures me that women like that are few and far between. Women may say outwardly that they are never consulted about the itinerary, but Andrew has found that most have no imagination when it comes to assisting in a decision that affects both of them. He always took this inability to mean a certain amount of selfishness on his girlfriend's part, as though she wasn't deeply enough involved with him to anticipate his interests or what would make him happy."

I thought I knew where Karen might be going with all of this background about Andrew. But if it ended up with her telling me that her boyfriend was only looking for a travel agent that cared, I was going to feel let down. I was hoping that there was more to this recitation than Ms. Columbus telling me that she could have her pick of travel destinations with her new lover.

There *was* more.

Karen continued releasing what had been bottled up for weeks, "Andrew's unwillingness to be in control had also spilled over into his sexual and fantasy life as well."

Okay, I thought, *if my attention had been wavering, it isn't now.*

"I'm not only speaking about who decides what position that he and his lover will be in during the act of lovemaking. I am referring to a specific type of foreplay that he needs to enhance the entire experience."

Her words make me think of the old joke, *What is Arnold Schwarzenegger's idea of foreplay?* The answer was, *Maria, wake up!* I decided not to interrupt by telling her the joke right then.

Karen had evaluated my reaction while she talked and concluded that I was still interested. "Mark, several weeks ago Andrew confided in me that he grew very excited at the prospect of being restrained prior to making love with a woman. With the way that he had led up to it and the way that he explained it, I was neither shocked nor surprised. I mean, I haven't been living under a rock during my marriage, although sometimes it's felt like a minimum-security prison. I've heard of this sort of thing before and I was aware that there is a shop over in Royal Oak that caters to people who are interested in this type of addendum to their lifestyles." Karen paused to see how I was holding up. I was being a very good listener.

"It was obvious to me that Andrew had put a great deal of thought into this over the past several years. What he *did* not and *has* not shared so far is how much experimentation he has done in the past, if any, or how receptive any of the other women he has dated were to this."

I said, "It's probably not something you want to ask a girl to do on the first date."

Karen smiled, "I must admit that I was intrigued from the moment he told me. I have since carefully considered why. Until recently I have always felt powerless. For 37 years I was always the thinnest or the weakest in any group. I never played sports in school, nor as an adult. I married right out of college and Dennis had always decided where we would live, what we would spend, and even what we would drive. It fascinated me that here was a man offering me total control in the bedroom or wherever else we were to act out his fantasies."

I began to pry, "So you're thinking about saying yes?"

Karen smiled sweetly, "Oh, my dear. I already have. Many times. I started the way I suppose everyone does. I took the sashes off two of his bathrobes and tied both of his hands to the headboard of his bed. I stripped down to my bra and panties while I ran my tongue over his chest and stomach. I left a couple of gentle bite marks around his upper thighs. I know from my own experience how sensitive that area can be. I think he began to realize just how naked and vulnerable he was at that moment and he became very excited…believe me! I also think that he began to wonder just how well he knew me when I started biting him…I mean…I could have bitten him anywhere I chose at that moment…although I suppose that not having his feet bound afforded him some protection."

I had heard some terrific confessions in my little studio, but this one had the makings of one of the top ten. Karen had worked her way through most of the entrée by now. My partially open jaw indicated to her that she had my undivided attention.

Karen continued, "After a half hour of this little game it became apparent that Andrew was in some discomfort just from wanting to complete the act so badly. I was unquestionably excited myself so I decided to take pity on him. I got off the bed but maintained eye contact with him and unhooked my bra and then just let the whole thing drop off. When I started to wiggle out of my panties I thought he would lose it right there. I climbed back on top of the bed and kept going until I was on top of him. He slid into me *very* easily. Mind you, I never broke eye contact with him the entire time that I was doing this. Now, I know I haven't mentioned what a considerate lover Andrew has been but I assure you that in the past he has always waited until I was ready. This is one time, though, that he could not and I was barely settled on top of him when the poor boy released."

I don't think that Karen had a best friend to tell about her encounters with her new boyfriend. She certainly wouldn't be able to count on her husband to listen. I was happy to lend an ear that day. Karen's well-modulated voice and carefully chosen words made the scene of her experiment come to life. She was very attractive and the thought of her astride her lover while naked (and very excited) was fascinating. She needed some reaction from me to show my interest in her tale. She needed verbal encouragement immediately.

"Wow," I said.

I thought perhaps she had told me everything by now. But she had not. And now that she knew I would accept her revelations at face value—that I wouldn't scorn her or react judgmentally—she felt free to serve me another course. The workout was a distant memory as Karen described her sex life over the past several weeks in detail. She sat down on a bench, as did I, and spoke in a low and completely mesmerizing tone of voice.

"We performed the act the same way the next night although he *did* last a little longer and I was able to satisfy myself as well. After each time I could think of nothing else the entire next day. Following the second night I set aside the whole day to prepare for the third evening. You know me well enough by now to agree that I have an extremely creative side, and I began to use these nights with Andrew as an outlet for my creativity. I spent the morning shopping for a black leather bikini with chrome studs lining the edges of both the bra *and* the panties. Actually, the panty was really only a modest thong—if there is such a thing. I felt much more secure wearing something of this nature than I ever have in the past thanks to your efforts over the past year. I feel as though my derrière has quite a bit of shape to it compared with last year at his time, and Andrew quite concurs. In the afternoon I procured several pairs of padded handcuffs, a padded blindfold, and four different types of paddles. I also purchased a minimal leather outfit for Andrew. It consists of little more than a triangular piece of softened leather in front to support him with some black rawhide strips that enable it to be tied around the back. Now I've already explained how well thought out Andrew's apartment was even before I began to redecorate, but I don't recall mentioning the walk-in closet to you. Andrew's master bedroom has *the* most spacious closet imaginable. The best part is that lining both sides is a series of rods for hanging suits or shirts or pants. The rods are affixed to the wall at various heights throughout the entire closet. Mark, the whole thing is tailor-made for anything we want to do in there. On the third night, we both had a couple of glasses of wine and I then slipped into the bathroom with all of my things. I put on the leather bikini and some black heels. I left all of my jewelry on and walked out of the bathroom dangling his leather thong in one hand and the padded blindfold in the other. I commanded Andrew to march into his bedroom and to put both of these items on and nothing else. I told him that after he had complied, he was to sit down on the bed and call out to me to indicate that he had finished preparing himself for me. It took him longer than I expected but I suspect that he had difficulty tying on the thong while he was excited. After nearly 15 minutes he called out to me as I instructed him and I gathered up the bag that I had brought with the remainder of my purchases. When I walked into the bedroom he was sitting on the bed blindfolded, practically naked, and awaiting further instructions. I commanded him to stand up, take a quarter turn to the right, and to walk five steps. I kept directing him in this way until he had found his way across the room to the closet. I guided him with my voice alone until I had positioned him with his back to a wall. He was most co-operative and had not uttered a word the entire time. I ordered him to kneel down in front of me and stretch his right arm over his head. I attached one set of handcuffs to his wrist and the other to the rod over his head and did the same to his left arm. I got very close to him while I was performing this task and he could sense where I was and would try to kiss my breasts or my stomach area. I used this infraction as a reason to reach behind and punish his buttocks with one of the paddles while I explained that "slave" was never to touch "Mistress" unless explicitly allowed to do so. Needless to say, I have never experienced this kind of power over another person, especially not over a man. Andrew has a slim, beautiful body from running and at times I just wanted to sit in a corner and gaze at him as he knelt there helpless. Instead, I got out a soft piece of rope and went around behind him again and tied his ankles together. Mark, I do not think that he could have risen to his feet even if he wanted to risk my paddle again. You will love this next part. I took out the key to the handcuffs and tied it to the end of a piece of string that was perhaps six feet in length. I took a piece of masking tape and climbed up on a footstool to fasten the other end of the string to the ceiling of the closet so that the key hung down across from his right hand and about two feet in front of it. I do not know why, but I became so excited at this point that I had to actually step out of the closet and take several deep breaths. After I was able to compose myself, I walked back in to where my lover hung. I found myself loving him very much at that time because of the trust that he had placed in me, and yet I was feeling rather wicked because he was having all of the fun! I checked the tape that held the string and then I spoke to Andrew. I explained that shortly I would be pulling up his blindfold so that he may evaluate his situation and see that although I had no intention of helping him, I had left him a possible way out. I also explained that I would be unfastening his thong as well and as the cool air struck him I did not wish to see any evidence of excitement or he would be paddled appropriately. Mark, I could already see that he had been in a state of three-quarter arousal practically the entire time, but I felt so naughty because I knew this would simply afford me with an excuse to use the second paddle with the holes in it. It had an audible whistle when swung briskly, and since it made so much noise my slave would also hear it coming before it landed. As I slowly pulled up the padded blindfold, I bent down and spoke into his ear, explaining that the key to his freedom hung just in front of him. While he stared at that and began to devise a way to get the key I reached behind him and pulled at the little bow he had made on the scanty piece of leather that covered him. It did not drop off immediately but instead allowed him more freedom until the cool air struck him. My assumption proved correct and the air brought him into a full state of arousal at which point I kept my word with the paddle. Poor Andrew could see quickly that the only way to bring the key to his hand was to blow on it to push it away so that it might swing farther back toward him. He blew on it once but then I stepped around in front again to explain that I would be removing my leather top and bottom while he tried to escape. I explained that Mistress had become quite aroused as well and she would lie on the floor directly in front of him and pleasure herself during his escape. If he took too long, I warned, then his opportunity to relieve his desire inside of Mistress would be lost and he would be left to his own devices. I unbuckled my top and just let it hang across my breasts while I unhooked my thong from each side. Andrew began to blow and the key began to swing back and forth until I thought that he might have it after five or six more tries. I *said* that I was feeling naughty, though. As my top and bottoms began to fall away I reached out and grabbed the key to steady it until it hung motionless once again. I know that seems cruel, but I wanted to buy a little more time to lie in front of him so that he could see that I meant what I said. I did lie down as promised—on my back—with my feet facing him while I used my bag of toys as a makeshift pillow. Andrew immediately began blowing on the key again, but he seemed more desperate and his aim was not very good on the first dozen tries. At first I only pretended to pleasure myself with my hand but after a minute I began to experience some genuine sensations as I watched my frustrated lover try to catch the tiny key. Mark, I have never been stimulated by visual messages. I have always been one to respond to caressing or scents or sometimes even auditory stimuli. But watching this beautiful naked man do everything in his power to reach me was causing me to get so aroused that I grew concerned that I truly *would* climax before he freed himself. There was an added element to this situation that I found very erotic as well. Even though I lie completely nude and exposed to him while I waited, I still had the power to stand up at any time and thwart or delay his escape by simply halting the momentum of the key once again. I enjoyed this feeling of power very much but at this point I knew I would enjoy receiving him equally as much. I purposely delayed my own pleasure by using both hands to caress my breasts, knowing full well that upon seeing this he would hasten to reach me all the quicker. Mark, after he got both hands free he crawled to me without even untying his ankles first! He entered immediately upon reaching me like he was starving for me. Again he did not last long, but this time he never withdrew. He just continued on until we both climaxed, right there on his closet floor, but his was for the second time without a pause!"

My studio's telephone was the lifeblood of the business. Established clients called it to make appointments or to change the time. Prospective new clients called to inquire about hours, rates, and to ask detailed questions. Producers from television news shows had been calling of late to offer free spots on the nightly news in exchange for an interview from one of the only two personal trainers in the state. My fiancée called in several times a day to schedule herself to help me—or to elicit my input regarding our upcoming wedding. For 45 minutes, I had ignored that phone. The answering machine had clicked on several times, but I didn't care. I was thirsty and hungry but I ignored it. Karen had overloaded my imagination until I was unable to react any longer. I could only sit and listen. Karen, tired and dragging only an hour ago, now seemed invigorated and delighted to have me as an audience. After a minute to let me catch my breath, Karen continued.

"Mark, we both found this original closet episode so satisfying that we repeated it again on several subsequent evenings. Of course, while Andrew was at work during the day I would take the opportunity to add to my bag of accessories. I purchased additional outfits for myself, naturally, comprised of as much chrome and chain and velcro as I could find. I purchased different styles of whips and riding crops also—always looking for the one that made the most noise without leaving any welts. Without trying to make you uncomfortable, I would like to add that I spent a great deal of time purchasing accessories for Andrew's...ah...genitalia as well. I bought products that I can use to...ah...weight him down with if he's not wearing the thong. I bought an insidious little device that consists of five chrome rings of descending size attached at intervals to a five-inch leather strap...it's called by different names but the package for this one said, "Gates of Hell." I will not go into detail on how I get it on him but once I do, I receive a great deal of satisfaction in knowing that he is wearing this extremely uncomfortable apparatus solely because I have commanded him to do so."

I never claimed to be a camel. I walked over to the cooler for a Diet Pepsi.

24

Jorgé could still not draw a breath and his chest hurt with a crushing pain. He watched as the man seated across from him stood up with a face that now showed both surprise and fear instead of dislike and determination. Jorgé could see no weapon but he was getting dizzy and *still* he could not breathe. He needed Paco now! Paco would be able to help him breathe. Jorgé turned his head to look for his aide. Still searching with eyes wide open, he died.

A .223 caliber military round from an AR15 had severed his aorta, and its impact and fragments had turned much of his chest cavity into mush. Jorgé would not see the village of his home or count his money ever again. But at least he had stopped sweating.

As Rico rapidly removed the barrel from the sniper rifle, he kept his gaze fixed on the figure slumped back in the chair at poolside. Rico smirked. The shoot would have been an easy one even if he had chosen the 20-inch barrel instead of the 24. He knew from long experience, however, that sometimes the intel that came from his clients was anything but. This particular mark was so wide that—with the longer barrel—Rico could have guaranteed a hit on some portion of his body from over two times the distance. The fragmenting round hadn't cost him any accuracy, either, especially when he had elected to use a 75-grain charge instead of the 65. At 2700 feet per second, the round could have covered a mile in under two seconds. At 500 yards Rico had only a two-foot drop to deal with. The report had been no louder than the slamming of a Mercedes car door by the time it had reverberated among the towers of the neighboring hotels, and was masked by the radios and hubbub at poolside. Rico would have been able to identify its origination within 20 feet had he been at poolside, but he doubted that the ex-military thugs that El Jefé paid to guard him had enough training or experience to even guess. The fifth floor vantage point had been the ideal choice. It was high enough to clear any intervening vegetation, but not so high as to have his sight line obscured by the pool boy's opening of the umbrella, which Rico had fully anticipated. He had also been prepared with a back-up scenario should the umbrella have still proved to be too low. He would have used his first shot to shatter one leg of the table, and as it fell his *second* would have shattered El Jefé's sternum. While some would have called it showing off, for Rico it would merely have been another multiple target hit, with the width of the second target making it as easy as sitting at the next table with an M16 on full automatic.

Rico continued packing up the pieces of the gun. He never wore gloves on these jobs because he still enjoyed feeling the cold metal in his bare hands. Taking the gun with him would guarantee that not only would it not yield fingerprints, but that the police would not glean any hair, fibers or any other materials off of it that might be useful. Besides, the 24-inch stainless steel floating barrel and its sight matched so perfectly with this gun that Rico was loath to break up such an ideal combination. In addition, no eyebrows would be raised by his eventual purchase of another. Supreme confidence jostled with caution as Rico recalled the dozens of marks he had erased over the last 17 years with impunity. Sure, he still took precautions by the bucketful, and had yet to even be contacted by any form of law enforcement—much less interviewed, charged, tried or convicted. Much of this was a tribute to Lieutenant Spina, who had kept abreast of any state-of-the-art investigative techniques and kept Rico apprised of them. But Rico planned well, too. Since the round had struck the mark exactly on target, it had distorted and fragmented into many pieces, making a ballistics match nearly impossible. Rico would keep the stainless barrel with the bore that had been so precisely machined that no instrument capable of measuring its variances existed—and would probably not exist for the next hundred years. The 1:8 rifling (one turn per eight inches) was ideally suited to every condition that Rico had ever encountered.

Today's disguise was tennis cap and togs, with the gun and scope packed tightly in towels inside a medium-sized piece of Samsonite. With his California tan, lean-muscled physique, and dark sunglasses, Rico carried two encased rackets along with the Samsonite that said either dead-serious amateur or touring pro. Rico pressed hard to click shut the latches on the suitcase, and pulled out a miniature pair of field glasses from one of the tennis ball cans in a racket case pocket. If he had chosen the other racket case, he would now be holding a 9-millimeter Glock with a 15-shot magazine. He stared through the glasses for one last look at the pool area.

El Jefé was still DRT (Dead Right There) and two of his soldiers were standing next to his corpse, leaderless, trying to decide on the next course of action. The three men in white suits were gone, and the rest of El Jefé's crew had disappeared as well, no doubt ditching weaponry into automobile trunks before the inevitable arrival of the police. It looked like El Jefé had died with his eyes open, and Time of Death had been 15 to 20 seconds after impact. Only just now were some of the other guests at nearby tables beginning to look over at the corpse of El Jefé with curiosity, as though the two men standing next to him had merely initiated a conversation to which he did not respond. There was no panic, no screaming, and the activities of the Hotel del Solè's poolside guests never even slowed. El Jefé's death, although untimely, was quick and without any screaming or flailing of the arms, and incredibly enough so far, no one present was the wiser. No one, of course, but his two remaining soldiers. They had made a decision, albeit a selfish one. They placed a newspaper across the open entry wound on his chest, and laid an arm across to pin it down. One man plucked El Jefé's sunglasses from the table and put them back on Jorgé's rigid face. Their former boss now looked almost tranquil…like a man in a flowered shirt who had fallen asleep while reading the paper in the relative coolness of an umbrella's shade. It would be left to the pool boy to attempt to wake him later on this afternoon, when he tried to find out if the dead man was thirsty.

Chris Olson—or Rico—looked around the hotel room one last time—more to recall if he had touched anything that would yield up a fingerprint rather than to see if he had left any object that would allude to his presence there. As had already been the case some 38 times in the past, there was nothing. That Chris Olson had only just checked in at 8 A.M.—and paid cash—meant that even a careless man would not have had much time to leave signs of his existence strewn about. And Rico…Chris…was not a careless man. The Lieutenant had once suggested that there was no reason that a careful, calculating, and innovative man could not last many years in this profession. The door to getting caught by chance would only open if Rico were to leave it unlocked. He had hinted at an appropriate age for Rico to retire as well—55 years of age—which coincided nicely with the Lieutenant's own planned retirement at the age of 60.

Chris Olson pulled a tissue out of his tennis shorts and wiped down the room key before he placed it on the bureau. He tucked both carrying cases under his left arm and picked up the Samsonite suitcase with his left hand. Using the same tissue, he unlatched and opened the door to the room, striding out into the hallway with nary a look in either direction—a man whose attention was focused on an early afternoon match that would never be played. He took a back stairwell down to the parking lot, a simple task for one so fit. When Chris Olson got to the rental car, the suitcase went in the back seat but the tennis cases—with the Glock on top—stayed in the front. Three spare 15-round magazines accompanied the handgun, not counting the full one already inserted into the grip. The magazines were loaded with Black Talon rounds, the infamous "cop killer" bullets that could penetrate an automobile door or personal body armor. Since his proficiency with a rifle was rivaled only by his ability with a handgun, Chris Olson would only be taken that day if he were confronted by *61* law enforcement officers.

Chris Olson arrived at the rental lot of Miami International Airport without being slowed by anything more threatening than a merging tractor trailer on I-95. He parked his car in a lot that would receive 300 other cars like it that day. An attendant walked over with a clipboard to check him in and commented briefly about the heat. He offered to have the final rental tally placed on Chris's Visa card. Chris agreed and pretended to sit and fiddled with a suitcase latch until the attendant went on to the next returning vehicle. Quickly, he wiped down the steering wheel, turn signal lever, gearshift knob, and inner driver's door handle. The key was still in the ignition and it too received some quick final attention before Chris gathered up his things and closed the driver's door with a bump of his hip. Chris double-timed it to the long-term parking lot, where his own innocuous Caprice Classic sedan waited for his return. He got in and pointed the Chevy back toward I-95. It had been a long drive from California earlier in the week and Rico was under no time constraints to make it up to Chicago for the next job. He had allowed for three days and intended to use every hour of it.

Rico remembered his last job in the Midwest. It was in Detroit almost five years ago. He had shot the mark on a Thursday and stayed on to attend a wedding. The wedding wasn't until Saturday and he hadn't picked up his date from the airport until Friday. He thought about her. Cynthia Kinney was the typical California model type. Blond hair, light freckles, and long, tanned legs got her all the work she wanted in the catalogs and media ads. They had dated on and off for a year. But Rico had not felt any closer to her than any of the others. Still, her friend and former co-worker in Detroit was getting married and Cynthia needed a date to attend what promised to be a well-choreographed event. She had flown into Detroit Metro on a Friday and Rico promised to pick her up at the terminal. Of course, she had asked him why he could not accompany her on the flight from LAX, but readily accepted his explanation that he was just beginning a two-week business trip on the road that could culminate in Detroit as easily as anywhere else. Cynthia might have been more disconcerted if Rico had volunteered that his Caprice carried a small armory in its trunk that would have been difficult to check in at the baggage counter of an airport. Had he further explained that the business trip involved killing a man in cold blood in Detroit and then waiting to see if another job gelled up in Chicago right after the wedding, she probably would have withdrawn her invitation altogether. And then Rico would have had to kill her.

"How can we be sure he is dead?" she asked.

"He had not moved for many minutes, *mi amor*."

"But perhaps he is only gravely injured. If he were to receive medical care in time, he may recover."

"My eyes are better than yours, my flower, and my left one is not swollen almost closed. I can see from here that his eyes are still open, and yet he remains still."

"If he were to survive this, I fear he would not rest until he found out who was responsible for this."

"He has been shot with a military round, precious one, and the wound is at his heart. Other men have been shot in the leg with this type of thing and still they have died. Besides, Miguel and Santo would not have stood there for this great a time if they still sensed breath coming from his body."

"Will they not have suspicions as to why you have not joined them?" Lorita questioned nervously.

"When they first called me on the radio, I said that I was chasing the man who fired the shot." Paco said soothingly. "The second time that they contacted me, I told them that I was up here in case there was an attempt on your life as well. I expect that I will hear from them again soon as they inform me that any effort to get him to a surgeon would be futile. I will tell them that you do not wish for them to be questioned by the police. I will tell them to arrange him so as not to draw immediate attention, and then to leave."

"Other people, they go on about their business as although nothing has happened. Even the couple at the next table has just left without looking back."

"They know what happened. They may have guessed how. But no one these days wants to get involved in such a messy thing." Paco continued on, "That is why men like your husband can operate with little fear of consequence. People do not want to be drawn in unless it affects them."

They were on the fourth floor of the Hotel del Solè, peering out from behind a gap in the drawn vertical blinds. The entire pool area was splayed out before them. She had watched the whole scene unfold—the three men in the white suits—the umbrella being opened, the leader of the men being seated by his aide. She had known that this would be the moment that her husband would be shot. When the man sat down—in the bright sunlight—her husband's guards would see no guns produced, but still they would not be sure...Lorita had known...but she still jerked back when Jorgé did—after the bullet had struck.

"He beat me, you know," she said.

"I know this, *mi amor*," he said. "You do not have to repeat this to justify our course of action. The men know this too. Some of them, they did not approve as well. You loved him once. You were faithful to him. You loved him before the money and the house and the gold. You did not seek these things. You sought only to be happy...and only with him. He abused the privilege of walking through this life with you. I give you my bond...I will never make the same mistake as he!"

"I love you, Paco," she told him.

He was standing behind her, both arms around her waist. She turned her face to look back at him. He met her face with his lips and gave her two gentle kisses, one on the swelling of her eye, the other, an even gentler one, on her carefully sutured cut.

"And I you, my precious one," he replied.

Her head clearing, she had begun to relax a little and collect her thoughts. "I did as you asked," she said. "I found the book of numbers in the smaller of his bags, and switched it over to one of my own. The book has many pages, but I think I already know which ones belong to the banks."

"Then let us leave this place, my love. We will go back to the house. When the police contact you, you will say that you fell and that you needed the services of a doctor. You will say that when you were leaving Jorgé told you that he would go to the pool for his meeting and then see you tonight. When this thing has blown over a little bit, we will get a man to come to the house to open the safe. He was a bastard to never have done the thing of honor and marry you. We will add your name to the documents that show the ownership of the warehouses. I will handle it with his lawyer and merely say that this is the way Jorgé wanted it to be."

25

Karen Columbus continued to catch me up on her activities of the last several weeks.

"This past week I have been perfecting a simple scene that has evolved from that first night in the closet. Andrew has very soft, very lush carpeting throughout his large living room. I like to don the most revealing outfit in my collection before I blindfold him and order him to lie face down at one end of the room. Sometimes I allow him to wear his thong, however, just as often I do not. I handcuff him behind his back and buckle his feet together with a recent purchase of leather ankle cuffs. I then proceed to the opposite end of the room and find a comfortable chair to sit in to observe his journey across the room. Sometimes I will read or paint my nails, but if he should make too much noise during his struggle I will interrupt whatever I am doing to walk over and spank or flog him with a selection from my bag."

In spite of her descriptive tone, Karen spoke matter-of-factly enough to convince me the evenings had occurred exactly as described.

"Now Mark, I encountered an unforeseen circumstance almost immediately during this scene and it required several different innovations before I could resolve it. You see, I miscalculated Andrew's degree of athleticism. At first, I would scarcely have time to walk across the room and settle in before he was halfway to me. I felt a tinge of guilt for flogging Slave until he hitched back to where he started. It was as though I were punishing him for obeying me too quickly. Before I allowed him to start again I attempted to impede his progress by placing a dining room chair and an end table directly in his path. He pushed the chair out of his path quite easily and simply began to go around the heavier table. Finally, my creative side devised a method to slow his progress considerably. I ordered him to await my return and stepped into the kitchen. I retrieved a plastic one-gallon milk jug from his refrigerator and emptied its contents into the sink. I refilled it with clean water and retightened the lid using a rubber jar grip to ensure that there would be no leaks. I took the jug with me across the living room into the master bedroom and went into my bag again. From it, I selected a soft, thin rope of suitable length, and I attached one end securely to the handle of the plastic jug. Now here is the clever part. I went back into the living room and ordered Slave to roll over onto his back. I removed his thong and looped the other end of the rope around his…ah…testicular area and then tied it quite tightly. I then returned to my chair at the other end and commanded him to recommence. He started off very briskly again for several feet until the rope became taut. It gave me great satisfaction to see the surprise and delight on his face when he found that progress would not be so trouble free this time. I asked Slave if he was experiencing too much pain and told him that if this was so we could end the evening now and I would see myself home. He shook his head *no* vigorously and spent the better part of an hour inching toward me, resting for awhile, and then continuing. Mark, as I sat in that chair all I could do was revel at the power that I held over this beautiful man. As he got closer I could not resist telling him *where* on my body I had hidden the key, and the steps he would need to take to retrieve it. Mark, after he finally reached my position, he satisfied me once just getting the key!"

From early childhood, humans learn to read the body language from other humans in an ongoing process. Babies learn that certain motions from their mother indicate that feeding time is near. Young children decipher the severity of a parent's angry expression to decide if a line has been crossed and punishment is imminent. In the schoolyard, a bully seeks out shy, isolated victims who are already "cut out of the herd" to pummel with verbal or physical intimidation.

Experienced policemen and psychologists teach women (and men) not to present themselves as potential victims. They encourage walking with head high and shoulders back, studying a potential attacker as if memorizing their features or assessing vulnerable areas for a preemptive strike. I have several theories as to why normally reserved people view me as approachable. One is that, due to the physical and sometimes superficial nature of being a successful personal trainer, I am a notorious people watcher. Malls, restaurants, parking lots and especially beaches are fine places to stare at people unabashedly. At these locales I can appraise their musculature, make assumptions about their level of physical activity, and mentally assign them a number corresponding to their percentage of bodyfat. If given sufficient time, I enjoy evaluating their gait for knee, ankle, or hip problems that may limit the amount or type of exercise that they are capable of performing. Many people tend to interpret this affable staring as a genuine interest in them and their well-being.

When listening to a client, I try not to interject too often with comments, thoughts, or solutions. I allow myself one raise of an eyebrow per minute, one knowing half-grin every two minutes, and a pointed but thoughtful question every four minutes. Whether or not this makes me a good listener is open to interpretation. One can talk to somebody in a coma without being interrupted, but being comatose does not make for a good listener. In less than two hours, Karen had obviously concluded that I could be trusted with the most intimate details of her personal life.

I'd had both male and female clients share information about extremely private matters with me before. On one unusual day *two* different female clients solicited my opinion about a part of their anatomy. Although they had never met, and their appointments were nearly four hours apart, the conversation eventually led to each of them asking me if I felt as though they needed a breast augmentation. Alone in the small studio, each insisted on showing me her "before" situation and requesting my input. In my opinion, one of the women needed it and one did not.

I did not consider myself to be prudish and was fully aware that many different subcultures, or scenes, existed and were pursued by outwardly average people. Karen's revelations were much more involved than just spilling the beans about an extra-marital affair. She was discovering herself as she became more immersed in a subculture that allowed and even coveted women who could play a dominating role over men. As she began to feel increasingly confident in a secretive society that admired convincing and creative role-playing, she began to research the ideas of others to decide if her creativity compared favorably.

Two weeks after the unexpected unburdening to me of the details of her secret life, I found myself alone again in the studio with her. While making her appointment, she had spoken of just getting in from New York. Before the previous client had reached his car in my parking lot, Karen spoke to me in a hushed tone.

"I do not think I told you that Andrew and I were going to New York for a specific reason. Prior to leaving we made inquiries about several 'clubs' that cater to people who are interested in BDSM. Do you know what that stands for? It stands for bondage, discipline, sadism, and masochism! These clubs have certain requirements that must be met before one is allowed to enter. Street clothes are discouraged—or should at least consist of leather and chain outfits. Single men are not allowed to enter unless accompanied by a female. There is a cover charge that is quite reasonable for regular attendees but very substantial for a couple that only intends to visit once. Once inside, there are rooms of various sizes that are set aside for specific types of equipment so that certain "scenes" can be enacted.

Andrew and I often observed men in dominant roles with their wives or girlfriends, or men who brought *compensated* companions to play a submissive or dominant role. I wore a long coat when we arrived, but underneath I was dressed in an outfit that left a great deal of me exposed. Both sides of my leather brassiere had a center portion that could be unsnapped quite easily. This left me wearing a brassiere that did not cover the center of my breasts. The bottom part of my outfit was more clever still. I wore a pair of black leather shorts. They fit my upper thighs and around my posterior almost perfectly thanks to you and our sessions here. But if I were to get too warm while I was exerting myself during a flogging session with Andrew, I could remove them quickly with only one hand. The shorts are comprised of two pieces of leather—one forms the front half and the other comprises the back half. Instead of having seams, though, the two halves are fastened together with zippers. If I am punishing Andrew for something—and get too warm—or if I just decide to increase the amount of visual excitement for him, I do not even have to stop. I merely switch over the instrument to my left hand and continue while I undo the zippers from both sides and just allow the shorts to fall to the floor! Mark, I have practiced this repeatedly in front of a mirror without missing a stroke. I must confess that when the shorts fall off and I am left with only a minimal leather thong covering myself the entire effect is very arousing."

I resolved to ask Karen to model the outfit sometime in the future. She continued on.

"On our first visit we checked our coats, but I never did remove my shorts. I was also wearing black stiletto-heeled boots that rose to just above my knees. Andrew really looked the part in a chrome studded black leather webbing that criss-crossed his torso. It *did not* cover much of his private area, because that part was little more than a small triangular piece designed to hold him in place...and not much else. On that first occasion, he also wore wide leather cuffs around his wrists and ankles, but on the second visit I ordered him to wear a chrome, studded, black leather dog collar around his neck with a sturdy steel loop for fastening the end of a chain or rope. We must have encountered over 200 people there on each night, and many were outfitted similarly to us. Some of the women had full black leather corsets and I thought I saw a man wearing one too, although I did not stop to inquire if that was his choice or his companion's. I did notice a great many men *and* women with piercings through their nipples, which I would *never* even consider for myself. We began to tour some of the inner rooms where every manner of equipment was being utilized. Now, the proper vernacular when referring to someone participating in a scene is very important. The one who is doing the flogging, spanking, tying up, or ordering around is call the domme, which is short for dominant. As you might suspect, the one who is being restrained or disciplined or trained is called the sub, which is short for submissive. Some people switch from one role to another with relative ease depending on what is agreed upon. I do not. I will only play the domme and Andrew certainly does not mind this arrangement! At any rate, it was my observation that an attractive, capable female domme is quite rare and extremely coveted by members of this subculture. On the first night I was more interested in the fixtures that were being used. There were padded tables with eyebolts at each corner and there were padded pommel horses with fixtures already attached to the legs. We observed stocks that kept the head or hands from moving about, and others that held the feet while the subject sat. One room had a medieval looking rack assembled entirely from carved wooden pieces. Another room had crosses of several types. Some of the crosses were in the shape of an X and one was on a pivot and could be rotated so that the sub's head could be pointed up or down or in any direction that the domme wished. I believe that some of the participants were those that do this sort of thing professionally, as they were putting on quite a show to the small groups of couples that paused to watch. In one of the rooms the centerpiece was a large solid wood wheel that lay on its side. The center was mounted on bearings so that the entire wheel could rotate like a children's merry-go-round at a playground. On the second night the wheel was in use with a beautiful blond woman lying on it, attached by her wrists and ankles. She wore nothing except for a blindfold and the tiniest piece of material that one could call panties and still be correct. There was a lit candle suspended over her on a rope and as a man spun her slowly on the wheel, hot wax would fall from the candle. The wax would land arbitrarily on different parts of her body and it was quite obvious from her expressions that it caused her some discomfort when each globule contacted her skin. Andrew and I watched for nearly an hour until finally her partner stopped the wheel and a man took her place on the wheel. He was fitted with an outfit similar to Andrew, except that he had a full leather mask around his entire head with small holes for the eyes, nose, and mouth. The woman that strapped him in was quite spectacular. She was tall and pale with long dark hair, black nail polish, and black lipstick. She wore a leather mask around her eyes and she had black leather gloves on—with only partial fingers—that zipped up nearly to her elbows. Her outfit consisted of a corset-like bodice that pushed her bosom up and out without totally covering up her magnificent breasts. She was very voluptuous, and the bodice and the manner in which she was laced up inside it was absolutely stunning. The bottom of the outfit looked as though it was laced together between her legs in such a fashion that one could catch glimpses of her private area. I do not believe that she unlaced it to access this area, however. I do suspect that there were concealed snaps located somewhere to better facilitate its removal. Her leather boots rose to her mid-thigh and added still further to her height. She held a short whip in her hand. As her companion spun on the wheel he would squirm when the hot wax hit him and then *she* would wait until he made a complete revolution before expertly using the whip on a selected area. After five minutes she stopped spinning the wheel to attach some long clamps onto his nipples. We were both amazed when she resumed spinning the wheel and was then able to flick the clamps back off with the whip. Her dexterity with this device was very impressive, and she would pause only when approached to pass out what I assumed to be a business card. I jokingly asked Andrew if he would like to take the man's place when they were through and I watched him contemplate my offer for a moment before he said no. He further went on to say that he would like to try it, but by now, there were too many spectators in the room for him to feel comfortable. I must confess that I looked down at Andrew and he certainly *was* intrigued at the thought of being the next claimant to the spinning wheel! Just as we were preparing to leave, the stunning woman with the whip called the man on the wheel "slave." She halted the wheel and demanded, in front of everyone, that the man kiss her boot! Mark, she placed her right boot up on this wooden turntable directly next to the man's head and told him that it was there waiting for him to his left. She waited until he turned his head and kissed the glossy black surface of it once. She called him a slave again and told him that if he thought that the one pathetic kiss was going to satisfy her then he was sadly mistaken. She struck him on the leg with the whip and demanded that he try again. He kissed her boot top a second time but lingered a little longer. This incredible woman then announced that this second effort was better, but that she had decided that she would prefer that he *lick* the boot top instead. Well…he hesitated, and that earned him two strokes from the whip! Mark, there must have been 20 people watching. I have never seen a woman who was so in control! I could not take my eyes off of her. I was enthralled! She had a complete masterfulness about her that was so spellbinding, no one in the group dared to move! I found the entire scenario to be quite erotic. After her slave had licked her boot top several times she leaned down toward him and asked whether he enjoyed what he had just done. He nodded slightly but that did not suffice, she struck his bare chest and said *speak slave!* Whereupon he said *yes.* She was still not satisfied and struck him again, demanding *yes, what?* He replied, *yes, Mistress Priscilla, I enjoyed that very much!* She replied, *that's much better, I shall reward your obedience with one more ride on the wheel!* She then stepped back down and gave the wheel a hard spin. As it spun she would deliver a stroke every 15 seconds or so. After a few more minutes she stopped the wheel and released the man. Some of the people who had been watching began to drift away to other rooms but the ones who remained seemed entranced. I could tell that Andrew was quite exited as well, but I suddenly became determined to speak with this woman if she would allow it. It was with some trepidation that I approached her, but as I walked up she saw me and greeted me with a pleasant smile while her slave stood quietly behind her. I prefaced the many questions that I had by telling her how impressed I was with her and how her entire demeanor just fascinated me. She thanked me and explained that she had actually been a drama major in college and this sort of thing had always come quite naturally to her. I asked her where she had purchased her incredible outfit and she replied that all of her outfits were handmade to her specifications by an American Indian craftsman in North Dakota. I asked her how long she had been doing this with her boyfriend and she immediately corrected me. She said the man with her was not her boyfriend…he was a client! She reached into her leather brassiere and pulled out a glossy black business card with raised gold lettering on it. As I took the card, I noticed that it was still warm from the heat of her bosom, and I found even that to be quite erotic as well! The card was really very simple. It had a graphic across the top depicting a multiple-tailed whip. The middle said "Mistress Priscilla" in a beautiful classic script. A phone number was near the bottom. She went on to tell me how she had been a professional Dominatrix for nearly five years now, and that her clientele was obtained entirely by word of mouth, and that most had utilized her services on a regular basis for quite some time. Well, Mark, this all prompted a hundred more questions. Before I could ask the first, she answered it. She said she charged $300 an hour plus travel expenses. I managed to ask if her clients ever requested any sexual contact from her. I observed that the man on the wheel had appeared to be extremely aroused and was wondering if they ever requested any relief from that situation. She responded to my query by stating that *all* of her clients understood in advance that there was *never* to be sexual contact of any kind. If they were cooperative, however, and they were in a more private setting, she *may* release them long enough to satisfy themselves. Then she smiled very sweetly and asked me to excuse her, but her session with her client was over and she was to meet with another quite soon. I thanked her profusely and told her that I hoped to watch her in a session again soon. Mark, never have I been so enchanted with a performance…and I have been to many conventional plays! This woman oozed sexuality and combined theater with a commanding presence that had me mesmerized. I was so inspired by her! Andrew and I went on to find a small unused room with a wooden set of stocks standing in the middle. It reminded me of the type described in the depictions of the Salem Witch Trails. There were several sections, all bolted together with pieces of flat wrought iron. The wood was very dark and had been sanded and shellacked to an extremely smooth finish. A person of normal height could bend at the waist and place their neck and wrists into spaces carved into a bottom piece. The top piece had corresponding spaces and could then be closed on top of the person and latched at one end, thus entrapping them. Mark, when I saw what it was I let out a little squeal and demanded that Andrew position himself in the device at once! He complied and I latched him in. I had a small riding crop with me and I was so inspired by Mistress Priscilla that I began to tease and taunt Andrew as never before. While I focused most of my attention on his nearly naked rump and on the back of his legs, I would occasionally pause and walk around to the front. The first time that I did so, another couple had walked into the room and were attempting to observe while being as unobtrusive as possible. The man seemed especially interested in me and while my ex-husband and I have been to nude beaches in the past, I have *never* exposed myself in a situation such as the one I was in. As I was saying, I walked around to the front of the stocks until I was finally in full view of Andrew. I asked him if he was enjoying his session and he said *yes mistress*, he was. I assured him that I was receiving great pleasure from our time in this room as well, however, I had decided to heighten it still more. His gaze was completely fixed on me and I reached up to the top of my leather brassiere and unsnapped the panel that covered my left breast. I told him I was going to allow him to suck on my left nipple and if I found it pleasurable then I would redirect my attentions when I returned to striking him with my crop. I reminded him that I knew full well which areas he liked it the most on, and that the crop would visit those areas the most frequently. As I have mentioned in the past, I have very small nipples but Andrew had no trouble in finding my left one with his mouth, and he rapidly brought it to a point. I was extremely pleased with his attempts, and Andrew and the other couple knew it as my breathing grew more labored. Reluctantly, I finally withdrew my nipple from his mouth and pulled away.

At this point, the couple was making no effort to be tactful, and was staring openly at the two of us! I resnapped my left side and moved back around behind Andrew. I kept thinking of Mistress Priscilla and continued to tease and crop Andrew as I imagined that *she* would.

Finally, as I was beginning to glisten from sweat, I commanded Andrew to spread his legs wide…and then wider still. It was quite obvious to all that he was aroused to the point where it was unbearable for him. I decided to end his misery with a series of staccato raps directly on the leather covering of his tiny thong. He shuddered repeatedly as he climaxed before he realized that I was not the only witness in the room, upon which he turned beet red! I won't go into detail about the mess that he cleaned up in the *coed* restroom. Suffice to say that as we were leaving the room, the another couple was getting ready to claim it…although *he* was eagerly latching *her* in! I think we most definitely inspired at least two people ourselves that evening!"

26

Taylor Flaska sat with his arms crossed and folded on the desk in front of him. His throbbing head was resting on top of his arms and his eyes were reduced to slits to further fend off the sunlight pouring into his office. He thought about getting up and pulling the blinds, however even the thought of the movement involved made his head hurt worse. Taylor, the Assistant Mayor of San Diego, was being crippled by his second migraine of the month. He felt like dying. He wondered if any politician had ever died in office of a migraine. He doubted it. The Mayor of San Francisco had died in his office back in 1978, but that was from a gunshot wound and seemed like a more noble way to go. Taylor considered reaching out to the intercom on his desk and buzzing Marcie in the outer office. She would be understanding. She claimed to have migraines as well. *Marcie* maintained that the latest school of thought said migraines were triggered by allergies. She had suggested Taylor introduce a resolution to the city council banning allergies in San Diego. At least Marcie was a very capable secretary.

Taylor had moved here 20 years ago after college to get away from the pollens and the winter weather from back east. A newly certified CPA, Taylor was very proud of the fact he passed his exam on the first sitting. Taylor had applied at every larger city in southern California that would take his application. He just wanted to work a 40-hour week, advance at a reasonable pace, and be within a sane driving distance of his college sweetheart when she started her job in Costa Mesa. The City of San Diego had called first. Twenty years later, he was still employed by the city, albeit in a far different capacity. A local businessman named Donald Barnes had decided to run for Mayor on a fiscal responsibility platform. He needed a city insider in his proposed administration, preferably someone with a background in accounting. It wouldn't hurt if the portly businessman's new running mate was slim and good-looking either. It would not even hurt if his new running mate was dating Don's daughter, which Taylor had been. The young lady in Costa Mesa had dumped Taylor 19 years ago, and the last he heard, she had four children—and the only accounting she did now was to parcel out their lunch money and make sure the household bills were paid. His parents back east didn't seem concerned about grandchildren. They were just relieved their son hadn't moved to San Francisco and turned gay.

Mayor Barnes and his Assistant Mayor had now been in office for five years, and last year's re-election had been a landslide and a virtual mandate to keep up the good work. *Who knows?* thought Taylor, *if Don ever tires of the office or strokes out, I may make a run on the same tried and true platform.* Taylor had used his job title with great effectiveness as a pickup line at bars. Even if Don's daughter had failed to be his perfect match, an important sounding job would expedite his finding the right one. He tried out a new line in his aching head, *Hi, Taylor Flaska, Mayor, is this seat taken?* He thought of another: *Hi, Taylor Flaska, how would you like to trade a key to your apartment for a key to the city?*

Taylor smiled through the pain. That last one had possibilities. He thought about buzzing Marcie when suddenly, he heard her voice. It sounded like she was saying, sure, sure! She wasn't, though. When the man she had been yelling at flung open the door to Taylor's office, he could hear her much more succinctly.

Marcie was adamant, "Sir, sir, you *can't* go in there! Mr. Flaska is *not* seeing anyone right now…sir, sir!"

Taylor picked up his throbbing head. The man was large, with a barrel chest that was sliding into his stomach—and red-faced. In spite of his partially blurred vision, Taylor recognized the intruder. His voice boomed off the glass windows and rattled the framed portraits of civic leaders—and even the smaller ones of groundbreaking ceremonies.

"Taylor! I need to jaw at you!"

"Mr. Flaska, shall I call downstairs for an officer?" Marcie inquired loudly.

Shaking his head no would have jarred his brain and elicited a scream. Taylor tried to muster a smile and waved her off.

"Mr. Assist*ant* Mayor, I'm pissed off and I wanna tell you why! And then I wanna ask you what you and Don are gonna do about it!"

Dick Senstock was going to be dead of a heart attack in five years…ten tops. Until then, he was one of the biggest contractors in the city…and today he was one of the loudest. His specialty was significant public works projects in the bottom quarter of the state, and he bid on San Diego's proposals regularly. He had a drawl that could have been from Southern roots but came out like the aftereffects of a bout with Bells Palsy.

Marcie had closed the door behind her and was now back at her post in the anteroom, determined not to let another invader breach her territory.

Taylor's migraine seemed to have subsided a little with this unexpected distraction standing in front of him. He had never noticed before what an ugly cuss Senstock was turning into. Dick did not seem inclined to sit, which was fine with Taylor; perhaps then he wouldn't stay to mar the décor of his office much longer.

"Mr. Assist*ant* Mayor, I realize we haven't talked much before, and we ain't that close, but that there boss of yours is avoiding me today and I gotta have some answers or I won't be able to swaller lunch."

It looked to Taylor like it would be the first time in a long time if that truly came to pass. "What's on your mind, Dick?"

"*Mis*ter Flaska, I'll get right to the point. I been doin' business with this fine city for a lotta years. Now, my reputation speaks for itself. I do good work. Stuff I did 20 years ago, people still got no complaints. So when I got to my office this morning, I sat down with the mail and divided it up into piles. I got a pile for checks so's I can have my girl take care of it right away. I got one for bills so's I can get 'em matched up too. I got other piles too but, Mr. Assist*ant*, I don't have a pile where I can put a slap in the face! But that's whut I got this morning in the mail. I opened an envelope from your fine city and got a letter sayin' you was sorry but my company wasn't gonna get the contract for the new waterworks project. I paid my money to ya'll and I bid what Don told me to bid, and now in your letter I'm being told I wasn't the low bidder on this one. Now, Mister Flaska, I already know'd that. I also know'd that I wasn't supposed to be. But that's not how it works! I don't give you guys a hundred grand just to be told that I'm playin' by the same rules as everybody else. Now, I didn't pay my money on the last two and I didn't get 'em. But that's because it wasn't my turn. I know'd that. But this time it was my turn to get it. I had my extra money wrote in and that money was spoken for for my new house on the beach. Instead I'm out a hundred and I can't even break ground on that cottage 'til next year."

Dick looked a little less red now that he had vented to somebody. Without being asked, he sat down and filled one of the average-sized chairs in front of Taylor's desk. With a couple of minor additions, Senstock would have looked like an obese gargoyle.

But Taylor was almost too stunned by the revelation he had just received to be revolted. Was this some kind of a set-up? He knew about the waterworks project from the endless consultant reports and the council meetings. Had this sort of thing happened before? What was the legal term for it? Bid rigging…that was it. How much did Don know? According to Senstock, he didn't just know about it—it sounded like he ran it. "I…I don't know what to say, Dick," Taylor spat out.

Senstock leaned forward, trying to act conciliatory but with a face that could scare a kindergartner back into diapers.

"Look here, Taylor…if I can call you that. It's just us menfolk sittin' here right now. I know you and Don and that council member and even that fella in Planning ain't getting' rich off of these deals. But another 25 grand a year in your pocket ain't hurtin' your retirement nest egg either, is it? Now ya'll know that the guy that bid low on this one ain't gonna do near the job that mah company's gonna do. Fact is, sometimes it's worth payin' double to get triple the job quality. Think how you and Don are gonna be burstin' with pride when that project comes up on time and pumpin' like it should. Ya'll be cuttin' that ribbon and smilin' ear to ear. Now I think what happened is maybe the wrong guy in Planning opened them envelopes last month and then the council okayed the wrong company. I don't know what kind of pull you have on this, but if Don ain't returning my calls I got to get the ball rollin' today so somebody can make it right. You unnerstand?"

Taylor was beginning to recover some of his lost poise. His eyeballs had stopped throbbing and the back of his skull was down to a dull ache. "Um…Dick, have you consulted with anybody else about this yet?"

"Well no, of course not. I mean, for the past five years it has just been Don but it always went good before."

Taylor continued to recover from his shock. He tried not to say anything incriminating. "Um…first, Dick, I've got to get hold of Don and see what happened. I have not talked to him yet today either. I'll get back to you as soon as I know more."

"Fine, Taylor, that'd be fine. Sorry to have barged in here like this and hit you between the eyes right off. It's sorta like my daddy used to say, though. *You don't wanna pay for the best room in the whorehouse and not even get laid!* It ain't so much the six figures I'm out…it's the seven figures I'm not gonna get!"

27

While Karen Columbus continued to gauge my reaction whenever she related her latest exploits to me, she no longer hesitated or held back anything. I was now privy to every detail and thought that was running through her head during her experiences. Her choices of words and mellifluous voice still made each story sound as though it were being narrated by a prim and proper schoolmarm.

During subsequent workouts Karen regaled me with stories of her adventures during two more trips to New York. Near the end of the stories of her last trip, she began to look at me differently. She acted as though she either expected more of a reaction from me, or was preparing to ask me something but was trying to decide in advance what my answer would be.

Finally, at the end of her story and her workout, she began to lay down some of the groundwork for her question. After ensuring that no other clients were going to require my attention, Karen lowered her voice and chose her words carefully.

"Mark, I am sure you are astute enough to have noticed that I have not mentioned my husband Dennis as of late. In as gracious a manner as possible, we have both agreed that our interests have drifted too far apart. Since I have never borne children, there are really no familial ties to bind us together. I still think the world of him and I am sure that he does of me as well. Sadly, we have mutually concluded that an amiable divorce would be the right answer and some weeks ago, with his blessing, I initiated proceedings."

I found it curious that Karen could tell me about the most intimate parts of her sex life but could not tell me that she had filed until now.

Karen continued, "Dennis has provided the both of us with a very comfortable living as far back as I care to recount. But the combination of our extensive traveling habits and the fact that we used to dine out at some very nice establishments quite often, has not left us as much in the way of savings as one might expect. It has been agreed upon that I will receive our beautiful condo free and clear and that I will leave his modest 401k untouched. While I shall not receive any alimony, he *is* eligible for a pension in several years and when he does begin to claim it, I shall receive half."

It sounded to me as though ol' Dennis had a few more bucks stashed away than he was alluding to, but I kept my thoughts to myself.

Karen went on, "I have been considering my own career options in great detail and I have reached several conclusions. The first is that although I am a successful interior decorator, I have never really strove to take on more than one client at a time. Thus my income from this endeavor has always been somewhat limited. While I charge 45 dollars an hour, I would have to drastically increase my hours in order to sustain my travel and spending habits. If I did so, I would then lack the *time* to travel *and* would have to curtail the amount of hours that I now spend with my aging mother, whom you probably remember is my sole remaining parent."

Karen glanced at me to see if I was giving any indication that I knew where this was leading to. I will admit I did not.

She took a deep breath and plowed ahead. "I have made extensive inquires as to what the market will bear in what I'm about to propose to you. In the City of New York, the going rate is from 250 to 500 dollars per hour to enlist the services of a Dominatrix. I have since had another chance encounter with Mistress Priscilla, and she has further elaborated to me about her rate schedule. The 300-dollar an hour figure she cited was valid only if a client was going to utilize her services for several hours continuously. For a single hour she might charge four or even five hundred, depending on her schedule in that particular week. She put it this way: *After all, it is just theater and the most sought after actresses are the most highly paid!*

"Now regarding the Detroit area, there are many wealthy enclaves—and many husbands and single men with decidedly unimaginative spouses or girlfriends. Priscilla herself has encountered several men from our area already, although because of the distance constraints none of whom which she would consider regulars. It is her feeling, and mine, that there would be a strong market for this type of service in the Detroit area if it were done discreetly enough. I feel as though the market would certainly bear $300 an hour for a single hour, and $250 an hour for a session that lasts for several. It's simply a matter of supply and demand, really. I believe there is a great deal of demand but no supply to speak of. Now, even though Andrew has business experience, I have elected not to involve him in this venture for several reasons. One of them is because our relationship has regretfully settled into that of a domme and her slave rather than that of boyfriend/girlfriend. As a result, I see no future for us as man and wife either. In addition, I have never *really* been on my own. My parents supported me during college and upon graduation, I jumped straight into a marriage with Dennis. I rather relish the idea of being completely independent from a significant other but as I previously stated, it has to be on my *own* terms. It has also crossed my mind that Andrew might be somewhat jealous if I began to practice "our thing" on other men with any regularity. I am quite sure that this would be a source of constant conflict between us. I saw signs of this in New York on the second visit when I was approached by other men on their knees requesting some time with me. That was the primary motivation for making this last trip by myself."

Karen took another deep breath. "The reasons that I seek to involve you are twofold: The first is your size and musculature. I intend to place several discreet advertisements initially, and am fully aware that some of the respondents may misread what I propose. I am also concerned that some of them may not intend to fully compensate me for my services even though I will insist on being paid in advance. While I would *never* involve you in any of these negotiations, your presence in the vicinity would no doubt have a calming effect should I need to indicate that you were nearby. You can assume whatever mantle you desire, but I would rather consider you as my bodyguard, for want of a more appropriate term. The second reason that I am requesting your involvement is because, through this fitness business, you have had a wide experience with people from all walks of life. I fully realize that your clientele is primarily upscale with a certain amount of discretionary income. This parallels the clientele I intend to develop. As I meet with these people initially, I would like to profile them to you and perhaps enlist you to some extent in determining their legitimacy. As far as your own compensation, should you decide to aid me in this endeavor, I will forward half of what I receive in payment over to you. Needless to say, once I feel comfortable enough to meet with a client on my own, I would keep my entire fee. During the initial meeting or meetings however, I would feel much more at ease if you were wearing a pager or listening device a short distance away."

Karen looked at me quizzically as I mulled it over. I should have been disgusted at her proposal. She was asking me to sit at some obscure location and read a book while she tied up and spanked men (or women?) for money. My studio was doing well. I was far from destitute. If any of my own clientele were to find out about my part-time gig they would probably quit in revulsion.

On the pro side, however, it was difficult to maintain the energy level necessary to bounce around the gym with enthusiasm for 45 hours a week. I had a wedding coming up and the expenses were mounting rapidly. One hundred and fifty an hour was very good money. I could justify accepting the job if I tried hard enough. Men who were bored with the sexual aspect of their marriage could find an outlet that did not involve the risk of contracting AIDS. I would be saving marriages and possibly lives! If I said no, then Karen may decide to attempt to develop her new venture anyway. If something went awry that I could have easily prevented, I might have regrets. I would be like a form of OSHA, ensuring the safety of her workplace. I agreed to do it.

"Good," she said, and her dark brown eyes lightened.

"Now, I've given my moniker a great deal of thought. For a number of reasons I cannot use my given name. So after working through a considerable list of possibilities, I have arrived at just one…Mistress Victoria!"

I told her that I liked it. It had a certain ominous tone to it. I told her it had just the right amount of syllables, too. Victoria continued, "I have been making many purchases in the past several weeks in order to increase the amount of 'accessories' that I am able to utilize when I roleplay with a client. After all, I don't want them to become bored soon after I take the trouble of getting to know them. I want them to experience a build up of excitement in the days prior to their session as they try to anticipate what I have in store for them. It also ensures that I will have more fun as I drop hints to them about new devices that await. I have written out some preliminary ads as well, and I have reserved a widely read position on the back page of an "underground newspaper." I do not mention my rates in any of the ads, but since the entire page is reserved for unique services, anyone who inquires will expect to be charged once they retain me. The contact number at the bottom of the ad is that of a new line that I have had installed at a vacant house. The house belongs to a friend of mine who owns multiple properties, and it is essentially condemned while he prepares to market the land upon which it rests. I have attached an answering machine to the line that allows me to check it from a remote location. I have registered the number to a fictitious name as well. I believe that it will be very difficult for anyone to decipher my whereabouts if I do not wish to meet with them. I am hoping for numerous calls, as I intend to be quite selective before meeting with a new client and expect there to be a weeding out process."

I eventually concluded that Kar…er…Victoria would have been pleased if her ad had garnered one dozen calls during its one week run. She phoned me at the studio to report with a squeal of delight that her machine had fielded two dozen calls the first day! The next day, she teetered on the brink of delirium when her machine reported 40 calls. By the end of the week Victoria's machine had once answered 70 calls on a single day. Only one-third of the callers had the moxy to leave a message…or maybe only a third had a return number where they could speak to her in private.

Victoria eventually returned most of the messages, and by month's end had agreed to meet with ten of the callers. From that point it did not take her long to develop a regular clientele. My jaw dropped more than once when I heard what position a specific client held and the details of his whispered desires. Within two months, Victoria had met with all ten and was seeing them on a semi-regular basis. Soon, all of her new clients were by referral only, and my presence was no longer required.

28

"Jesuuus Taylor! I was gonna tell you!" Mayor Barnes was trying to force a laugh.

"When, Don, after our tenth term in office? You've been doing this five goddamn years now! And the thing of it is, every piece of shit that's been doing it with you and the others thinks that I'm in on it too! You know how I finally found out? It was like a perfect storm. The head of Planning was out sick and the wrong guy opened the envelopes. Then you're out two days getting your vasectomy redone. Who the hell ever heard of that anyway?"

"Boy, you don't think I planned on having that last one at my age, do you? Especially not with that little chippie in Parks and Rec. I shouldn't have had my own doc do it in the first place. But he said he'd watched a couple. He said nobody ever plans on those little tubes growing back but sometimes the ends miss each other so bad they just do. I think this other guy's got it right though. Now I've just got 18 more years of child support and I'm home free!" Mayor Barnes said sarcastically.

"I've had two days to go through the records, Don. Five years. You averaged four times a year. What have you taken in so far, about two million?"

"That's sounds about right. Don't worry, I've been holding your share for you. Comes to about $400,000 by now."

"What were you going to do Don? Wait until the FBI arrested us and then write me a check for bail money?"

"Well, actually, Taylor, I'd have a problem doing that right now. You see, it's expensive living in this town and with the two youngest girls just finishing up college right now—I might have $75,000 or $100,000 in cash—I'd have to owe you the rest."

Son-of-a-bitch, he never even thought I'd find out!

"How does Marion feel about you stealing two million dollars and the city getting screwed over for about 25 million?"

"Well, now son, she doesn't have to know. This was for her daughters too. I think if she knew about this—or my new baby boy—she'd be pretty upset, but she'd stand by me."

~~~~~~~~~~~~~~~~~~~~~~~~~~~~

She'd stand by me. Mayor Barnes' words were still ringing in Taylor's ears. Well, maybe Marion Barnes *would* stand by her husband if she found out, but she would be swinging a baseball bat! Taylor was still furious and wished he had one right now to knock some sense into his boss. It was two days later. They were sitting in the steam room at the Mayor's Executive Health Club. A police detail stood outside the thick oak door. Any sound that penetrated *out* was masked by the Muzak on the speaker over the officer's head, and Mayor Barnes knew it. It was the perfect venue for discussions that needed to be kept one-on-one.

"Why the steam room today, Don? Did you want to make sure I wasn't wearing wire?"

"Yeah. Something like that."

"Don, I haven't told a soul about this yet. I can't believe it myself. I want to walk out of here this afternoon after hearing that somebody put you up to this…or maybe you were blackmailed somehow. Don, I want to hear how the man I trusted—the man who approached me six years ago and asked me to help set this town right—didn't dream this up on his own. Together, you and I were supposed to be guarding this city's coffers…getting these fine people more bang for their buck…planning out the future. Instead, you're looting them—and half the contractors for 100 miles think I am too. Don, at least tell me this is part of an FBI sting. Tell me that they've got bigger fish to fry and that you're cooperating with them, and pretty soon a bunch of dirty contractors are going to get indicted and we'll be heroes in the press when this all comes out."

"That's not a bad way out, son. Except that I haven't exactly gotten the ball rolling on that one yet."

"Well, Mr. Mayor. I've never told you what to do yet. Not in six years…five of them spent running this city. I've always let you lead—spoken only when asked. But I'm telling you now, that's the only way we're going to play it. That's the only way I'm gonna stay on board this ship. We'll talk to the Feds. We tell them about the Planning Head and the Council President and the hell with them! Let them go down with the next two or three contractors greedy enough to keep doing this. We're going to come clean, put a spin on this, and who knows—maybe even stay in office a couple of more terms. Even if we don't, at least we won't be doing time in the Federal Pen. The only downside to doing it my way is that you won't be able to keep any more payments in the sting…you'll have to give it back. And you can keep my share of what you've collected so far—I'm smart enough to know that I wasn't going to see it anyway—even after I stumbled onto this mess. But you know what, Mayor? That's the difference between us right now. I wouldn't take it even if you *hadn't* spent it. With all due respect to your office—but not you anymore, Don—I'm not suggesting we get this in the open…I'm *telling* you. I'm only 42. I'm too young to spend the next 20 years in the Pen. And you're 55. You're too *old* to do the time!"

Mayor Barnes was silent. He had never seen his protégé dig in his heels like this before. When they first announced their candidacy, Taylor Flaska was 36 and already had 14 years with the city. So the voters had someone on the ballot that they had already entrusted their tax money to. And his lean, sandy-haired good looks hadn't scared away any female voters, either. With Don's gift of gab and self-confidence and his "fiscal plan" for a city reeling with Defense cutbacks, they had been the right candidates at the right time. And in spite of Taylor's accusations, they had not done the city any harm, Don reasoned. In fact, they had attracted enough high-tech business in their new industrial parks to put real money back in the city's bank accounts…in fact last time he checked there had been a significant surplus. But all of that seemed to be lost on Taylor right now—full as he was of righteous indignation. It was easy for him to stand on the soapbox and preach. He had no wife, no family—he drove a city-supplied car. Being elected Assistant Mayor had even been a salary bump for him. For Don, even with the Mayoral Mansion and the limo and the other perks, it had been a cut at a time when his daughters were looking at colleges. And the wife had been spending money like they were finding it under their pillows—what with the gowns and the jewelry to impress the citizenry. They always had to be the first to bring out their checkbook at every charity event, and lately it seemed like everybody was begging at once. Of course, Mr. Flaska had his own way of making an impression on the citizenry—at least the female portion of it. Mayor Barnes had heard that more than one young lady had succumbed to the aura that went with Taylor's job title, which would explain why there had not been a rush to sound any wedding bells at City Hall yet. Perhaps Mr. Flaska had other motives for going to the Feds other than those he stated. Maybe he envisioned some heroic whistleblower role for himself to get his clean-cut image on CNN so he could lure the young ladies from a bigger, national pool. Whatever Taylor's true motivations, Mayor Barnes was going to need to buy himself a little more time.

"Okay, my boy. I can see that you're right on this one. I give, I give. But before we put this whole thing into action, you've got to allow me to pretty things up a little. If the FBI decides to start looking into things before they play ball with us, they might find a discrepancy or two or three in my bank accounts. I'm gonna need a little time to switch things around…maybe start up some new ones at different banks. Might need to take out a personal loan now, too, in case things heat up and they look too hard at my cash flow later. Truth is, I'm still gonna have to put Debbie through her last year of college and I don't think Marion is going to slow down just because her husband of 33 years asks her to. You've been out to our place in the mountains—I don't think you'd want to see us give that up if we didn't have to?" The Mayor wasn't accustomed to begging. The closest he got to it in his political duties was negotiating. Don knew that he did not have much wiggle room with this one. But the time he was asking for meant the difference between a comfortable retirement or spending the next 20 years rooming with a large, lonely man named Bubba.

"How much time do you think you need?" Taylor asked cautiously.

"If you could give me two months, I should be able to get out some good detergent and scrub everything down pretty good. That may sound like a lot of time to you, but you must know by now that we don't have any more major bids coming up for at least that long, and there can't be any sting unless they see something worth using their stinger on."

"And on the sixtieth day from today we both go in?"

"Together, with maybe an attorney or two."

The Assistant Mayor and his Mayor shook on the deal, just as the Mayor's incisions were beginning to ache again.

29

Although Mistress Victoria had pared back her workouts to only once or twice per week, each visit to my studio brought details of a particularly unique encounter. On one of these visits, Victoria's brown eyes were flashing as she began describing the previous night.

"Mark, I have to tell you about the most special time I had last night. One of my regular clients is very happily married, but has some fantasies that I have been fulfilling for him quite satisfactorily. Although I think he still loves his wife very much, he claims she is lacking in imagination. They are both young still, and they have been so engrossed in their careers, it is my opinion they neglected to set aside time for each other's adventures. My client had a desire to involve his wife in one of our scenarios at their home and I agreed to do it. I have no idea how much he clued her in but he indicated to me several times that he had received her tacit approval. It had just become dark when I arrived in the driveway of their home. This man holds a high level accounting position at one of the Big Three automobile firms and I knew that he was well off, but his home was even more sumptuous than I had anticipated. When I got out of my Cutlass, I had been asked to walk around the back and let myself in through a large wooden gate. The gate was part of a tall privacy fence that encircled their backyard, but I believe that their heavily wooded property extended all around for some distance more. They did not have any neighbors in close proximity to them.

The temperature was still in the high 70s, but I wore my full-length trench coat anyway until I had closed the gate behind me. Mark, the only word that I can use to describe the backyard is exquisite! There was a large kidney-shaped in-ground pool in the middle of the yard. The water in the pool glowed and I remember thinking how inviting it looked. White concrete walkways and a sunning area encircled the pool. The walkways meandered out in every direction as well. One led to a wooden deck in back of the house and one took a roundabout path to the gate where I had let myself in. There were two more walkways that curved their way between the stands of trees that were growing throughout the backyard. The walkways were illuminated by hundreds of small lanterns that were planted every ten feet or so along each side. This lighting gave the entire yard an ethereal glow that was stunning. As I approached the pool, I observed my client in a lounge chair at one end. He was wearing only a swimsuit and I think that he had been watching me from the moment that I entered the gate. I walked over to a patio table near him and set my leather bag of equipment on the surface of the table. I removed my long trench coat at that point and folded it in half along its length before draping it across the back of a chair at the table. My client was still staring at me from his chair but now I began to return his stare while I unzipped my leather bag and reached in to remove some items. I myself was wearing a black leather half-bustier and leather shorts that were so brief that the cheeks of my derriere were peeking out the bottom. As you have observed in the past, I have a substantial amount on top and I *adore* this bustier because it pushes everything up even further until my cleavage is completely overflowing!"

I had seen Victoria in the bustier before. Overflowing was the perfect word to describe the situation.

She continued. "I had removed just a few items from my bag, gazing down at him all the while, when I arrived at my riding crop. Without breaking my stare, I grasped the crop and motioned with it for him to stand up. As he did so, I plucked two leather cufflets off of the table and ordered him to buckle them around his wrists. When he had finished, I set my crop down, picked up a coil of rope, and looped one end through each of the rings that were attached to the cuffs. After tying the end around itself securely, I picked up my crop and the coil again and led him over to the nearest tree with a suitable branch. I ordered him to stand under the branch while I threw the entire coil over it and watched it land behind him. I cropped him on his buttocks twice and ordered him to raise his arms over his head while I pulled hard on the rope. When I had taken out all of the slack in the rope I cropped him once more and demanded that he stand up on his toes as high as possible. At this point I dropped my crop and used both hands to tug on the rope as hard as I possibly could. Then, keeping the rope very taut, I wrapped it repeatedly around the trunk of the tree. I was near the end and only needed to loop it underneath itself twice. I stepped back for a moment to admire my work. As he hung there I walked up to him and suggested that he might be more comfortable without the swimsuit and I gave it some downward tugs until it fell down around his ankles. I ordered him to step out of it and after he did I kicked it with my boot over to the tree trunk. I do not know if he works out in his pool but he has a rather slim body and I stood back to admire it. I remember asking him how he liked being stretched out and put on display for Mistress, and he answered that he liked it if it pleased me. I told him that I was pleased so far but that his naked buttocks were presenting such an inviting target for my crop that I could not resist. I stood in back of him and began with some light strokes. After each stroke I allowed the crop to linger and I dragged it across his skin around to his most private and sensitive areas. Several times he turned his head in an attempt to watch me, but a more vigorous strike and a sharp rebuke were all that it took to face him forward again. After three or four minutes, I observed that his attention was focused on a glass doorwall at the rear of his home. I asked him if he was expecting an audience tonight, and he said that his wife was home and he had seen the draperies move behind the glass. I asked if this was the first time that she will see him this way and he said yes. I peeked around, and his excitement at the prospect was becoming quite obvious. A moment later the glass door opened partially and a pretty woman with short dark hair stepped out. She was about five and a half feet tall and had a cute little figure. She was wearing a swimsuit bikini with a modest bottom but a top that pushed her medium-sized breasts together very nicely. She was staring at her husband and then back at me, and as she drew near I marveled at her pale, perfect skin. Her tummy was neither perfectly flat nor did it protrude. The curve of her hips complemented her legs perfectly, and it looked to me as though she found the time to walk whenever possible. After she had absorbed what was happening under the tree limb, she turned and began to find the steps in the shallow end of the pool. I do not know if she had planned to swim…I think that it was a spontaneous decision. She had a precise, graceful stroke that was a pleasure to watch. After several laps she must have arrived at some conclusion about the evening so far, and she stopped swimming and stepped up and out of the shallow end. As she walked toward us this second time, water was streaming from her hair and down her shoulders and arms. Her large dark eyes were still moving back and forth to me and her husband. She was breathing lightly from the swim and her breath had a light, minty aroma that I found exciting. We had not heard her speak as yet, and I asked her if she enjoyed seeing her husband become more aroused as she approached. She looked down at him and in a soft voice, she responded yes. Now that she was out of the swimming pool, I felt better able to proceed with the scenario that my client and I had envisioned over the phone. Not wishing to make any abrupt movements, I sidled over to the patio table once more and returned with two more of the leather cuffs. With a smile and a wink, I told the woman that her husband and I would very much enjoy seeing how these looked on her. We had arrived at a significant moment in our scene, and the pretty brunette wife looked down at her feet for a moment as if contemplating something. After a moment she took a deep breath and reached out with her right hand. I handed her the cuffs and lent some assistance with the first one as she buckled it around a perfect, porcelain wrist. Mark, the contrast of the black leather against her pale skin was so breathtaking that I had to look away to her husband for a moment! He was watching as well, and had by now arrived once again at full attention. I left the woman to fasten the other cuff by herself and once more drifted over to the patio table. When I saw that she had nearly finished her task, I picked up the second coil of rope and walked back to her. I was delighted at her level of compliance and told her so. I dropped the coil of rope to the ground at the bottom of her bare feet and gently reached out to grasp her hands, one in each of mine. She allowed me to turn each hand over slowly as I admired the metal studded cuffs around her wrists. I looked over to her husband as he hung there and asked him whether he thought that they looked perfect on her. He nodded yes and she smiled ever so faintly. That smile emboldened me to ask her another question. I explained that the swimsuit complemented her lovely figure well, but that I kept imagining a beautiful pair of breasts beneath the top and wanted to know if I could remove the top portion of her suit to see if I was correct. She hesitated for several long seconds before a little nod of her head told me yes. Small water droplets were still escaping from her hair when she nodded. Gently, I stepped around behind her and unfastened the clasp to her top. She had dropped her hands to her sides my now, and I met with no resistance as I stood behind her and slipped the straps down and over her beautiful arms. I walked back around to face her. The night air had already begun to affect her wet nipples, and they responded very quickly. In a quiet voice I told her that I was right, she had very beautiful breasts. Without asking, I bent down to pick up one end of the rope that lay at her feet. Still without asking, I grasped first one wrist and then the other, quickly feeding the rope through the metal loop on each. As I tied the cuffs together, I began to explain that when I had removed her top I realized she was still very wet from her swim. I told her I had an idea that would assist her in drying off as I did not see a towel anywhere. I tossed the rope over the same tree limb that supported her husband and raised her arms above her head with my free hand as I pulled it taut. Although she had been finished with her swim for several minutes by this time, her breathing was steadily growing more rapid. My other slave's eyes were nearly bulging by now as he witnessed this new proceeding. Soon I had the rope very taut but I did not demand that she go to her toes like her mate. I wrapped the rest of the rope around a different tree trunk that was still very near. I commented aloud how she looked like a spectacular piece of sculpture that had been hung up to dry. I pointed out that a gentle breeze was blowing sporadically and would soon evaporate most of the wetness from her gorgeous skin. Again without asking, I walked up to her and turned her hips enough so that she was now directly facing her husband. She was nearly panting by now as I took possession of her completely. I hooked my thumbs inside the waistband of her bikini bottoms around each hip and pulled downward. I had worked them down six inches or so before I had to pause and reach around behind her to stretch them over her buttocks. Once I accomplished that, I was able to rapidly work them down her legs to the ground. I could not resist looking up as I did so. With her arms over her head her bosom had lifted up as well, and I was sure that I could see her heart pounding beneath her left breast. She was closely cropped and I could smell her dampness and her excitement as I sweetly ordered her to step out from the bottoms around her ankles. She complied and I tossed them over to the tree next to her husband's. I let the couple face each other while I walked back over to the table and selected my long-handled paddle. Her skin looked so smooth and divine that I did not want to risk leaving even a temporary mark on it with the crop. She was quivering by now but I passed her by and walked over to her husband while mentioning that this paddle was a favorite of mine because the grip was so comfortable. I asked if either wanted to try gripping it, but then smiled and apologized for being silly because obviously they could not right now. Then I told them that they would each get a chance to try the other end instead. Mark, this paddle causes a great deal more noise than discomfort, but I enjoy watching my slaves' faces when I approach them for the first time with it. I swung it backhanded for the first one, but even so the slapping noise resounded amongst the trees. I quickly switched to a forehand for the next several slaps and then paused to inspect his backside for any signs of undue redness. The couple hung only about four feet apart from each other and I could see her quivering turn to a tremble as I stepped over to her. If she expected me to ask anymore, she was mistaken. When I got to her I instead turned to her husband and asked if he wanted to see her paddled. Mark, I was completely unsure as to whether he had suggested a scene similar to this to her or if it was *she* who had hinted to *him* that she would be a willing participant. But I did know that I would have to take it easy on her initially regardless of how inviting her beautiful buttocks were. She was trembling so hard that I was concerned she may faint at the very first stroke! I delivered a light one and she exhaled in a huge gasp, but did not cry out. Her trembling lessened as I delivered another one on the opposing cheek. After two more she was still panting hard, but even her quivering had ceased. I followed up with a half dozen more after that, but I did not expend much effort on any of them. I left them both to ponder their circumstances for a moment and went back over to the table. I have an assortment of bells that I like to use when a slave is ready for more difficult training. I selected two that were attached to springy clamps and walked over to my male slave. I clamped a bell onto each of his nipples. I had never seen him so aroused before. He was a full inch longer than I had ever seen him…not that he was small. I believe some of it was due to viewing his wife's predicament, and the rest was from *being* viewed by his wife. Once the bells were on securely, I walked behind him once again and warned him that if I heard the bells ring after I struck him, I would make the next stroke harder still. Well, it is almost impossible not to move a little after being struck with that paddle, and I heard the bells nearly two dozen times before he figured out how to keep them quiet. I verbally applauded his efforts and walked back to the table. I also have a set of bells that are attached to tiny nooses made out of nylon line. As I brought them over to her, I explained that I had a special set of bells for her but we would not be playing the same game. Instead I would release the rope as soon as I had secured her bells and expected her to stand quietly until I could let her husband's hands down as well. She complied and I went over to the table to select my rubber whip. I love this one because it has 30 rubber tails coming out of the handle and makes a wicked whooshing sound as it is swung through the air. The tails do not make much noise as they connect, but I have grown very adept at twirling it rapidly with my wrist and arm. I can strike the same area with it four or five times per second, or just once every two seconds with more rapacious blows. I had attached the small nooses from the bells very tightly around her erect nipples, and she had remained motionless. She had her head down and was inspecting her adornments when I released her husband's rope from around the trunk."

30

"What's the matter, *Mister* Assistant Mayor?" Colleen asked sweetly. Her light freckles were arranged in a polite but inquisitive smile. Her flaming red hair cascaded in curls and ringlets to just past her shoulders. She was half turned to face him from the passenger seat of his BMW as he guided it through surprisingly light traffic on I-15.

They were on their way to a long weekend at the Mayor's family "cottage" that was nestled in the mountains of Big Bear. Taylor realized with a start that he had not said anything in over half an hour, and Colleen was not the kind of woman that you ignored if you were hoping to score later on. But the Assistant Mayor of San Diego had a lot on his mind in the last month, and burdening this young lass with any of it would be counterproductive to the purposes of this getaway. With only 30 days to go before he and Don went to the Feds, this might be his last vacation for awhile. He had already had three migraines this month, and Taylor hoped the solitude of the Mayor's mountain retreat would help ease some of the tension that had become his constant companion. The second reason for this getaway, of course, had much to do with the fact that this alluring young lady had been resistant to his every attempt to…consummate their relationship. Taylor had high hopes that three days of "playing house" up amid the picturesque beauty of the mountains might change her thinking a little. He was accustomed to one night stands—followed by his promises to call—and even girls that took two or three dates before giving him the signal…but this hold-out of hers going on two months was a puzzle he was growing increasingly frustrated with. On top of it all, Taylor was getting jumpier from two unusual incidents in the past week that had him seeing ghosts behind every bush. He was still trying to decipher the meaning of the piece of masking tape over the peephole in his apartment door.

"Nothing's wrong, Colleen, really…at least nothing that a few days of staring out a picture window looking at what you would swear is a painting won't cure. You are going to love it up here, I guarantee it."

"How often do you come up here?"

Now there was a loaded question. It really meant, *Do you bring your other conquests up here or am I special?*

"Until now, the only time I've ever been up is to meet up with the Mayor and his family." Taylor wasn't the first politician to ever tell a lie. If he survived the sting operation politically, perhaps he could get re-elected in his own right someday and tell a few more. Suddenly he had a chilling thought; what if the masking tape wasn't just a prank?

It had been 2 A.M. on a sleepless night and he'd been lying in the dark on his front sofa when he heard a scratching at the front door. He got up to investigate and as he drew near, it sounded more metallic than a cat's claws would have—as though someone were inserting and then withdrawing a key in the locks. He had not actually seen the knob turn—but heard the metal on metal tap as the hardware on the door met that of the security hasp on the frame. Taylor had that one installed at the advice of the police department—it was identical to those found in motel rooms—and it could not be opened from the outside. Taylor finally realized that there was an attempted break-in in progress and began shouting as he went for the phone. A squad car was at his buzzer in one minute flat. The investigating detective, Sergeant Robert Costa, was as perplexed as Taylor as to why he would be singled out for such a bold B & E attempt. But Detective Costa was more curious about why Taylor had to unlock the door for the responding officer. If an unknown person had unlocked the door and was trying to gain entry until thwarted by the extra lock—and then scared off—why did they take the time to re-lock it again? Perhaps the Assistant Mayor had been half asleep and mistaken? Perhaps it was nothing more than a prank by some teenager in the building?

If it was a prankster, as Detective Costa had inferred, then he was making a concentrated effort to have a good laugh at Taylor's expense. Just two nights ago he and Colleen had driven the BMW up to Santa Ysabel to meet her friends for dinner. After handing his keys to the valet, Taylor experienced a sudden chill despite the 80-degree temperature. Colleen had noticed his involuntary shiver and laughingly asked if he was apprehensive about meeting her friends. Her comment evoked a guffaw from him that she had not heard for weeks and the incident was forgotten—until dinner was over. The two couples exchanged pleasantries as they bid each other good night and stood awaiting the valet. It looked to be a long wait, however, as the restaurant seemed to disgorge all of its patrons at once, and Taylor impulsively plucked his keys off the board and headed toward the lot. The chill came back and he began to shiver with a vengeance, until a stray headlight beam fortuitously illuminated the ground beneath his car. The shivers paused in their travels from his lower back to his shoulders, and instead his knees weakened. There they were—standing erect beneath his tire like little steel soldiers—three roofing nails placed on their heads. A closer examination revealed that while the points were already in contact with the tire, they had not yet begun to penetrate. Nor were they meant to...until the instant that someone began to back the car up! After six inches in reverse, the long barbs would have driven themselves home, with any hissing being masked by the sporty cars exhaust note. How far Taylor and his date would have traveled this way was difficult to say. It would have been ten, perhaps 15, but probably not more than 20 miles before the handling became vague enough for him to pull over. Taylor's imagination had raced at the time…was this another, but more elaborate prank?…or was this designed to leave him stranded on a lonely stretch of road? The chills returned as Taylor speculated as to the whereabouts of the prankster. He and Colleen had obviously been followed. But who was doing the following? Taylor scooped up the nails and studied nearby cars for observers. He half expected Dick Senstock to leap out of one and demand a progress report regarding the next time he would be allowed to loot the city's bank account. But the heavyset contractor was nowhere to be seen. Taylor had turned the nails over to Detective Costa in the morning without voicing his suspicions as to who or why, but knew in advance that they would not yield any prints. Taylor wasn't sure if he was being warned or stalked. The chills seemed to come more frequently now—he got them almost every time he left his office or apartment. He suddenly craved being among crowds of people—or at least not finding himself alone.

It was when Taylor had gone to Mayor Barns with his suspicions that he had received not only a truckload of reassurances that the beginning of the end was near, but also a set of keys. *Mi casa es su casa,* Don insisted as he explained that Taylor would actually be doing him a favor this weekend by saving him the trip up to check on things.

If there was one thing that Taylor was grateful for, it was the fact that his chills had gone away ever since leaving San Diego. He looked over at the latest candidate for the title of Mrs. Taylor Flaska. God, she was beautiful. In profile she reminded him of a young version of the red-headed actress Julianna Moore. Maybe after the upcoming thing with the Feds was over he could start thinking hard about some sandy-haired or even red-headed little clones. This young lady seemed to have an unpretentious appeal and seemed very patient. She would probably make a fine mother. A wife and children would also present a wholesome image if Taylor were ever to head the mayoral ticket himself one day. Of course, he would also have to interview her between the sheets before making any final decisions. Colleen had readily agreed to this trip, however, and Mayor Barnes had made it clear that any wines in the house that struck their fancy should be tasted immediately.

They arrived just before dusk as the last rays of the dying sun glinted on the tiny grains of gravel embedded in the roofing tiles.

It had been a winding journey up the road to the house—which at first looked like a toy stuck into the mountainside, and Taylor was able to point it out to Colleen more than once. But as they finally pulled into the private driveway, Colleen gave out a little gasp at the unexpected size of their final destination. It had originally been designed to look like a Swiss-style chalet but last minute changes from Mayor Barnes to accommodate both his daughters and political guests had swollen it to a six-bedroom, five-bathroom affair that dwarfed the other "getaways" around it. The front half rested on columns plunged into the mountainside, and four balconies jutted out. Extra large windows across the exposed side further detracted from the original chalet look but did not fail to impress Taylor's red-haired guest. While Colleen stood staring at her new surroundings Taylor silently walked over to her, took the young woman's hand, and pressed the keys of their borrowed retreat gently into her palm. Then he popped the rear deck lid of the BMW and gallantly scooped up both of the valises. He successfully slammed the lid down with one elbow and they both started up the drive together. Colleen opened the door with the first key that she tried, and held it open for Taylor as he deposited their luggage just inside the door. In a flash he was back out again, making her giggle as he scooped her up with a flourish and carried her across the threshold. She reached up and kissed him, and they did not stop until several seconds after he had set her down. Remarking aloud at the tasteful décor, Colleen followed Taylor as he carried their luggage upstairs and into the master bedroom. They did not bother to unpack immediately, but instead opted to head straight out the doorwall to the balcony. Their view took in not only a considerable portion of countryside, but in the not-too-far-off distance a commanding view of Big Bear Lake as well, which brought another gasp from the enchanted young lady. Together they sat on a divan until evening took over and the first stars presented themselves in the clear sky. Taylor found a bottle of wine and together they shared it until his hunger pangs told him that he might want to do something about dinner. The massive freezer in the kitchen yielded two boxes of crepes—one of cheese and one of strawberry filled—and soon Taylor was sautéing them in a pan in between ramping up the sound system. The entire house was instantly filled with the sounds of Kenny G, and Taylor turned off the stove before padding upstairs to inform his intended about the status of their repast.

The upstairs seemed chillier than before and Taylor made a mental note to check for a top floor thermostat after dinner. As he rounded the door into the bedroom, he smiled outwardly when he noticed Colleen's bare feet and legs on the bed. To his delight, they were attached to a completely nude woman that lie on the bed, and illuminated only by the glow of a bedside reading light. Taylor suppressed a chuckle when he saw her legs parted slightly but her hands down at her sides in a pose of surrender—as if to say that the time was now and she did not intend to resist him. His gaze traveled up her long, lean form to her breasts. Although not large by any means, they were nicely formed and still stood up well from her chest. His tie had disappeared as soon as he got in his car that afternoon to pick her up, and he loosened still another shirt button before he went to her on the bed. He finished his inspection of her naked body and looked over at her face with an approving smile. Instead, he froze in horror. Her lightly freckled face, once so pleasant and innocent, was now a purple and blue contorted mask. One eye was half open and bulging, the other completely shut. Broken capillaries spiderwebbed across her cheeks and forehead. Her purple lips were distorted into a grotesque sneer as though her soul had left her body and she did not care.

The blood drained from Taylor's head and his knees weakened as his heart threatened to stop pumping altogether. He needed to sit or brace himself in order to continue standing, but could not will his arm to touch the bed. As panic welled up inside, his eyes were drawn now to her neck and the dark bruise of thumbprints in the mottled skin that covered her crushed windpipe. As he rocked unsteadily, he felt something under his feet. He looked down and saw that he was standing on what used to be Colleen's clothing, except that it looked as though it had been sliced off of her in pieces. The growing realization that he was being set up for murder started to creep into his consciousness. Taylor knew he needed to sit down and think. His next several moves would be critical to not only his political future, but his freedom as well.

Taylor blinked hard. If this was a horrible dream he needed to wake up from it right now. Even the migraines would have been welcomed back at this point if that's what it took to bring him back to consciousness. Suddenly, the back of Taylor's neck tingled as a chill surrounded him. With his next breath the room's temperature seemed to drop. Taylor spun around. A tall figure was standing in the doorway! In the dim light the man looked like an apparition—the face immobile and expressionless. As Taylor's eyes refocused, he stared at the wavy brown hair and the skin on the unshaven face as it stretched over high cheekbones and a square jaw. The eyes, intense and unblinking, were set well back under the brow, making it impossible to determine if they were brown or black. The apparition's upright bearing and posture reminded Taylor of some of the military men that he had seen in the city—ramrod straight and square shouldered. The apparition was dressed in black jeans and a black T-shirt. Muscle bulged beneath the shirt's thin material, and the short sleeves were stretched to their limits trying to conceal arms that looked as though they could bend steel bars. Taylor gasped. The figure held a knife in his right hand, the kind of knife that you only saw in Navy Seal movies when the heroes swept silently down to slash the throats of their prey. Just when Taylor didn't think that his situation could get any worse, the figure tilted his head. It made the thick muscles in the neck flex beneath the taut skin as the unfeeling eyes continued a cold appraisal of their quarry. Somehow Taylor found his speaking voice, and as he did so he began to move slowly away from the bed.

"Listen, I don't know what Senstock told you but I haven't said anything to anybody! I'm fine with whatever he and Mayor Barnes decides to do. Just let me get out of here and I'll say I was never here and I never saw you!"

The figure moved again, slowly starting toward Taylor in a motion that was less walking than gliding across the natural wood floor. Taylor moved slightly toward the open bathroom door and the figure altered his path ever so slightly to cut him off…then stopped. Taylor continued backing up again on a path that would soon take him to the glass door and the balcony.

"Look, whatever they're paying you—I've got money—I can pay you more!"

The figure started to advance again. Taylor backed up a step onto the thick cushion of an area rug by the balcony door. He thought of trying to pull open the door and attempting a dash out onto the balcony to scream for help, but the figure had now begun to float toward him again and was no farther than ten feet away. Taylor remembered seeing a movie once where the hero had confronted a knife-wielding assailant by wrapping a jacket around his arm to parry the thrusts. But the recollection worsened his terror as the absurdity of his besting this forbidding creature in hand-to-hand combat took hold.

"Look, if you're doing this to scare the hell out of me it's working. If there's anything I've got to do to walk out of here with a warning please say something and I'll do it!" Gingerly, Taylor began moving to one end of the area rug but the man/ghost angled over to cut him off as fluidly as ever…and drew even nearer. Frustration mixed with panic now as Taylor realized that he had been isolated to an eight by ten foot piece of woven fiber. Out of the corner of his eye he spotted a dark object. It was Colleen's suitcase, set casually down by the balcony glass. Desperately, Taylor formulated a plan. If he could turn, step, and grab it rapidly enough, he might be able to scoop up the piece of luggage and fling it at his attacker. With luck, the apparition would be distracted enough for Taylor to slip by and get out the bedroom door. This thing didn't look like it could be outrun, but with a head start Taylor might win in a quick dash to the BMW. He steeled himself for a quick move…right…now! He turned and began to move to his right when he suddenly felt a searing pain in his side. A powerful hand pinched his throat together as he felt the blade lacerate his kidney and twist around through other adjoining organs until his knees buckled. The hand continued crushing his larynx as he collapsed into a heap on the rug. He tried to expel air through his imploded windpipe but succeeded only in staring up at his killer as the light in his eyes flickered out.

~~~~~~~~~~~~~~~~~~~~~~~~~~~~~

    Rico kept his hand on the mark's throat until all life had ebbed away. Rico had anticipated a pathetic last-minute lunge for the suitcase 20 minutes ago as he was extinguishing the redhead, but he elected to let it sit. His physical regimen had left him even stronger and faster than when he was back in 'Nam. He knew from nearly a week of recon that the mark, while slightly younger, spent too much time in the office to even qualify the final act as sport.

    All of the massive hemorrhaging had been internal and a minimal amount of blood oozed out of the entry wound. Rico had kept the mark cornered on the rug as he moved in and had kept the thrashing to a minimum, but he carefully checked the surrounding wood floor for spatter anyway. It took less than five seconds to arrange the corpse along one end of the rug and ten more to roll it up. Again the floor was meticulously inspected before Rico squatted down and forced an arm between the floor and the rug. From there it was a simple matter to scoop the load and thrust upwards to a standing position. The trip to the BMW was much shorter than any hike through rough terrain with a full pack, and Rico popped the deck lid with the keys he had found on the bureau.

Time of death to time of departure was about three minutes, and Rico pointed the BMW in a direction that generally led him back west. Five miles from the chalet, the BMW passed the wooded area where Rico had stashed the motorcycle that had brought him to within hiking distance. He would return in his van and pick it up at his leisure early Sunday—long before his mark was missed. The ride to Eternal Rest Memorial was uneventful, but in case it was not, a .22 Ruger with a full suppressor lie on the driver's floor. By 2 A.M. Rico arrived at the long, curving driveway that led to the funeral home but bypassed it in favor of the entranceway to the cemetery itself. The BMW drove sedately through the cemetery until it reached the crematorium. Rico parked in back of the squat building and walked to the side. He found the new pane of glass still in its cardboard sheath under the same bush where he had stashed it with the caulking gun. After breaking an existing pane of glass in the window above, Rico reached in and unlatched the window. In one smooth motion he boosted himself through the opening. Once inside, he opened a cargo door in the rear of the masonry structure. Rico popped open the trunk once again and carried his bundle to the crematorium's furnace. He slid the body in on the rollered grating, and closed the top door. To be thorough, he set the electric timer for 120 minutes before pushing the button on the electronic igniter. An audible sparking ensued, and a moment later a hiss of gas. The furnace ignited with a dull roar. Methodically, Rico set about caulking the new pane into the window before cleaning up the shards of broken glass and relocking the window. The rear door was self-latching, and soon he was parked outside of the cemetery proper. He checked the area for signs that his visit had aroused any suspicions. Finding none, he drove to LAX and dropped the glass shards and the caulking gun into a dumpster before driving the BMW to a long term lot and wiping it down. His second five-mile hike took him back to the nondescript warehouse lot from where his evening had officially begun.

31

"After I had released my male slave, I turned my attention back to his pretty brunette wife. I asked her if her beautiful bottom was stinging and she shook her head no. I told her that I would give her still one more opportunity to fall asleep tonight with a sore bottom. Her eyes were still downcast whenever I spoke to her, but when I asked her if she was aware that her husband had remained very aroused, she nodded her head yes. I asked her if she agreed that he was in desperate need of relief and again she nodded her head in the affirmative. I could not resist teasing her further. I walked to her and began caressing her about the shoulders and the tops of her breasts with the tails of my rubber whip. I accidentally on purpose allowed one of the tails to tinkle the bell hanging from her left nipple. Her panting returned to an audible level once again. I was taller than her in my boots and I leaned forward to murmur in her ear. I watched her eyes jump from my cleavage to that of her own naked breasts. I asked her in a low voice whether she may be in some distress herself. When she did not respond I asked her if she wished to be checked here in front of her husband. I was bluffing, of course, but she shook her head no and her eyes grew wider. I whispered back that I thought that she, too, was very excited and that she would welcome some relief as well. She hesitated, and then finally nodded yes. I stepped back and said, 'Good!' I said that I would give them both the opportunity to satisfy each other. I told them there was one stipulation. I said that at no point did I want to hear any bells ringing. I explained that any ringing would interrupt my enjoyment of this quiet backyard, and I would deal with it severely…whereupon I swung my whip through the air to emphasize my point.

"I explained that both would be allowed to use their hands as best they could to facilitate his entry into her, but that unfortunately they would both remain bound. I told them that I wanted to leave each unable to protect themselves adequately should I hear the bells tinkle. I walked over to one of the patio chairs and turned it around so that it was facing our little group. Then I walked back over to my female slave and grasped a section of her rope with my free hand. I was tugging firmly as I led her over to the chair. She was taking small, timid steps and I allowed her to do so. Her bells tinkled as she walked and I knew with certainly that her attempts to silence them in the next minutes would fall short. I motioned to her husband to approach, and he obediently and eagerly complied. His bells made noise as he approached us and I gave him a whack across the front of his thigh as a warning. When he arrived at her he wasted no time in resting his hands on her shoulder and pushed gently until she began to bend over at the waist. She seemed very shy, and I was only able to see the back of her head as she would not turn it to face me. As she bent over, she needed to maintain her balance by stretching out both arms and resting her wrists on the back of the pool chair. I was standing off to the side and it was at this point that I almost lost it. Mark, when she was fully bent over at the waist I could not help but notice that her breasts were hanging down and the bells were dangling down as well. I am sure that I caught her looking down at them also as her mate began to slowly probe her with his erection. Gradually, she widened her stance and he reached down to grasp and guide himself into her. I heard his bells make noise and lashed him across his exposed backside. I watched the muscles in her naked bottom tense when I did so, but her bells remained silent so I dealt her no punishment. He continued entering her with more caution, and I stepped back once again to admire the side of my female slave's right breast as it hung free. Her damp hair hung down, partially obscuring her face, but I could see the muscles in her thighs tense rhythmically and her lower tummy undulate as she expelled each breath. Her mate's patience was rewarded. He had entered her fully without another sound from his bells. I was impressed by his self control and told him so. Slowly, he began to rotate his hips around in a circular motion while he stayed deep inside her. I was quite entranced by the effect that it had on her. She gasped out loud and in less than a minute she began a shudder that began at her feet and went right up her legs to her torso. By the time it reached her shoulders her bells began to give her away and I stepped forward to keep my promise. I was sorely tempted to lash underneath at her exposed breasts but did not want the strings that attached the bells to become entangled in the tails of my whip. Her right flank was completely exposed so it was my only logical target. I was loathe to interrupt what must have been an unusually hard orgasm for her, but on the other hand did not want to lose control of the situation even at this late juncture. I did not seek to inflict too much pain—so instead I used that rapid twirling strike that I described earlier. Mark, my little reminder seemed to have the opposite effect on this woman. She began to cry out, not in pain but in ecstasy. Her shuddering grew even more violent and soon she began to thrust to the rear as if to take even more of her mate inside her. He did not have any more to give, but her thrusting set off his bells as well. *Rules are rules*, I thought, and I started striking his backside and flank in an alternating fashion. While I did so he began to meet her thrusts with his own and he began to become more vocal also. I alternated between the both of them with my whip but either they were oblivious to it…or my actions merely served to heighten their passions. He climaxed while hers was still continuing. I was glistening from my exertions and finally stopped reprimanding them. As he finished his knees began to buckle, as did hers, and he gently pulled her down to the ground with him. Only then did their motions completely cease. Never in my life have I viewed anything up close that made me want to satisfy myself so urgently. It took every ounce of professionalism that I had to refrain from touching myself. Instead I walked over to them as they lie gasping for air and unbuckled their leather cuffs. I gently unfastened their bells as well and just bunched up everything into my bag. I left wordlessly, but as I got to the gate I could not resist a backward look. They were already intertwined in each other's arms as they began to get their breathing under control. I was resolute. I was going to go home as quickly as possible and only then give in to my own overwhelming urges after what I had just seen. But Mark, I barely made it to my car! I threw my bag and my trench coat in the back seat and as soon as I sat down I was no longer able to ignore the tingling between my thighs. I know that the tightness of my leather bottoms may have been a contributing factor but the main instigator was that scene that I had just participated in. Mark, I was about ten miles from home and I did not think that I could make it! I looked around, and the driveway and immediate area were unlit. I was able to roll my shorts down enough to attain access to myself. I had such a head start that it did not take me long at all to alleviate my problem! I finally felt relieved enough to pay attention to my driving, but on the way home my mind kept returning to the scene that evening and the possibilities should they ask me to direct another time. I will not elaborate on what occurred immediately upon my arrival at home but I will tell you that I was far too agitated for dinner as the sensations built up once more!"

32

It was Monday evening.

"Mayor Barnes!"

"Mister Mayor!"

"Mayor Barnes!"

Police Chief Ryan Pellerin spoke again, "As I said, the Mayor has a prepared statement that he would like to read. He may have time to field one or two questions at the end but I would urge every reporter to wait until that time. Most of your questions will not be able to be addressed simply because the Bear Lake Police, the County sheriff, and the State Police have only been investigating this current situation for less than eight hours now. We intend to check into every possibility, but will not have any definitive answers for weeks, or perhaps even months. Thank you and now here is your Mayor."

Mayor Barnes moved to the podium as the flashes went off and the cameras whirred. He leaned forward slightly into a gaggle of microphones. He cleared his throat. "I realize that the following statement may leave more questions unanswered than answered, but please bear with me because a man that I have always considered to be a close friend and confidant may soon be accused of perpetrating a heinous deed before he has a chance to tell his side of the story. The Bear Lake Police Department has confirmed the identity of the deceased woman as Colleen Kimball. She is predeceased by her parents, and her brother Frank Kimball has been notified and given our most heartfelt condolences. She was a valued employee of the City of San Diego Parks and Rec Department and she will be sorely missed by all. This office will issue further details about funeral arrangements as they become available."

Mayor Barnes turned the page and cleared his throat again. "Last Friday my friend and colleague, Taylor Flaska—whom you are all aware is also the Assistant Mayor of our beautiful city—came to me with a request. He told me that due to the pressures of his office he was suffering from terrible tension and it was manifesting itself in the form of blinding, recurring headaches. A few of you have been to my little chalet at Bear Lake for various functions, as had Mr. Flaska. He asked me if it was going to be occupied this past weekend and I said it was not. At this point, I would like to stress that I had no idea of his intentions, nor do I know at what point he managed to secure the spare set of keys from the desk in my office. Although I considered us close and knew him to be a relatively young, good looking single man who met many women during the course of his active social life, we never discussed his personal relationships. While the death of Miss Kimball is of course being investigated as a homicide, I would like to stress that the authorities would only like to find and speak with Mr. Flaska right now. I consider Taylor to be a civilized man. I think that the rumors in the press and on television at this point are premature. I have heard suppositions that Miss Kimball spurned his advances and the situation escalated out of control but no one knows at this point *what* occurred up there. I want to believe that Mr. Flaska had nothing to do with her demise and that when he is found, a plausible explanation will surface. Until then, I am sure you are aware of the many vital functions that Mr. Flaska performed for this city. As his position cannot go unfilled for any length of time without causing our citizenry undue hardship, I will submit the name of an interim Assistant Mayor to the Council at tomorrow night's emergency meeting. Dick Senstock is a name known to many of you for the many important construction projects that he has been responsible for in and around our city. Since we have an unprecedented number of new ones coming up, it has come to my attention that no one is better qualified to guide us through these projects, from beginning to end, than this experienced man. I hope that you and the rest of the citizens of our piece of paradise here in Southern California will support me in this. Soon you will see why I believe that the trust that I intend to place in Mr. Senstock is so well-deserved."

Now Mayor Barnes stopped reading and looked directly at the television cameras instead of the reporters. "And now I would like to appeal directly to our television and radio audience. If you have seen Mr. Flaska or his black 1994 BMW, please give your local police department a call immediately. And Taylor, if you are watching this right now, I urge you to respond to my plea without delay. My wife Marion and I care about you and do not want to see you injured. I am sure that there is a logical explanation for your actions. Please contact the authorities before anybody else gets hurt. I promise that Marion and I will stand by you, and together we will see this thing through. Thank you."

"Mayor Barnes, is it true that Taylor Flaska's unpacked suitcase was found at the scene?"

"I cannot comment on that."

"Mayor Barnes, have any other young women come forward to say that Mr. Flaska had sex with them against their will?"

"Mr. Mattson, I have not received any information about that."

"Mayor Barnes, have the police determined if Mr. Flaska had relations with Miss Kimball *after* her demise?"

"Mr. Wollenwebber, that question is too base to be worthy of an answer!"

Police Chief Pellerin stepped over to Mayor Barnes' side. "I think that's all the time that the Mayor has for now and I also think that you will agree he has been *very* forthcoming. I will call other conferences this week when we have more to tell you. Thank you."

33

Some of Mistress Victoria's stories clearly belong in a category labeled *Things That Make You Go Eeew!* She often saw a side of people that I did not…and most definitely did not want to. In retrospect, I believe that she had three reasons for describing some of the more interesting scenes to me. The first, as was the case with the couple in the backyard, was to titillate and perhaps boast a little about her own ability to improvise. She obviously enjoyed playing her role to the hilt but I think that, like many actors, she "really wanted to direct." I think that the second reason she used me as an audience so frequently was due to my former role as her bodyguard. It gave her a measure of security to keep me apprised of some of the stranger requests that she received. For the same reason, I continued to receive many personal details about her clients such as their names, professions, and the location of their homes. I am sure that she derived some measure of security from the fact that someone she trusted knew where she kept her appointment book and her clientele list. Once, when the topic of our conversation turned to weirdos, she spoke of a threat that she was prepared to recite if a situation began to turn sour. Only half in jest, she told me that she would say, "I have a large friend with a gun who knows your full name and where you live!" Fortunately this situation never arose and I attribute it to the fact that new clients were gleaned only from referral. I was surprised weekly as the peccadilloes of corporate heads, community leaders, and well-known entrepreneurs were revealed to me.

I believe that the third reason for all of the tales—and the thoughts that ran through her head while they were occurring—was the simplest. Mistress Victoria needed to vent. Surely she must have found some of the requests to be hedging into the realm of the disgusting. While she took great pains to keep everything discreet and above the law, I was aware that she received substantial financial offers for sexual liaisons. Her personality was so complex that even if the transaction had been legal, she would still have declined—no matter how mind-boggling the figure. Mistress Victoria had at least two close girlfriends that I knew of, and I still believe that each was convinced she was only a very successful interior decorator. She dated and traveled with a man 20 years her senior who was kept completely in the dark about the true source of her income. I concluded that I remained her only confidant for quite some time.

Returning to the category of "…Eeew!"…the Mistress arrived for a workout exactly one week after the backyard story. As other clients left for home, she became steadily more talkative. She began speaking about the previous evening by telling me about a new referral.

"Mark, I have got to tell you about this young man that was referred to me by the head of an extremely large law firm. The older man has been a client of mine from day one and a very generous tipper, I might add. I thus had no reservations when a very pleasant young attorney from Oakland County called me up and used my established client as a referral. As I have mentioned previously, many of my clients are interested in accessorizing their session with me. I attempt to supply them with as many of these accessories as I am able, not only due to the markup on my cost, but because my sources are doubtlessly quite superior to that of my clients and when *I* receive an order, my client's discretion is assured. It simply would not do for an automobile executive's churchgoing wife of 30 years to open a UPS delivery box containing three sizes of anal plugs…now would it? I also know from experience things that the client cannot possibly know—such as which blindfold eradicates all vision the most effectively, or which ballgag is the most…or the least…comfortable. A lot of leashes, collars, and items of restraint are of course reusable after only a wipe down with some disinfectant, while some of the attachments that I use on a male client's privates require a thorough soaking afterwards. I do absolutely draw the line at butt plugs, however. I will supply them, but after it has been utilized for two or three hours blocking a client's orifice I insist on leaving removal and disposal entirely up to him!" Mistress Victoria made a face to indicate her feelings about the subject.

"Getting back to this young attorney though, I was somewhat surprised when he showed up for our very first session carrying a black rucksack that looked completely filled. Our discussion on the phone had covered spanking and sharp rebukes for his desires to wear female undergarments. I fully expected him to produce a set of pantyhose or lacy bikini briefs but *not* an entire wardrobe! He rented a suite for our session at Guest Quarters. When I arrived, he met me at the door and requested some time to prepare before I pretended to walk in on him. He had already paid me for two hours and the session began the moment I walked in the door, so I was quite content to watch cable television in the living room area while he prepared himself in the bedroom. Richard was dark haired and had a long surname like Tomasinobeni. He could not have been much over 30 and was not altogether unpleasant to look at. I do not recall specifically what type of attorney he was, but I remember him mentioning that he did defense work. I seated myself on the sofa and watched CNN for 15 minutes before scooping up a pair of handcuffs and tucking them into the rear waistband of my shorts. I knocked on the door to the bedroom and called out, "Richard, are you in there?" Upon hearing no response from inside the room I opened the door wide and stood in the doorway. He was lying on the bed in full regalia. He was wearing items that must have been purchased from a Victoria's Secret catalog or some other merchant of risqué underthings. His chest and legs were completely shaved and he wore a pair of nylon hose. His crotchless panties were encased by a black garter belt and the garters were clipped onto the tops of the hose. I almost exchanged my look of pretend horror for a smile when I saw the lacy black anklets that he was sporting just above the feet of the hose. What stopped me from ruining the scene, though, was my fascination with the decoupage negligee. It covered an actual white corset that he was laced into! I think he was already wearing the corset underneath his shirt when he answered the door, because it looked as though donning it had been quite an involved process. He was wearing white, lacy, fingerless gloves that looked so delicate that I have no idea how he got them on without their tearing. He was using one of these gloved hands to cover himself between his legs. In the anticipation of my "surprise entry," I was certain that there had been some degree of manipulation." Victoria made another face.

"I acted shocked and then angry. I was wearing thigh-high heeled boots that sunk into the carpeting as I strode over to the bed, but I must have looked quite tall to him. Richard froze open-mouthed and his face actually reddened with shame. I backhanded him across a thigh and ordered him to roll over onto his stomach. Roughly, I grasped one wrist and pulled it behind his back before I slapped a cuff on it. I sneered as I asked him what his colleagues at the office *and* in court would say if they saw him like this. After I had cuffed the other wrist I ordered him to lie still until I got back. I quickly returned with my bag. I had already received a glimpse of the anal device that protruded from his backside, but I swear to you that it was not until I returned and began to use my paddles that I noticed the wire! It snaked into a battery pack that was tucked into the back of his hose. I whacked and whipped and spanked his rump and thighs for quite some time until my shoulders began to grow tired. I assume that his electric device supplied him with many additional sensations as well. Finally, I had run out of ways to verbally humiliate him and every area of physical contact was beet read, if you will pardon my pun. I placed the keys to the cuffs in his right hand and commanded him to toss the keys and cuffs back into the living room after he had finished himself. I timed it. Six minutes later the cuffs, with the keys in the lock, slid out the door. Without saying a word, I packed up my bag, donned my trench coat, and left. Of one thing I am certain. I would not retain that man to represent me in a courtroom if he were doing it pro bono and I was only charged with littering! It was not until just prior to bedtime that I realized I had been washing my hands every hour on the hour! Even this morning, the whole mental image of that session kept coursing through my brain!"

34

I MET NORMAN BAIGHTS nearly two years before he died. I had recently sold a large house in Sterling Heights, Michigan in order to purchase a much smaller one two miles away. The downsizing allowed me to extend my temporary retirement from the fitness business from two years to three. It also allowed me more time to spend playing *Mr. Mom* to my daughter Rachel while the wife went back to work.

It was a cold but sunny November afternoon in 1994, and I was on my driveway, standing in front of a 1989 Dodge Caravan and peering under the hood. My friend Glenn Grenadier had sold it to me after his nephew had rearranged the front end. I was evaluating the amount of bending and welding necessary to straighten the minivan's uni-body frame while mentally planning the purchase of a new hood, fenders, and grill in the spring.

I had seen many ugly motor vehicles before in my lifetime. Some had been chewed up by rust so badly that they looked like a rolling x-ray. Other Detroit designs looked like they were sketched out first by Helen Keller—and then put together by a troupe of epileptic clowns. Some designs were just an assembly of large squares. My old friend Mike Horace once pulled up into Glenn's driveway in his brand new Chrysler New Yorker. As he stepped proudly out of his gun-metal gray monstrosity, Glenn shouted out from the garage, "Hey Mike, I see you got your new car, why don't you take it out of the box and let's have a look at it?" Mike left immediately, ostensibly to run an errand, but the car dealer would not give him his money back.

If I had ranked these ugly vehicles over the years, the one that Norman drove into my driveway that afternoon would have made it into the top 20. It was of mid-'80s vintage, and it was manufactured during one of Japan's first attempts to turn a front wheel drive economy car into a minivan. Japan had begun adding enough zinc to the steel mix of its cars before Detroit did, so there was very little rust. Robin's-egg blue looks very appealing on some things—the most natural being an actual robin's egg. On the square-fendered minivan wannabe, however, it looked like a vehicle that had begun its life as blue but had then spent the last 30 years broken down in the Mojave Desert—bleaching in the sun. Initially, there may have been a target market for this eyesore. I was able to picture a Japanese family driving it quickly through the city until Godzilla squashed it. I could envision a bespectacled, balding and impoverished college undergrad driving it back and forth to the library while waiting to hear about his application for a teacher's aide position. But the man who stepped out of this design failure did *not* look as though he belonged in this type of car.

Norman was 6-feet, 1-inch tall with a dark shock of jet black hair and thick, dark eyebrows. His black eyes glared out from beneath his brow and his black mustache twitched as he sucked on the remainder of his cigarette. Far from ugly, he had that Romanian gangster look that many women find appealing. In his cotton jacket and baggy jeans, it was difficult to tell how fit he was but my first impression was that losing 15 pounds wouldn't cause him any undue hardship. I have known people with even the most pleasant countenances to be quick to anger, self absorbed, and as mean as a bag of constipated snakes. My initial impression of Norman was that trouble had found me and was striding across the pavement of my driveway to bring grief and pestilence into my world. But the natural scowl was quickly and consciously altered into a well-practiced, casual smile as he approached. The first words out of his mouth were friendly, disarming, and to the point.

"How ya doin'? I'm your neighbor from just down the street there," he said with a vague stabbing point of his index finger. "I guess we've both got a couple of mutual friends so I figured it was about time I got my ass down here and introduced myself. I'm Norm."

In a single—again practiced—motion, Norm flicked his smoldering cigarette onto the brown, dormant grass along the side of my driveway and proffered his right hand. I shook it and told him my name was Mark.

He said, "Yeah, I kinda knew that already because your buddy Tim Raven knows a guy who works for me, Jeff Hazey."

The first name was a workout buddy of mine who would become the first employee of my fitness studio the following year. I had heard the second name mentioned previously by Tim. I began to let my guard down and my shoulders relaxed as Norm simultaneously reached into his jacket pockets for a pack of Marlboros and a butane lighter. I acknowledged knowing both men.

As he lit his next one, he studied me for a minute.

"Yeah, man, it's ----in' cold out here today compared to yesterday. I've known Jeff for years from when we both used to work retail, but then I got into other things and he got into other things and we left that ----in' place, only he got stuck managing that little apartment complex even though he knew it didn't pay nothin'. I told him too, but all he heard was 'free rent' and he took it not thinkin' it would be as much hassle as it is and pay shit besides!"

Norm was already halfway through his next Marlboro. I was growing curious as to how he could talk so quickly after taking such deep drags on his cigarette.

"The stuff that I got goin' took off right away so I got with him and explained that it wouldn't be exactly working *for* me since he could make his own hours and sell as many or as few cars as he wanted to. Now I'll do five cars a week and he's ----in' happy as hell that he hooked up with me again. I've got him helpin' to clean 'em up and prep 'em and then when we sit 'em out for sale he's gotta meet the people there after they call. One thing about a used car, if that ----er drives right then it's ----in' sold the first time!"

I had never listened to somebody use the f-word as a noun, a verb, *and* an adjective with such gusto. I knew instantly what Norm was talking about because of my background as an ex used car salesman. I also assumed that he was referring to "curbstoning." A curbstoner is a used car dealer that purchases a car through contacts or newspaper ads—or even from approaching someone with no current intention of selling their car. In Michigan, the Secretary of State's office requires used car dealers to maintain a commercial place of business, keep a logbook on every purchase and sale, pay yearly fleet insurance, and collect and forward sales tax and transfer fees to the state government.

Curbstoners take a lot of shortcuts. They work out of their homes or apartments—or sometimes just the back of their car. Titles are "jumped" as the curbstoner transfers it from one owner to the next without ever plating, registering, or recording the transaction. When I met him, Norm was setting his cars out with a "For Sale" sign in the window on Mound Road, a main thoroughfare one block from his house. The car being offered usually graced the front yard of a ramshackle home facing this multi-laned highway. Eighteen thousand vehicles passed by Norm's "outdoor showroom" every day. One or two always stopped. The people who called the cell phone number on the sign were directed to either Norm or Jeff and were soon met with the keys in tow to rev engines and test the radio. Jeff's blond hair and cherubic good looks, combined with his affable demeanor, gave the prospective buyer the confidence that they were dealing with the only honest seller in the city. The car had always been vacuumed and shampooed, waxed and polished, and patched together with any mechanical band-aids necessary to survive a four-mile test drive down the smooth, wide road. Norm's selling technique varied greatly from Jeff's, but was nonetheless even more successful. The savvy curbstoner liked to approach a wary buyer with the same carefully rehearsed friendliness that I had witnessed during our first encounter.

After an initial disarmament of the buyer's suspicions, Norm would spend the next half hour, hour, or the entire evening persuading them that the car would sell immediately to the very next person to inquire. He convinced them that the inquiries were coming in fast, expressing amazement that he hadn't received three more in the time it took to check the oil. Sooner or later the exhausted buyer began to reach for a wallet or a checkbook for some deposit money just to shut Norm up. The majority would also have been persuaded by then that there wasn't another used car in the entire state available for less than $50,000. When the buyer returned with the cash that Norm insisted on to complete the transaction, an observant few might notice that the place reserved on the title—for the vehicle's owner and his address—never began with *Norman Baights*. Norm was always prepared for this discovery with a lengthy, detailed dissertation on how he was selling the vehicle for his mother, grandfather, married sister or church pastor. He *could* and *would* carry on for as long as necessary about the upkeep and babying the car had received during its pampered stay with the previous owner.

"Now Jeff realized right off the bat that he was one lucky mother----er to be working for me. We've been friends for years now, and you can ask any of my friends and they'll tell you that I always take care of 'em."

The second cigarette lie smoldering in the grass and a third was being pulled out of the pack. I could see my daughter inside watching a video and my wife was not due home for hours. Norm looked like he intended to hang around until I agreed to run for President of his fan club, and I wasn't even wearing a watch to glance at.

"I mean ----, that's the way I ----in' am and I can't change and I don't want to try. If a friend needs something I've got and I find out about it, I'll just give it to 'em and I won't ask a single ----ing question. I know that if I treat 'em that way then they won't think twice about doing the same for me. If my friend's car breaks down and I have two cars, he gets one until he can get his fixed. I don't know what the hell Jeff does with all the money I give him, probably blows it all on ---sy for all I know, but if he's broke he knows he can come to me and I'll advance him 10 dollars or 20 or a ----in' thousand!"

A fourth cigarette was cast to my lawn to join its comrades, and soon a fifth was being selected for the lighter.

I wasn't sure what the purpose of all of the profanity was. I had heard plenty during my years as the proprietor of an auto repair facility. I had occasionally uttered a cross word or two myself as I pulled a 600-pound engine out of a car or stuffed a transmission into an aperture of limited dimensions. Crushing a finger or striking one with a hammer was universally recognized as an appropriate occasion for expressions of feelings that were not intended for delicate ears. Busted knuckles, cuts, and burns from metal that moments ago had been glowing from the flame of an acetylene torch were all acceptable reasons for a spontaneous outburst of foul language.

Nor were the hardcore gyms that I enjoyed visiting sacrosanct from large men with potty-mouths screaming at each other. I have also known women to express themselves in this manner. One of the strangest and most vile tirades I have ever witnessed was at a hardcore gym in California between a red-faced, veiny body builder and a big hairy woman named Jake. Even as a teenager I briefly dated a thin young woman named Kim who supplemented her vocabulary with some very foul words.

While working as a guest relations engineer at one of my fitness client's drinking establishments, I had often encountered inappropriate language. A great deal of it was directed at me when I escorted drunk combatants out through the main entrance and down a concrete staircase.

I could not imagine that Norm using such a large dose of profanity when urging a car buyer to make a purchase, so I was left to conclude that these vulgarities were his way of impressing me. It had already occurred to me that the "neighborly" visit from this man who resided ten houses down had an ulterior motive of some sort. Since he had asked me no questions of a personal nature, I assumed that he had already gathered all of the necessary information from another source. I asked myself what sort of impression he was trying to make on me. Was it that of a tough but fair businessman? Was he going to try to make me swear my allegiance as a loyal friend by day's end? My suspicions were further aroused when the subject continued on used cars.

"Y' know, the whole ----in' problem with people is that they don't wanna work anymore. They want it all ----in' handed to 'em for nothin'! I bust my ass finding these deals and then I can't find anybody to help me out. Five years ago, I could stop by at a buddy's house with a car that needed brakes or a water pump or a radiator and he'd drop what he was doing to help me out. We would work on it together until it was dark or midnight or whatever and the only ----in' time we'd stop is if I went to get another 12 pack or a pizza or if his wife needed something from the store. When I went, I wouldn't ask for money either. The both of us would just work on the goddam thing until it was done. Then if he needed something that I had a day or a week or a month later he knew he could just come over and ----in' pick it up, no questions asked! I got *racks* full of used tires in back of the garage, and if he needed one or two or whatever we'd just pick out the size and put 'em in the trunk. So instead of payin' some asshole at the store $150 for a couple of brand new tires he'd be all set just because he knew me! I used to know a guy who'd do nothin' but sand and paint cars in his garage all night for a couple of hundred bucks a car. Yeah, he worked his ass off, but at the end of the week he'd picked up an extra thousand or so and I'm telling you that money was tax free! I'd *still* be using the guy if he hadn't started twitchin' and jerking around from the paint fumes. He stopped painting but by then it was too ----in' late, and after he got too sick to go to work at his day job I would think nothin' of stopping by with some burgers or a six pack to see how he was doin'! Now I'm just surrounded by lazy mother----ers. Jeff's apartment managing job doesn't pay him shit and he just lives in that two bedroom dump. I tell that ----er if he would just get off of his dead ass and hustle he could get himself into a house, maybe not like I've got but at least he'd be putting his money back into something."

I would soon discover Norm had bought his house near the end of my street from a desperate family—for not much more than the value of the land. Hours after closing on the property he had begun to barter, wheedle and cajole until construction on a monstrous addition began to turn a quaint ranch into a sprawling one. Garages and driveways were planned and added. Meanwhile, Norm continued to accumulate tools and supplies to refurbish the cars that provided his money supply. With his empire now occupying nearly an acre of land set right in the middle of suburbia, Norm assembled a motley crew of laborers to repair, buff up, and shampoo his findings in a five-car sweatshop at the back of the property. He imported a Russian wife because the American women just wanted to spend his money. He began to spend more time on his teenage hobby of golf, working his way into ever more elite foursomes as his handicap spiraled downward. He sought out players that always bet on the outcome, and a good week on the links brought Norm an extra $500.

I gradually discovered, f-word by f-word, that Norm's visit to me that morning had two purposes.

"So Mark, what year is this ----er anyway? It looks like an '89."

"It is, Norm. This ----er is an '89," I replied.

"It's not hit too bad, I guess. 'Course, bending that radiator support out might not be all it takes to straighten 'er out. Once the frame bends on these ----ers they're a bitch to get right again."

"I've had some success in the past with just a steel I-beam, a chainfall, and some patience," I reassured him.

"Oh, well if you're gonna try this yourself then I see why this piece of shit has been sittin' around so long. 'Course it's gettin' older by the day sittin' here. It's November now, in two months it'll be 1995 and this ----er will be another year older and worth even less."

I was grateful that Norm had stopped by that day to tell me what month it was since the insurance agencies and real estate offices in the area hadn't yet begun mailing their yearly blizzard of calendars. If not for this thoughtful man in front of me, now lighting a sixth cigarette, the entire Christmas season might have passed by—with me unaware.

"'Course I gotta frame guy who might be able to straighten this ----er out. I buy and sell a lot of these ----ers but they gotta be standin' tall before some soccer mom will take it. This ----er's got all the seats in it so it won't work as a cargo van."

Norm checked the odometer and exhaled a cloud of smoke into my minivan.

"Fifty-five thousand miles, that's not too bad. Damn shame it's got a cloth interior though, everybody wants leather."

I liked the crushed red velour interior far better than the vinyl seats, and I was ready to wager that potential buyers would too.

"It's got the V-6 instead of the four, but even with these miles you don't know if they changed the oil regular or not on the ----er, you ever start 'er up?"

"It runs fine," I responded.

"So, if you don't mind me askin' what did you give 'em for this ----er, five hundred? Six hundred?"

"$12,600. Do you think I paid too much?"

Norm broke into a grin and threw number six into the grass while he began to reach for number seven.

"Oh, I get it. You don't wanna say. That's okay. But you can ask *any* of my ----in' friends that whatever they tell me stays between us. I'm the same ----in' way. I'll tell a friend anything he wants to know, but I don't expect him to go runnin' off at the mouth about it. You didn't pay more than a thousand did ya?"

Warily, I replied, "I would have to check with my accountant on that one, I diverted some funds from one of my offshore oil wells to buy it, but I can't remember if it was in pounds or Deutchmarks or what."

"Ha, ha, ha, heh, you're funny. I like that. Okay, I respect any ----er that wants to keep his business to himself. All I'm sayin' is that if you don't have the time or if this ----er turns out to be too much of a project for ya then I'll take it off your hands for cash. Remember, the longer this ----er sits around, the less it's worth."

As the months went by I would gradually realize that as skilled as Norm was at selling a car, his true talent lie in purchasing. He bribed a circulation manager at *The Detroit News* to furnish him with a coveted copy of the Sunday Classifieds on Saturday. Within minutes he would laser in on the two best deals and call startled sellers all evening until they promised to meet with him. Once there, Norm "beat 'em up" for hours until their evening was ruined and they took the pittance that he was offering to get him off their driveway and out of their life. On the rare occasions when Norm wasn't the first one to call about the car, he still "worked 'em" with a huge assortment of psychological gambits. Smoking like a brush fire, Norman enjoyed working the seller to the point of exhaustion. In the process, he convinced them that there were hundreds of better offerings in the newspaper and that he was the only person who would ever take the trouble to drive out to look at this heavily flawed used car that they were trying to foist upon the public. Often he brought an underling whose sole job was to remain silent while peering underneath the car and shaking his head negatively in a concerned manner. Using sleep deprivation techniques first perfected by the North Vietnamese—while sometimes fortifying himself with a line or two of cocaine—Norm blanketed the seller with a patter that eventually made them agree to anything.

In the ensuing months, I would observe as he applied his car buying techniques to purchasing real estate.

Ever watchful as he drove through unfamiliar neighborhood side streets in response to a classified ad, Norm's head would turn violently enough to snap his neck when he spotted a parked car without a plate. Norm's full attention would be instantly diverted to his new prey. A car with no license plate meant a car that was unwanted, unneeded, and ready to be given away to a deserving curbstoner. Norm would pound on the door and, in the absence of any answer, leave notes offering to pay top dollar to remove the eyesore from the driveway or yard. Norm was not above pounding on adjoining doors to obtain the vehicle's full "story," or even the owner's home phone number from a gregarious neighbor. Owners of unkempt real estate could be subject to the same onslaught if Norm were to sense an imminent buy. Tall grass, peeled paint, or newspapers collecting in the yard or on the stoop would unleash a fusillade of persistent inquiries about the ownership status of the house. If a deal could be made, the ink on the contract would still be wet while Norm phoned every transient carpenter or drywaller within a ten-mile radius. Promises would be made, bartering would begin, and on the day that the former owner vacated, a ragtag squad would descend upon the property to hammer, nail, paint, and caulk until a "For Rent" classified ad might be placed. Within days the former tenement would be a cash contributor in Norm's budding real estate empire. Even his blond wife would be enlisted as a day laborer in the frantic push to turn a liability into an asset overnight.

~~~~~~~~~~~~~~~~~~~~~~~~~~~~

At least one dozen cigarette butts lay strewn about my dormant lawn and driveway. The donated butts gave my landscaping the "bus stop" feel that it had been lacking. Norm had finally accepted that the minivan was not currently for sale.

Norman now began a second tack in his efforts to take advantage of his new found friend, neighbor, and ashtray.

"I dunno what *you're* finding, but these ----in' cars I've been buyin' lately have been gettin' ----in' harder and harder to work on. Houses are one thing. You can get a couple of sheeny guys in there who say they can drywall or paint or whatever and you just don't pay 'em 'til it looks decent. But these ----in' newer cars are all electronics and computers and shit and unless you got all the meters and tools for workin' on 'em you're screwed. You gotta be a ----in' genius to figure out what's wrong with these newer ----ers, otherwise you're just paying hang tag…you know, list price...for new parts and puttin' 'em on, hoping that fixes it. The only other way is to take it to the dealer and they see ya comin' and ram it up your ass. I can buy these ----ers smart, but by the time I pay to have it painted and get it runnin' right there isn't anything left over. Now, lemme ask you a question. Your buddy Tim says that after you sold your gym you went back to repairin' cars in your garage sometimes. Were you doin' this just for the money or because you needed something to do or what?"

"It's always nice to have a skill to fall back on," I answered.

"See, that's smart. But what would be smarter is if ya turned that into some dough. What I'm thinkin' is this. I *pass* on a lot of deals 'cause they're runnin' bad or the climate control isn't workin' or there's some ----in' noise comin' from the engine and it's got overhead cams and fuel injection and shit. Now I could do more of these deals if I could find somebody like you to go in on 'em with me. Y' know—I'd find 'em and put up the money and you get 'em runnin' right. Then we have Jeff or me sell it and split up the money and then you get paid off for whatever you got into it. If we ran it that way we could really kick some ass. We could do five cars a week together easy and make a ----in' ton of money."

The thought of working on only one car per week with an exotic problem made me nauseous. I would rather spend a week locked in a closet with my first wife and her attorney—without any breath mints for either of them. To be saddled with a mechanical puzzle every day of the week was unthinkable. The thought of any business affiliation with this chain smoking con artist was giving me the urge to have my lungs screened for tumors and move to Brazil. I could only imagine the look on my future ex-wife's face as she came home from work every day to a line-up of broken cars on our driveway and the grief it would bring. My next fitness studio venture was developing from a gleam in my head to a distinct possibility within the next year, and I had been intensifying my workouts. There was no time for any additional ventures. I needed to firmly decline Norm's offer without making a permanent enemy of the neighborhood wheeler-dealer. I needed to stymie any possibility of a partnership without cutting off all communication forever.

"Let me get back with you on that," I replied.

Norman took my rejection well. So well, in fact, that several days later he and Jeff pushed an old white Mercedes down the street and up into my driveway. His persistant pounding on my door left me little choice but to peek my head out to see what new crisis awaited me. The Mercedes he had purchased might have a few years and a lot of miles on it, he admitted, but the body was flawless. His parents were retired and looking for economical transportation while wintering in Florida. The white Mercedes fit the bill perfectly, he crowed. The only hitch was that it wouldn't start. Norm had located a shop that would rebuild the starter for $100 instead of $300. So now the only fly in the ointment was that the same shop wanted $150 to pull the starter out of the car and put it back in. I popped the hood and peered in. I told Norm that it looked tricky, but as a favor to him I would do it for $90. As soon as my parasitic new friend left, I phoned the same shop and described the car and the problem. The owner said he would charge me the same price that he quoted to Norm 24-hours ago…$100 to rebuild the starter but $250 to pull it out and replace it. I could tell immediately that Norm valued trust and friendship above money. I upheld my end of the bargain anyway and replaced the starter, remembering an old mechanic's trick that shortened the job and still made it profitable.

After completing the job, I started the Mercedes and drove it down the street to Norm's house. He answered the door and perhaps out of guilt, I thought, offered to buy me breakfast. We drove two miles to a little hole in the wall that, from the road, looked more like a homeless shelter than a restaurant. Norm and I elbowed aside more than one seedy character to slide into a dilapidated booth until the protruding cushion springs halted our progress. He crowed about the $1.95 breakfast special until I ordered one after he did. Although the tattoos on the waitress' forearms were offensive, the sausage and eggs were edible. During breakfast my new friend began to work on me.

"I sure appreciate you gettin' to that ----in' starter right away. It's goddam good to know that there's still people that'll come through for ya in a pinch. That's how *I* am. Everybody takes me for granted until they ----in' need somethin'. But when all hell breaks loose who do they come runnin' to? Norm Baights, that's who."

The waitress interrupted with a coffeepot. As she reached across the table to Norm's cup, her forearm flexed and the muscular man and woman in her tattoo appeared to fornicate.

"So I always settle my debts right away, too…anybody'll tell ya that. What do I owe ya on the Mercedes? I think we said 70, right?" Norm said casually.

"No, it was 90." I replied.

Norm stared at me with his head tilted and a suspicious half smile. It was so convincing that he must have practiced it in a mirror.

"Naw, really? I thought we agreed on half of what the shop was chargin'. If they wanted $150, it was 70…well…75 dollars. Now am I ----in' wrong?"

"I'm sure it was 90 dollars, Norm."

I wasn't biting and he could continue with the act no longer. He looked down to jelly his toast.

"Well, okay, if you say so. Guess I gotta trust ya. That's the way I ----in' am. I keep on trustin' somebody until they give me a reason not to. I'll tell ya what though. I saw where that blue van you're drivin' could use a couple a tires in the back. If ya want, I got a set at the house that I could show ya. I mean, it couldn't hurt to look. These tires are used but they're worth 150 dollars *all* day long!"

"I intend to sell the van," I said, "I'll just stick with the 90 dollars."

"Okay, okay, that's fine," he replied quickly. "But sometimes ya ----in' gotta be open to a swap cause you'll come out *way* farther ahead than if you went to pay *retail*." Norm spat out the last word as though it were blasphemous.

"Norm, that's why they invented money. They needed a system to help determine the value of goods and services. The barter system doesn't always come out evenly for all of the parties involved in a transaction."

Norm agreed and went on to offer me some side trim molding to fit the wrecked minivan in my driveway in lieu of the 90 dollars. I politely declined as the waitress brought our bill. The total was $4.80. Norm left five dollars on the table and stood up, fumbling for his car keys in the pocket of his jacket. As he started to walk away, I flipped open my wallet and grabbed a dollar, leaving it next to the five. It would be several years before I would again meet a tightwad of Norm's equal.

In the car, Norm continued on, "I'd give ya the ----in' 90 right now but I don't have the whole thing on me. I thought it was 75, I'm not shittin' ya, but after buying us both breakfast I'm coming up short. I've got it back at the house, though, and we're headin' there anyway. My wife's going grocery shoppin' as soon as I get back and I've gotta get some cash out for her too. You gotta meet her. She is ----in' beautiful. I put up with a lot of shit from my friends because of her. Natasha is tall, blond…she's a ten, I ----in' swear to God! My friends all ask me, *Norm, what the hell is she doin' with you?* I tell 'em that you gotta get 'em young. I met her when she was just 19 and just came into the country. She was drop dead gorgeous and when she came in to the ----in' appliance store everybody, I mean *everybody* was hittin' on her. I started *workin'* her until she went out with me. I knew not to let anybody else near her until I could move her in with me. Even then my buddies would hang around my place, just waitin' to make a move on her! Mark, when you meet her you'll see why…you will just shit your pants!"

I hoped that Norm was wrong about my pants but when we got

back to his house I followed him inside. The interior of the ranch style home was clean and modern, although not lavishly furnished. The kitchen was the first room we walked into after going in through the side entranceway. I pulled out a chair and sat at the table while Norm went to find his wife. One minute later he returned with a tall, thin blond in tow. She was wearing dark blue jeans that looked as though they had been sprayed onto her out of a paint can. She was wearing a loose white blouse with half sleeves and metal snaps that fastened down the front. At 5-feet 9-inches, she had the slightly stooped posture that some tall women have after being teased during their school years. Her hair was bleached blond and her small, thin nose, strong chin and perfectly spaced brown eyes made her very pretty. As she walked into the kitchen she seemed shy but I surmised that she might be cautious after ten years of being introduced to the flotsam of Norm's friends and business associates. I stood up and extended my hand as Norm said, "Mark, this is my wife, Natasha."

I locked eyes with her as she extended her hand and said, "Everything that you told me is true, Norm. She is as beautiful as you said she was."

Natasha said, "Hello, nass to meet you," and blushed almost imperceptibly.

Norm looked a little surprised and said, "Yeah, what did I tell ya?"

Natasha busied herself at the kitchen sink. Norm opened his wallet and put $50 on the counter beside her. He pulled out another 50 and two 20s and handed them to me, wincing as though his right arm was part of the deal. I accepted the money but wondered why he had taken it from his "stash" and put it into his wallet first…

I turned to leave without making any accusations and Norm said, "Talk to your wife and maybe the four of us can get together for dinner or something."

I said that I would.

35

Martin's cell phone rang as he began to step into the fitness studio. A big but nervous man, the shrill ringing from his pocket caused him to let go of the handle and plunge his hand down into his pants quickly to retrieve the little device. If it was the wife, no one inside the studio needed to know his marital status. If it was business, he had all the more reason to answer it outside. The number came up private.

"Afternoon."

"Yeah, it's me. Lissen, I still can't find a good way to get ta her. All she does is go from da house to da coffee place, or da house to da hair place. Every other day she goes straight to da boat. Da only time she's by herself is in her car. Even when she walks she goes to dat high school and walks real fast around da track but dare's always somebody dare, like kids or sumptin. I'm tellin' ya, dis Summer broad is never alone for long. We gotta nail her soon, Marty, 'fore she gets lost again in Florida or sumptin. Probably da best thing is to break in to da house during da day if she's in it."

Martin Fife sighed. Benny was causing him a great deal of stress these past two months. He could feel it as the stress threatened to build into another heart attack. The only thing worse than having his first heart attack at 39 would be having his second one at 40. Taking on Benny as a partner last year was supposed to help stave off the second one for awhile until the Doc could get his cholesterol under control—but the fat fuck was going to bring it on even sooner.

Irritated, Martin answered. "Hey, I said not to use any names over the cell phone. Somebody can triangulate in on us and listen to every word we say. They can record us. These things aren't secure."

Martin had gotten into the University of Michigan on a football scholarship. At 6-foot 1-inch and 240 pounds, Martin had been a standout at Grosse Pointe North at every position he tried. While his academic career was far from stellar, his first two years of college ball had him convinced that the NFL draft awaited him. Then, in his third year, the other young men began to catch up to the burly linebacker. Their years in the weight room began to pay off. They got bigger. They grew stronger. Worse still, they seemed to get faster and Martin did not. He started to abuse his body with diving tackles and risky plunges into the surging line. At the Ohio State game, on the third play of the second half, Martin threw himself between two sprinting linemen to tackle the runningback. The runningback's knee came up between Martin's legs. A 290-pound teammate of Martin's—charging from the other direction—smashed both of them into the ground—but not before Martin's knee buckled backwards. Searing pain emanated from his knee and his crotch for weeks. It still amazed Martin that a loose testicle, smashed between cup and leg, would merely be listed as a "groin pull" on the injury roster.

"OK, OK, but da boss said dat he wants to see sumptin happen soon. He says dat da broad is in too tight wit da old man. He wants her in da hospital by next week!"

Martin winced and waited for angina pain from his chest, but none came.

After two operations the pain in his knee had diminished a great deal, and after a year of rehab he could jog on it. It would never be stable enough to play football again, and Martin didn't care to. He had enough passing grades in his Psych classes to get an interview with the Grosse Pointe Shores Police Department after an uncle vouched for him. The academy had been easy compared to football training camp, and soon Martin was endlessly patrolling a two-mile strip of Lakeshore Drive in a shiny squad car.

36

Over the next several weeks Norm plied me with one "business opportunity" after another. Cars with greasy engines that had ceased to run were dangled as bait to encourage my involvement in loose partnerships and alliances. I declined as rapidly as the offers surfaced, and signed up to work on my buddy Doc's race boat instead.

My wife Tara and I did give dinner with Norm and Natasha a try. Over the course of the meal Norm's vehement complaints to the waitress grew fainter as it became clear the manager was not going to strike the tab. After one brief tirade about dessert not coming with the meal—while Natasha rolled her eyes in embarrassment—the check was presented. Norm looked at it as though it were a large cockroach, but remained motionless.

I reached over and picked up the bill. After a brief examination, I looked at Norm and said, "Your end is about 20 bucks."

The statue came back to life and asked to check the bill. I handed it over. Norm scrutinized the bill like a forensic accountant, and his thick eyebrows furrowed as he searched for a way out. After two or three minutes, he raised his eyebrows in triumph.

"Mark, Natasha didn't have a Diet Pepsi but you *and* Tara did. Our end of it is more like $18, buddy."

"I thought we might both leave a tip," I replied.

"After the way they treated me? Not a chance!" Norm was steadfast. I calculated 15 percent of the total and left it.

Boating season waned. It had been nearly three years since I had closed my last fitness studio and the urge to get back into business as a personal trainer was building once again. I began to lay plans. I would begin with at least two trainers already on board. A workout buddy, Tim Raven, assured me that he would be interested. At 35 years old, I was confident he would mix well with the older demographic I intended to pursue. Almost as importantly, Tim had only grossed $7,000 in the previous year as a house painter. I thought that $25,000 a year to start would be a nice jump, and he readily agreed.

My next employee would logically need to be female, I decided. Since people find it difficult to heed exercise advice from a personal trainer who belongs in the main tank at Sea World, I had to be discerning. I had recently met a young lady at my church who solicited my advice about automobile repair. She had explained her funds were limited and that the repair was extensive. In between my searches for a new studio location, I repaired the car for half of what she had been quoted. Andrea was very tall, very thin and very blond. After the work on her car was complete, I broached the subject of employment in the fitness industry. Andrea was very enthusiastic. My wife Tara was not nearly as excited about Andrea's employment with me, however. Tara sprayed holy water at me whenever the opportunity arose, and I often awoke to lit candles surrounding the bed as my beautiful wife tried to cast the devil out of me. Eventually, I determined that Andrea was only 22 and cooled to the idea of clients working with her.

I finally located the perfect unit in a strip mall only three miles from my house. Negotiations with the landlord were well under way but I still needed a female fitness trainer.

On a Monday morning I awoke to Norm pounding on my door. He had just purchased a car from a widow by convincing her that the brake system was defective and had been recalled. On the way home an indicator light on the dash notified him that the battery wasn't charging properly. My presence was being requested for a consult. An hour later, I wandered down the street and met Norm at the large garage at the back of his lot. I had diagnosed the problem when Natasha walked in to ask Norm for five dollars in gas money. He opened his wallet with a grimace. Norm counted out five singles, staring at them as if trying to memorize their serial numbers.

Natasha seemed grateful, smiled at me, and walked back to the house. I watched her walk for a minute and then spoke to Norm.

"Hey Norm, does Natasha work out?"

"Naw, not really. I mean she does some ----in' aerobics tapes with the TV set on and stuff but she's just naturally that way. Her sister Sherry is the same ----in' way, too. My wife is a knockout without ever workin' out or nothin'. She's got no ass or hips though. I tell her that all the time. When we go shoppin' though, I see how all the assholes watch her when they don't think I'm lookin'. I just tell her that if she wants to hook up with one of them that's fine. She gets one suitcase for her shit and she knows not to let the door hit her in the ass on the way out. She'd never do it though. I practically took her off the streets and gave her everything she's got. I buy her clothes twice a year. I got her a ----in' minivan to drive. She's got it made and she knows it! Besides, she's crazy about me and I make sure she stays that way by makin' damn sure she doesn't know anything else!"

"Has she ever had a job?" I asked.

"Oh ---- yeah. She worked with me for a while at the appliance store and somewhere else before that too. But those other guys at the store were ----in' *dogs* and I knew what they were after, so I made her quit when I went out on my own here."

I took the plunge. "I'm going to open another fitness studio and I already know that half of my clients will be female. I'm going to have to hire a female trainer that's over 30 and in good shape. It pays very well and I think that your wife has a lot of potential, but I would never approach her without asking you first."

"Well shit, I never thought about something like that. She was gonna take some ----in' nursing classes at the college, but after I paid for books and tuition I'd be out thousands. By the time she graduated and bought new clothes and got a job somewhere I'd be so ----in' far in the hole that I'd be lucky to *ever* see the profit zone. Whattaya need her to do for you at this gym?"

I explained that it was more of a fitness studio where a client would be matched with a trainer for their entire hour. I talked about the machines and weights that I had already ordered. Details about the equipment fell on deaf ears. Norm began to hammer out a salary for Natasha as he imagined the paychecks flowing into his account.

The next morning I received a phone call from Natasha.

"Mock, thees ees Natasha. Norm says you maybe have job for me? How I learn vat to do?"

I was glad to hear from her so soon.

"I have a workout area set up in my house for now," I replied. "I work out Monday, Wednesday, and Friday in the afternoon for about an hour. If you like, you can meet me here and I'll get you started on the weights and machines so you'll know what you're doing by the time the studio opens."

There was a long pause and some murmuring in the background. I soon realized that Norm had been listening in on another line.

"Norm tells me to ask you vat does thees pay while I vork out at your haus?"

"Nothing. I'm training you for a job and a career and it doesn't pay anything until the studio opens."

There was another pause and more murmuring.

"Norm vorried I can't cook for heem or get car part when I train at your haus."

"Well, it's only for three hours a week. If he can't spare you I'll try and find somebody else."

Natasha promised to call me back, and the next morning she did. We set up her first workout for five o'clock that afternoon.

My first course of action was to address the "hunch" in Natasha's posture that had caught my attention on that first day in the kitchen. Natasha was 5-foot-9. I had encountered the posture problem in tall female clients more often than male clients. My best guess was that there was some stigma attached to being the tallest child in grade school or middle school, especially if the child were female. Telling your daughter that "all of the boys will catch up by high school" doesn't have much of an impact when high school is still five years away. Natasha had always been very thin as well, and over time admitted to me that other classmates had been quick to point out this fact.

~~~~~~~~~~~~~~~~~~~~~~~~~~~~~

 A pulldown machine is little more than an overhead bar—attached by a cable to a stack of weights. The weights can be adjusted from as little as 15 pounds to as much as 250. The idea is to sit down, reach up, and pull the bar down 10 to 20 times. I had a pulldown machine at the house. I set the weight at 20 pounds and showed Natasha how to grip the bar. She pulled it down to her shoulders 12 times and assured me that it was easy. I set the weights at 30 pounds and told her that we would pause for a minute before doing another set. We had officially begun to strengthen the upper back and shoulder muscles that would eventually correct her posture. In the ensuing years, Natasha would develop muscles across her upper back that rippled when she flexed them. In her late 30s, Natasha would be able to perform enough chin-ups to embarrass a platoon of Navy Seals, and look far better while doing them. I added a bench press routine to her program as well. Over time, she could lay on a bench and push the equivalent of her own bodyweight into the air several times. It was a feat that most sedentary men could only dream about, and never failed to impress and amaze a studio full of clients.

 We worked on her long, thin legs by squatting with a weight bar across her back. After gradually building up her bony knees, we squatted deeper and deeper with weights that increased every month. Her glutes (tushy) began to lift and develop shape and form. Her thigh muscles flexed and tensed with every step that she took in a stride that looked as though it had been borrowed from a cheetah.

~~~~~~~~~~~~~~~~~~~~~~~~~~~~~~

The first time my wife Tara came home from work to be greeted by my new protégé, she was polite. The second time, Tara was less than thrilled. By the tenth time, Tara started to mutter a word under her breath that began with the letter "d" and rhymed with horse. Fortunately, my new studio was nearly ready to open by then.

In a figurative reading of the tea leaves—as I tried to gauge my new endeavor's success—one incident stood out. Well into the evening, Tim was painting an inside wall of the nearly completed unit. Weight machines and treadmills lie strewn about in various stages of assembly. Tim was startled by a pounding on the front glass. A man was attempting to get Tim's attention. The man had a wallet in his free hand. After Tim opened the door, the man walked in to explain that he had heard about the new facility and wanted to sign up right then and there for one year. Tim took the man's name and phone number, and told him to keep his money until we opened.

Two weeks later we opened for business. Tim and I were as popular as milkbones on the Iditarod, and soon we had a loyal clientele.

Shortly after we opened, I began to allow Natasha to work with clients on occasion. Her own workouts continued to transform her physique as she attacked the weights and machines with an intensity and fervor that belied her runway model looks. After two months she was working for twenty hours a week as business continued to boom. I paid far too much attention to her workouts and too little attention to my collapsing marriage. Upon arriving home at night, I was often hunted down and pelted with Holy Water balloons. My church pastor, an ex-Detroit cop, powerfully built ex-workout partner, and one of the finest and most moral men I have ever met, excommunicated me in a two-page letter.

37

BY THE TIME he turned 30, Martin had issued 22,143 traffic tickets, with only 240 going to actual residents of Grosse Pointe Shores. Out of the 412 arrests that Martin had made, all but two were for outstanding warrants, drunk driving, possession of marijuana, or a little cocaine. One of Martin's two important arrests was a suspect in a murder case who was later acquitted. The other was a large man who grew belligerent about being arrested for outstanding child support and succeeded for a while in wrestling Martin to the pavement. But help soon arrived in the form of 20 other officers from the Shores, the Woods, and the Farms and the man was zealously subdued. Immediately upon the man's discharge from St. John's Hospital, he was charged with the attempted murder of a police officer—since most of the officers present agreed that the man was trying to grab Martin's gun. The warrant was voided once it was discovered that the Detroit resident had actually overpaid his child support by several thousand dollars. The attempted murder charge was consequently reduced to simple assault and a jury in Wayne County acquitted the man after 15 minutes of deliberation.

Martin took some small measure of pride in the fact that only one of his arrests had been that of an actual Grosse Pointe Shores resident. The drunken woman had plowed into two cars at the intersection of Lakeshore and Vernier and her transgression could not be addressed with only a warning. Martin always took his oath to protect and serve the 2,900 Shores residents very seriously and not to step on any rich or influential toes in the exclusive community.

There were no bank robbers to chase, however, due in part to the community's lack of banks. The absence of retail stores in the community kept retail fraud and daring daylight robberies to zero. After logging eight years and 195,000 miles (the majority of it at 25 miles per hour), Martin was far from making police chief. It would also be some time before he would be considered for promotion in the seniority-heavy department. His wife had just given birth to their third child. Acquiring a larger house was becoming a pressing concern. At $48,000 a year, a move into Grosse Pointes Shores was nothing more than a hallucination when one considered the $450,000 price of a starter home.

~~~~~~~~~~~~~~~~~~~~~~~~~~

"Okay, but da boss says dat if we can't do what dey ask den dare gonna find somebody who can."

Martin still wasn't sure why he had said yes to a partnership with this thug. One thousand dollars a day plus expenses meant that this contract was a lucrative one. Now, however, the focus had turned from background research and observation of the subject to a demand that some action be taken to discourage a continuation of the relationship between the old guy and his girlfriend.

"For starters, he's not our boss. He is a client. We have other clients. We even have clients who only request activities that are legal."

Martin knew better than to give out that kind of detail over a non-secure line, but this hood from the Bronx was straining at the leash. Benny was also salivating at the thought of the $250,000 bonus if Summer was unable to continue the affair for any reason. Martin himself had been hoping more for an extortion type of conclusion, but if Summer was sleeping with anybody else, she wasn't letting Benny photograph it.

"Look, all I'm saying is dat dare not gonna keep payin' our bills unless we do sumtin!"

Martin wondered if they'd pay his legal bills if they tried a

Nancy Kerrigan and got caught. He didn't think so. The loss of his private investigator's license was not an appealing prospect either.

The same uncle that had gotten Martin started in law enforcement had given him part time work at Fife Investigations when his family kept growing. In spite of his department's policies against performing outside security work, Martin kept a low profile and took all of the spousal surveillance cases that Uncle Richard no longer had the stamina (or the prostate) for. He had tailed executives with their secretaries, documented chat room affairs that turned into the real thing, and even videotaped a cliché "lonely housewife and the pool boy" tryst for a suspicious husband. The curvaceous lady of the house had felt protected by the tall hedge surrounding her yard as she sprawled naked on the diving board of her in-ground pool. The young man had just finished his second year of college and was fully servicing the tan Grosse Pointe Park homeowner every Wednesday at one o'clock in the afternoon. Martin was determined to fully document one of the encounters.

Many of the older homes in The Park have three stories, and one of these was for sale just two houses away. Posing as a real estate agent, Martin obtained the lockbox code and set himself up in a gabled third floor bedroom. He was able to use a copy of the video for years at area bachelor parties. His new parabolic mike had provided a matching sound track of astounding clarity as well. The divorce was ugly, but not nearly as bad as that of the Grosse Pointe Farms trucking company owner. His late night arrivals at home had raised the suspicions of a wife that hadn't received any matrimonial deliveries from the man in over two years. An investigation revealed that the man was, in fact, still at the office on the nights in question—receiving loads from two of his truck drivers—on the office couch.

After a two-year apprenticeship under his uncle, Martin was qualified for his own P.I. license. A switch to full-time would mean leaving the police department. The decision was tragically made easier when Uncle Richard suffered his fourth heart attack while on the toilet and died at the age of 49.

38

CLIENTS WERE INSPIRED and motivated by Natasha as she pushed them hard while laughing at their excuses. I soon discovered that my employee and protégé had a sense of humor, as well…except that it was rather nasty.

A significant portion of our clientele was older and some were taking medications to correct blood pressure or other conditions. A husband and wife couple that worked out at my studio regularly had recently celebrated their sixtieth birthdays. They were outspoken, pleasant, and obviously adored each other. I envied their 40-year marriage and their sunny outlook on life. I had been doing squats with the husband, albeit with a light weight, when I should have perhaps chosen something less strenuous. He was a little pale and resting on a bench when Natasha strode into the studio to begin her shift. She acknowledged my client by name, whereupon he fainted and collapsed in a heap onto the studio floor. His devoted wife grew less distraught after his eyes opened and he was again able to speak. The ambulance arrived within one minute. They carted him away to the hospital for a work up, and he resumed his workouts the following week.

Natasha, however, took great pleasure in teasing me about the incident. When we were alone in the gym, she would sit on the same bench and yell out, "Mock, Mock, who am I?" until she caught my attention. When I looked over she would purposefully fling herself off of the bench, collapsing in a motionless heap on the floor.

We drew a little closer together on those days.

Some said that Natasha was without empathy. Others might maintain that she had an uncanny ability to analyze and explain. Natasha was sitting behind the studio's front desk on a cold February evening several months after we opened. Across the desk, the two chairs were occupied by a physician and an investment banker. Natasha's pen was poised impatiently above the appointment book. Both the doctor and banker were trying to recall their evening schedules two days hence. The doctor thought that he could make it at six o'clock, but then asked Natasha to erase his name and write it in at seven instead. The banker grew increasingly frustrated that he could not remember whether he had other plans in the next 48 hours. The physician offered that he believed that he had Attention Deficit Disorder as a child and that it had been neither diagnosed nor treated properly. The banker turned his head in amazement and confessed that he had always felt the same way. They both lamented about how school would have not been so difficult had they received the proper help. They mutually commiserated about how ADD had affected not only their personal relationships but had held them back professionally as well.

These two men, from different cities, backgrounds, and generations barely knew each other until then. But in a few short minutes they had formed a bond. Each felt a little better after talking to a fellow man with a self-diagnosed learning disorder.

Natasha set her pen down and looked at each man.

"Did you ever theenk that the both of you are just stoopid?" she inquired.

I could not help but overhear. Fortunately by then, I had many other clients as my fondness for Natasha continued to grow.

Shortly after her impromptu analytical session, Natasha was behind the desk when a very nice couple walked in. Both appeared to be in their mid-30s and decidedly on the plump side. The man took great pains to make it clear that his wife was the one who was interested in joining. He was only there to write the check for the program. He was happy with who he was and unconcerned about his appearance. He did not care what he looked like, he declared.

"Maybe thees is true," Natasha replied, "but you *should* care because other people steel must look at you."

~~~~~~~~~~~~~~~~~~~~~~

When Norm was first presented with the possibility that his wife could be paid a nurse's wage without him enduring the expense of nursing school, he was euphoric. Visions of being able to withdraw completely from the automobile reassignment business while *Natasha* brought home the bacon danced in his head. He immediately began to devote more attention to his already well-honed golf game, making quick jaunts to Florida when Michigan winters intervened. He combed the classified sections of the local newspapers "For Sale by Owner" columns hoping to add to his real estate empire. At 32 years old, Norm seemed to be on the fast track to an early retirement—filled with putting greens and televised sports.

~~~~~~~~~~~~~~~~~~~~~~

At first, Natasha dutifully rendered her paychecks unto Caesar. The first hint of a crack in Norman's master retirement plan came in the form of smoke. The smoke was produced in great volume, however, and emitted from the tailpipe of the ancient minivan that Natasha was allowed to drive. In its early years it was red. Before becoming Natasha's sole method of transportation, its form had morphed into a misshapen collection of rust, dents, ill-fitting doors and skewed bumpers. The faded interior was ripped and torn, and the radio's static made it sound like a transmission from Mars. During one ill-conceived attempt to patronize a subshop's drive-through window, the smoking exhaust left the cashier coughing, wheezing, and dizzy. The classic Camaros and Chevelles that graced their home's garages were not to be driven by anyone other than Norm himself—as he had declared long ago. The minivan's only real value to Norm lie in its ability to eradicate locusts from farmers' fields…and to get Natasha to work.

Many of our clients, however, drove Jaguars, Mercedes, or Infinities. On one sunny afternoon, several studio patrons remarked how the contrast between one client's hulking new Lincoln Navigator and Natasha's listing minivan was startling. In a sea of shiny paint and chrome, the van stuck out like a pariah.

Soon, Natasha was careful to wait until the last client had left in their car before venturing out to start hers. I usually waited with her, chatting and waiting to see if the battered bug bomb would start at all. When it did, I usually followed her home, watching the van spew like a special effects machine at a rock concert.

One night I suggested that it might be time to find a different car. Natasha responded strongly and with not a little anger.

"Oh, I cannot. My Norman, he ees such a cheap ass!"

"But you're working. Why don't *you* buy something?" I inquired.

"I haff to geeve whole check to that bastard," she explained.

I had not intended to delve into the financial end of their marriage, but now I was intrigued. "How much does he give you back?" I asked, suspecting I already knew the answer.

"Dat prick geeve me nothing. Only eef he need grocery or car part. Eef I get change I put gas in van crappy ees all."

I was beginning to sense that there was trouble in paradise. My qualifications to intervene in Norm and Natasha's marriage were exemplary. My wife was now following me around the house nightly reciting Gregorian chants in hopes of driving the devil out of me. When her friends saw me they urged me to seek marriage counseling *before* they said hello. Her mad money had grown from a nest egg to a fund large enough to hire Johnnie Cochran. My second marriage was heading into the station with no brakes, following the trainwreck of my first. I plunged ahead anyway.

"Natasha, why don't you take your paycheck directly to the bank and cash it? Then deposit most of the money but keep some of it for yourself. If he confronts you about it, explain that you had an emergency and needed a few bucks."

"Eet will cause beeg argooment. You ever try argoo with Norman? Get in two verds, zen he yell and svear for hour!"

I explained the term "emotionally abusive" to Natasha. I pointed out that though my own marriage was circling the drain, there was no yelling or screaming in our household. Neither Tara nor myself were forced to tolerate constant threats of sudden homelessness. It would soon be over without a shot being fired.

I was wrong, of course. After a time, Tara approached Norman and declared her suspicions about my friendship with Natasha. Norm was apoplectic. He grilled his wife like a prisoner of war. He demanded to know if her recent distance from him was a result of a new love. He ranted at her insolence and ungratefulness after he had worked so hard to provide her with food, clothing, and transportation. In her own defense, Natasha pointed out that Norman had a couple of character flaws that were in need of improvement. This only caused her husband to fly to a new level of rage, however, as he screamed to be informed about her current status with me.

The next morning the knocking on my door brought me out to a pacing Norman Baights in my driveway. A sullen Natasha slumped in the passenger seat of the ugly Nissan while Norman explained that things just didn't look right. Natasha had been coming home too late. She had been skimming money from her paychecks without telling him where it was going. She wanted a newer car. He didn't have these problems prior to her working at the studio. Before she met me, she had cleaned the house and his cars and had cooked their meals on time without questioning him. The fitness studio, with its friendly people driving their new cars, was poisoning his wife's mind. She must quit immediately. He was ----in' sorry, but that was his final decision. He said good-bye.

Life must not have been very pleasant in the Baights household over the next week. The first call I received from Natasha was to inquire as to whether she was still allowed to use the studio when nobody was there. I had not changed the locks. I told her that she was still welcome.

Like an Amish husband who has allowed his cloistered wife to visit the big city for the second time, Norm had relinquished too much of the leash. The second call that I received from Natasha was to request that she be rehired part-time. I readily agreed. Norman began to grace the studio with unscheduled visits at odd hours to check on her. He sleuthed in the parking lot after dark, hoping to observe an impassioned embrace. But Sherlock Baights came up empty, and gradually returned to golf and his television set.

Although I saw Natasha regularly at the studio once again, I received a third call from her a month later. It was a warm day in July and she mysteriously asked if I would meet her at a local park. I agreed. When I arrived, she was already sitting at a picnic table. We had the park to ourselves. I was very curious and spoke immediately upon sitting down.

"What's up?"

"I geeve Norman letter," she said. "It vas four pages long. I say how cheap he ees. I say how mean. I say he sheety lover but I say eet nass. I say how I used to lavv heem ten years ago when we married, but now tired of being slave. He know now I do not clean puke and tresh from crappy cars he buys. You see, in letter he cannot interrupt Natasha. I leeve on keetchen table. He probably read right now. But Natasha vorry. I say vee need to talk to counselor. Vee need to make changes. But maybe I go home and he just lock me out. Say I have nathing. I haff little money saved…not much."

Finally, I had the opportunity to expound about a subject that I was an expert on. I knew a lot about divorce law. I had one under my belt and another one ripening on the vine.

"Natasha," I said, "I have tried to stay away from questions about your personal finances. But I have a pen and if you have a piece of paper, we'll total your marital net worth right now."

We listed the houses. We estimated their current value. We deducted the mortgages. Classic cars, savings bonds, certificates of deposit and cash were discussed and appraised. Other than two very small mortgages, there were no outstanding loans. There were no credit card balances. On the other hand, there certainly wasn't any expensive jewelry or furniture to be concerned with. I sat at the picnic table, engrossed in the numbers, while Natasha interrupted periodically as she recalled additional assets. When I was finished, I circled the final figure and pushed the paper to her side.

"I'm no C.P.A." I said, "but according to our accounting you and Norm are worth quite a bit for a relatively young couple. The final figure here is just over $400,000!"

Natasha didn't seem surprised.

"Thees ees good," she said. "but vat does all thees matter. Norman say I ever leeve heem I get clothes on back, nothing more."

"I would disagree, and so would every judge in the state. You've been married ten years. There's no prenuptial agreement. He did not have significant assets when he entered into the marriage. You get half."

Now Natasha seemed surprised. Norm had successfully brainwashed her over a ten-year period and, in this sunny roadside park, it was all unraveling. I meddled further.

"Of course, if it came down to dividing it, I'm sure he wouldn't part with your half willingly. There would be legal fees, and it's inevitable that he'll make claims that you have overvalued some items, which would mean some independent appraisal fees."

In for a penny, in for a pound. I was on a roll. Best of all, I did not charge a fee for my unlicensed legal services.

Natasha had been correct, of course. The "Dear Norm" letter had set off an avalanche of questions, accusations, and propaganda.

Acting again as her unlicensed legal counsel, I cautioned Natasha to copy every bank receipt, document, and title pertaining to any asset that we had listed. She did so, and soon checks that she wrote began to bounce after Norman cleaned out every bank account and cashed in every certificate. Eighteen thousand dollars disappeared from their safe, and classic cars mysteriously wound up in his parents' barn. Norm's parents, whom he had previously loathed, became the new caretakers of his and Natasha's cash and titles as well.

Meanwhile, on the reconciliation end, Norm insisted on frequent marriage counseling to shore up his crumbling marriage and convince Natasha to renew their vows. Renew them, at least, until he could devise a way to liquidate and convert their real estate to cash.

Natasha became increasingly emboldened and began depositing her paychecks directly into her new checking account, accumulating a retainer to enlist a real attorney in what promised to be a war.

In the middle of an unusually rainy October, Norm fled to Florida with two divorced male friends to play golf. But there would be no respite on the links for his marital woes as his cohorts explained the equanimity of the judicial system. Norman wasn't the first married person to hide assets prior to a divorce, they cautioned. The judge would see right through every attempt, they warned. In the end, after submitting huge fees to his attorney and hers, they told him, Natasha would receive half. Norm and his advisors drowned their conclusions in fermented hops and barley and they all phoned Michigan frequently during crying jags to beg for a reconsideration. Natasha, increasingly repulsed by the sniveling and groveling, grew more steadfast and resolute. Due back on a Monday, Norm surprised Natasha by flying home on the preceding Friday night. He followed her about the house, whining like an abandoned puppy, until she was forced to seek refuge at her sister's house. She returned Saturday morning to more of the same, and left him sitting on the edge of the bed, crying at his misfortune. She drove to a children's birthday party, and from there phoned me at my studio. I asked her how she was holding up.

"Oh, Natasha fine," she said "but Norman, he cry whole time and say ven I come home I find cold, dead body. I tell him do not talk of thees things. Think of vat *you* say and tell him not get sympathy from Natasha. He ask me vhy not make lavv. Say he lavv me. I cannot answer. But Mock, I have question for you."

I told her to fire away.

"You say you get divorce soon. Eef I get divorce too, we become better friends maybe?"

"That would be called a rebound relationship," I cautioned. And anybody with experience in these matters will tell you that it is a bad idea, and will probably never work out. "But yes, I would absolutely consider becoming better friends."

"Good, Natasha see counselor on Maanday vith Norm. I say then I vant divorce. Go to lawyer I find. Tuesday, serve peppers."

I hung up, realizing that I wouldn't be placing any personal ads after my divorce.

The studio was busy for a Saturday and I didn't arrive home until 3 P.M. As I turned onto my street, my attention was drawn to a fleet of police cars and EMS units at the other end. I could see Natasha standing by a patrol unit with her arms folded while a policeman wrote on a clipboard.

There was no longer any need for Natasha to break the bad news to Norm at Monday's counseling session. In fact, there would be no counseling session for the couple to attend. Natasha had arrived back on the block an hour ago. Her half-hearted search of the house had not revealed the whereabouts of her soon-to-be-ex husband. But a quick look inside the ugly blue Nissan on the driveway did. Slumped over against the driver's side door was the corpse of Norman Baights. The shotgun lay at an angle across his chest, his big toe still jammed through the trigger guard. She summoned the police, and while the house and grounds were thoroughly searched, there wasn't any note of explanation to be found.

It would be almost two years later when Natasha had a conversation with Norm's sister that shed some light on the final event. When they had been children, she said, little Norman would play every board game to win. If it looked as though the eventual outcome would not leave Norm on the winning side, he would toss the board into the air before the game was over…and walk away.

It took Natasha's attorney two years to pry her assets from Norm's grieving but greedy parents. Putting it all into the past, she sold everything and moved 20 miles away into a small house on the lake.

Tara moved out soon after Norman's death, releasing me to become better friends with my widowed neighbor.

After Norm's funeral, Natasha returned to the gym—and her workouts—with a vengeance. She continued to re-sculpt her already hard physique with an eye that grew more discerning every day. She renewed her focus on her back muscles until they rippled beneath her dark tan. When she so desired, she could flare them out from her sides, giving her torso a v-shape seen only on Olympic-caliber swimmers. She attacked the weights as she pumped up her shoulders. Her ramrod straight posture was soon so far removed from that of her former scoliosis look that she now appeared to be six feet tall. Freed from the tyranny of her marriage, she slept like a beautiful corpse—and ate ten times as much as any supermodel—without gaining a pound.

For my part, I introduced her to upscale restaurants and slinky, clingy dresses. As shallow as ever, I would trail her from ten paces back at normally sedate fine dining establishments. As Natasha followed the hostess, I would watch the tables erupt into activity. Husbands would stare open mouthed at the statuesque blond beauty as she strode through the dining room. Wives would jab their husbands with elbows and even forks to return their attention to the table before any fantasies began to take root. No matter how refined in appearance, businessmen lined up along the bar were reduced to giddy smiles when Natasha, blond-maned and braless, acknowledged their existence with a smile. The men were so intent on undressing the statuesque beauty with their eyes that their brains could no longer spare electrical impulses for their breathing reflexes. They would slump to the bar in mock faints, giggling like shy schoolboys.

I took my voyeuristic act on the road as well. I told her the yellow stretchy tank top that I bought her would allow her to blend in perfectly on the streets of Chicago's business district. But the material proved to be too thin and the July day too sunny. I was proved to be wrong. Men in suits stopped walking or talking. Construction workers were too stunned to catcall or hoot. A bus bumped a car into an intersection as both drivers gawked. At the Chicago Mercantile Exchange, the trading floor grew hushed when Natasha peered over from the balcony above.

39

Ten years to the day after Martin hired into the police department, he inherited Fife Investigations—and retired from the force. Although he occasionally employed a couple of part timers or the off-duty cop in need of extra cash, the ex-patrolman tried to handle most of the commissioned tasks by himself. He continued to cultivate a regular clientele of the well-heeled and their errant loved ones from the 49,000 residents of the five Pointes. He wallowed in the pig slop of the wealthy community's marital breakdowns, and was well compensated for it. Martin soon raked in over $350,000 a year and he, with his wife and six children, moved to a large house in the Farms. He had paid $850,000 for it, and reveled in the fact that his new house was within a stone's throw of the Shores, his old patrol ground. Former clients referred new ones, and combative divorce attorneys enlisted his services for their freshly signed clients. The wronged or suspicious residents of the Pointes placed a great deal of trust in their native son, and already the 39-year-old P.I. had experienced an explosion of repeat business. Former clients married to a second—or even a third—wayward spouse re-enlisted his services. Business owners paid well for employee background checks.

Martin tried to balance family life with 65-hour workweeks. But soon, a chain of events was set into motion. A familial history of sky high cholesterol cropped up. It quickly warned Martin of its presence with gripping chest pains for six months prior to his heart attack, which he ignored. Post attack, his cardiologist sent away vials of Martin's blood to the lab twice until both readings came back at 412 m/d. Martin now had four stents placed in various arteries to keep blood flowing to his heart muscle. After the operation, Martin's doctor explained to him that his 65-hour weeks were no longer possible. Martin needed to begin distributing some of the workload to others to keep up the flow of revenue while he tried to regain his health. Martin began a search. A Mr. Benjamin Dumasolli was in town and inquiring about establishing a firm of his own. An alliance was formed. But Benny was not from Grosse Pointe. When purity was necessary, he was unfiltered. When the situation called for tact, Benny was crass. What had worked on the docks of New York was not suitable for the Pointes. But Benny was ready to work 100 hours a week for a piece of the action. Now they were both looking for the right time to scare—or beat—the lust out of the richest man in the state's mistress—for a quarter million dollar bonus.

40

WHILE I DERIVED an inexplicable pleasure from watching men...and some women...mentally undress my female friend, I reserved the physical undressing of Natasha for myself. For a time, I occupied myself by literally tearing her clothes off, until her wardrobe of old tee shirts and jeans was exhausted. She seemed to enjoy this immensely, so I pulled a page out of my own book of kink and found her an old pair of sweatpants and a sweatshirt—size extra large. Late one night at the studio, I told her to go into the changing room and put on the outfit—with nothing else underneath. I had just had a tanning bed shipped in. It came by truck, affixed to a wooden platform that measured eight feet long by eight feet wide. While Natasha changed, I dragged the wood from the back alley into the gym. I laid it down at an angle. When she came out, I laid her down on the platform and told her to stretch her arms above her head. After she did, I took a staple gun and tacked the loose material of the sweatshirt around her entire perimeter to the platform. I used a *lot* of staples. Even with her super human strength, Natasha could not free herself. I grabbed some scissors off of my desk and took over an hour to cut her out of the sweats, being very careful not to snip at anything important. She seemed to enjoy having her outfit removed in this manner very much.

Unfortunately, I could not always be with my blond, hardbodied friend. Business was brisk and I had to attend to it, and in spite of her nasty sense of humor and outspoken habits, something about Natasha hinted to the public that she was approachable. Not surprisingly, the section of the public that received these hints was predominantly male. They followed her in stores, parking lots, and while she drove her new Lincoln in traffic. I could not always be there to watch over her, but I knew that Smith and Wesson could. I obtained an application for a concealed weapons permit for her. She laughed when I asked her if she had fired a gun before. Her father earned his living in the old country as a hunter. And *his* father had done the same. The hunting lineage stretched back for eons. I suspect that somewhere along this bloodline, one of her ancestors invented gunpowder. After careful consideration, we selected a .38 caliber Smith and Wesson Airweight as her carry piece. At a weight of about two pounds, her high tech, hammerless titanium pistol was polished to a high sheen and would have complemented much of her jewelry. Would have, that is, if she had worn it on a chain as an accessory. But nobody would ever see this piece of gleaming metal unless it was too late. We ordered concealment purses and holsters to go with every outfit except her string bikini. She practiced withdrawing her new gun until she could aim and fire it faster than I could say *dead rapist*.

We broke in her S&W at the firing range, and I watched her pump round after round in tight clusters of holes on paper targets. On the full-scale silhouettes of a man, Natasha took obvious delight in grouping her clusters around the crotch area. When I suggested that she may want to aim a little higher up with the intention of hitting a vital organ, she laughed. She said, "Vat more important then za von I am shooting at?"

It wasn't until I explained that her choice of target areas was causing me some personal discomfort as well that she smiled and shot bullseyes through the heart.

At the gun range, Natasha loaded her gun with "wad cutters" to make bigger, cleaner holes. But we decided that when she carried her gun in public, she would keep it loaded with hollow points. A hollow point bullet is aptly named. Each lead bullet is cast with a snout that is dished severely inward. Several tiny notches are cut into the tip that is left. When the bullet impacts a gelatinous mass such as human flesh, it "explodes" or separates into smaller pieces as it enters. The greater number of pieces gives the projectile a greater chance of finding an organ or severing a major artery. This subsequently causes more damage and increases the targeted individual's chances of dying.

Many police officers carry hollow point rounds because there is less chance of a "through and through." A through and through can be undesirable given the potential of striking an innocent person who might be standing behind the perp, but still in the line of fire.

I accompanied Natasha on the day that the County Gun Board set to review her application. In the small anteroom, a three-man panel was seated at a table in the front. One man was a State Police Lieutenant. A second man was a Lieutenant of the Macomb County Sheriff's Department. The remaining man represented the Macomb County Prosecutor's office. All three were shuffling paperwork when the Assistant D.A. called Natasha's name. She wore a dark, conservative pantsuit and her most sensible dress shoes. As she strode to a small table in front of the men, the shuffling of the papers increased to a rapid pace. Natasha sat in front of the Gun Board. The Assistant D.A. cleared his throat and asked Natasha why she wanted an unrestricted permit to carry a concealed weapon. She replied that she wished to carry a gun for her personal protection. The Assistant D.A. thanked her. Ten seconds later he called for a vote.

The State Police Lieutenant voted no because he had been instructed by the Chief to always vote no. The Chief interpreted the United States Constitution's Second Amendment differently than many people. His wife, friends, and anybody else that the Governor sent to him were awarded a permit, but complete strangers could not be trusted.

The Macomb County Sheriff's Lieutenant voted yes. In the

absence of any criminal record or a Charles Manson stare, the Lieutenant has been advised by his Chief to vote yes. Crime in the county had decreased every year since the policy began, and in Natasha the Chief had just cultivated a loyal voter.

The Assistant D.A. voted yes for many of the same reasons. The vote was two to one. Natasha was issued a plastic coated permit on the spot.

When we arrived back at the parking lot, I opened the trunk to her car. She found the box with her new Smith and Wesson. She loaded it up inside the car.

It was a bitterly cold Monday in February of 1998 and I had just recently sold my fitness studio. Michigan was bleak, dreary, and a documentary on the cable news channel was showing Princess Di's wrecked car for the 1700th time. Her lover, Dode Fayez, was on the radio. He was also on the dash, the windshield, and the rear view mirror. Natasha was complaining that her tiny, cold heart was having trouble pumping warm blood to her extremities. I suggested loading up the motorhome and heading south before she suggested that we get on a plane without our guns and fly to somewhere. By that afternoon we were entering Kentucky, and by late evening we were wearing light jackets in Northern Georgia. At the end of the next day we were hooked up in the side yard of a friend's house in Boca Raton. We rented a convertible, locked up the motorhome, and headed down to Miami. We ended up in South Beach, eating at Cuban restaurants and shopping in the warm sun. During the hottest part of the afternoon, we took a long stroll up and down the beach itself. I was prepared for the Cosmopolitan atmosphere that permeated the area. People from every country in Europe lolled in the sun or took refuge underneath their brightly colored cabanas. What I was not totally prepared for was the extreme poverty demonstrated by these European women. Apparently, many of them could only afford to purchase the bottom half of a bikini. They seemed determined, however, not to let their lack of funds deter them from doing every activity they would have done had they been able to buy both halves. I assumed that even the bottom portions had been heavily discounted at the shops as well, since many of them had very little material to speak of. I asked Natasha if she thought that some of these women would welcome a charitable donation to purchase a top half as we watched two of them wade out of the ocean. She said that they might be offended by an offer to help. Her thoughts were confirmed when we came upon two dark-tanned and topless Spanish women playing paddleball on the beach. They stood 30 feet apart in the hot sun, vigorously swinging their paddles as they batted a white ball between themselves. This activity had drawn a small crowd of men in addition to Natasha and me. The men's chivalrous nature no doubt necessitated that they stand by in case an errant ball find its way into the ocean water. I realized then, however, that if the two women could afford to purchase a paddleball set then they could have afforded bikini tops. My concerns abated, we went to select the nightclub that we thought best suited to attract celebrities for me to gawk at.

As near as I could determine, the most famous individual in the hotspot that I picked was a man who had once dated Robert DeNiro's hotel maid. Natasha and I left sometime after midnight. Our car was parked in a lot with a reasonable long-term rate on the outskirts of South Beach, but it was a perfect night for a walk. As we neared the car, something in a shop window caught my eye and I paused to peer in. Natasha saw a break in the moderate traffic and crossed the road to the parking lot that held our car. By the time I had finished looking, a light had changed somewhere and traffic was brisk for a minute thus delaying my own crossing. But soon I was able to bolt through a gap and lope across the street. Even in the dimly lit parking lot, Natasha was easy to pick out. She was 50 feet from the car and had her set of keys in her left hand. To my chagrin, there was a second party in the lot. He was dressed like *Ghetto Gangsta Meets*

Homeless Man. It was late and the attendant had decided that he was not going to collect any more fees…so the guard shack was empty. I was still 200 feet from the lot and broke into a run. Gangsta was cutting across the lot at a trot and closing fast on Natasha. My gun poked me in the side as I ran but I was not yet inclined to pull it and race down the sidewalk with it visible. Natasha was nearly to the car, but Gangsta had closed the gap to less than 40 feet. I hit the parking lot at a dead run. I could see Gansta's hands by now and they looked empty. I planned my first strike based on his hands remaining that way. I got ready to yell to Natasha. At the precise time that I did, Gangsta's head turned and he saw me coming. I will never be mistaken for a midget, and his eyes bulged wide. He changed course immediately, veering off at a right angle. He held up both hands so that I could see his palms and said, "Hey, that's cool, that's cool, man…no problem here."

I downshifted quickly from run to trot to walk. Natasha was standing at the locked passenger door. She smiled at me like everything was wonderful. She did not have her key out anymore and was instead waiting for me to unlock the car with the remote. She pulled her door open and the car's interior lights shone into the lot. My eyebrows rose involuntarily. The light glinted off of her .38 as she palmed it. Whatever Gangsta's career path was, she had been about to cut it short. She had been *waiting* for him! As she ducked into the car, she returned her S&W to a pouch on her belt without saying a word. On the ride back to the motorhome, the topic never strayed from dining or shopping.

Part II

41

It was early August in 2002. I was in a deep state of self-therapy following a roller coaster ride of life-plan derailing proportions. I had just spent the last three years and four months reluctantly exploring an alternative career path. My career opportunities had ended in chaos and disappointment. One of the trainers at my most recent fitness studio on the edge of the Pointes—who was sure that she had her thumb on the pulse of every denizen—had spent a great deal of time in the past week patiently explaining how I would soon be the *scourge* of the Pointes as well. At any moment—according to her—I would to be sucked into the maw of public opinion and spit back out again as a pariah…no longer worthy of employment by any of the 49,000 people that comprised the Pointes.

In the space of 40 months I had "progressed" from personal trainer of the richest man in Michigan and his lovely wife—to their chauffeur, bodyguard and boat captain. Unfortunately, the last eight months of my sojourn had consolidated my roles into that of a pimp and gypsy psychologist. The tattered shreds of a reputation that had been resting on increasingly shaky ground no longer provided enough fabric to sew back together a quilt of credibility, I was informed. In fact, the gloomy assessment at the time was that I did not have enough fabric left to construct a brassiere for Paris Hilton. Now, as I contemplated my next move, I found solace at my fitness studio. In spite of the business suffering from a post 9/11 recessionary spiral—

and a road improvement debacle in front—I was determined to boat, tan, barbecue, and work out until the disappointments were just unpleasant memories.

I had ignored my daughter and my friends so severely that shopping at Forever 21 and lunches at old haunts and greasy spoons sounded very enticing. I boated and floated around shallow Lake St. Clair. I spent long lunch hours at Crews Inn in Harrison Township, watching retirees boat up the Clinton River while I sampled the different noon-time specials from the ingenious Chef Steve.

Once again, I was lowering the bodyfat percentage of Southeastern Michigan and patching up old relationships. A friend that I used to talk to nearly every day had been relegated to once a week. I corrected the slight. Another friend that I had enjoyed weekly conversations with had been of necessity demoted to once a month. I apologized and called regularly again. Once more, my cell phone rang with familiar phone numbers. Even friends who only called when they needed something began to phone more often.

I expected this August afternoon to be little different, and had my phone programmed to "the same ringer tone for all callers" as I worked out with clients and eagerly fielded calls. Thus, I didn't mind at all when the phone clamored for attention yet again in the late afternoon of that day. I excused myself from a lady on the leg press machine and strolled over to my desk to peek at the caller ID. But it was bad news. It was a number that I hadn't seen for three weeks. Memories that I had been trying to suppress came bubbling to the surface. Frustration, betrayal, empty promises, and the threat of financial ruin manifested themselves through the ten digits on the little screen. I could ignore it, but if I did, the numbers would only appear again in 20 to 30 minutes. When it rang again, I could walk over, check it, and back away without picking it up. Eventually though, the message reminder would sound off, indicating a voice message. The female voice would allude to something of great importance, and hint that not returning the call immediately would result in catastrophic consequences. Further avoidance would eventually result in calls to my home phone, where a caller ID device did not shield me from intruders.

I picked it up. "Good afternoon, it's Mark."

"Hi, Sweetie, oooh, I haven't talked to you in so long. God it's good to hear your voice. I'm so frustrated with Max I could scream. He's up to his same old tricks again. Mark, I don't think he stopped drinking in time. I think he's losing it, I really do!"

"Hi, Summer, oh, I'm fine I guess."

"Oh, I'm sorry, Sweetie. Here I've ignored you for weeks and then I just call you and unload. But there's nobody else I can talk to about this. Bernadette went to the chiropractor to have her neck adjusted and the next day she had a stroke! Mark, she's only 41 years old and now she's lost 50 percent of her peripheral vision. She should not even be driving and she's got to take care of Barry full time now that his MS is getting worse. Anyway, she's got her hands full and doesn't have time for me anymore!"

Summer was Maxwell Lexington's mistress. Maxwell was arguably the wealthiest man in Michigan—a state already chock full of automotive barons. Until recently, I had been in the part-time employ of Mr. Lexington. I became acquainted with Summer over a period of months while we transformed her physique from that of a sexy but chubby socialite into that of a well-toned Aphrodite. Maxwell's retail empire enjoyed a stranglehold on the competition in the lower half of the state and the mogul had accumulated billions. The power and the money had driven Summer into a frenzy, and she divorced her husband of ten years to be unencumbered in her pursuit of a 71-year-old prize. I had an unusual dual role of Relationship Counselor and Step-'n-Fetchit until I decided that a trail of broken promises would lead to either financial ruin or insanity. In spite of Summer's repeated intonations about not burning any bridges, I realized that the only way out of this unprofitable, three-way relationship was to set this bridge on fire, and then nuke it! Only this nuclear reaction would guarantee that no attempts were made to rebuild either the bridge supports or the foundation.

"Y' know, Summer, the last couple of years would make an incredible story. I've been working on an outline of the main points of interest in my head while it's all still fresh."

"Oh, it *would*, wouldn't it. Anyway, I'm sorry I haven't been in to work out. Max has been keeping me so busy. A lot of times I don't know if we're going out on the boat that day until the last minute. He's been making some changes…some *major* changes at Corporate. I can't say why, but a lot of people aren't going to like those changes either."

Max had eight children—four were involved in the family business. A fair statement would be that out of Max's 4000 employees, these four would welcome change the least, especially if it were Summer-induced or related.

"I have got to get in to see you. I mean I've been powerwalking on the track whenever I can but I've been eating too. Can you believe that we still boat up to the River Crab almost every time we go out? I mean, if we're going to eat on board I've practically got to tend to everything myself. Captain Lance has a first mate but she's really young and I think she's just his girlfriend. I'm not even sure she's 18."

"Probably not. Not too many 18-year-olds are entering the eighth grade."

"Mark, stop it. I know you don't like him but Max has to use him. Max has him on salary and it would be pointless not to use him. I know you re-arranged your business to keep your part of the deal but you've got to see it through Max's eyes. His family blames you for us and they hate you! They wouldn't have set foot on the yacht if they *even thought* you were going to be there!"

"How many times have they set foot on the boat?"

"Well, they haven't yet…but the thing is that if they wanted to then Max would have had to go out and find a different Captain!"

"I had a substitute ready in case that happened. I told Max, he knew it."

"Look, what are we arguing about? I need to see you. I think I'm only a couple of pounds up but you know where I get it. My butt never does stick out like some do but it feels wide and my lower tummy is starting to pooch out again. Do I still have some visits left on my card? I'll just tell Max that I have *got* to see you three times a week and he'll have to work around *us* for a change. He's in a meeting with Dale Ladd, his company president, so we have at least a couple of hours. Are you going to be there?"

Woody Allen once said that 80% of life is in just showing up. While it was true that Summer had a mysterious hold over Max, the inverse was that Summer would also do anything Max asked her to in order to get another tentacle around him. Whenever Max began to shower Summer with promises, she flew to him like a jet-propelled moth.

Summer was a raven-haired ringer for the actress Madelyn Stowe, who most recently appeared on screen as the wife of Mel Gibson in *When We Were Soldiers*. At 5-foot 7-inches tall, Summer's weight could bounce from 133 pounds to a scone-assisted 144. While Summer was not a big eater, she had never met a piece of white bread that she didn't like. Her suspect infatuation with Max was coupled with a determination to become a permanent part of his lifestyle. This total absorption had resulted in a waning of her interest in any exercise program. Two years ago, our workouts together had almost returned Summer's physique to its glory days as an entertainment engineer at the Windsor ballet across the Detroit River, but it was now regressing once again.

~~~~~~~~~~~~~~~~~~~~~~~~~~~~

In the first *Rocky* movie, Rocky is a down and out prize fighter who, through a twist of fate, gets a shot at the heavyweight championship of the world. Upon learning of this, he seizes the opportunity to get in the best shape of his life. He's absolutely focused. He's goaded from behind by the memories of a dozen failures. At the same time, Rocky is pulled forward by a goal…the goal of being on an equal footing with the Champ. The ensuing

Rocky films find Rocky, for one reason or another, complacent during the beginning. Then, predictably, something sets him off and he trains like never before. Each film is filled with life lessons and set to very inspirational music that would have made Mahatma Ghandi, Mother Theresa, *and* Liberace take up the sport.

By no means was Summer down and out when I met her. She was married to a 45-year-old successful Greek real estate investor who could still set the hearts of most Grosse Pointe socialites a flutter. I often caught male drivers slowing down to watch her step out of her white Mercedes whenever she parked in the front lot of my gym. Sometimes the Coast Guard chopper that flew training exercises over my gym would stop and hover, mistaking the glints and flashes of Summer's jewelry for distress signals. But after ten years of marriage and a lot of dinners on "The Hill," Summer was no longer as thin when she first married. Even after our first meeting, however, I remember watching the 39-year-old strut back to her car in a pair of Gucci's, and thinking, *Hey, would you like some fries to go with that shake?*

Summer wasn't interested in boxing, though. Her arena was men, and the ten years of marriage was just some time off between bouts.

When a professional boxer retires from the ring, he might try managing another fighter. When Summer, at 29 years old, married and retired from stripping, she decided to give social climbing in Grosse Pointe a whirl. She retained the right decorators for the interior of her husband's classic home on Windmill Drive. She shopped at the stores that touted the most sought after designers (and to Summer, a *sale* only referred to that big white sheet on top of their neighbor's boat.)

Social climbing in the Pointes is difficult, after all, without the right equipment. Instead of rope to pull yourself up, you need money. To insulate yourself from the howling elements of gossip and rumors, you need loyal friends. The *right* friends can also serve as reliable guides to help negotiate the treacheries and unknowns of the sheer wall that is being attempted. The *right* friends can also be stepped on at the most opportune moment in order to reach the next level.

A good climbing partner can make the ascension easier. A husband who is successful, witty, handsome, and from the right stock can make all the difference between reaching the top and a nasty fall. Summer made several attempts to assault the mountain of social acceptance in the tightly knit crowd of "Ins" in Grosse Pointe society. She lacked, however, one of the most important criteria of a successful climb. Summer lacked an adequate base camp. A good base camp for the serious social climber in Grosse Pointe is important when the ambitious socialite needs refuge during foul weather. A good base camp for a social climber in the Pointes requires several items. Parentage is important. A family history of auto barons, real estate magnates, manufacturing dynasties, or even a respected line of physicians from in and around the area can be an oft-mentioned part of the social resume. If the surest way to be rich is to inherit, then the surest way to be accepted in the hierarchy of the Pointes is to have parents that heralded from there and were already accepted. Education is important. Private prep schools such as *Liggett* and the *Academy* place one immediately into the plus column. Grosse Pointe North and South high schools were the preferred choices unless one was an exceptional athlete, in which case one was expected to attend *Brother Rice* or *Bishop Gallagher*. The University of Michigan is a perfectly acceptable alma mater, although any Ivy League Schools are more so. Joining the right clubs such as Lochmoor or the Yacht, Hunt, or Little Clubs never hurt the cause when social climbing was the goal.

Unfortunately for Summer, her parentage was also in doubt. Through no fault of her own, she was adopted by a couple in a tiny Western Michigan town. Her school choice was limited to the single school that all of the local farmers' children attended. Her adoptive mother did all of her socializing at church and her father did his at the VFW hall. Aspiring socialites have overcome such inauspicious beginnings in the past, but never after giving birth to a "love-child" at the age of 19 the way Summer had. It didn't take the tongue waggers long to calculate that the age of her son did not equal the number of candles on Summer's anniversary cake. Repeatedly thwarted for promotion in the social pecking order and bored with "back to college" courses, Summer sought a new challenge.

Like a prizefighter contemplating a return to the arena, Summer needed to get back into winning form. A tennis league, weight-training at my studio, and powerwalking with her friends pummeled her curvaceous figure back into competitive condition. Like Rocky, Summer had a tunnel-vision motivation and more importantly, she had a conquest in mind. Max was 70 but still virile when they met. Summer worked hard to become more desirable by the day. He was confident, powerful, and very rich. She was beautiful and captivating with an entrancing smile, a sly wit, and an inquisitive nature. When queried by her husband as to her whereabouts, she used words like *friendship* and *mentor* to explain her relationship with Max.

Now Summer was about to enter the seventh round of a 12-round bout—just past the halfway point. She had won several rounds—reviving the sex drive of her geriatric boyfriend—and drawing declarations of love during their most intimate conversations. But Summer had lost a few rounds as well. Max's eight offspring had rallied around their mother and loudly and repeatedly declared their vehement opposition to Summer's existence. This had caused Max to scrutinize Summer's intentions with suspicion. With her divorce from Chuck, her husband, fully underway, Summer now sought a guarantee of future financial support from Max. She could not, however, convince the wary billionaire to commit to a contract. The recalcitrant Max would not even earmark funds for a temporary "love nest," and they made do with the sumptuous aft-cabin on his 58-foot Michigan yacht. The wealthy man, for his part, made little effort to shower his love bunny with baubles. Refusing to fully step into the sugardaddy role, he maintained that he preferred her to be unadorned with anything mined from the earth. Her fortieth birthday was recognized only after many prompts by a gauche looking gold ring destined to be melted down and recast. Obviously ordered over a car phone on the way to the office, its odd companion (considering the circumstances) was a gold necklace and a gold cross encrusted with small diamonds.

Now it looked as though the referee had called for a time out. My guess was that Summer intended to use this time wisely. She intended to fine tune the product once again by getting back into her workout routine. In the rarefied atmosphere of professional golddigging, maintaining the product is a full time job. Eight hours of sleep is not enough. The day must be interspersed with a nap or two to keep a fresh appearance. Hair, nails, and tan are maintained with appointments carefully juggled around the rich man's schedule. Eyebrow and bikini waxing, botox treatments, and collagen injections for the upper lip can require a day or so and should thus be scheduled during the lover's business trips. More serious—but still essential—maintenance such as breast work, eye lifts, laser treatments on the face, and liposuction require scheduled downtime, arrived at by mutual planning. Workouts at the gym are a long term precaution and as such are moved several notches down the list of priorities. The downtime after a workout must be factored in as well, since showering, hair treatments, and the reapplication of makeup must be seen to for several hours immediately after.

Summer pleaded with me. "Mark, I've got a few hours while he meets with Dale. He may want to continue our discussion afterwards or he may just go home to Elizabeth…I don't know. Anyway, I've got to start making time for me again. I need to do things for myself. He's put me through so much with this divorce. Do you have any time this afternoon at all?"

"My five-o'clock asked if they could move to six."

"Oh, that's perfect. Mark, I will *be there* at five!"

True to her word, Summer's car pulled in promptly at 5:25 P.M. Wearing Burberry shorts, a striped tank top, and talking a mile a minute on her cell phone, the slightly tubby temptress strode across the lot and into my studio.

The human body cannot remember pain. The brain can recall the exact circumstances of the event that caused the pain, but there is no memory center that restimulates the nerves involved in the incident. If it could, my tush would have sent a jolt right to my brain as Summer walked in the door and clicked shut her cell phone. If my body could have remembered all the pain, I would have avoided the perfunctory hug and the air kiss from her.

"Sorry I'm late, Sweetie, I was talking to my attorney. She thinks Chuck is playing games with his assets. She says she got a forensic accountant to go over everything. She also says that if we had been married just one more year I would have had a much better chance of breaking the prenup. The problem is that all of the properties have liens on them from banks. Really, the banks own everything!"

"Where did the money that they borrowed go?" I asked.

"I don't know," she answered. "I just told her to settle."

"At least it'll be over and you'll be free to date at last."

"That's not nice. Anyway, speaking of dating, guess who's been calling me every day?"

"President Clinton?"

"No. Seriously. Darren's been calling me again. Mark, he's promising me the sun, the moon, and the stars. His new deal is that if I marry him and we have a child, any prenup will be *void* after ten years! Can you believe it? Mark, he's worth *at least* 50 but it might be more like 150! But I don't know. I'm just not *attracted* enough to Darren to spend the next ten years with him."

Apparently it had not occurred to Summer that if the prenup expired, *one* of her options might be to stay married. She wasn't generally very good with numbers, but *was* adept at dividing large ones in half.

Darren Ruby was from New Jersey. His net worth of 240 million dollars came from the moving business, but in the past few years he'd been buying up mini-storage businesses. His business partners were somewhat shadowy figures whose last names all ended in a vowel. Still a young man at 50, Darren strongly resembled, physically and feature wise, the actor Dom DeLuise. He resembled Dom, that is, if the balding actor had received thousands of hair grafts to the top of his pate. Surgically transplanted from follicley lush donor areas in the back of his head, the hair grafts now grew on top and gave the portly millionaire a natural looking hairline.

Darren's adoptive parents were of Jewish descent, and thus Darren spent the first 25 years of his life with an unusual Hebrew surname. Friends and enemies alike came up with nicknames for Darren's last name. Business associates mispronounced it severely. Telephone solicitors butchered it beyond recognition. So when Darren married Deborah Ruby, he changed his surname to hers. Darren and Deborah Ruby prospered and raised two children to adulthood. They also adored each other until the day she died of cancer at age 50.

Wealthy beyond belief, but despondent and consuming more calories than any two men, Darren notified his "business associates" that he'd be spending more time in Florida. Darren liked to watch boats. He bought a two million dollar condo in Boca overlooking the Intracoastal Waterway. In high school and college, weighing 140 pounds less, Darren used to be on the tennis teams. He wrote a check for $55,000 and joined the Boca Raton Resort and Club. From his 15th floor condo's living room, Darren could peer down and spy on the Club's tennis courts. Any female players meriting thorough scrutiny were brought closer into focus by swinging around a telescope that Darren often used for watching boats out on the Atlantic Ocean.

One clear morning in February of 2002, the Itasco revealed a dark-haired woman darting back and forth on court number 14. Her leg muscles flexed beneath her tanned skin, and her short tennis skirt ruffled in the breeze that her quick movements created. When she stretched up to hit a shot over her head, the skirt could no longer cover her clean white panties. The woman was playing with a doubles partner. The man was heavyset with a white shock of sweaty hair that was pinned to his head by the band of his eye goggles. His movements had only a fraction of the range of the woman, but they were, in contrast, calculated to use only a minimal amount of energy to reach the ball. The woman raced from sideline to sideline in the backcourt, while the older man returned anything within reach like a human backboard. As Darren stared through the lens, his heartbeat became more rapid as he realized who the woman reminded him of. She had striking similarities to Deborah, his beloved wife! A woman's age is difficult to ascertain at 1200 feet, even through a $5,000 telescope, but the way the beauty carried herself suggested that she was at least 30 years of age. Darren returned his attention to her partner. Although the man's face was relatively smooth, the legs and wrinkled arms gave up clues as to his age. The bowlegged gait that the man used to amble about was not the result of years of ranching, however. It was the stance of an older man, and gave Darren hope. The woman was undoubtedly down here visiting her father after…a tumultuous divorce?…the loss of a job elsewhere?…or was it perhaps some other calamitous reason after which a white knight of means may successfully introduce himself?

Fifteen minutes later Darren was in front of the tennis counter at the Boca Club. The sprawling complex contained a marina, a hotel, and an entire golf course within its heavily fenced and patrolled territory. The tennis club, however, was known not only for the professional tournaments that were sponsored, but for the expertise of its teaching pros that was offered for 12 hours each day.

"Good morning, Mr. Rrruuby," the girl behind the counter sang out.

"Morning, Marlita. I don't have a match set up today. I was hoping that perhaps somebody's partner didn't show or begged off."

Mr. Ruby could be a most generous man. It would be worth Marlita's time to stare long and hard at the morning sign up sheets.

"Noooo, I am so sorry [and she meant it], everybody who was scheduled today has made it so far."

Darren's wallet was out now. A $100 bill was drawn out by a chubby thumb and forefinger. "Oh," Darren sighed, "that's a shame, I was hoping for a game this morning. I just got word from my secretary that I have a couple of hours now, but no more time at all this week." Marlita's eyes widened. In Mr. Ruby's hand was two days of her take-home pay.

"Perhaps, because of your situation, Mr. Rrruuby, there are steps I can take. Allow me to make a call." Marlita scanned the possibilities at eleven o'clock. Stopping for only a second to check a phone number, she dialed. She explained to the hotel guest that she was very sorry, but the pro that was slated to be with him at 11:00 was running quite late today due to a personal matter. Would he be so understanding as to come in at 12 instead for the next available pro? Apparently the answer was a positive one with Marlita beaming and thanking the cooperative guest as she hung up.

"Good news, Mr. Rrruuby, Erik will be available within ten minutes. I know you like to work with him very much. I will go down and tell him of the change."

Marlita was $100 richer and Darren was now paired with Erik, the club's top teaching pro. It should be a simple matter to find a court near or adjacent to number 14.

Court number 16 was the first court east of 14, and for the moment seemed to be available. With a shrug and a knowing smile, Erik agreed to bypass number 18 and settle in at 16. Soon, the staccato rhythm of Darren's and the pro's rackets added to the racket sounds and footfalls coming from the adjacent court. Darren was slow to serve and slow to retrieve errant balls today and Erik, smirking, could see why. The busty beauty on court 14 wore an outfit that was an attention grabber. She seemed to be all legs and bosom as she lunged and slashed her way around the backcourt. Her competitive spirit almost made up for her shortfalls in experience and skills. Her determination and will complemented the craftiness of her partner, Max Lexington, and together they might be a force to be reckoned with in a year or so. At the moment, however, they were being trounced by a 75-year-old Jewish strip-mall mogul from New York. His partner was a tall, older bleached blond in desperate need of a leg lift. Although she was thin, the leathery, mottled skin of her legs shook, rippled, and bounced as she expertly worked her team's backcourt. Sadie had joined as a member with her beloved Herman before he had passed on 20 years ago. Unfortunately, her days of using the club as a place to meet new boy toys had also passed on. It no longer made a difference how much of Herman's money still lie safely offshore or how high Sadie had her face and eyebrows lifted. Tightening the rest of Father Time and Mr. Sun's ravages was now approaching the realm of major surgery, and might endanger the health of the aging but frisky widow. The male escorts had made her feel desperate and cheap. Their gender preference was always a concern to her anyway in a HIV riddled world, and the lingering erections and bloodshot eyes of the last two suggested the possibility of Viagra. That a 25-year-old man would need Viagra to make love to a lusty woman when she herself needed no artificial preparations was in itself a mystery to her.

Darren's attention was further diverted when the brunette goddess paused during a break to trot over to a viewing area west of court number 12. She spoke briefly to a bored looking blond man seated at a table. He had the look of a guy who would shun the box of HoHo's that Darren ate every night and who had spent entirely too much time in weight rooms. The white knight's quest may be over before he undertook it if the 40-something man were to be his adversary.

The smitten storage-king was beginning to think that perhaps he had completely misread the situation presented through his telescope until the blond man came back from an errand. He held a cup of ice in each hand and walked briskly across court 12 to hand the cups to the bowlegged gent and the goddess. Upon further examination, the pumped up spectator didn't fit. His shirt and shorts made him look like a thug who suddenly realized that staying cool in the hot Florida sun may require cutting up his blue jeans somewhere above the knee. Belonging to the Boca Club meant that one had a predilection for golf or tennis…and a discerning taste that demanded the best venue around for pursuing them. This man looked as though a racket or golf club would feel more comfortable in his calloused hands if he were to be allowed to beat a transgressor with it. Belonging to the Boca Club might be viewed as a right of birth had one's parents belonged to the venerable resort. The squinty-eyed blond spectator, however, gave the impression of one who had just offed his parents to avoid attending family get-togethers.

Darren decided this man possessed neither refinement nor the money that he himself used to substitute for his own lack of culture.

Darren's conclusion brought with it some measure of relief. The woman had obvious refinement. She carried herself with a self-assurance that could only have come from an East Coast finishing school. Darren had arrived, financially at least, 20 years ago—and any future mate would be required to have a certain sophistication. The long procession of bimbos he'd been dating the last six months had done nothing to help him forget the death of his wife. South Florida was rife with pretty golddiggers and at first, at the urging of his local friends, Darren had entertained several. Nightly Darren and his cohorts filled large round tables at the best Boca eateries with friends, recent acquaintances, and the occasional lady from an approved escort service. The table would groan with the weight of every item on the menu, and at Darren's insistence each was to be sampled by all. A typical bill for the gregarious millionaire would be in the thousands. However, none of the women he met at these impromtu fêtes were marriage material. They made him uncomfortable when he first brought them up to his condo. He could feel the appraisal books in their heads come out as they first added up the value of the sumptuous furnishings. They usually waited until the end of a short tour before calculating the square footage and hence the retail value of the unit itself in such a desirable area. The more classless ones—the ones who could not comprehend a number bigger than the size of their implants (400cc)—asked outright. And Darren would give them a truthful answer. He enjoyed watching them flush as they tried to contain their excitement. He also knew then that the tour would end in his 800-square-foot master bedroom.

Most of the interviewees lacked style. They all lacked substance. South Florida was a Mecca for beautiful young ladies with fond memories of Spring Break. Their migration from the northern climes occurred every day. They would find, much to their disappointment, that the only jobs awaiting them were minimum wage and mundane. Darren could have an endless supply of clean, wholesome girls at $200 a throw. He could buy a daily companion for only $35 an hour. For that price, he could put ten on board the Viking yacht that he had just placed a deposit on. In fact, he could keep the women on board the yacht 24/7 for less than the yacht's daily operational expenses.

But none of the women would be like this one. Not one would have that alluring smile or those feline brown eyes that smoldered with a competitive fire. Darren had decided that the bodybuilder could not possibly be the woman's paramour. Somebody of his ilk would be more comfortable with a muscular Germanic type. A lady like this would make the perfect armpiece for Darren as he re-entered the societal structure of the exclusive coastal community where his mansion now lie empty. Darren needed an introduction. Erik, intent for the moment on improving the millionaire's serve, was pretending not to see this.

Darren had always been lucky in business. Lucrative deals flocked to him like Michael Jackson to a Menudo concert. Now, after a one-year drought, luck extended itself once again into his personal life. The brunette and her bowlegged partner set their rackets on chairs and strolled over to their opponents. The Jewish strip-mall king was meeting grandchildren at the airport. The blond with the epidermal layer that drooped down to her ankles was packing up as well. A minute of rehash and good-byes later, Max and Summer returned to their rackets. The blond man remained seated. The couple intended to stay for a while. Smoothly, seamlessly, the seasoned pro winked at Darren and moved to the edge of the court.

"Mr. Lexington, Miss Sevalas, perhaps you'd care to volley with Mr. Ruby and me for a while?" A moment's hesitation was followed by a quizzical look to each other before Max spoke, "Why yes, Earrek, that would be fiiine with us."

More formal introductions were made and Darren had his toehold.

Darren's next mission was to determine the exact nature of the relationship between the older man and his ravishing partner. Initially, the body language from either contributed little to any conclusion. The smile from one, the courteous *nice shots*, and the polite respectfulness of personal space could have come from two partners assigned to each other at the front desk that morning. The savvy businessman also knew that it could be a front the two put on to disguise their relationship from other club members. The swarthy man with the camera that watched their match so intently from the railing of the clubhouse's second floor might be a second reason for the casualness. Or the relationship may simply be a platonic one.

The newly arrived team scored easily and often in spite of Darren's 300-pound bulk and the pro's half-throttle efforts. Summer's increasingly frantic machinations did nothing to close the gap between their skills. Playing the net, Darren began some preliminary overtures by offering his new objective the occasional word of encouragement or advice. Her polite smiles and responses indicated her appreciativeness of the unsolicited tennis lesson. Max's snowballing silence demonstrated a growing dislike for the tips…and for Darren.

Billionaires do not become so without a competitive nature. It became clear to Max that he could not prevail on the court *and* that his opponent had a thinly disguised fondness for his partner. After a lifetime spent reading people in order to turn their strengths and weaknesses to his economic gain, Max saw through Darren like an x-ray machine. Darren and his cohort might win every match, but Max knew he would walk away with the prize. He would start by laying it out for the opposition in one deft move. Max waited. Erik aced a serve. The billionaire waited a little longer. Summer augered a lobbed return into the net. Darren suggested that the busty Summer lean over a little further when she awaited a serve, and Max began to grow impatient. Finally, a sharp return from Erik in his backcourt had Summer racing to her left in a desperate attempt to reach it. Her steps were perfectly spaced as she doubled up her grip and swung her racket in a vicious backhand. The ball sped back diagonally across the top of the net and caught the corner of her opponent's court with such speed that not even a hasty burst from Erik got him there in time to volley it back.

Max seized the moment. Spinning around and taking two quick steps to Summer, Max exclaimed, "Nice shot, Babe!" No sooner had the compliment raced through the Florida air to Darren's ears when Max also threw an arm around his partner's waist and drew her to him. There was neither struggle nor protest as the beaming "Babe" allowed her collagened lips to be directed to Max's sundried ones. The reveling retailer planted a direct hit on his mistress in a congratulatory—and obvious—reclamation of his concubine.

That Darren was meant to observe this staking of territory—cloaked within a display of affection—was quite apparent. Max's triumphant smirk, immediately post-kiss, left no other interpretation. The cold blue eyes behind the older man's goggles assessed the potential suitor's reaction.

Inwardly, Darren's reaction was one of despair. Gone was the fantasy of a newly divorced daughter visiting her aging father at his seaside condo. Totally eliminated from the realm of possibility was the chance that the couple had just been randomly assigned to play together two hours prior. The old guy definitely wasn't her priest.

Any type of savvy businessman/mentoring luscious young protégé was probably off the table as well.

Darren however, had faced indomitable situations before…and always found a way to be the tape breaker at the finish line.

Another glance to the balcony would have suggested that the swarthy observer shared Darren's despair. Although his camera lay at the ready in his thick hands, the quick and sudden public display of affection had caught him off guard as well, leaving the event unrecorded.

42

As Martin Fife closed his cell phone and spun to re-enter the studio, his thoughts returned to the client he was working for at the moment.

Martin, still in a state of denial, had checked himself into St. John's Hospital only after ten percent of his heart muscle had already died. Within 20 minutes, he had found himself being pumped full of anti-coagulants, and within two hours he was having a tube inserted through an artery in his right leg. The catheterisation procedure pinpointed the first of three blockages within minutes—all were adjudged to be 95% or greater—and two days later three tiny stents guarded against a recurrence. Martin was discharged 24 hours after his surgery—but not before a former acquaintance had re-introduced himself.

The name of Martin's surgeon was David James Campbell. With death looming imminently, Martin had not made the connection with the *Dr. Campbell* as it appeared on his physician's nametag and his old high school teammate. Dr. Campbell, for his part, recognized his old buddy immediately but elected to postpone any reminiscing until Martin's survival had been assured.

In the hour preceding discharge, Martin and David relived the blocks and the tackles, the wins and the losses, and the cheerleaders that grew prettier and more adoring with each re-telling.

Dr. Campbell openly expressed his surprise upon learning that his old teammate had worked as a policeman in the doctor's own neighborhood for so many years without their paths crossing. David grew quiet and contemplative for a moment, however, when Martin revealed what he was currently doing for a living.

Eschewing the services of a hospital orderly while still abiding with St. John's protocol, Dr. Campbell himself wheeled Martin downstairs to where Mrs. Fife sat waiting in her car. The two alumni of Grosse Pointe North shook hands and vowed to remain in touch long after Martin's follow-up visits to the surgeon's office were necessary.

Six weeks later, Dr. Campbell would be the first to make good on their mutual promise to communicate in a capacity other than that of doctor/patient. Although the subject matter was to be quite different from that which Martin had originally envisioned, it was nevertheless well within his scope of familiarity.

David Campbell had met his future wife, Jillian, while satisfying residency requirements at the very same hospital where he now practiced. After the end of a Saturday shift, David had stayed on the hospital grounds to attend the official opening of the new Oncology Building. Still wearing his white hospital coat as he worked his way through the crowd, David's eyes locked onto the pretty blond. She was sitting with her family and assorted other dignitaries atop a newly delivered stage in the Cancer Center's parking lot. Jillian's own attendance was prompted by the fact that her father, a wealthy retailer, was funding much of the center.

Now, ten years later, the hard-working physician had growing uncertainties about his beautiful wife.

Six weeks to the day after Martin met Dr. Campbell, albeit under some touch and go circumstances, he received a private call from his old teammate. The subject of running down and tackling a man with an air-filled piece of leather would not be broached even once.

David Campbell began. "I know that we discussed the probability of easing you back to work after a certain period of recuperation from your myocardial infarction. I should be the last person to make demands of you or add to your workload, but I have a personal matter that has been of some concern to me for the last two months. I am approaching you with it not only because of your expertise in this field but because I remember you as someone who could always be relied on."

Martin was intrigued.

The doctor continued. "When we were catching up I remember mentioning to you that I have been married for ten years now. While there is a ten-year age difference between Jillian and myself, I have always felt that we were well suited to each other. I know I did not mention her maiden name to you. It's Lexington."

Martin gave a low whistle. "You mean one of Max Lexington's daughters?"

David responded with an uneasy grunt. "Yes, I know. It looks like I married an heiress. But I assure you, she wants for nothing. I switched from pediatrics to my present specialty long ago and for me, a 60-hour week is not uncommon."

"So where do I fit in, David?" Martin asked.

"Martin, in the afternoon, over the past two months, Jillian has been…uh…missing in action. It's not *every* afternoon, and it doesn't ever seem to be for more than a couple of hours."

"If you'll pardon my saying so, David, a couple of hours is plenty of time for a pretty lady to find trouble."

"That's why we're having this conversation, Martin. I don't want to believe it. She hasn't given me any indication that she's unhappy with me. I found out quite by accident, you know. One of Jillian's sisters paged me at work because she could not locate her either. Since then I've made a regular habit of calling her at times I normally would not. The earliest she'll pull her disappearing act is around noon. The latest is around four."

"Any ideas, Doc?"

"None. But I'll pay you your regular rate to give me some."

"Have you thought of just asking her?"

"Yes. But let's face it, Martin. If it were something innocent, she would already have told me by now. I'm afraid I'm at the point where my imagination is beginning to run away from me. I keep asking myself whether she's found someone else. Or if she hasn't, is she out looking? I need to know, Martin. This next part is difficult for me to put into words, but I'm afraid that my suspicions are rapidly growing into an obsession. It's starting to affect my work. I can't afford for that to happen. My patients need me to be at the top of my game. Your own cholesterol readings are still over 300. *You* need me to be at my best."

"You're looking for more than just knowing where she goes, aren't you, Doc?"

"I'm afraid so, and believe me when I tell you how awkward it is for me to ask you this. Jillian has never met you before, and she has never heard me mention your name. All I'm asking you is that if she's *not* seeing anyone…I…ah…need to know if she would like to."

"I'm sorry, Doc. If you're getting at what I think you are—me following your wife and then hitting on her—well, I gotta tell you that professionally, that's about as low as a P.I. can stoop."

At the end, Martin and the doctor agreed to take one step at a time, beginning with Martin starting regular observation of the heiress the following morning.

43

I knew how Jillian Campbell spent her afternoons three or four days a week. I knew—because she was with me—or at least in my studio, working out with me or Michelle, my manager.

Our paths did not cross until her fourth visit, but I recognized Max's daughter immediately when I walked in the door. At 5-foot 6-inches, Jillian was ten pounds heavier than the night I drove the heiress, her husband, and her parents to a downtown Auto Show premier. Her parents, of course, were Max and Elizabeth Lexington—my former employers...until Summer had shown up.

Diffusing what could have been an awkward situation, Jillian smiled and signaled me over to the treadmill she was walking on. She still resembled the actress Kim Basinger, in spite of the extra weight. I approached her slowly, deciding whether to begin with apologies or explanations. Jillian broke the ice by beginning first.

"I'll bet you're surprised to see *me* here. You probably thought all eight of us blame you for what my dad is doing to my mom. I did for a while too. But then I remembered something. A few years ago my father had eye surgery and couldn't drive himself around for a while."

"I remember that too," I replied.

"Did you ever meet his last PR lady, Meliss Taurissy?"

"Just once, when I drove your parents to the State Capitol for some luncheon."

"Did you think she was pretty?"

"I remember that she was a brunette and wore her hair up. I was obsessing about that and didn't notice much else."

"Did her hair bother you?"

"I just don't like it in general when women wear their hair that way. I worry about rodents and their offspring living in there without the owner's knowledge."

"I don't remember you being so funny when you drove us to the Auto Show."

"After working for your father, I needed either a sense of humor or a lobotomy."

"You should have tried to develop the sense of humor."

"Now look who's funny."

"Did my father ever say anything to you about Meliss?"

"Now that you mention it, he asked me at least five or six times in the weeks after the luncheon what I thought of her."

"Do you think that he was having an affair with her?" She asked suddenly.

"I think that sometimes old lions need to prove to themselves that they can still hunt," I sidestepped, although not well.

"So you do."

"Hey, look what I've got here in my hand! It's your workout chart, Mrs. Campbell. What do you say we get started?"

~~~~~~~~~~~~~~~~~~~~~~~~~~~~~~

I managed to limit the conversations between myself and the former Miss Jillian Lexington to topics pertaining solely to her workout—for the rest of the hour.

She made her appointment for one o'clock the following day and picked up not far from where she had left off. "You didn't recognize my name in the appointment book, did you?" She asked.

"I never knew your married name," I reminded.

"I could try to convince you that I began working out here because

I've gained a few pounds since I've gotten married. David and I are also trying to get pregnant and I'm on two different prescriptions that are supposed to help—but they're not helping me keep the weight off."

"You look slimmer today than yesterday…and more fertile," I offered.

"I'm not working out here to have my ego stroked by some jokester, either. The truth is, the only reason I started here is that I knew that Summer Sevalas works out here too. I thought maybe I would run into her without her realizing who I am."

"I don't see her here much anymore," I cautioned.

"I'm sure you don't. She's too busy whoring around with my father and crushing my mother." There was a long pause, "I hate her, you know."

"I'm not surprised," I said.

"I hate her for what she's doing to my mom and what she's done to our family. And my father, he's always preached morals and God and faith and…and family. I don't hate him yet but I think I'm starting to."

"I'm sorry." I tried a subject change. "How about we try the ab machine?"

"Did you know that just three years ago my parents were into marriage counseling at their church?" Jillian asked.

"A lot of couples are helped by marriage counseling." I replied.

"They were the counselors," she informed me.

"I was afraid of that," I said with a wince.

"I just wanted to see what was so special about this particular one. I wanted to see for myself if she was really so goddamn beautiful that a man would just throw away his marriage and his family and his respect in the community for her."

I continued to meet at the studio with Jillian on a regular basis. Fortunately, Summer's visits during this period ranged from infrequent to nonexistent—consequently it took very little juggling of the schedule to ensure that the two did not meet. While there was a fire hydrant located in close proximity to the studio, I hesitated to purchase the necessary hoses and fittings. I had carefully estimated the amount of damage to the equipment and mirrors inside the little studio should a chance meeting—and thus a catfight—occur. I weighed the dollar amount against that of the water damage that separating the two with the fire hose would entail. I instead resolved to redouble my efforts to divert such a disaster from happening on the property.

Eventually, Jillian's venting abated enough for us to concentrate our efforts on her workouts until a funny thing happened. She began to lose weight and tone up. The heiress and I finally reached a tacit understanding—she would bring up the name of her father's mistress no more than once per workout. For my part, I willed myself to suppress any look of panic every time that front door opened.

~~~~~~~~~~~~~~~~~~~~~~~~~~~~

In spite of our understanding, Jillian had the occasional bad day—when her venting would exceed the allotted amount of time.

After one particularly vexing weekend in which a close friend spilled out details of her father's indiscretions, Jillian came in fuming. "Mark, it used to be the case that the only thing my father could do to make me angry was to lie to the public. I would turn to the back of my morning newspaper and see one of his weekly ads splayed across the entire page. They're beautiful ads, really, with a *reason* for the weekly sale in big, bold letters and very vivid, well thought-out photographs everywhere. But I majored in marketing in college and it disturbs me a great deal every time I see him offer a discounted price. Above the sale price is a price that purports to be the list price…although the State Attorney General told him that he couldn't *call* it the list price anymore. He always calls it something else…but the *inference* is the same. Nobody reads these ads every week. He's hoodwinking the public into believing he's *ever* sold one at the list price. *Nobody's* ever actually bought an item at the higher price…they would be paying five times his cost! One of his ads the other day had a door mirror on sale for $99, and that's probably a fair price. But my God, Mark, right above it he claims that he usually sells it for $299, and that's just a bald-faced lie!"

"I'm sorry you feel that way," I consoled. "I was thinking of visiting one of his outlets for the pre-Labor Day sale, but now I think I'll pass."

"Don't think that I haven't put in my own two cents worth," Jillian went on, "because I have. I bring it up to him about once a year, but he's so predictable. Every time I mention it, he'll just shut me out for a few months. No phone calls, no conversation at family get-togethers…nothing. I just wish there was some way that I could get through to him…something that I could do to retaliate. I'd like to make him see that he can't just lie with impunity…and embarrass and humiliate my mother in public by stepping out with that golddigging slut—parading her about whenever he chooses!"

44

Summer was pulling down on a bar attached to a cable while she talked. It was a warm-up set and in spite of being on repetition number 15, she was still able to talk. I was not impressed, however. If a pathologist was performing an *autopsy* on Summer, she would still be able to speak.

"I'm so glad you could take me today, I really am. I *miss* not working out with you. I need this. All we do is eat and, well…you know. I need a good friend to talk to even if I don't always agree with what you've got to say."

Her last statement was true. A month ago I'd made the mistake of suggesting to Summer that she look for work. Her return glare was that of an angry witch appraising her victim for a ritualistic castration.

"Not that there's anything wrong with doing it every day. I mean, Darren used to *demand* it at least once a day when Max was away. And you know what they say about Jewish men. *They* try the hardest to please their women. Mark, Darren would go down on me for hours if I let him! That's more than I can say for Max! 'Course it's not his fault. He simply wasn't brought up that way! It's not something that men of his generation talked about or did."

My eyes blinked rapidly as I tried to load in any movie reel other than the one I was watching. The information that Summer so casually fed me was unwelcome and seared my imagination in horrific flashes. I would have squirmed less during a discussion about hemorrhoids. "We're going to have to work legs and abs today too, Summer."

"Oh, I'm sorry, Sweetie, am I making you uncomfortable? Who else can I talk to about this? I can't ask Max to go down on me the way Darren does. Max has no idea what I do when I'm in Boca and he's in Michigan. One potential problem is developing, though. Remember I said that Darren has been calling me every day? Well...he says that he wants to come up here to see me. I keep telling him he can't. I say that I'm too involved in the divorce right now...which isn't true...it's nearly over. He says it doesn't matter, I can turn the whole thing over to his lawyer if I don't like the way it's going. Mark, can you imagine? How would I keep those two separated? Even if Darren stays at the Townsend in Birmingham I can still only spend half the week with him if I'm seeing Max."

"I suppose that if you suggested a threesome then one or both would be offended?"

"Mark, don't even *joke* about this. I need to make a decision soon. Darren says if I were his, he would *shower* me with gifts. He says I would never have to worry about money again. But Mark, sometimes when we're in bed he can be so rough! I mean, he knows what he's doing and he's not selfish if you get my drift. But when I'm on the bottom I feel like I'm being smashed. He's like a 300-pound bear on top of me...fur and all!"

"Summer, you really don't have to explain everything to me."

"Who else can I tell, honey? Before I ask for your advice you need to know the good *and* the bad. Now Max, on the other hand, is much more gentle and loving. And believe me, for *his* age and lack of different partners, he knows what he's doing too! But I can't *trust* him. And Mark, it's all about trust. He says I can trust him, but what has he shown me? He's broken it off with me more times than I can count. I can't wait around for him to reconcile his feelings about me...and about his wife Elizabeth. Look at the baggage he's carrying...his wife...eight kids...and how many grandchildren. I've confronted him about that too."

"I don't think his wife has any intention of setting him free so that he can share his life with you. I think she's just being selfish. Could we get a warm-up set of squats?"

"Mark, Elizabeth knows everything, she knows about me being at the house when she was in the hospital for her foot surgery. But that's because her kids and Robert the butler were spying on us and reporting back to her. Max says he's quietly put the word out for a new house manager. He says he can't stand to even look at Robert anymore. Robert chose sides. He chose Elizabeth but he forgot who signs his paychecks."

"I'm sure he felt good about getting tangled in the middle."

"Well, honey, I *know* he didn't. But listen, I think the kids put him up to it. And I'll tell you something else. I think the kids are having me followed. I will *not* go anywhere without my cell phone and people around. Two days ago I was at Grosse Pointe South. I figured it would be safe to powerwalk around the track with the football team there getting ready for the season. But there was this car, Mark. It was kind of big and a little older. I don't know what kind it was. I think it was maybe an older Cadillac or Lincoln or something. I'd been walking for about 15 minutes when I noticed it. I wouldn't have noticed it at all except that my father used to have cars like it. The windows were tinted somehow so I couldn't see inside. It had a yellow or orange license plate but I was too far away to read it. Mark, I've seen this same car over on The Hill when I met my friend Tishelle Gaudette there when she was having those erratic periods…and that discharge. I told her I thought her last boyfriend should be checked by a doctor but she wouldn't listen. Anyway, I saw this same big car in a metered parking spot across from Lucy's Tavern. I also saw it in a parking lot at the marina when I was running late to meet Max at the yacht. Mark, I wouldn't have noticed it except that I almost hit it!"

I thought to myself, *in that case you've probably noticed half of the cars in the city.*

Summer was finally on her second set of squats. Yachting,

snacking, and fine dining on the St. Clair River were adding to the size of Summer on every bodypart below her waist. Forty sets of squats would have helped to offset the swelling of her fat cells. We only had time for five sets though, and I exhorted her to focus on her workout and make every set count. She would have none of it and was determined to use the hour to elaborate about the two millionaires in her sex life. There was a yin and a yang to the whole situation and Summer was intent on making me privy to every detail as if I would be dating whichever one she didn't choose.

~~~~~~~~~~~~~~~~~~~~~~

When I was a small boy, I was drinking from a cup of milk on the back porch of my house. Lunch was proceeding along quite well until my second sip. In mid-sip I opened my eyes to find my lips touching a spider-like creature with a huge pair of wet wings—floating in my damn cup! Repulsed beyond words, and immediately traumatized, I swore off milk for a month and my favorite cup forever. In 1960 there were no counselors for victims of bug trauma and as I grew older, my phobias got worse. My saintly, fastidious mother compounded my fears by patiently explaining to me where the germs and microbes waiting to sicken me liked to lurk. In public places my name became *don't touch that* and I soon became able to assess the degree of danger in any particular bacteria riddled surface by gauging the different looks of horror on her face. At home forks, plates, glasses or straws were never to be shared among siblings or parents. Any food item that fell on the pristine kitchen floor was to be treated as hazardous waste and disposal procedures were to be implemented forthwith. Spiders, flies or bugs that breached our sterile environment died a quick death and all traces of their existence were sanitized away repeatedly until the room was again safe to enter. As a teenager, my first kiss was passionless and bereft of any concern as to whether I was doing it right. Instead, my first smooch was only the beginning of a tense waiting game. For the rest of the movie I sat on a germophobic death row, cringing as I speculated as to what type of bacteria had leaped from Molly's lips to mine. I survived the evening without contracting dengue fever or any other exotic condition. When a naïve Molly eventually offered to let me kiss her in areas below her chin, she had to be quickly discarded and replaced with someone more sanitary.

My first job as a bicycle mechanic resulted in greasy hands that could never touch a sandwich until thoroughly cleansed, and even so the "handle" of the sandwich could never be consumed. A job as a store detective was safer from a toxicity perspective, but care had to be taken if a shoplifter, reluctant to be detained, attempted to bleed on me. My disease avoidance rituals only became more fervent after I opened a car repair business. I had to deal with dirty black grease, unwashed floors and countertops, and food that became tainted the minute it hit the open air…but that only describes my first wife's kitchen. The mechanics that worked for me were even sloppier. A used car salesman that I hired to help me with the adjoining lot was so slovenly that his apartment resembled the inside of a dumpster—if it were shared by a McDonald's and an adult book store. No matter how busy I might have been with a mechanical crisis, I always abandoned my shop at lunchtime to dine out. I calculated that I would fare better at a Detroit restaurant—inspected by Health Department officers only once a year—than with lunch at my office or (God forbid) at home. I also took the precaution of adopting a personal policy that any soft drinks I consumed on the premises were never to be set down until empty or discarded. This private resolution was enacted the day I broke up a fight between two of my mechanics concerning drinking on the job. Their work bays were adjacent to each other. The mechanic in bay two caught the mechanic in bay one strolling over to sip on his Pepsi bottle one hot summer day. I was torn at the time as to which sickened me more—the shared drink or mechanic number one's hacking cough.

When I sold my business and temporarily retired to the suburbs, I bought a house with a crawl space. A plumbing problem soon developed and I traced it to somewhere under the kitchen floor. After a second plumber failed to appear, my wife Satan began to speak in a low gravelly voice about not having any water to cut her whiskey with. I slid open the outside door to the crawl space and, armed only with a flashlight, peered in. There was only a two-foot clearance between the dirt floor and the cross members that supported the floor of the house. Every spider that was indigenous to Michigan—and any surrounding states—had set up a permanent encampment in the crawl. A couple of species of Brazilian Rain Forest Tarantulas were visiting for the summer as well. The vast displays of webbing left the tangle of pipes at the far end of the space difficult to make out. As I planned the possible path that I would crawl with my tools, I observed that few spiders ventured near the floor. They were intimidated by the giant centipedes that roamed it.

    I thought about going back into the house and trying to call a third plumber, which meant I also would face down Satan. I would have to slap the whiskey tumbler out of her hand and lecture her about the dangers of alcohol. While I was committed to this righteous path, I would flatten her cigarette stockpile beneath the tires of my Cadillac—while leaning out the driver's window to admonish her about the dangers of smoking. But hiding all of the kitchen knives, unloading my guns, and sleeping with one eye open for the next six months held little appeal for me at the time, so I remained outside.

    I traipsed to my garage and selected my plumbing tools. With fresh batteries in the flashlight and a powerful spotlight, I returned to the crawl space to confront my phobias. I reasoned that people spent thousands on psychiatrists to assist them in confronting their fears, and that shock therapy could total thousands more. In minutes, I would receive all of the benefits of both…at once…for free. There was grunting, grimacing, groaning and cries for help, but I told Satan she'd have to hold it until the plumbing was fixed. It took six trips and one hour, crawling across an insect and arachnid infested no-man's land. In one fell swoop, I confronted and conquered half of my phobias. I would now be free to laugh at multi-legged insects as I smashed them with the heel of my hand. A fly on my dinner no longer meant throwing out the entire meal. I had crawled through my fears like a man and stood up a champion.

Ten years later, at the age of 36, I would begin to stare down the second half of my list of "things that gave me the willies." I was sitting at a table in a restaurant. Across from me sat a little blond angel in the form of my three-year-old daughter, Rachel. It was just the two of us and I paused in my gluttony to stare and marvel at the three-foot tall vision of perfection that God had entrusted to me. She maneuvered her chicken finger as daintily as her short, chubby digits would permit. My meal was salty and my water and Diet Coke glasses were empty. The waitress had been AWOL for some time, no doubt applying for a job at the post office where she could still ignore me but receive better benefits. My daughter pursed her perfect lips around the straw that emerged from her nearly full glass of pop. She took a tiny sip, her second of the night, and I watched a few bubbles meander up the clear tube. Perceptive beyond her years, she looked up with clear blue eyes and took in my parched plight. Speaking as clearly as a cool desert night, Rachel slid the glass toward me and said, "Want some?"

A moment of decision had arrived. Surely this cherub's body could not harbor a single germ. Bacterium lurking in the immediate vicinity were undoubtedly blinded by the glow of purity from this creature and unable to find their way inside. I could seize this opportunity as a moment for spiritual growth…as a time to demonstrate unbridled trust. I could also use the idle straw in my empty Coke glass to inhale some of her pop. But I elected not to. I refused to be labeled a coward or as a parent who would not sacrifice for his offspring. I leaned over. I sipped deeply. Rachel's rosy round cheeks glowed as she smiled. The tables had turned at last. She had taken care of her *father's* needs for a change. Unbeknownst to her, she had also assisted her father on a larger scope. This beguiling child had directed me to a path. If that path were followed to the end, I would be freed from the rulebook of rituals that I adhered to in my efforts to ward off unseen biological threats.

~~~~~~~~~~~~~~~~~~~~~~~~~~~~~

Eight years later I was well along on that path. Summer continued to itemize every detail of her two love lives. She had completed a third set of squats and had begun to explain how one clever woman could service two rich men in the same Florida city.

"So, Mark," she initiated while I began to cringe. "Remember last February when I was down in Boca with Max? Well, I was with Darren at the same time if you catch what I'm saying."

I did not want to catch anything from her.

"And they're *both* very demanding. These are two men who are used to having it their way. Well…I had plans with Max for the day but I had slept at my own place. I think one of his daughters was over the night before. Max was supposed to call in the morning as soon as he was free and it was still only ten o'clock but I hadn't heard from him yet. So my cell phone rings and it's Darren!"

I thought I saw where this was headed, but hoped that I was wrong.

"So, Mark, Darren is wondering where I was the whole day before. He said he kept calling my cell but of course I had it off and in my purse. I just told him that I was with my girlfriends and I didn't notice until this morning that my battery was dead. Mark, he insisted that I come over to his place. He would *not* take no for an answer! See, that's one of the big reasons I'm afraid to commit to him at all. He can be kind of a bully until he gets his way. I mean, Max is that way too, but he sort of badgers you into doing what he wants or just keeps questioning you and explaining his side of something until you finally give in. So I grab my cell phone off the charger and *fly* over to Darren's condo. When I get there I'm not even in the door when he grabs me and starts to maul me! I told you he's rough but Mark, he's practically *ripping* my clothes off *before* the door is closed! I know I'm supposed to see Max within an hour or so and I *don't* want to get all hot and sweaty and smell like his cologne with no time to take a shower. Worse yet, I'm worried that he's going to tear something and I didn't bring a change of clothes with me after flying over there so fast. So *I* start breathing heavy like I'm *enjoying* being raped. I tell him how much I've missed him but I *have* to leave my cell phone on because my girlfriend had a biopsy and I agreed to go with her to the doctor to go over the results."

I said to Summer, "Ah, the ol' can't have sex now because my girlfriend might have cancer excuse."

"Mark, I'm serious. I was in a bind. So anyway, I managed to get down on my knees and started to unbuckle his pants."

I really didn't want Summer to continue on at that point. I looked above her head at the studio's ceiling fan, wondering whether she might stop talking if it came loose and decapitated her.

The fan was mounted far too securely and Summer continued on.

"So we hadn't even made it to the bedroom yet and I'm unbuckling *and* reaching in at the same time. He's *very* interested by then."

I thought, *please don't tell me how interested...please...that will only lead to a description of the dimensions of his interest and I don't want to know.*

To my horror, Summer elaborated further. "I thought about taking him in my mouth right there in the middle of his living room, but just then my cell phone started ringing. Well, Mark, you *know* who that was and I was hardly in a position to reach into my purse and *answer* it!"

Summer's appointment was up and I looked desperately at the front door for my next client.

"So I stood up but I left my hand down there and kept...uh...massaging him. I started to walk him backwards to his bedroom but that damn place is so big my cell phone started to ring again before we got there. My purse was way over by the front door so at least it was fainter. Finally I get him into the master bedroom but Mark, it was so funny because his pants kept dropping until they were around his ankles so by then he could only take little baby steps backwards, and when the back of his knees hit the edge of his bed he just fell over onto the bed."

I thought that Summer might let up if I changed my look from one of mild disinterest to that of a mental patient in a catatonic state. Oblivious to my distress, she plowed on with her story.

"I climbed up on top of him and he started groping up the leg of my shorts to try to finger me but I kept moving my hips away. I had the whole thing in my mouth by now and he was going crazy…telling me to marry him and he would take care of me forever and I've got to tell you that was making me pretty wet. So then my phone starts ringing for a *third* time and I haven't even been there ten minutes yet! I don't think Darren even heard it, he was so wrapped up in me!"

I wanted to wrap Summer up myself, but I was out of fresh cement.

"…and then he just released…and he was moaning and almost bucking me off of him. I'm not going to tell you what I did with it but I knew that if I didn't get over to Max's right away that it was going to be war! Mark, I didn't have time to talk to Darren after he was finished or to hold him and there was no way I was going to stick around for him to take care of me so I just leaped off the bed and said that my phone was ringing even though it had stopped. I got to it just as it beeped to say that somebody had left a voice message. I played the message and you know who it was and boy was he pissed! I just yelled out to the back that it was my girlfriend and it was an emergency and that I'll call him as soon as I got to the doctor's office. He just laid there and I don't think he could even talk yet so I just left."

I had made it. The story had essentially been about how Summer had given oral gratification to a large hairy man in Florida while another male suitor phoned her incessantly. It was not a story that I would be retelling to my children and my children's children, but I made it to the end. With the passage of time and perhaps a closed head injury or two, I would eventually forget about what I'd heard. But suddenly, I was thrust about halfway into a Ginsu knife commercial on TV…you know…"BUT WAIT, THERE'S MORE!"

"Okay, Mark, now here's the funny part, but it's a little gross, too. I'm driving like a madwoman down the coast on A1A and I'm practically dumping out my purse on the seat looking for some gum or some mints or anything after swallowing you know what! Horns are beeping at me and I had to keep swerving back into my lane and I couldn't find anything to chew on! I'm frantic but there aren't any drugstores along that stretch and the way my cell keeps ringing, I know I don't have a second to spare anyway. So it takes me about ten minutes to get to Max's condo and he still hasn't given me a key to the outside door but the guards at the desk know me so I *fly* by them as they just wave me on. The elevator door is open and nobody else gets on with me so it goes right up to his penthouse without stopping and I'm jumping off before the doors are completely open. There were no mirrors along that whole ugly hallway to check myself so I decided to just make a run for one of the bathrooms as soon as he opened the door. Well Mark, I took a deep breath and just tapped on it and Max flung the door open, and if you could have seen the way his face lit up…he was *so* surprised! Mark, it's not like I could rush past him and say *excuse me, darling, I've got to go brush my teeth right now!* I don't even keep a toothbrush there anyway. I had no choice. I just wrapped both arms around him and gave him a big wet kiss! I told him I missed him and I would have called first but my cell phone battery died! You see Mark, I had no choice! Considering where I'd just come from and what I'd been doing, don't you think that's gross? Don't you?"

I was wrong, I thought I had made it through the story undamaged, but had not. Just recently I had drunk out of a client's Pepsi can by mistake. Not one, but two sips were ingested. I was able to easily suppress the old feelings. Three years prior I had an old 90-pound Doberman. Young Dobermans are susceptible to bouts of diarrhea. Old Dobermans are even more so. During an "episode" the dog would stagger from room to room looking for (to her credit) an open door to the yard. The cleanups were arduous but an excellent test of rehabilitative progress for a registered germophobe.

In my mind, I had officially been off of the list for some time and now considered myself to be merely "contaminant conscious." I found the last two minutes of her story to be repulsive. Most of my favorite adult films would now be verboten. Some of my most cherished dirty jokes would have to be filed away into the archives forever, lest I be reminded of this horrible tale. Most importantly, I would never kiss a woman again unless she had continuously been in my physical presence for at least 30 days.

Summer went merrily on her way with a lighthearted skip in her step after her workout/counseling session. I stayed behind to deal with the traumatic effect of her latest revelations. I hoped to never meet Darren. As for Max, there is a pop culture game out which dictates that all actors are six steps away from appearing in a movie with Kevin Bacon. For instance, Michelle Pfeiffer has never appeared in a movie with Kevin Bacon but she did star in the movie *Wolf* with Jack Nicholson. Jack Nicholson did appear with Kevin Bacon in *A Few Good Men*. Thus Michelle Pfeiffer has a "Kevin Bacon rating" of two (while Jack Nicholson has a rating of one). Knowing this, someone with a mild obsessive compulsive disorder may have difficulty looking at Michelle Pfeiffer without thinking of Kevin Bacon. I liked to think that I had as many OCDs as the next guy. I was confident that I would not be able to look my former employer Max in the lips ever again.

45

Max owned an 82-foot yacht. He (or his company, rather) had paid $3.2 million for the boat in 1997. His Azimut never failed to impress when it pulled into any port on the Great Lakes around Michigan. Its crew of two proudly wore crisp, khaki pants and Izod shirts emblazoned with the name of the boat. Motoring up to a dock was an event by itself as the captain skillfully throttled the large boat's engines and bow thrusters to ensure the most gentle arrival possible. Upon securing the lines, the crew would activate a hydraulic gangplank from deep within the ship. Impressed guests and beaming owner alike would disembark in complete safety—no matter what their state of inebriation may be at the time. The yacht and its crew wintered in Florida, waiting for a call from Max's secretary or the pilot of his private jet to indicate that their services may soon be required. On the rare occasions that Max ordered his yacht out from its berth, the destination was seldom more than a scenic four-hour trip down Florida's Intracoastal Waterway to an upscale waterfront eatery. On the rarer occasions when members of his family accompanied him, the destination may offer a little more variety such as a day spa or a unique shopping plaza.

In the world of South Florida yachts, however, an 82-foot boat is not considered to be particularly large. Entry level size is 65 feet. The law requires a licensed Sea Captain for anything bigger than 65 feet. Max had a dream. The billionaire dreamed that he would purchase a boat in the 120-foot range and staff it with a sharply dressed, respectful crew. His dream included full time employment for a European-trained gourmet chef operating out of his new yacht's galley. The chef would be available day or night to cater to every gastrointestinal whim of Max and his guests. Max's dream also revolved around a number one guest, his faithful mistress, Summer. Together they would cruise slowly up and down the Intracoastal Waterway, smiling smugly as they received ooohs, ahhhs, and accolades from impressed onlookers.

If wining and dining at dockside cafes grew tiresome, and Max and his beautiful companion became bored after viewing a thousand miles of waterfront houses and condos, the Bahamas beckoned.

In the Bahamas, clear blue waters entice scuba divers, para-sailors, jet skiers, and adventurers who merely want to explore the countryside on a moped. In addition to the aforementioned activities, miles of sandy beaches, punctuated by Tiki Bars, cry out to be walked on. But Max only swam occasionally in the indoor pool—eschewing the outdoor one—at his mansion. He thought that para-sailing involved special wind-driven boats for wheelchair users, and jet skiing looked very bumpy. The closest Max ever got to motorcycles was when they pulled up to his Mercedes at intersections, unless one included a 24-hour consideration of investing in a string of Harley Davidson dealerships. Beach walking held little allure either…unless a treadmill could be installed on the beach. Even Tiki Bars were pointless as the now teetotalling Max preferred to drink his favorite grapefruit juices from the inventory on board his yacht. There was another tiny flaw in Max's dream of traveling with his entourage of servants and concubine in a new 120-foot floating hotel. His yacht broker had to sell the old one first. Perhaps an imaginative individual can envision a hardworking citizen arriving home after battling rush hour traffic and declaring to their spouse, "Honey, I've had enough. We won't go camping this summer. I found a yacht for only three million cash!" But that individual can rest assured that this happens infrequently, hence the abundance of yachts for sale and a dearth of buyers. Huge boatyards shelter hundreds of "offered" yachts, docked nose to tail. Photo advertisements in yachting periodicals howl about the new engines and interiors of the thousands of boats throughout their pages, often culminating with the words "make offer."

As every wily South Florida yacht broker knows, prospective buyers need to fall in love with a boat the very first time they lay eyes on it, or the chances for an eventual sale are small. Max's 82-footer was reminiscent of a giant Orca, with black and white paint accentuating the sweeping lines of the yacht. It looked powerful and it was, with a top speed reputed to be in the low 40s at full throttle. Inside, the sumptuous appointments of the cabin's dark cherrywood and black oak interiors spoke of a quiet refuge on the water paralleling that of the finest hotels surrounding the Port of Monaco. The main dining table alone could seat 12 comfortably amid its settings of gold, silver, and crystal. A table on the aft deck could service another eight while full wet bars at each level supplied beverages to all.

In spite of the fact that at five years of age the Italian made yacht would soon be in need of a major maintenance update, Max's broker found a buyer. Two point six million is considered a bargain in the world of "sport yachts," but Max had grown tired of the expensive mechanical malfunctions. The unspoken fact that this magnificent boat was undersized—when compared with the amount of toy that a man worth three billion dollars could afford—was a growing concern as well. The new buyer had a demonstrated net worth of only 12 million. After a year on the market the broker had matched the boat with a buyer, pocketing a $260,000 commission in the process. Max, for his part, agreed to hold one million in paper on the boat. This meant that the new owner was only able to come up with $1.6 million in cash and that Max had agreed to finance the rest. This also meant that Max would have a GPS tracking unit secretly installed on the boat prior to the final transaction taking place. The sales contract stated the yacht was not to leave U.S.

waters until the final payment had been rendered, and it was the broker's duty to monitor its whereabouts to ensure that the agreement was abided by.

Finally Max could turn his attention to finding a new yacht more befitting to his economic status. Some day, the new owner would discover that his acquisition had a top speed of only 36 miles an hour versus the 44 advertised. That particular voyage of discovery would be costly, however, as the boat that he still made $25,000 monthly payments on guzzled diesel fuel at the rate of $500 an hour.

Max's Michigan boat was only one year old. At 58 feet in length, it was small by yacht standards, but truly a bargain at 1.2 million dollars when new. Earlier in the year, I had briefly been Max's yacht captain for this fine boat. Eager to get my hands on the helm of a 40-mile per hour luxury motoryacht with a million and a half dollar list price, I had rearranged my life. I hired additional help at my studio. I cancelled all summer vacation plans with my daughter. I arranged for additional help on board my new charge to assist in navigating, docking, and guest services. I asked Natasha to be patient…her captain would return from the sea by fall. I tutored myself from every manual that I could find about the boat and its electronics. I was well aware that this knowledge may be required within days or even hours when my impulsive boss notified me that a run was imminent. After two days in complete charge of this spectacular piece of floating machinery, I was summarily replaced.

The new captain, it was explained, would be starting with a clean slate. Max's family was not allied against the new servant, as he was not the one responsible for enabling their fickle father and grandfather to stray from their beloved mother. Summer was opposed to the hiring of the new captain, she assured me. He could be hard to locate during the morning to prepare for a spur of the moment voyage. He could be slovenly, with the culinary aftermath of a long day on the water still strewn about the cabin and deck by the onset of the next outing. Worst of all, Summer suspected that he was directionally challenged, as his estimated time of arrival at a dockside destination could miss the mark by hours.

Unfortunately, the million dollar boat did not belong to Summer, it belonged to Max, no matter which of his company accounts had covered its cost. I had handled my pink-slipping without loud protestations upon the advice of Summer. I had also tolerated my surprise dismissal without wrapping the new captain in anchor chain and bumping him over the side…which would have been frowned upon by my attorney.

After three years of tenuous employment, I only wished to return to my gym-rat roots and make my way in the world.

After several weeks of silence from Summer and Max, my healing process had been interrupted. Chaos followed Summer like financial advisors following a lottery winner. She was in the last half of a prize fight and she had just lost her trainer after he'd been thrown out of the arena. Summer wanted her trainer back in the ring with her, but didn't know how to go about it. Her story about juggling Darren and Max was her way of putting out feelers to see if a reconciliation between us was possible. But Summer knew men, and she knew that I was building a protective wall between us as quickly as I could take delivery on the bricks and mortar. Summer knew her plan needed to evolve. She called me early the next morning.

"Hi, Sweetie, it's me. Say, Max is going to be out of town for a couple of days and I was wondering if you could do me a favor?"

"Please don't ask me to kiss you."

"Oh…ha, ha…wasn't that gross? I hope I didn't ruin the rest of your day but Darren had been calling me and I was *dying* to tell somebody. Two nights ago I was at Lucy's Tavern over on Kercheval and I ran into Tishelle, you know, my friend the makeup artist? Anyway, I started to tell her but she has some sort of rash she got from this guy she's been seeing and the itching was driving her crazy. Finally she went to the ladies room and when she came back she said that there was blistering you know where and she had to leave."

What pre-qualified me to hear about all of her friend's gynecological problems I had yet to figure out.

"Anyway, thanks for listening to me yesterday. I have an idea that you might find interesting, though. Max won't be using the 58-footer for a few days while he's out of town and I thought that maybe I could ask some friends and you could ask some friends and we could take the boat out tomorrow. Or if you didn't want to bring anyone and it was just my friends I would gladly pay you for captaining for the day. I don't think that Tishelle can go but I could ask Marcie and Connie. Marcie offered to let me move into her house during the divorce, but I think part of it is because she's got the hots for me, if you know what I mean. Connie has been doing my nails for ages and she's just a riot although I think that breathing all of those chemicals every day at work is making her a little crazier every year."

Summer might have had some flaws but being a cheapskate certainly wasn't one of them. When she offered up an olive branch she presented it thoroughly and—to her way of thinking—enticingly. Although my own huge, *Miami Vice* type of offshore boat was running well, it was getting long in the tooth. I valued it at $50,000 or so…one twenty-fourth of the price tag on the boat that Summer was dangling in front of me. My hackles rose slightly as I realized how Summer was trying to win back my friendship. Offering to pay me to spend the day meandering about Lake St. Clair in a new yacht was a blatantly transparent way of getting me back in her corner to coach her during the last rounds of the prize fight. Summer obviously thought that I was lacking in pride and character and could be won over with some material gesture.

"Is Max okay with all of this?" I asked.

"Oh yes, Sweetie," she replied. "I've already talked to him this morning and he said that as far as he knows, both tanks are full and ready to go."

Part two of her peace offering was the single friends she mentioned. I thought that inviting Tishelle might add excitement to the day. We could measure the diameter of her blisters at the beginning of the voyage and re-measure at the end. This would not only indicate whether or not her prescriptions were effective, but would emphasize the danger of sharing a towel or a toilet seat with her. Marcie sounded as though she might be happier spending the day working as a women's locker room attendant. If we extended our day trip past sunset, Connie and her chemically modified personality might provide worthwhile entertainment as she howled at the moon. I decided to approach Natasha regarding her attendance as my guest. Her reply was not as enthusiastic as I had hoped.

"Why vould I vant to go with zat beech and her sheety friends?"

"So that I won't be perceived as a single male, available for an afternoon fling or worse."

"I know you don't faak any of dese vimmen…you vorry dey giff you disease."

We were in Natasha's Corvette and she was driving when I asked. The muscles in her shoulders and right arm rippled as she gripped the wheel. Her cold brown eyes narrowed to slits as we talked about my golddigger acquaintance. It was exciting to watch her blood begin to simmer. I wasn't in danger yet and I found the growing nastiness of her mood fascinating, but before the mood changed from thin ice to volatile, I fought down my intrigue and shifted course. If I didn't change my tactics forthwith, I would be driving in the morning to the yacht by myself.

"As you're aware, my relationship with Max has cooled quite a bit within the last month. I gave it everything I had for three years, but when I asked to be compensated on a regular basis, he grew very fickle."

"He ees a cheep-ass!"

"Well, yes. There are some who might see it that way, myself included, but the fact of the matter is that he has a million dollar boat that he is not using at the present time and we do not."

"I like boat you haff already Maak, ees fast and ees loud! Eet looks like big peenis!"

"Well, thank you. I like my boat very much too. But Natasha, this is a rare opportunity that anybody who loves the water, like we do, would and should jump at. Summer will have no clue where she is the instant we leave the dock. We can go anywhere we desire. The tanks hold $2000 worth of fuel and they're full. We'll go and get lost and pretend Summer isn't even there!"

"Vee stop in middle of lake and lie nude een sun like on your boat?"

"Well, uh, no. Much as I would like to do that with you on this boat, it would send the wrong message to the others. That might also be counterproductive to you accompanying me. I don't think Summer's friends are as obsessed with maintaining their physiques the way we are. If they decided to join us we might be saddled with some unpleasant memories."

"I zee." She pondered for a moment. "Seence Max get rid of you, you have been veddy nice to Natasha. Alveys spent time vith me. You feed me at nice restraants. You know vat else," she smiled coyly. "I go vith you."

My own shoulder muscles began to relax as my girlfriend consented to going as my escort. Her eyes were wide open again. She looked across at me with a last minute demand.

"But nex day you take me to range and vee shoot our gahns. Vee do not go for months, Natasha get rusty."

I smiled at her and reached over, stroking the back of her neck under her blond mane. I swore to her that we'd go to the firing range and shoot until we were completely covered in gunpowder residue.

46

On the cusp of his first workout, Martin was already talking to Benny for the third time that day. He was almost shouting. "We're not talking about what's going to happen to *anyone* on these phones. I'm at the gym now and I've got to go in, doctor's orders. I'll see you later at the office. This conversation is over."

Staking out Dr. David and his wife Jillian Campbell's Grosse Pointe Farms home had been a relatively simple matter. An estate was being offered at the bargain price of $950,000—and it was only five doors down. Martin parked his Escalade in the driveway of the vacant home and did his utmost to play the role of *successful real estate agent awaiting a prospective client.* His wait bore fruit in only an hour on the first day—but Jillian's entire route encompassed a CVS pharmacy and her parents' home on Lakeshore Drive.

Martin's second day of watching Jillian had been significantly more productive. After a brief stop at the dry cleaners, Jillian had pointed her Lexus to a destination quite familiar to Martin.

Now, getting to know her would be greatly simplified—after he joined.

Martin clicked his cell phone shut and continued his entrance into the fitness studio. It was 11 A.M. There were five people in the small studio, and all were women. He was greeted by a pleasant little brunette and for the first time since his playing days, felt out of his element in a gym. He still weighed the same as when he played ball, but now his chest seemed to be sinking down into his midsection. His shoulders were still broad, but when he glanced at the dumbell rack they didn't feel thick or strong anymore. The perky brunette introduced herself as Michelle and encouraged Martin to sit at the front desk. After a dozen pointed questions and a short spiel about how wonderful he'd feel after he left, she herded him toward a treadmill. During Martin's 20-minute walk on his treadmill, a couple of women came and went. None of them remotely resembled Jillian Campbell. After 45 minutes of energetic instruction and precision note taking, Michelle declared Martin's workout to be over. Martin checked his watch. It had gone by fast. For the first time in weeks his stress level seemed lower. At $1000 a day, staking out this gym might not be such a bad gig. Martin sat down at the front desk and signed up for two more sessions.

Since his eleven o'clock workout on Monday had resulted in nothing more than a pleasant afterglow after having paid some attention to his declining health, Martin made Wednesday's appointment for 12. Several women and two other men crossed Martin's path in that early afternoon, but Jillian never appeared. He and Benny had lurked in vehicles across the street many times in the recent past watching Summer arrive and depart from this same facility. It crossed the P.I.'s mind there was a remote possibility he would run into Summer here as well, although they hadn't tracked her to the gym in several weeks. Martin's mind stumbled ahead to the scenario of Summer and Jillian working out at the same time as the P.I. Together the two accounts paid $2000 a day, so for that hour the P.I. and his clogging arteries would be performing the tasks of two detectives.

On Friday, Martin had scheduled his workout for one o'clock. He arrived at 12:45 and was on a treadmill at 12:50 when he hit pay dirt. Jillian, with her blond hair pulled back in a ponytail, appeared at the front desk in blue spandex workout attire.

As Martin prepared to try a new tactic, he mentally recapped the week's futile efforts to catch Jillian with another man. She had chatted quite amiably with a druggist, but the man looked to have one foot in the grave and Martin couldn't envision the conversation leading to a tryst. The bag boy at the grocery store seemed to be quite taken with Jillian, and might have been in his mid-40s—thus somewhat closer in age. He spoke with a terrible lisp, however, and Jillian's responses seemed to be more out of politeness than lust.

Martin quickly introduced himself to the pleasant housewife as she hopped aboard the treadmill next to him. He wasted no time in engaging the subject in a little thought-provoking conversation. She proved to be quite easy to talk to.

It was becoming clear that Martin need only switch on the macho charm act and Jillian would be drawn to him the way they used to be in college. He might have to allow for a couple of "dates" before she spilled everything to him. The dating could not be allowed to go on too far, of course, because Martin was, after all, a married man. He resolved immediately that even if Jillian eventually threw herself at him, he would keep her at arms' length. A nagging voice reminded Martin that consummating any relationship was not an option anyway, given the frustrating diminishment of his erectile function. The same heart medications that staved off another major episode were putting a serious crimp in his sex life.

Martin shed a silent tear about his inability to perform any longer, and promised himself to get the information that the doctor requested. After he wrapped it up he could give Benny a breather for awhile. The slob from the Bronx had been working their firm's bread and butter case for months now, and they were no closer to the bonus than when they started. Their employer's growing agitation was becoming apparent in every phone conference.

The morning dawned foggy and sunless. Fortunately, by the time Natasha awoke the fog had begun to lift. By ten o'clock the last remnants of mist were burning off and we packed coolers of sugar-free soft drinks and bottled water. Although Natasha's last hopes of being released from her promise to me were disappearing as the sun assumed control of the day, she was upbeat and happy, matching my own mood. We loaded the coolers and took her Corvette to the Grosse Pointe Yacht Club. I knew the sleek new sports car, although impractical for hauling, would receive nothing more than a nod, a wink and a wave from the geriatric gate guard. My more practical cargo van, on the other hand, ran the risk of being stopped and scrutinized, as though illegal aliens were packed under the dash and hanging from the suspension. Asking for no explanation and receiving none, the guard gestured us through. The Yacht Club had an area of 40 large boat wells set aside for yachts of 65 feet and more. We slid past to a section of wells reserved for 50 footers and up. The *Old Salt VII*, illuminated by the prim and proper Grosse Pointe sunshine, lie waiting for us beneath its canvas.

We begun unzipping and loading at exactly eleven o'clock. By 11:15 A.M. the huge diesel engines rumbled to life. We finished reeling in the boat's electric shore cords by 11:25, and had all mooring lines off and wrapped by 11:29. At 11:30 we eased out of the well and glided slowly through the man-made harbor. Summer had explained that it was still her custom to be met by the boat at a nearby harbor...for the sake of discretion. There were 49,000 people in the Pointes, and I guesstimated that one-tenth had already heard of the relationship between Summer and my former boss. This led me to question whether there was any further need to be discrete, but there was speculation that one of the dockhands at the Yacht Club had not yet heard, so I cooperated. Ten minutes later, we approached the harbor shared by Colony Marine and Emerald City, docked, and waited for our guests well ahead of the noon rendezvous time. By 12:15 Natasha and I had been docked for half an hour. At 12:20 I shut off both engines. At 12:35 my cell phone rang. It was

Summer. She and her friend Connie were leaving the house and should be with us in ten minutes. Around one o'clock, Natasha began to simmer at the untimeliness of our shipmates. I was looking for ways to suppress a mutiny by 1:15 when a white Mercedes squealed around a row of parked cars and barreled toward us. The passenger side mirror survived a close brush with a lamppost, and the Mercedes angled into a parking slot opposite the boat.

A flash of sunlight glinting off of a chrome wheel cover caused another car to catch my eye. From 150 yards away it appeared to be a slowly moving Cadillac…a Sedan DeVille. It was a charcoal gray four door and it crept another 50 yards closer to us before slowly turning left toward a row of parked cars. In spite of the sun flooding the parking lot from a now cloudless sky, I could not make out any of the Cadillac's passengers. The side windows were obscured with the same adhesive film used to darken the insides of limousines. As the Caddy inched into the sole remaining open slot in the row, it became apparent that the rear window had the same treatment as well. Nothing, however, covered up the bright yellow license plate affixed above the rear bumper.

Apparently, Summer had not conjured up the mysterious Cadillac after all. The timing of this newcomer's arrival and the match to Summer's description of the car at the high school were beyond coincidence. Summer popped the rear trunk of her Mercedes with a remote and began unloading small trays of sushi. I slid behind the radar arch of the boat and stayed focused on the Cadillac. The doors stayed shut. I had no way of knowing if the engine was still running. A quick glance toward the rear of the boat found Natasha standing with her arms folded, glaring at our passengers as Summer directed Connie to a large Christian Dior bag. Seeking to diffuse a potentially hostile reception from my first mate, I began to step sideways along the deck toward her. I intended to break the ice by pointing out the location of our secret observer and then recite a recent column from "Miss Manners." Before I could clear my throat and begin, Summer and Connie were teetering along the dock well within earshot with their hands full. Natasha reached over the rail, scrupulously avoiding Summer to grab a heavily loaded Neiman Marcus shopping bag from a wobbling Connie. Setting the bag onto the deck and extending her other arm in a continuous motion, Natasha grabbed Connie's hand and hauled her easily up onto the deck. Natasha directed her new charge forward, leaving me to heave Summer and her perishables aboard. With a quick "Hi, Sweetie, sorry we're late" and a hasty air kiss, Summer found her own way forward and down below. Seconds later, Natasha reappeared by my side on deck. I slid past her to the pilot's seat and restarted both engines, rechecking the gleaming gauges once the rumbling became steady and constant.

Once again my gaze returned to the row of cars, watching for movement. I decided to alert Natasha and took a breath to speak.

"I see ze car," she said. "It ees a '92 Cadillac Sedan DeVille. I saw eet come in lot right after dat beetch. He follows her. Daht plate ees from New York, yes?"

"Uh, yeah. I think it is. How did you know what year that Caddy is?"

"Ven I was married I use to half von. Natasha *love* that car. Make me feel reech. Leather was very nice. Norman sell it von day. He use money to buy him membersheep at golf course. Daht prick buy me minivan instead. Minivan smoke out exhaust pipe." Her eyes narrowed to slits.

We continued watching the charcoal spy-Cadillac.

"Natasha," I ventured, "I always had one question about that minivan. I know the police found the shotgun on the floor of the van the day that Norman decided to …uh…check out. And I remember that his shoe was found off, and he could have used his toe to pull the trigger that way. But I remember you saying that you drove by yourself to that birthday party. If you didn't drive your van, what did you drive?"

Natasha turned to me and her eyes grew even narrower. "Norman vas sheety to Natasha. Natasha hate minivan. Don't vorry. You are nice to Natasha always. Life much better now. Natasha *never* get rid of you."

Reassured by Natasha's spontaneous outpouring of affection, my attention returned to the Cadillac once again. Before I could begin to untie the lines that bound the boat to the pilings, the driver's door of the dated luxury car swung open. As I started on a front bow line, a large man got out slowly from behind the wheel. By the time the second bow line was free, the man was strolling along a dock toward a small boat. In spite of the 80-degree heat, he was wearing a dark jacket and long, dark colored pants. The olive complexioned skin of his face was partially covered by a pair of dark sunglasses. He was carrying a paper bag in the crook of his right arm that could have contained a six-pack and a submarine sandwich from the party shoppe at the Marina's entrance. Natasha had already untied the two rear lines and our boat floated freely between the two docks, with both diesel engines rumbling at idle and the exhaust notes reverberating against the steel seawall. Firmly ensconced once again in the captain's helm chair, I eased the dual throttles forward a half-inch, and the transmissions engaged the props. With a gentle lurch, the boat squeezed out of its temporary well and into the main channel of the marina. A quick glance to my right indicated that no boat traffic would hinder our progress to the lake. A quick glance to the left...revealed a small boat of 22 feet with a white deck and a dark red hull...bobbing in the channel about 100 feet back. The boat had a little cuddy cabin in front, but it wouldn't have been anything more than a place to get out of the sun when anchored. There was no canvas to shield the driver from the sun, and the rays exposed him like a giant cockroach, his rumpled black hair sticking out from his giant head. As he stood behind the windshield of the small boat, I guessed his height at 6-feet 2-inches, with a weight of perhaps 280 or 300. His body was rapidly making the transition from burly to fat. Bringing attention to this fact was the 35mm camera that was attached to a strap around his fat neck and rested squarely atop his burgeoning paunch. I previously had contact with this type before;

they played football during high school, kept the same eating (but not exercise) habits into adulthood, and then sought to regale me with stories of their glory days. I was staring at the same man who had pulled up in the Caddy not ten minutes ago! Suddenly, I had an awakening. Perhaps it was the camera with the long lens attached to it. It might have been the thick black mustache and the shades hiding part of the swarthy, fleshy face, but my memory finally spit out a photograph. I had seen this guy before in Florida at the Boca Club! He had not been wearing the jacket, but the same camera atop his stomach back then had caused me to pass him off as an ugly tourist. Natasha's periodic glares in his direction told me that she had noticed the boat and its ponderous pilot as well.

My last sighting of "tall, dark and pit-faced" had been while he stood on a balcony that protruded from the clubhouse of the tennis facility. I had not acknowledged him then, and I made no effort to do so now. Our boat had continued its progress into the main channel, and it was time to temporarily engage only the left engine as I hit the bow thruster. The huge pleasure boat began to turn on its axis to the right, and after seven seconds it was pointed out to the lake. For two seconds, I bumped both throttles at once from neutral to forward, and we glided through the 700 feet of canal that separated us from open water. I had prepared myself for a fusillade of compliments from Natasha regarding my capable handling of our magnificent yacht, but she only drifted over to where I sat and said, "I theenk thees asshole in back of us is here to follow us, yes?"

My eyes drifted over the front seat where her fanny pack with its Smith & Wesson five-shot airweight lie. My own pouch with my .45 Beretta was tucked into a cubbyhole to my immediate right. I felt safe enough. It was broad daylight and we would not be the only two boats out on the lake. If I had any concerns at all, they were for our hefty follower's safety should Natasha perceive that he was interfering with her day. I explained about my Florida encounter and my revelation as I connected the dots between that one. Natasha agreed to ignore instead of confront, and by then I was out of the "no wake" zone and throttling up the diesels of our gleaming white yacht.

~~~~~~~~~~~~~~~~~~~~~~~~~~~~~~~

Benny belched and broke wind at the same time. The windows in the Sedan DeVille were all up, but the powerful ventilation system would take care of the aftermath in a hurry. Benny loved this car far more than the little econo-cars he had been renting earlier in the year. He had used a lull in the case a month ago to drive the ten-year-old luxury car back from New York to Michigan. The vents poured fresh, cool air into the car to replace the last clouds of methane gas coming from the driver's seat just before Benny's eyes teared. Benny was downing far too many of the onion and bologna packed party subs on this job, and his digestive system was telling him so. The party store's sign on Jefferson always drew him like a beacon, and when he walked in, the subs under the glass counter greeted him like old friends.

His 60-inch waistline was a far cry from where it had been during his days playing varsity football. Morris High had never seen such a mountain of a man move so quickly through enemy lines to crush the other team's quarterback like a bag of grapes—Benny mused—recalling an article in the school paper. He might be a step or two slower and a few sizes bigger, but all he'd been doing for the past 25 years or so was eating and sitting. He'd been in great shape by the end of the Police Academy too, but ten years of patrol and 15 more of P.I. work meant that it was time to get back to his fighting weight again. Benny would, too, as soon as this case was over. Maybe tonight for sure he'd do some pushups or something when he got back to the motel room. He'd been banking almost 300 clams a day for over six months now, following this broad around as she went from bed to boat to the back seat of a Benz—and the top floors of hotel rooms. This piece of ass got banged more often than the drums in a rock band. But Benny was putting away a nice little nest egg for himself. He couldn't know that with no health insurance he'd soon be spending it and more on the lesionous polyps growing ever larger in his lower G.I. tract. At one point Benny had watched this broad while she banged two millionaires and her ex-husband on the same day. A rumble of new gas shook Benny and came out both ends again. *Geez, these pills the doc gave me aren't doing their job any more*, he thought. He placed a fat, hairy finger on the power window button just in case, but the surging blower motor prevailed once more before things got too dicey. Benny checked his watch.

He'd just left the broad and her skinny blond girlfriend as they went inside some deli. They didn't leave the blond's house until 12 noon and he could tell by the way they were both dressed that they'd end up at the boat. The broad was predictable, but she was never alone. Benny knew they'd take a half hour at the deli and then make maybe one more stop. He already knew where she'd go to meet the boat. Benny wondered if the old guy would be on the boat waiting for her as usual, or if maybe she'd have to wait for him for a change. The little scanner in Benny's car crackled as Summer used her cell phone again but she was just telling the captain that she was coming. His voice sounded different, though…like maybe he had allergies or something. Benny had been tailing the broad long enough to know that he had at least half an hour before he had to be at the marina.

Benny pulled into the party shoppe's lot. It was a nice day and all, but if he never took that damn rented boat out again it would be okay. For one, his high school in the Bronx never did get a swimming pool and Benny didn't care much for the water. He could float if he had to but he felt stupid trying to swim more than a few feet. It embarrassed him to think that a guy who was such a strong, powerful athlete in high school couldn't swim a lick. He didn't even take his shirt off much anymore since the day the girls on the beach started laughing at the jungle of hair growing on his back. He resolved to get it waxed or something once he got back in top shape. Benny was in the party shoppe now and handed over a 50 to cover two subs, two bags of chips, and a 12 pack. The guy behind the counter slid over a dozen packets of mustard with his change. Benny scooped them into the bag and in doing so, noticed the equivalent of a whole packet dried up on the front of his shirt. There wasn't a lot of time for laundry when you were working a case undercover like this. The huge stain was too high up on the shirt to hide it by tucking it in, and his pants felt too tight to accept the shirt tails anyway. Benny shoved his change into the pocket of his jacket. Maybe when he got back to the car he'd put the camera strap around him. The camera should hide the mustard stain in case he saw any cute broads at the marina that needed his attention.

 Benny didn't want to release again in the party shoppe where the owner knew him and was grateful to get back to the car. He waited until he sat back down and then left the driver-side door open for a minute before settling back in. Maybe he'd drive over to the marina and check to see if the boat was there yet with the old man. Benny checked. The boat was in the usual spot, waiting for the broad, but today Benny got a little eye opener. The original captain, that Mark guy, was on the back deck with his knockout girlfriend waiting with him and acting like she was going too. Benny had watched her before through the wavy windows of the little gym and was getting to like looking at the tanned muscles on the tall blond dame. She looked damned good in her dark shorts and tight tank top. Benny remembered girls like that being all over him at Morris, especially when he wore his varsity jacket. He could have his pick of them again once this job was over and he had a few bucks, especially if he did a few sit-ups first. He'd choose smarter with the next one, remembering back to the last bitch that left him when the money ran out. The bonus would be nice too…if that goddamn Martin would let him earn it. Maybe Marty would like to spend the day in the hot sun, cooped up on that little rented washtub, waiting for the broad and the old man to get it on. *Sure would like to get my hands on that blond dish,* Benny thought. He'd show her why they called him "Benny the Banger" back at Morris. She was probably a wildcat but she'd meet her match when he got hold of her. Her damn boyfriend wouldn't have any say in it either, although he was looking more like an NFL linebacker than a fuckin' boat captain these days. Benny wasn't afraid of him. Back in high school he'd rip the head off of bozos like that and hand it back to them on a platter. Benny brought his camera up to his right eye, looking through the telephoto for any sign of the old man. If he was there, he was below, and there was no sign of the regular captain either…the red-haired guy. Benny shifted to train the lens on the blond dame's tanned cleavage. After this was over he might still find a chance to make her beg. Benny looked down onto the part of his lap that wasn't covered by stomach. The wrapper for the first sub lie opened and empty. *Jesus*, he thought, *I finished that one without even realizing it.* He crumpled the waxpaper and tossed it over the seat onto the back floor of the Caddy. It didn't have far to fall before it landed on top of the other garbage already piled back there. It was starting to smell. If Benny scored with one of the broads he saw lying on the boats on weekends, he'd have to clean the car out before he took her anywhere in it. Maybe Marty could cover for him one day next week if he asked one out. The only problem with that idea was if Marty had to go out in the little boat all day. He could have a heart attack out in the middle of the lake somewhere and by the time they found him he'd be stiff. Benny would just have to keep up this end of it until they got the bonus. The surveillance from the Caddy wasn't too bad…at least he had the big mason jar for when his eyes began to float. Thinking of it, he looked down on the floor on the passenger side and resolved to empty it tonight. The problem with the little surveillance boat, though, was that when Benny went down below, he couldn't fit into the crapper. That left him to hold it or hang it…over the side, that is, and hope the wind didn't blow it right back on him like yesterday. Benny's stomach rumbled but nothing came out. He started up the Caddy and swung it out into the only lane that led out of the marina. He'd wait for the broad and her skinny freckled friend somewhere out front. Maybe they would call the whole thing off rather than get this late a start. Benny, for one, wouldn't minding taking a pass on spending the whole day out on the water in that shitbucket that he used for surveillance. It would be better if he could trade places somehow with the old man and spend the afternoon doing the broad down below. Benny had let himself down there one night and it was *nice*. There was a lot of dark wood. It was a real five-star set-up, especially that big back bedroom. After he finished her, he'd make a point of asking the old man how *he* liked bobbing around like a cork in the hot sun all day.

Benny's car took him back to the front of the marina. When traffic on the main road cleared, he pulled straight across into the parking lot of a restaurant called *Waves*. He'd wait there for somebody to show up. The Waves sign marquee said that this Friday night the band was J.D. and the Racketeers. It sounded like a '50s group. Benny had seen cute broads walking into the place before. If Summer turned in early on Friday night maybe Benny would try his luck in there. He liked '50s music. He sat and watched for an hour before Summer's white Mercedes passed by. Benny wanted to take a leak without using the mason jar but didn't go into the restaurant, thinking that maybe the old man had slipped by him and they'd be leaving right away. The Caddy had been running the entire time and he dropped it into drive, waiting for a break in the traffic on Jefferson. Benny slid into the marina not 30 seconds behind the Mercedes and found a spot close to his surveillance boat. He'd finished both bags of chips and six of the beers…which went right to his bladder. He sized up the situation and decided that maybe they were getting ready to go without the old man. He grabbed the remaining sub and beers, got out of his car, and headed straight for the surveillance boat.

The little boat reeled and rocked as Benny swung one leg over the side and onto the deck. His nose was greasy and his shades slipped down. He pushed them back up on his face. The P.I. threw the paper bag and its contents on the back seat and fumbled with a fat hand for the keys in his pants. He kicked the life vest to under the passenger seat and, sticking the key in the ignition, fired up the boat's engine. It roared to life and Benny released the two poorly tied lines that held him to the dock. Shifting into reverse, he backed out quickly, smashing a piling with the side of the boat hard enough to startle another round of methane from his colon. Bearing down in reverse toward a Bayliner docked directly opposite his well, the gaseous P.I. threw the throttle from reverse to forward without a pause, and the little boat's abused transmission obediently accommodated its odorous commander with a clunk and a whine, averting a collision by millimeters. Upon rounding the corner of the feeder channel into the main channel, Benny found neutral once more and drifted, idling, while awaiting his subject's departure.

47

I CONTINUED BRINGING up the throttles until the big boat planed out. Natasha and I, after the aggravating but not unexpected delay of our trip's onset, discussed the merits of setting course for a trip around the top of Michigan to Chicago. We knew that Summer and Connie might stay below anywhere from five more minutes to several hours, depending upon what a recently opened bottle of Chardonnay instructed them to do. We imagined their surprise at finding the anticipated three-hour cruise turning into forty-eight. We assumed that the words *mutiny* and *kidnapping* would be bandied about frivolously at first, and then with increasing emphasis. The situation would naturally take a graver turn as their cell phones came out—only to be flung overboard to avoid getting a Sheriffs' Patrol or Coast Guard boat involved. We debated whether the grubby pilot in the little boat that followed far behind had enough fuel for a trip of 650 miles by water. Our plotting was interrupted when Summer and Connie came up from below, crystal wine goblets in hand, for a breath of fresh air. I slowed our pace to 25 miles an hour and set our course for one that I had followed many times during my employment with Max. I knew from experience that our estimated time of arrival would be 3:34 P.M., give or take 20 seconds. Summer and Natasha donned bikinis and formed an uneasy truce. They alternated between the rear deck's sofa and the bow's front sun pad, depending upon the position of the boat relative to the sun. Connie, her tiny bosom already sporting a pushup bikini top, sat next to me at the helm. We sat in complete shade, protected by a partial hardtop that covered the front half of the rear deck.

Years of boating and baking in the sun had given me a brown hue that was in startling contrast to the fair-skinned Connie. I guessed that after five minutes of afternoon sun she would freckle, 20 minutes would result in severe burns, and in an hour she would have blisters the size of weather balloons. I surmised Connie was well aware of her ultraviolet sensitivities and was content to sip fermented French products and chat with the captain of the ship. The chatting was one-sided at best. Over two hours I was informed she had experienced several devastating sunburns as a child that required prolonged hospitalization. The same doting parents that had left her outside—cooking for too long—had broken up when she was young because of her father's over-consumption of fermented American products. In contradiction to today's headlines, Connie was molested by a Catholic priest at least twice as a young girl. I assume the holy man later realized his mistake and moved on to his more natural prey of young *boys*. She attended college and then nursing school, where she met her future husband, the doctor, during her internship, at the age of 20. He was 40 and looking, and as soon as his divorce was final they married. Connie gave birth to a nine pound boy five months afterward and things went well enough until her car accident at the age of 35. Her closed head injury, in retrospect, altered her personality. Her rages at her husband were the sole cause, she now realized, of his flirtations with the nursing intern at his office. In the subsequent divorce, Connie got the house in Grosse Pointe Farms—mortgage free. She intended to begin a refresher course in nursing school as soon as her medications were able to get the seizures completely under control. Until then, she earned pocket money by working 15 hours a week at her friend's hair salon. Her son, now 18, informed her that his father's new wife gave birth to a full term baby girl shortly after his wedding to the intern. Connie had some regrets about that situation, but only because she had always wanted a daughter.

On the way to the boat that morning I had received a phone call. My daughter wished to attend a slumber party Friday night. She wanted me to wait until Saturday to see her. I had been a little down...until Connie's life story. Now, out on the open water in my yacht, fish leaped out of the river to smile at me. Seagulls cooed instead of screeching. The sun sparkled on the water ahead as if to mark my path. My stunning girlfriend lie on the bow of the boat in her tiny American flag bikini, turning heads and dropping jaws. I looked over at Connie's arm, surprised that an I.V. bag of liquid Prozac wasn't connected directly to a vein.

As we hove to within a half-mile of the River Crab, I signaled to Natasha for help with the lines. Connie began to detail the main points of her 18-year-old son's battle with drugs and alcohol, but I busied myself with docking maneuvers in the river's current.

There was a lack of boat traffic and wind that afternoon. At no point, for a change, was my million dollar plus craft in danger of being pitched into the rocks that guarded the entrance to the River Crab's boatwell. I backed into it on my second attempt. Natasha claimed to be very impressed as she fastened the stern lines, but I knew if I had made it on the first try she would have indicated her pride in my yachtsmanship by pinching my glutes. Pinchless, I waited until the bow lines were secure before shutting down the engines. A few mid-afternoon diners ooohed and ahhhed out of the restaurant windows while I waited for Summer and Connie to change into more suitable dining attire, so I acted as ownerlike as possible. An incoming cell phone call helped me to further the charade although it was only Marilyn, the cleaning lady at my studio, berating me for forgetting to leave her a check.

Gazing southward down the river from whence we had come, I spotted the same small red boat that had followed us out of the marina. It was slowly bearing down on a short dock that jutted out into the wide river six properties away. A real estate sign in the backyard of the property announced that it was for sale. The small boat bobbed more vigorously than we had in the light river chop, and collided energetically with the pilings that supported the dock. My rotund "shadow" scrambled to get a line around a cleat on the dock. As the small boat rolled from side to side in the wavelets, it struck the dock again and I distinctly heard words that rhymed with "duck misfit" waft up the river. On his third try my fat follower managed to secure a line. After what seemed like enough time to tie fast the Queen Elizabeth II, Admiral Nelson managed to loop a line around a listing piling. During the securing of the bow line, three hovering sea gulls and I were treated to the most vulgar display of white, hairy butt crack that any of the four of us had ever witnessed. The most sensitive of the gulls crash landed on shore and wobbled around on the beach, retching and quietly shaking its head.

Lord Nelson crawled up onto the dock, his camera banging into it lens first. The fat man waddled ponderously up the dock and into the backyard of the riverfront home. As he left my line of sight, I turned toward the steps that led below just as Summer began to emerge. She was quite chic in Versace and Vera Wang and Connie soon followed in a snappy little number from Target. My fears that the afternoon would be marred by a seizure from Connie were beginning to dissipate. I stopped trying to envision the end of an Armani sarong being shoved into Connie's mouth by her friend to prevent any tongue biting as the unlucky woman thrashed about.

Although it was my custom to order a carryout and dine aboard the yacht in these situations, I had reconciled myself to the probability that Natasha would insist we eat indoors at the "adults" table. We took a roundabout path across the docks and passed through an outdoor patio eating area replete with umbrella shaded tables before reaching the side door. For seating purposes, the side door was considered to be the front entrance and a smiling hostess nearly gangtackled us. The well-known restaurant was only ten percent full at this time of day, and a coveted window seat along the river was easily obtained. While I was able to keep a close eye on the boat from my perch, I was painfully aware I could not have the best of both worlds. A seat near the kitchen would have meant less "travel time" before the food arrived at our table, hence less likelihood for opportunistic airborne bacteria to land and breed on my selection. But the kitchen doors were far away from the coveted window seats, and I knew all three women would want a view of the river as they ate. I longingly watched the doors swing open and closed in the "back" of the restaurant…which was actually the front, as Summer and Connie stuffed crackers into their mouths.

48

Benny cursed. The last 20 years of this Private Investigator crap hadn't involved nearly as much ass-kicking as he had thought it would. All he did was follow people and take pictures or pick up the phone and do background checks. He had watched *Mannix* on TV as a kid. After that it was *Banacheck*. George Peppard was one cool guy. Tom Selleck had got into some real scrapes as *Magnum P.I.* too. Even James Garner in *Rockford Files* had the chicks hitting on him as he drove that Firebird around at breakneck speeds. Benny had found out the hard way that most of this job was just bullshit! It was just about scraping by from job to job while you were mostly asked to watch people go about living their lives.

Benny remembered when his bladder used to behave like it was the size of a basketball. He could still recall holding it for six or eight hours at a time when it looked like a subject was about to slip up. Now, it was all mason jars and extra-large Burger Prince cups, and Benny had trouble waiting even an hour before "draining the snake." When he mentioned it to Martin, the only advice he got back was to have his "prostrate" checked. Benny didn't survive and conquer the football wars of the South Bronx only to have some homo doctor stickin' fingers up his ass. He already looked down sometimes and saw blood in the crapper after he was finished…he didn't need some guy with a piece of paper hanging on the wall making things worse!

Benny knew right where the two boats would end up as soon as the musclehead captain turned to the left with the broads. The P.I. wished he could have just taken the Caddy and ridden in comfort. He'd followed the boat to this joint a dozen times before behind Summer and the old man. Sometimes the old guy would stand up for a minute and look back over their wake toward Benny in the surveillance boat. The detective always wondered at that point whether he knew he was being tailed and acted extra cautious. But the old man wasn't on board this afternoon. It was just that jerk-off captain and those three broads. Benny hoped it'd just be a matter of time before they anchored and started screwing around. He'd get photo ops for sure then. It'd be nice if they brought the whole damn orgy out onto the back deck where Benny could snap enough pictures to confront Summer with while he enjoyed watching the tall blond get down at the same time. On second thought, if Benny were on board the first thing he'd do is kick the musclehead overboard and get the foursome going himself. He'd had enough of this watching and never participating crap. Once he had the blond and the brunette screaming and thrashing he'd come up with a task for the redhead too. Only after he was finished would he lay it on the line with Summer and collect on the bonus. 'Course, there was always a good chance that one of the broads would have liked what she got that day enough to hook up with him for something a little more permanent. Benny finished the last beer and threw it down below with the others. There had to be a couple hundred empties down there by now—mixed in with the sub wrappers and empty bags that kept them from rolling around much. It was getting pretty rank down there, and he knew he'd have to get some dock service or somebody to take care of it soon.

Benny cursed himself again for not just taking a chance and riding up in the Cadillac as the yacht began to veer toward its usual destination. Docking this tub was a bitch and Benny especially dreaded the climb up the hill to the main road. It looked like a docking was coming up, though, and Benny reached inside his jacket to check for the Glock pistol in the shoulder holster. He still had the one that took the older 14-round clip and it felt heavy when the strap cut into his flesh. In his profession though, you never knew when you'd come across a crowd of bad actors and he felt good having the extra bullets to take care of business.

Benny waited until the yacht was docked before he pointed his own craft toward the vacant property and its unused dock. He nearly overshot but the dock slowed the boat down in a hurry. As his second attempt to tie a line failed, Benny cursed loudly. Maybe it was the heat or maybe it was the beers, but Benny was feeling more nauseous every time he tried to hook up here. He hated making this trip every other day and he resented this boat. He didn't like the way Summer ran her life, he didn't like the musclehead driving the boat today, he had gas again—and he was getting pissed off.

After Benny finished securing the boat he scrambled up onto the dock. The boat bobbed up a little higher without the well-fed P.I. on board. As Benny reached the land side of the dock, a bundle of gray and white feathers on the beach caught his eye. A seagull was staggering around in circles as though drunk or sick. Benny considered putting it out of its misery with a bullet, thought better of it, and tackled the hill to the main road instead. After negotiating the 200-foot hill and crossing the six front yards that lay between the house and the restaurant, Benny was sweating like O.J Simpson at a knife show. He was pissed off and he was tired of hanging around near the restaurant's parking lot while everybody ate and had a good old time. He decided *screw Martin and his chicken shit professional attitude*. This situation was starting to call out for some sort of action to be taken. The subs and chips were long gone. Benny didn't sign on for this case only to starve to death. Today he'd eat outside on the patio, and if Summer saw him there she couldn't do a goddam thing about it. His P.I. identification was in order and his gun permit was current. From past experience, he knew dinner could take an hour or it could take four. He'd sit outside and make sure any good looking broads got from the parking lot to the main door okay. Only one other couple sat in the 15-table patio area. Benny picked a spot in the middle and signaled to the waitress. She scribbled frantically as the P.I. ordered from the bar and followed up with two appetizers and an entrée from the menu.

~~~~~~~~~~~~~~~~~~~~

Natasha was making a valiant effort to socialize, but did not get her eyebrows waxed twice a month—and thus could not comment on the absolute artistry that was required. I watched Connie begin a seizure, then realized my mistake when the only fly in the entire restaurant flew out of her right ear. The salads and appetizers were excellent, but as the conversation turned to the top three manicurists in the Pointes, I felt it was time to check on the boat.

"I'll go vith you," said Natasha hastily. In a moment of pity, I didn't argue. We excused ourselves from our tablemates and bee-lined to the main door. Natasha exited first and hung a quick right to where the yacht was docked. As I pivoted to follow her, a seated figure caught my attention. Up close, the patio patron looked like a cross between the enforcer in a low budget Mafia movie and a spokesmodel for *Cardiac Arrest Monthly Magazine*. Lobster bisque soup dribbled among the dark two-day stubble on his chin as it sought to join a yellow stain that was partially obscured by the 35mm Ricoh camera resting across his potbelly. His spoon had ceased its travel halfway to his open mouth, and in spite of a pair of outdated dark shades it was obvious that he was staring at Natasha. The tight muscles of her glutes were contracting rhythmically as she trekked downhill on the slanted dock and Secret Agent Slob sat motionless as he ogled. I changed my course and readied some unkind words for Charley's Riverfront Crab's outdoor dining guest. Snapped out of his reverie by a waitress depositing another load onto his tabletop, the sloppy sleuth noticed my approach. Cocking his head toward Natasha and back, he broke into a rotten toothed grin and, setting down his spoon, grabbed his crotch area with an obscene motion. With his left hand he pulled back the crumpled left lapel of his dark jacket, revealing the handle of a gun hanging in its shoulder holster. Still smiling, he pointed back and forth, first to the gun and then to me. I slowed my pace and glanced around. One other table was occupied. Two waitresses chatted ten feet away. The sun had reached its zenith and flooded the patio with brilliant light. My own .45 Beretta hung on my hip in an innocuous fanny pack with the safety off—only two swift motions away. He wouldn't pull his gun before I got there. I wanted to spoil his meal and his ability to chew the next 20 meals, but I had reservations about any offensive actions in broad daylight. I had concerns about the four witnesses too. Four witnesses might get the story straight when law enforcement officials got to the scene. I could go with one witness…perhaps two, but *certainly* not four. Frustrated, I veered around a table and back to the docks. A loud guffaw reached my ears from behind me.

 I used to moonlight as a guest relations engineer at a drinking establishment on busy Friday nights. I specialized in patron entry management (at peak times I made them wait in line) and crisis intervention. I witnessed some arguments that ended with a drunken macho man flailing his arms and yelling, "Lemme at 'im!" while being restrained by his 90-pound wife.

 My fat antagonist's bravery knew no bounds in front of the four witnesses. But they wouldn't always be present. I would wait. I got to the yacht and Natasha sensed my anger. As I explained my non-confrontation, I stared ahead at the little red boat tugging on its lines. I ceased venting and asked Natasha to go back to the table in five minutes and cover for me. She smiled and nodded. I wouldn't have to wait. I could fire the first salvo soon. Working my way back on the dock to the seawall in front of the restaurant, I pretended to diligently check a boat line. But after my inspection, I continued to walk along the seawall and the front of the restaurant—away from the boat. Upon reaching the opposite end, I turned the corner and sprinted along the side, heading up the hill to the main road. At the main road, I kept the pace below a sprint to establish a "health nut out for a jog" scenario. The property's "for sale" sign came up quickly and I raced up the driveway into the backyard. Scrambling down the slight decline, my feet hit the dock seconds later and I slowed to a "concerned boater checking on his pride and joy" pace. A quick peek in the cuddy cabin revealed no one amid the heaps of garbage on the tiny floor. I moved straight to the engine compartment in the rear and heaved on the diminutive sunpad until I could determine how to open the hatch. It was up and propped in moments and without looking around I crawled down into the small engine bay. The engine, a 454 Crusader, filled much of the compartment and I fought to stay focused while I wedged myself around an exhaust manifold and deeper into the hold. Expelling air from my lungs to buy more wiggle room, I plunged my left hand toward the bottom of the hull and the twin bilge pumps. I traced wiring with my fingertips until I was sure. Grasping hard, I pulled forcefully. The insulated wiring resisted and cut into the fleshy part of my fingers, but I gritted my teeth and pulled even harder. The wires gave way with a jerk, but my arm was too confined by some thick water hoses to slam back into anything. I wiggled my arm out and checked my work. Both bilge pumps had at least one wire pulled out. Retreating from my claustrophobic position with great effort, I partially straightened up and opened the outer zipper on my fanny pack. Next to a spare gun magazine for the Beretta lie my Leatherman Wave® multi-purpose tool. Its ingenious design boasted of everything from razor sharp knives to pliers to a nail file in a stainless steel folding tool set. I was only interested in a knife blade. Choosing quickly, I unfolded one with a point and plunged it into the top coolant hose of the engine. Working the blade around easily, I removed a quarter-sized chunk. Now, when the engine was running, water would still flow through the block, heads and exhaust to cool them. But lots more water would gush out of the new hole and into the bilge, only to be allowed to accumulate there by the disabled bilge pumps. I did some math. A gallon of water weighs eight pounds. I didn't think that two gallons per minute would be an unreasonable amount to expect from the breach in the coolant hose. Sixteen pounds of new ballast per minute should start to make a difference in a mile or two. An experienced boater would soon notice a sluggish ride from his craft. An inexperienced boater would be oblivious until the steadily rising water level in his bilge shorted out the ignition wires and stalled the engine.

The question that was begging to be answered, of course, was how severely I wished to test the Obese One's level of experience. His leering grin flashed into my memory as he pantomimed his intentions for my girlfriend. Frame two popped up next as I recalled the butt of his gun and his greasy finger alternately pointed to the Glock and my chest. A black anger welled up inside of me. His apparent obscene intentions for Natasha might have been nothing more than bluster mixed with wishful thinking. His indication of his eagerness to shoot me in the chest would be interpreted by many as a death threat. Combined, the two could not be overlooked or ignored. Involving the police would result in nothing more than I said, he said. Perhaps it was all nothing more than a misunderstanding. It would nevertheless have to be cleared up at the earliest possible opportunity. This evening would be convenient for me. A yacht in the middle of a lake would be the ideal location. With a little luck Summer and Connie would be below exchanging the names of their Astrologists.

Unfortunately, my desire for a meeting meant that merely disabling the little pursuit craft would no longer suffice. The plastic output hose of the starboard bilge pump led to an outlet port in the side of the small boat's hull. The port was only four inches above the boat's waterline, and probably less with old two-ton aboard. I grabbed the plastic hose with my left hand. I slashed it wide open with the blade in my right. Now it was no longer vandalism in order to make a statement. It had attained the status of sabotage. And it was sabotage with a purpose. I tucked away the knife blade back into the steel handle and returned the whole tool to my nylon fanny pack. After closing the hatch, I hopped back onto the dock and walked to the end as though I had forgotten to bring the potato chips. Halfway up the hill I picked up the pace, and by the time the main road came up I broke into a brisk run. Thirty seconds later I reached the restaurant property, and thirty seconds after that slowed it to a nonchalant walk on the dock. The pudgy hands of my newest nemesis were wrist-deep in his breadbasket as I strolled back up the ramp and through the patio area. I ignored his hasty attempts to re-establish eye contact for Act II of Pantomime Theater.

The entrées were just arriving. As was typical, Natasha's dinner *looked* better than mine, but my whitefish was bone free and had been removed from the pan at exactly the right moment. Summer and Connie turned the conversation to their teenage sons…both seniors at Grosse Pointe South. They railed at the unfairness of a system that labels a student as an Attention Deficit Disordered, non-conforming, dope-smoking slacker and then places him in classes that fail to challenge him academically. I participated minimally in the conversation and Natasha said even less. Two more hours and four plates of Tiramisu later, Summer and Connie polished off their second bottle of wine. When the bill was presented, Summer's reflexes were still surprisingly sharp as she snatched it from the tray. I protested half-heartedly but Summer's charge card whirled from her wallet in a quick, well practiced motion. She would not allow her tablemates to contribute toward the tip either, and after another half-hour Natasha pointed out that the daylight outside was beginning to fade.

The four of us began to wander out to the docks, with Natasha leading the way, followed by Summer and then Connie. I brought up the rear and looked into the now illuminated patio area to see if the corpulent thespian had anything else to add before we met again. He was still seated at the same table but, although he saw us, was too engrossed in his cellular phone call for an encore performance. I have never been one for different varieties of macho posturing, and I am usually loathe to prepare my enemies by telegraphing my intentions, but I could not resist an ideal opportunity. I was just outside of the patio area and still felt the pair of puffy eyes boring into me. Spinning around on my heel, I pointed for a moment to the overweight watcher. After I was sure he saw me point, I broke into a swimming motion…specifically a crawl stroke. His conversation ceased momentarily and he stared at me as though I had grown antlers. A waitress noticed my theatrics and smiled but I continued by holding up just two fingers on my right hand and then pointing to my own chest. Confused and mouth agape, he continued to stare. When I was sure that my last two motions had registered, I spun around again and caught up with the group. Five minutes later, the yacht's engines rumbled to life as Natasha untied one line after another. Pulling out of the boat well was considerably easier than backing in. We were soon back out into the river with smiles and waves to the several impressed restaurant patrons that interrupted their meals to walk down and see us off.

Benny would have liked it better if he could have spent the evening eating at a table in the restaurant's bar. The way the bar was situated, though, meant that he couldn't see who came and went out of the main door. He definitely couldn't see the boat from there, and he didn't want to miss any photo ops in case the old man showed up after all.

When Benny was on his second bowl of soup, the musclehead's hot blond girlfriend came outside unexpectedly and turned toward the boat before Benny even had time for a howdoyado. She was pretending to ignore him but that's what these dames were taught to do even when they obviously needed a good shtoopin'. Three seconds later the musclehead came out too. He spotted Benny right away. The P.I. took advantage of the eye contact to give the dumbass a good idea of how he intended to take care of business once he got with her. Proving that he was even dumber than he looked, the musclehead changed direction and started walking around the tables toward the P.I. The jerk-off was bigger than he looked on the boat. Benny would have wiped the floor with this guy anyway if he tried to start something, but the lobster bisque was better than anything Benny had eaten in a week. When the guy took two more steps, Benny, quick as a wink, pulled open the side of his jacket and showed the big pussy where he was going to plant the first two rounds. That stopped the chicken-shit right in his tracks and after a minute of thinking about his death the coward turned tail and ran down the docks to cry to his girlfriend. These guys were all the same. They acted like big shit in front of their women, but when a real man stood up to them they started shaking and then ran and hid. The muscleheaded pussy had probably never seen or held a gun before and didn't know how to handle it. A lot of people were like that though. They got together to form anti-gun groups and piss and moan about the people that knew their way around 'em. That ball-less wonder running away down the dock was probably their leader and Benny couldn't wait to smack him around, gun or no gun, next time they ran into each other.

The chow was great at this place and Benny, between cell calls to Martin and hitting on the waitress, had no problem killing a few hours. The little hottie was just starting to warm up to him when the passengers on the yacht started to file out. Summer was talking a mile a minute and clueless as to how soon the burly P.I. was going to enter her life. Maybe when these two rich guys found out about each other and dumped the little tramp it would be Benny's turn for a little action before she found another Sugar Daddy. But Benny wasn't gonna pay her ticket no matter *what* she was like under the sheets. She would have to find some other chumps once this situation went south. The tall blond and the chicken-shit musclehead weren't even looking at Benny as they came out, as if he was invisible behind his cell phone. The musclehead pussy just kept looking down, pretending to watch where he stepped, until he got to the beginning of the docks…then he did something weird. While Benny tried to convince Martin that tonight was the night to rattle Summer's cage, the musclehead turned around all of a sudden and pointed right at Benny. Then without saying a word, the moron makes like he's swimming through the air. To finish making an ass of himself, he holds up two fingers in his right hand and points to himself with his left. Maybe the wimp went nuts with embarrassment over being called out and backing down earlier. Maybe he busted a nut lifting weights yesterday and shouldn't have mixed painkillers and booze at dinner. If Benny caught the guy alone back at the marina tonight he'd be sure to ask him what the pointing was supposed to be all about in between smacks. The best that Benny could figure, the faggot wanted to go swimming with him. Maybe the weightlifting sissy swung both ways, but he'd find out the hard way that only women tasted Benny's manhood…homos tasted his knuckles!

The break was over and it was time for the experienced P.I. to get back on the job. The waitress didn't say yes when he asked her out, but she didn't say no either. She'd hopped over pretty quick whenever he whistled for her and hustled back to the kitchen pretty good for everything he asked for. He'd get a yes out of her next time, which could be tomorrow. Her smile when she gave him the bill and asked him to come again soon told him everything he needed to know. He paid his bill in cash and left her the full ten percent tip. She was maybe 20 pounds too heavy, but Benny would get her to lay off the fries or something once she started to get serious about him.

By the time the investigator got back down to the red boat, the yacht's engines were warmed up and the lines were off. Benny watched it pull out as he untied the ropes from his private dock. The little boat's engine fired up long after the yacht reached the middle of the river, but Benny didn't care. They never went very fast at night and they always took the same way back to the marina, although Benny wasn't sure if there *was* another way. It was getting dark fast, but following them at night was easy. He could see the running lights from a mile away and they usually had the cabin lights blazing with the main door wide open. Tonight he'd play with their heads by keeping the lights on his own boat off. The musclehead wouldn't have any clue where the P.I. was until he popped the boat back into its spot at the marina, ready to kick ass and take names. The little boat clunked into reverse and Benny gunned it into the river lazily, backing it up for 100 yards before bothering to find forward and spin it around. With a roar he took off for the now distant lights of the yacht, shoving the throttle all the way forward to see how fast he could hit 45 and catch up.

This asshole was going a lot faster than the red-headed captain did at night and it took a couple miles before the little boat started to get close. Benny zigzagged in the yacht's wake and checked his cell phone to see if he'd entered the five mile stretch where he could get a signal. He had, but instead of making some calls he decided to play with the musclehead's mind by flicking his running lights on while he zigged and off while he zagged. Benny wondered if the guy was freaking out when the boat jumped his wake and disappeared on the left only to reappear on the right. Three more miles went by and the game was starting to get old. A small fishing boat was crossing Benny's path and the idiot didn't even change course until Benny flicked his lights on again. It was getting dark and Benny looked down at his fuel gauge now that it was lit up. It said half a tank but when he looked over to the middle of the dash the speedometer was acting goofy. Benny still had the throttle wide open but instead of saying 45 miles per hour the speedo said 40. *It was probably that jumping back and forth that threw it off*, Benny thought. *The yacht's lights seem a little farther away but that could just be I took longer in going from one side of the river to the other.* Benny straightened out his course and decided to bear down on the yacht until he could see the whites of the musclehead's eyes. He checked his speed again. The lying son-of-a-bitch speedometer claimed he was down to 38. Before he went out tomorrow, he'd have the numbnuts guy he rented this tub from put in a brand new speedo at his own expense, and do it yesterday! At least Benny seemed to be gaining a little on the yacht. Too late, he thought back to how he ought to have used the can one more time in the restaurant before he shoved off. He checked the speedo again. It said 35 miles per hour. Benny thought, *Jesus Christ, if the speedo is breaking down this fast you've got to wonder how accurate the goddam gas gauge is right now!* Benny considered looking for a place to pull over along the edge of the wide river. A look at his cell phone told him that he'd lost the signal again. The speedo said 30 miles an hour now and the P.I. looked ahead. He had almost caught up to the yacht! He could even see the muscle freak's silhouette in front of the big boat's instrument lights. He couldn't make out the blond dame though. She might be down below changing into something see-through—something that the burly P.I. would have fun ripping off of her. The speedo said 28. The engine sounded funny, more like it was starving for gas. *Screw this boat,* Benny thought, *I'll head for shore, tie it up somewhere and call a cab. In the morning I'll call the owner, tell him where I left it, and tell him that it's his problem, not mine.*

The little boat had closed the gap between itself and the big boat to 200 yards. There was no wake coming from the yacht anymore. In fact, the yacht had stopped moving altogether. As if following the example set by the large boat, the small boat settled down into the water as well. The engine had stalled. The boat glided for 100 feet more toward the yacht, but then ceased all forward progress. An eerie quiet was disturbed only by the quiet chugging of the yacht's diesels at idle.

Suddenly an ear-piercing wail split the quiet air. A stall alarm had gone off on the small boat's dash and was demanding its captain's attention. At the same instant, Benny noticed that his shoes were soaked. He turned off the ignition switch and clicked it on again, trying to restart the engine. It turned over once, then twice…and then it no longer responded. Benny's ankles felt wet. But he'd been in tougher scrapes than this before. The burly P.I. flicked on the light in the small cabin and rummaged around for the emergency kit. The light revealed a flashlight affixed to the inner wall of a storage compartment…and then the light went out. Benny fought down the first surge of panic, but empty beer cans and other floating garbage clustered around his legs at the knees, vying for attention and starting a second wave of the jitters. Remembering the flashlight's location, Benny snatched at its position until it dislodged. Clutching it nervously, the wide P.I. waded across the tiny cabin and rapidly squeezed himself out through the hatch—back onto the safety of the main deck. The flashlight jumped to life after his right foot slipped forward. The floor was tilting toward the rear of the craft, and Benny had to grasp onto both front seats as he eased himself toward the rear engine hatch. The life vest bumped his shin just below the knee as it floated in the back portion of the boat. Benny scooped it up and tucked it under his arm. He could feel a jet of water streaming out of one of the drainage holes in the deck. The drains normally whisked away the water from waves that crashed over the bow routing it harmlessly into the bilge, where it was pumped back out. Now water was flowing *in* from the holes, which meant something was wrong with the pumps. The boat seemed to angle back a little more sharply every minute. Benny had watched the owner open the hatch to check the oil. His hands were trembling as he pried open the engine cover to assess his situation. Hatch open, he aimed the flashlight inside. The water was churning from the right side into an engine compartment that was already full! *Jesus Christ!* Benny panicked. *I'm sinking!* The engine had disappeared underwater and the boat leaned back at an alarming rate, trying to add Benny to the flooded compartment. In desperation, the quivering P.I. floundered toward the front of the boat, now thigh deep and soaking wet as he splashed and cried out in a guttural yell.

Struggling to put on the life vest while still clutching the flashlight, the panicky P.I. soon found that the straps across the chest were not and could not be adjusted to fit a man of his girth. Water that had always looked so blue or green while he resented being forced to travel on top of it looked inky black as it bubbled up past his thighs as the boat continued to swamp.

Shaking from fear and the chill of the water, Benny suppressed a sob as he looked wildly about for help. It might have just been the wishful thinking of a desperate man and yachts don't have reverse lights, but the musclehead's yacht seemed closer than he remembered. Maybe Mark had slowed down for some reason and saw that Benny was in trouble. Maybe Mark wasn't such a bad guy after all. Benny had often sat in Fishbones' parking lot across the street to watch Summer but also noticed that Mark had a welcoming smile and a handshake for everybody else who walked in. Benny could sure use a strong hand now. It looked like the muscleman was still trying to back up. *What luck!* Benny exulted. *I don't know how much water these boats can take on without getting in trouble. Maybe there's a Styrofoam bottom or something I don't know about. Sure would be nice if Mark gets here in time and I can just grab his hand and step off!* Benny heard a muted waterfall sound as water suddenly began to pour over the side rails. He stood shivering on tiptoe, waist deep and clinging to the back of the captain's seat. Like a miniature Titanic with just one sobbing passenger, the front bow of the little boat began to point at the night sky. In two more seconds, the rear half of the boat was immersed and pulling on the rest as it sought the river bottom. In two more seconds the captain's chair—with the captain alternating between screams, cries of anguish and sobbing—reached the choppy surface as well. Benny's hands slid off the seat back and his crying ceased for a moment as he took in a mouthful of water. He expelled it in a burst as the tip of the bow silently slipped beneath the uneven surface of the river. His tears mixed with the cold water splashing cruelly into his face…but he was floating! The life vest tugged unevenly but valiantly underneath his armpits and more than offset the weight of the gun, spare ammo, and ruined cell phone. His clothes felt heavy, like they were trying to suck him down, but his bodyfat and the life vest were working in tandem to keep his bulbous head above water. Benny prayed that Mark would get to him soon. He rocked in the waves and strained to see the yacht, imagining the relief he'd feel once he got safely on board and introduced himself to his new friends. He saw a new set of running lights coming toward him. He stopped crying. *They're sending out a boat for me and it wouldn't look good to have my new friends see me cry.* He knew that the bigger boats often carried a little boat on back to get around on if they were anchored somewhere. Mark's yacht had a huge hydraulic swim platform in the rear capable of carrying a good-sized "tender" and lowering it into the water in seconds. But Benny had never seen a tender on the back of Mark's yacht…and the little boat coming at him seemed to be going way too fast! It was a big river, but Mark must know exactly where Benny had gone down. He appreciated the speedy effort, but the rescue boat was coming right at him and between the engine and the pounding of the hull was making a lot of noise and waves! The rescue boat was only about 100 feet away. There were no searchlights either, just a green light on the front. Maybe there was some trick to finding a man overboard at night. Maybe it was easier to get him in the boat when you made a lot of waves near him. Mark probably had some gadget in the boat that had Benny's exact location lit up on a screen. Mark was really close now and coming on fast…he must just be messing around because of the thing on the patio!

 The bow of the high powered fishing boat, cutting through the air at 52 miles per hour, just missed the bobbing screaming object. The rear section of the boat, however, traveling at the same rate of speed as it skimmed the surface of the water, struck Benny a glancing blow.

49

ALVIN BEAM LOVED his fishing boat. It was just one year old and the twin 100-horsepower Mercs gave the flat-bottomed boat a top speed of 65 miles an hour. Alvie, a nickname that he couldn't shake as a boy and lived with as an adult, had bought the boat brand new last year. He had purchased the boat, and the new EZ loader trailer the salesman had recommended for it, with "gratuities." Alvin, at only 40 years old, was a department head at City Hall—in a city very near to the Pointes.

The citizens who were elected to the Planning Commission and the Council were honest and thorough, but could be stubborn and particular as well. Occasionally a building contractor would apply to the Commission with a plan that might not meet their approval. The proposed building may not be surrounded by enough space for parking. A planned use may not meet all of the requirements the city's forefathers had envisioned for the parcel when first mapping out the commercial districts. Alvin was very pro-business in his director capacity, and often told the contractors so. He saw himself more as a liaison between the hardworking contractors and the red tape of City Hall. Alvin worked diligently to cut through this red tape for every businessman, and for his diligence he graciously accepted gratuities. While Alvin would *never* accept such a gratuity in person, he *would* provide the address of a "consultant" to where the envelope might be mailed. The consultant's address was in another city altogether. Alvin's girlfriend lived in this other city. Her street name was identical to that of the consultant. Even the apartment number matched up. Many of the businessmen liked to thank Alvin for his help with large gift certificates. But even more of them expressed their thanks with envelopes full of cash. The post office warns against sending cash in the mail, but Alvin and the people he helped were risk takers and ignored the warnings.

Alvin's new fishing boat had been purchased with cash from this year's grateful businessmen. The down payment on his beautiful cottage—on the St. Clair River near Marysville—had been purchased with cash that Alvin had thriftily and carefully squirreled away over nearly four years. Alvin remembered with a smile how he had been over $2,000 short two days before the closing due to escrow demands. He recalled how he and his girlfriend had hustled from store to store over the weekend, cashing in gift certificates that had been socked away for a rainy day. Alvin smirked with satisfaction at having the foresight to insist on a land contract (albeit with a huge down payment) so that his name would not appear on the tax rolls in Marysville for many years.

Alvin knew every intricacy of how properties were recorded and deeded—as well as every code and ordinance in his own "jurisdiction." Alvin was adept at using his knowledge when a business in his fiefdom violated a code or ordinance. As necessary, he would instruct his minions to fan out and cite those who scoffed at the City's rules, regulations, bylaws, or customs. The ordinance officers would howl like a clan of orangutans at the infraction—be it a cracked step, an incorrectly parked car, a missing exit sign or a barking dog. Next, Alvin ordered the writing of the dreaded warning notice, which sufficiently spurred many a criminal business owner to take corrective actions. If they did not, or could not, a ticket would be issued. The cataclysmic results of the ticket were a trip to the District Court across from the City Hall. There, the sly judge would find a way to rule for the City based on the sometimes vague law that the City wrote, and the business owner would be duly fined. Of course, the violation would still need to be remedied, or the owner would be re-ticketed and threatened with jail. A savvy business owner could wisely avoid the entire time-consuming process by forwarding a gratuity to Alvin Beam's consultant. After the gratuity was noted, the problem would go away. Alvin enjoyed his position with the City very much. He also enjoyed fishing on the Belle River at dusk as a way to unwind after a hard day of protecting citizens.

~~~~~~~~~~~~~~~~~~~~~~~~~

Alvin had left the office early that day. Traffic was light and the drive north took less than one hour. The fish took their time getting caught, though, and it was dark by the time Alvin started back. As he rushed back up the river the wind tickled his beard and the occasional errant bug slammed into his boat's windshield.

While freighters were still a common sight on the river at this time of night, pleasure yachts were not. The big white one that floated directly in his path did not appear to be moving—or preparing to do so. The wind whistling in Alvin's ears made it impossible to tell if the captain of the vessel was even running the engines, although without first consulting a freighter schedule it would be foolhardy not to. As Alvin approached he could see light through several of the main cabin's portals. This was obviously a party yacht and demanded a closer look to see if any bikini-clad women were on the back violating any local ordinances. Alvin buzzed the yacht at 52 miles per hour, knowing well that the small wake created by his 2500-pound boat would have little effect on the behemoth. Only two celebrators were on the rear deck as Alvin flashed by, and one of the shadowy figures waved to Alvin with both arms. Alvin smiled and waved back, wondering how much alcohol you had to take in to dance on the rear deck of a yacht in such an idiotic fashion. Alvin cut sharply around to the rear of the yacht and was preparing to slam his throttles forward still more when his hull hit something… hard.

During daylight hours, it would not be unusual to see a large dead fish floating down the St. Clair River. But Alvin had never seen a fish large enough to make his boat jump sideways 12 inches. A log can be impossible to see in the water at night, and if large enough, can make a small boat change course substantially upon impact. But Alvin knew that logs did not scream just prior to being struck—nor for that matter did large dead fish. Alvin yanked back quickly on the dual throttles and his boat rapidly settled down into the water. As he craned his head around to see where he had been, he spun the wheel at the helm as well. His worst fears (well, not his worst fears...no one had questioned his consulting fees yet) were realized. In the black waters, a dim light from cottages on shores reflected off of a yellow life vest floating in the water. A dark, wet mass rose several inches out of the vest.

Questions popped into Alvin's head faster than at the end of a Presidential Press Conference. Was this a party guest from the yacht? Had the yacht captain spotted someone floating in the water and begun a rescue? Had Alvie Beam interfered with that rescue? Worse still, had the outstanding public servant killed somebody? Alvin looked across to the yacht for guidance...all was still. His fishing boat was now once again upon the floating object, albeit this time at a trolling speed. There was still no motion on board the yacht—save for a flickering of the lights down below as unseen bodies shifted about. Alvin arrived at the still object in the water. It was human...or had been...and in spite of the thick black matted hair Alvin decided that it was probably a man. Alvin, feeling frightened and self-conscious, knew he had to start somewhere.

"Hallo, are you okay?" *No, he was apparently not okay*, and Alvin felt like an idiot for asking. Fear started to grip him. He needed help.

"Hallo on the white yacht! Is anybody around?" Again Alvin felt like a dolt. He knew somebody was on board. They had just exchanged waves with him two minutes ago...or were they warning him...perhaps waving him off. What he should have shouted out is,

Hallo, I might have just killed somebody when I ran my boat too near to yours. Could you come and take over this mess because I don't want the local police prying too closely into my personal life?

There was no response from the yacht. Alvin would have to go it alone for now. There were no flunkies to send out…no rules to hide behind. It was time to step up and be a man for once. Taking a deep breath and summoning his resolve, Alvin reached over the side of his boat with one arm, grabbed a shoulder strap on the life vest—and pulled. The object started to rise up out of the water…about four inches. This man had been—or hopefully still was—huge! At 140 pounds, Alvin's only chance of pulling him on board was with a construction crane! To make the situation worse, it felt as though the life vest was beginning to slip off when he tugged upwards. If he could pull forward from the front of the vest… an idea flashed through his brain. Rummaging beneath a seat, he found a spotlight. Holding it with one hand, he pointed it at the accident victim and grabbed the loose end of a line. He looped it around the strap of the vest. Now he could tow the victim to the back of the yacht and get some assistance. With luck, none of the partygoers would think to ask Alvin his name in the excitement of hauling their new guest on board. Alvin looked up to shine the spotlight on the rear deck of the yacht…but the yacht was much smaller now. Someone had been in the captain's chair and had slowly idled it down the river until only its steadiness in the water gave away its size. Alvin eyed his fishing boat's ship-to-shore radio. A mayday call would bring the Coast Guard in minutes. It would also bring a Sheriff's Patrol boat—and reporters and questions. In 15 minutes Alvin would be either a hero, a suspect, or both. A torrent of questions from the police would lead directly past the $36,000 fishing boat. Its registration would indicate that its owner's summer residence was a riverfront cottage worth ten times the boat's value. An inspection of the cottage would also reveal an S500 Mercedes Benz nestled on one side of the expansive garage.

Alvin brought the spotlight up to the area directly around the victim's mouth. Tiny water droplets glinted in the rays as the man's jagged breathing expelled them. This unfortunate situation was still only an accident, it had not yet evolved into a negligent homicide or worse. The breathing also meant that simply cutting the life vest straps, untying the rope, and continuing his return trip home was not an option. Alvin determined that the Canadian side of the river was closer. It also had more cottages with beaches. Moving his throttles forward into the trolling position, Alvin began a five-minute crossing with his charge in tow that felt like five hours. The fishing boat made a beeline for the first beach Alvin saw. Twenty feet from shore, Alvin hit the switch that pulled his engines up slowly until the propellers were barely under water. The floating man's feet touched rocks and sand long before the bottom of the boat did—after ten more feet the boat was dragging the yellow and black mass through shallow water. Alvin untied his line from the life vest and backed out into deeper water, lowering the engines and propellers back in as he went. He turned off the boat's running lights, clicked the switch that said P/A on his radio, and picked up the mike. With his other hand he sounded a blast on the little boat's air horns. Nothing happened on shore. Three more blasts produced the same results. Alvin laid into it, sounding one long blast after another until porch lights were turned on and residents began to step out. Alvin shouted into the mike, "There's a man drowning out here, he needs help!" A minute later, flashlights appeared and people headed toward the river. There were shouts, waves, and pointing as men waded past the beach to the partially floating victim. Satisfied, Alvin pushed the throttles to forward and crept away slowly at first, waiting until he was half a mile away to slam both levers forward and turn on his running lights. At 65 miles per hour, he was back at the cottage just ten minutes later.

50

The light on the river was fading fast. As both captain of the ship *and* a guest, I was enjoying the trip significantly more than I had on previous trips as captain and lackey. The near confrontation with the mysterious "slob in black" had not marred the journey. In fact, my plan to sort things out with him on my terms had added an element of anticipation to the return trip. The waning light reminded me of the past three years of knowing Max; I could still view diffused rays from the setting sun in between buildings and trees on the west bank. Occasionally, a hardy shaft of orange would escape through a low gap in the treeline to glisten off the waters for a moment. Inevitably, though, the day would fade into history, in spite of my best efforts to squeeze every bit of memories from it.

I was in no hurry to take my yacht back to the marina, particularly since this would probably be the last time. I asked Natasha to find out if the other two guests would be interested in a short trip up the Clinton River for a dockside nightcap at the Crews Inn. She came back up with an affirmative answer just as the little red boat showed up on my radar screen. Five minutes later, I had a positive visual confirmation when Natasha said, "That fat-ass follows us in hees boat."

I kept the yacht's speed up over 35 miles per hour. The faster I went, the faster my "tail" would have to go to follow me. And the faster he went, the faster his engine, and consequently his water pump, would have to rotate. I estimated that it would require at least an additional 500 pounds of river water before the boat's waterline reached the outside discharge for the starboard bilge pump. If the waterline became that high, water would start to pour into the boat—whether the engine was running or not.

Discarding any pretense of anonymity, the captain of the red boat began to intentionally jump the huge wake that my yacht threw behind it. Crossing my trail at severe angles, my not-so-subtle shadow jumped the wake with his boat on first the right side, and then the left. To further ensure that we noticed his strange actions, he turned off his running lights as he neared the left side, and kept them off until he reached the right. Although my speedometer said 35, his shenanigans began to slowly increase the gap between our two boats—as he covered a much greater distance with each change in course. At the exact moment that twilight became night, the red boat stopped jumping and zigzagging. It had dropped well behind and settled into a straight course directly in back of the yacht. After two minutes, the red boat had not made any progress as far as gaining on our position. Natasha watched while I scanned the radar. We both reached the same conclusion. Our tail was slowing down dramatically. Pulling the throttles way back, I cut our speed to seven miles an hour to allow the small boat to catch up. It never did. I shifted back still further—to idle—and our forward progress nearly halted. Our pursuer still did not demonstrate an inclination to close the gap between us. Gently, I moved the throttles to reverse. As the yacht began to slowly make progress backwards against the mild current the river offered, the running lights of the boat behind us winked out for the last time. After a minute, the hatch cover came up and a thin beam of light played about the general area of the engine compartment sporadically. Natasha, adept at giving birth to sentences with double meanings, observed, "Somebody broke hees boat."

The boat was past the point of being broken. The entire stern sat low in the water in an extremely unhealthy posture. The craft also began to turn in the current until it was gently being pushed broadside down the river. The thin beam disappeared, and a shadowy figure moved erratically about the deck. Trying to peer into the night, I imagined that the figure waved at me as if to say that *everything was under control and there was no need to approach any closer.* The little boat tilted to the rear even more severely, but reassured by the friendly wave that everything was copasetic, I returned to the helm to re-check the radar. There was a small blip at the forward edge of the screen but it was two miles off our bow and no immediate threat. A calm voice from the stern of the yacht said, "Front of boat go up in air like leetle Titanic and fat Rose jump off."

Apparently the situation behind us was less stable than I had concluded it was. I slowly continued my reverse course, mentioning to Natasha that I would like her to take the helm as we reached our soon-to-be new passenger. Mentally, I rehearsed proffering my left arm to his right as he clambered onto the swim platform—this would leave my right arm free while occupying his gun hand—and allow me to reach inside his jacket to relieve him of his weapon. Naturally, I would toss his gun onto the rear sunbed. In case the police became involved later into the night, I might need to demonstrate how my stowaway had pulled a gun on me—while I had been unarmed. Quietly, I slid the hatch to the main salon closed and latched it, wishing for Summer and Connie to remain oblivious to any evolving situations on the main deck. I rechecked the radar. The faraway blip had become a speeding boat—1000 feet in front of us! Looking up, I had an immediate visual sighting as he bore down upon us! As my finger moved to the air horns, the speeding boat changed course slightly to the east on a path that would miss our yacht by 100 feet. I held my finger above the horn switch until I could determine where his new course would take him. When he began to pass, I could easily determine that we were being buzzed by a fishing boat with only a captain aboard. The boat was powered by two substantial outboard motors and appeared fast. A center console type, it looked like a miniature ocean-going vessel and was probably packed with all of the latest electronics and live bait wells. I stepped over to the port side of the yacht and tried to wave him off, using both arms in an arcing motion. I waved like the ground controller on an airport tarmac as he tried to avert disaster. The driver of the fishing boat waved back and began to curve around in an arc that would take him behind the yacht.

The St. Clair River, like most, varies in width and depth along its entire length. According to my charts, the point at which the red boat's mishap occurred was 36 feet deep. It was 2,600 feet wide. Boats seldom cruise less than 300 feet from either shore, which leaves 2,000 feet of navigable width in that part of the waterway. My yacht, large by Michigan standards, was nevertheless only 16 feet wide. Thus, my guests and I were utilizing less than one percent of the available width of the river that night. The floating object of my search and rescue operation was at most three feet wide. He thus occupied only one-700th of the river's width. The fishing boat was about seven feet wide. There were approximately 299 *other* places on the river for him to safely pass by the floating shipwreck survivor.

The speedy fishing boat hit the guy at about 55 miles an hour. One could argue that it was a glancing blow. It could be maintained that a cushion of water had started to push the victim out of the way immediately prior to impact. A case could be made that the life vest provided some padding at first between impactor and impactee. Fate could be cited as the reason that one of the propellers didn't slice off a body part and mix five liters of high cholesterol blood with the abundant waters of the St. Clair River. I struggled to keep my eyes open, although I was wincing harder than a hypochondriac in a tuberculosis ward. The boat jumped a foot to its left. The driver's hand was on the throttle and instinct caused him to pull back immediately and coast to a stop. I pushed the yacht's throttle levers to neutral. The four engines from our boats and the tiny waves lapping at the hulls were the only sounds on the quiet river. I waited for the fishing boat's next move. If floating man wasn't dead, then he was extremely unconscious.

My new prescribed policy—toward all people who threatened to kill me and rape my girlfriend—was that they were to suffer a severe head injury. It had been my intention to achieve this in a different manner, but the end result was almost identical to the one that I had planned. The driver of the fishing boat had spun around and was idling toward floating man while shouting across the water at me as though I might be ready to engage in a dialogue. He reached floating man and brought out a spotlight. After a brief test to determine whether one man could pull a water-logged, unconscious 300-pound man into a boat unaided, he began to tie a line onto the life vest.

There was no name on the back of my new yacht as of yet. The only identifying registration numbers were on a temporary tag in a side window. They would only be readable with the Hubble Telescope. I slipped the throttles into forward. The yacht began to slip quietly away. We idled along at four to five miles an hour. The fishing boat did not seem to be aware of our disappearing act, but Natasha was.

Some of my acquaintances have hinted that Natasha was not the most gracious of hostesses. A guest at the house would suffer from cracked lips, a swollen tongue, and delirium from dehydration before Natasha would offer soda or ice water. Besides me, her closest friend was a wolf-like guard dog that lay outside her bedroom door and seldom slept. If one was in need of warmth, understanding, and sympathy, they were better off seeking out a crematorium operator. But I am by no means inferring that Natasha was *totally* incapable of sympathy. As the fishing boat shrunk to a tiny black shadow on the river, Natasha sensed my pensive mood and said, "You are sad because leetle boat get heem before you do?"

"Something like that," I answered.

"Eef he leeve, nobody know it vas you."

"That's true," I admitted.

"But you like to do it yourself, like feex car without mechanic."

"You know, I think that explains it well."

"Vat did that asshole do, make Mock so mad, make him break boat?"

I explained the encounter with the leering slob on the patio, and that I remembered him from Florida as well. I told her that I also felt as though someone had finally given him a thumbs up to injure me if I got in between him and Summer. When I described what he had proposed to me for her, my girlfriend's eyes narrowed to slits.

"That man was a peeg. Now that Natasha know thees things, she theenk you let heem off too easy."

We were interrupted by a pounding from the inside of the main cabin's door. Natasha stepped over, unlatched it, and pulled it open so that our guests could rejoin us.

Summer emerged from the abbreviated stairwell first.

"Hey you guys. Locking the door on us, huh?" Summer smiled coyly. "Were you two doing something that you didn't want us to see?"

Natasha and I tried to arrange coy smiles on our own faces. It worked. Connie staggered up the stairwell behind Summer, ricocheting off both walls as though trapped in a slow motion pinball machine. Summer spoke again, "Listen, you guys, I have no idea where we are right now." I shot Natasha my best "no shit" look and she turned away, suppressing a smile while busying herself with an empty wine goblet and two crumbled napkins.

"Anyway," Summer continued, "I would like to have Connie home by midnight if that's possible because she has a class tomorrow morning."

"It's eight o'clock and we could plan on docking within two hours if that would be acceptable," I replied. Noting that Connie had been mixing wine along with any medications that she was taking, I suppressed the urge to add *that will give your friend plenty of time for a couple of seizures on the ride home.*

51

On Monday morning Martin turned his cell phone on at 8 A.M. There were two messages on his voicemail. The first sounded ominous. It was from their employer on the golddigger case. Upon returning the call, Martin quickly learned that the man had been contacted by an investigator from the Ontario Provincial Police. His business card had survived a prolonged soaking inside the wallet of a large man found in the St. Clair River. The large man, while still alive, was comatose in the intensive care unit of Sarnia General Hospital. Martin and Benny's employer had kept his wits about him, steadfastly maintaining that he had once contacted Benny about doing routine employee background checks...and nothing more. The investigator had thanked him for his time. Their employer then made it clear to Martin that a man in his position would tolerate no more phone calls from police agencies. Harshly worded questions regarding Martin and Benny's competence were raised. Martin was made aware that the services of his firm would no longer be required. He was also reminded that their last bill, a substantial one, would remain unpaid until their employer required them for one last task. Until such time Martin was not to contact him in any manner.

Martin winced as he hung up. The next recorded message came as no surprise. A Canadian police investigator had some bad news for him...

The rest of the week went downhill from Monday morning. One hour of Monday afternoon was spent getting rebuffed by Jillian Campbell. On Tuesday, Dr. Campbell's office manager called Martin to inform him that his services were no longer required. On Wednesday, an attorney from New York called. He had been retained by Benny's mother to determine whether her uninsured son had been acting in the employ of the investigation firm at the time of his boating accident. On Thursday Martin's wife informed him that he no longer provided her with the companionship and sexual excitement that she craved, and she was sorry but his heart attack had made her realize just how short life could be. She suggested a trial separation, and she and the children would like to remain in the house if he didn't mind moving out for a time. On Friday, Martin checked himself into St. John's Hospital with severe chest pains.

52

On the day after the voyage with Summer, I arrived at my fitness studio just before noon. An hour later, the road in front of it reopened.

I had originally selected the studio's location based upon the upscale traffic I observed while using its vacant parking lot. Over two years I had built up a moderate amount of clients with workout facilities in their Grosse Pointe homes. The parking lot became a place to read and relax in between appointments. After two months it occurred to me that the building was located close enough to this wealthy community of 49,000 bodies to justify opening a Personal Training facility. I was correct. The studio opened in June of 2000. Business took off like a sequoia tree on Miracle Grow.

The road and drain construction began in April of 2001. Just as suddenly, business hit a plateau. Clients fought through mud and equipment obstacle courses in their Jaguars and Mercedes. Complete closures occurred hourly as end loaders, bulldozers, and gravel trucks blocked the road. For 17 months, ditch diggers and dozer operators relieved themselves in front of the studio. They parked their equipment across any opening or access promptly at five o'clock, not to retrieve it until days later if it rained. A small family-owned ice cream shop lie immediately to the north of my studio. Its owner and I would spend time together standing in front of our businesses, co-miserating about the length of the simple project and the suspicious lack of relief from the city that collected taxes from us. My studio had benefited from a few months of time to establish itself. But the new owner of *Family Treat* was stretched to the limits financially and was forced to quietly offer it up for sale while he struggled to remain open.

The road finally reopened in August of 2002. In September of that year, the same city that let my calls for assistance go unheeded began to demand that I begin landscaping an area that for nearly a year and a half had resembled a war zone. My attorney filed suit two weeks later. I settled in for a protracted war of motions, counter-motions, depositions and discovery demands.

In the meantime, my November birthday hit me unusually hard. I began writing a novel that covered a 20-year period that would have left a saner man on tranquilizers and Prozac. But I began writing as a catharsis instead, and by mid-December had accumulated 45 pages. Also in mid-December, Summer began to call me again.

A late November cold spell had turned the thoughts of every Michigan resident to Florida. Several hundred lunatics who permanently reside in the Upper Peninsula might take exception to the above declaration, but I would counter with a statement that my Aunt Barbara made to me about the opposite extreme. My Aunt Barbara lives in Phoenix. During a 115-degree day, this wonderful woman was able to look me straight in the eye and recite the state mantra.

"Oh, it's a dry heat," she maintained. "As long as we are done golfing by 7:30 in the morning, it's not too bad." That said, the wicker patio furniture spontaneously erupted into flames, igniting the two large rattlesnakes coiled beneath one chair. The point is that I admit the possibility of becoming acclimated to conditions that may seem hostile to an outsider. This acclimation, however, doesn't mean that one has to accept the situation.

It was 12 degrees outside on December 17th when my cell phone rang. The casual listener may not have noticed that the ringing sounded more ominous than the one preceding it. For a non-believer in horoscopes, the occult, E.S.P., and an unbiased judicial system, my spine was tingling like a pet pig in a Bob Evans restaurant.

The phone's caller I.D. confirmed it. The number was Summer's and she was reaching out from 1500 miles away.

"Hi, I'm cold and can't answer the phone right now, please leave a message," I monotoned.

"Very funny. Hi, Sweetie, long time no talk to," Summer replied. "I'm down here in Boca Raton on Max's yacht right now but I am so bored I just needed to hear a friendly voice."

"I'm sorry, my teeth were chattering. Did you say frozen or friendly?"

"Oh, I know, honey. I talked to Connie and she says that it's absolutely frigid up there."

I knew I could count on Summer to make me feel better about my situation.

"We've been affected down here a little bit, too. In the morning, when I do my powerwalking on the beach, I've had to wear a sweatshirt. The temperature has been just struggling to hit 70 by noon and I think our highs have only been 75 or 76 by mid-afternoon!"

I was at home writing and wouldn't discover the clogged furnace filter for another month. My toes were cold. I wondered how long they had to be numb before turning gangrenous and dropping off. I wondered if Summer knew that it was cloudy in Michigan and I was miserable—and would change the subject.

"It's normally around 80 even at this time of year and then we'll cloud up and get some rain for an hour. The problem is that it'll clear up right after and then with the sun it'll get real humid again!"

"Humid sounds good right now," I hinted.

"Oh, don't get me wrong, it is! Anything is better than being up there. In fact Max is up there right now. He's got business to attend to but he's made it *very* clear that he's going to skip the whole Christmas thing with the family. He says they have *not* been very understanding about what he wants and now he's *so* sorry that they all have their trust funds and feel as though they can say whatever they want. You know who has been the most supportive though? It's the one that he's had the most run-ins with."

"Larry?"

"Yes, Larry, the oldest. I think he felt very bad for his mom at first but I think that Max has been getting to him and winning him over to his side. You know that those giant stores that Larry was running have closed for good now?"

"Suburban Classics?"

"Yes, the buildings are up for sale and they're nearly empty. Max and I had a huge blowout a week ago after I told him he never thought about me. He always says that he loves me and he'll take care of me but he never does anything about it. He was getting so furious at the kids that he scheduled a meeting with his attorney about making some *major* changes to the will. He said that I'll be taken care of in it but I screamed at him and told him that I do everything on his timetable until I don't even have a life anymore. I told him that I need some assurances *now* before I find myself out on the street. I like the condo I'm in now with the ocean view and it's for sale but I don't think I can swing the $450,000 that they want for it."

"Perhaps something a little less pricey?"

"Why should I, Mark?" Apparently my question pushed a button. "Why the ---- should I have to tighten my belt just to get by when he spends money on himself like he's ----in' printing it up? I'm turning in the Mercedes and I ordered the exact same one so it's not like I'm throwing money away. I'm not even able to get to my trainer for my workouts because my life has to revolve around him 24/7! Even when my friends visit me down here I time it so that they leave soon after he flies down so as not to interfere if he wants to go somewhere. He lets them stay on the yacht and they normally love it because the staff is on board to wait on us hand and foot although we've been having some problems with them. You remember that he let Boomer and Kaycee go and he got that other couple? The new captain is fine and his wife is also a French chef with the accent and the whole nine yards but we've been having trouble with her. She's developed cancer and I don't know how serious it is but she's got to keep taking time off for doctor's appointments and chemotherapy and she's becoming *very* unreliable!"

Summer's caring and warmth came through the earpiece of my cell phone and was helping me to push the chill away…or was the opposite true and I had now contracted hypothermia from her?

"I mean, Max is still keeping her on salary even when she takes time off like that. He's not using the boat this week but my friends and I should *still* be able to expect a reasonable level of service and when she's gone like this we have to fend for ourselves. This new yacht is 105 feet. That's over 20 feet bigger than the old one and the captain is busy with mechanical stuff and lining up the cleaning services and keeping everything presentable. He doesn't have time to take over the cooking *and* make the beds *and* do the laundry."

I thought of asking Summer if she could cook, but I have also wondered what it would be like to run with the bulls in Pamplona. Spending the winter on a 105-foot yacht in Boca Raton may sound appealing to some, but apparently not to an aging golddigger. To the north lie the toney shops of Palm Beach, to the south Ft. Lauderdale and South Beach boasted of a nightlife that could be tantalizing or tawdy. But for Summer, the competition for men with obscene net worths was too fierce on Florida's Gold Coast.

~~~~~~~~~~~~~~~~~~~~~~~~

I have a friend I call Doc. Dr. Mike looks like a cross between Johnny Carson and Harrison Ford. Doc is in his early 60s, but his racing boats and Harleys have left him with a mental condition that makes him act 25. Doc's sole acknowledgement of his age is that he leases an oceanfront condo in Ft. Lauderdale every year from November until March. From there he blasts across the state on his motorcycle, lines up tennis matches with his cronies, goes too fast on the water, or finds decadent nightclubs where the dress code is leather.

Sometimes I need to get away from my own opinions and so I drive down to Ft. Lauderdale to seek out those of Doc. I call it "The World According to Doc." Hanging out with him for a week is like spending time with Rush Limbaugh, Evil Kneivel and Paris Hilton. I call him Doc mainly because I refuse to call him by his full, preferred nickname: "Anatomically Gifted One."

During a February session of "The World According to Doc" we were ensconced at a beachfront table in Ft. Lauderdale. Doc explained how it was our civic duty to be there—admiring the bikinied women as they walked or rollerbladed past. They worked hard year round to wear their skimpy, clingy outfits in public, but it would all be for naught if chivalrous men like us did not put forth the effort to ogle them.

The same session went on to expound further on the unusual number of pretty women in Florida. According to Doc, most of the young, attractive women living on Florida's east cost are transplants. Their first experience with the land of temperate winters is when they are in high school or college and travel south for spring break. Their Daytona Beach, Ft Lauderdale, South Beach, and even Key West memories are of endless beaches, endless parties, and adoring men.

Midwest winters with their snow, ice, and frostbitten extremities soon pale in comparison. Soon after their graduation from high school or college, they begin looking for a reason to move. They comb the help-wanted ads from afar. They seek out the extra room at Aunt Myrtle's Florida condo, or they beg a brother or friend for shelter until they get established. A lucky few immigrate to Florida with a job already promised, although at a fraction of the salary that its northern equivalent offers.

The job market in South Florida is very competitive due to the influx of immigrants from other countries who will accept anything *and* a disproportionate number of frugal retirees. Tourism only pays well for an elite few and the ludicrous cost of real estate near any coastline bursts many a bubble. Many of the young ladies, however, have had a savory taste of the area and the weather—and are tenacious. Cheaper living is available farther inland, but the murderous summer heat can make a northern girl's outdoor forays unbearable.

According to Doc, many of the more attractive girls learn that they can continue to experience the good life on the Gold Coast secondhand by working for escort services. The services are abundant in certain areas and are tacitly accepted by the communities as long as they adhere to written and unwritten guidelines. Most accept Visa and Mastercard and, while I had no interest whatsoever in the cost, Doc insisted on informing me that the average was $35 an hour. Of course, a 50-50 split with the "agency" was also the norm. It is thus that a well-to-do gentleman can pick up the phone and fill his own—or a leased—yacht with a bevy of beautiful young women eager to spend a day on the water. At the end of the day, when it is time for everyone to disembark, negotiations might take place between some of the young ladies and the owner or his guests. These negotiations would be for services that the agency did not advertise and was not entitled to a percentage of. Doc speculated that the average price arrived on was $200 in cash plus tip. On several occasions I have been reminded of the motto of many wealthy Florida men: *If it flies, floats, or ----s, lease it!* My spontaneous laugh whenever I heard this was nothing more than a way to disguise my disgust at the statement.

When Doc wasn't busy looking for a macho activity or an outdoor dining/female review location, he dated. Childless, and with all of his ex-wives still living back up in Michigan, Doc was free to prowl South Florida in his Mercedes—armed with certain criteria. His first requirement was that a prospect be younger than himself. On an extended motorcycle trip, every bit of storage space counted and there was seldom room left over for a walker—no matter how compactly it folded. Doc's second requirement was a degree of athleticism. A tennis game's pace can slow dramatically if a partner is forced to stop for pizza breaks, angina pain, or prosthetic limb adjustments. Doc was quite blunt about the third feature that he desired in a woman. He called it "cash flow positive," but I think that he would have been satisfied with a downgrade to merely "self-supporting." Doc's cynicism was not entirely without merit. Within weeks of saying I do, one of his previous wives had chopped off most of her hair, gained 40 pounds, stopped selling real estate and renewed her addiction to the daily soaps. Doc stepped up and assisted her oldest daughter in paying for college but drew the line at adopting her twin seven-year-olds. After a year of marriage and discovering a drawer full of love letters from her new boyfriend, he filed for divorce. She countered by demanding $100,000, health insurance for five years, and veterinary care for her dog for the rest of its life. Although Doc settled for only $23,000, his view of romance was skewed forever. Nowhere was this take on the intentions of potential dates more strongly reinforced than on Southern Florida's East Coast. Doc claims to have been attending a soiree on one occasion when he witnessed a tipsy young lady extend her hand to introduce herself and say, "Hi, my name is Diane, and just what is *your* net worth?"

~~~~~~~~~~~~~~~~~~~~~~~~~~~~

During Maxless weeks, the newly-divorced Summer had surreptitiously engaged in more than one foray into the dating world. As she combed the landscape for a new source of income, she grew frustrated. Her only dates seemed to be the leftovers or castoffs from other prowling golddiggers—or worse, men who earned *less* than $100,000 a year. Summer would initially describe a future prospect to me over the phone as being confident, sexy, or in possession of either gorgeous eyes, hair, or smile. They were snappy dressers, gregarious or witty—until they picked Summer up in their Oldsmobile Aurora or Ford Crown Victoria. Minutes later they became overweight, narcissistic, emotionally unavailable, or just plain short in stature. Summer's ventures into the world of dating in South Florida quickly taught her what most of the golddiggers already knew. She claimed the crop of single millionaires had been carefully scrutinized and well picked over. Although Summer had a slight advantage in that her divorce settlement had left her self supporting (albeit in a lifestyle that would be unacceptably frugal), she also had a distinct disadvantage. She was on the cusp of turning 40, and sooner or later the subject of age was destined to come up. Her carefully-honed ability to make a man of any age feel like he was the only man on the planet was offset as his thoughts constantly returned to guessing her age. She was acutely aware that, with a 20-year-old son away at college, she had no "baggage." But gravity, diet, and sun worship were beginning to exact a toll on the raven-haired goddess at a time when her competitors had a five to 15-year age advantage.

She began to lament the demise of her marriage that December. Two days after the first call, my cell rang again and her number appeared on the caller I.D. I answered.

"Hi, Sweetie, it's me. Sorry for calling so late but I just got back from the *worst* date! I met him at the Boca Club while I was playing in a foursome and he was pretty good. Even though he was on the other side, he gave me a tip on gripping my racket and I immediately started to attack the ball better. After the match was over we started talking and I tried to get out of him what type of business he was in—and he said he was in the jewelry business. Well, he had a cute smile but it was his dark curly hair and gorgeous blue eyes that made me keep staring. He was maybe an inch shorter than me but I figured that if he asked me out I just wouldn't wear heels. I commented on his beautiful Rolex and right away he said something about the almond shape of my eyes. I didn't tell him that I had anything done to them. He looked to be in his mid to late 30s anyway, and I wasn't ready to say anything that would give away my age. We stopped inside the main building at the little kiosk inside the atrium and we each had a scone and a latte and I found him to be very charming and he wasn't talking incessantly about himself."

I bit the inside of my right cheek to keep a comment from escaping.

"So we're done with our lattes and he's hinting around to getting together on Friday and we walk out to the valet, but I figure that I'll just wait and see what he's driving. I purposely fumble around for my ticket in my purse, knowing that if the valet gets his first then chances are they'll retrieve his car before mine. Well, it works. They get his first while he's still hinting that we should go out. Mark, the valet pulls up in a silver Mercedes S500 just like the one Max had. The car could not have been more than a year old and right then I told him that I would meet him Friday evening at this little café in Meisner Park. He was very classy and he even gave me a quick peck on the cheek when we said good-bye. So I meet him at the café but I was running a little late by maybe 20 minutes or a half hour at the most. Now Mark, I kid you not about this but the first thing I notice is that the Rolex is gone and he's wearing a Timex! So we're chatting and I decide to ask him what happened to the Rolex. Well, he sidesteps for a minute and then he says something about it being in for repairs. Well, right away that raises some flags because if he owns a jewelry company or even a chain of stores why can't he just pick out another Rolex from the case? Or, why doesn't this guy own two Rolexes or even three? So I try to pin him down on what he does and he starts sidestepping again and finally he spits it out and says that he's affiliated with the Parc chain of jewelry stores. Well, my friend Kim is a buyer for that chain for *all* of Florida so I ask him if he knows her. Mark, he turns kind of pale and says that he doesn't and I tell him that I don't see how since she's been there five years and he comes back with the fact that he only works at the one store right in Meisner Park. The subject got changed after that and I said that I'd had a long week and we said good bye and he asked if he could call me. I said sure but I gave him my home number and you know that I never answer that. Then I did something kind of sneaky. I waited until he paid the bill and got up to leave before I headed to the ladies room...but I never went in. Instead I gave him a few seconds head start and followed him out the door. I was really suspicious and I just have an intuition about some things so when he turned right, I did too. He went right past the valet stand to where he had parked in the street but Mark, get this...he wasn't driving the Mercedes anymore! He got into a Chevy Malibu and just drove off! A Chevy Malibu! I could not help but be pissed off at the way that I had been misled! Well, I keep my friend Kim's phone number on me because she said she could get me a position at Parc's Jewelry anytime so I called her as soon as I got my car. She tells me the opposite of what this guy said! She says that she knows him! Mark, he's just a sales associate at Parc's and has been for years and that's *all* he is! I told Kim where I met him and she said that the initiation may be $50,000 or $75,000 at the Boca Club right now—but years ago it was cheap and that his dad had passed away but his mom was probably still grandfathered in for some discounted yearly dues. She said that some older people just like to use the golf course there instead of the public ones. Mark, I'm thinking even the Mercedes that he was driving the day we met belonged to his mother! How much do you want to bet that he lives with his mom too?"

Suddenly, Summer had a moment of remorse over her long-winded diatribe about the perils of dating. There was a pause, during which I could feel her conjuring up a question to ask me to show that she cared. The questions were always personal and easy to answer...it was the pithy comment that always followed that required willpower to ignore.

"So Mark, what's new with you? How's it going with Natasha?"

"We are getting along famously," I answered, "now that my obligations to Max and you have subsided up here."

"Oh, I know. But remember he told me that we would be nowhere without your friendship and I know he's grateful. He said he would take care of you, you know."

"That's what I'm afraid of."

"Seriously though. You should watch out for Natasha. I think she's got a little bit of a nasty streak in her."

"I'll try and stay on her good side."

"So, Mark, what do you do all day now that we're gone? You should come down here and visit."

"I'm still writing my book. I've got 60 pages handwritten, which would be about 45 pages typeset."

It was time for the pithy comment.

"Oh, you better not be writing about me and Max! I'm afraid it will never get published anyway."

"But I am." *And it will.*

"Well good. He's treating me like shit anyway. He says he loves me and then does *nothing* to make sure that I have a future with him! He's talking about getting me some furniture, though. He says they have to have everything out of the Troy Suburban Classics store in a week or two. I told him what I wanted. I think he's got a buyer for that building."

I turned to prayer. *Please God, I don't want to help.*

God was too busy.

"Y' know, Sweetie. If you're coming down soon anyway and you wouldn't mind, maybe you could drive a truck with some of my furniture in it. I mean I'd pay for the truck unless you can use one of Max's."

"Whatever week that is I think I'm busy."

"Oh, c'mon, Sweetie, it'll be fun. I miss you. We can hang around like old times and besides, I need somebody to get me going on my workouts again. Have you driven a truck before?"

"Yes, but I usually rent a car or take my motorhome and drive down so that I have wheels when I get there."

"Oh we'll just use my car or if Max is down here you can have my car to yourself."

I preferred a Mercedes to a Cavalier by twenty to one, but Summer's enticement still fell far short.

"Look," I said, "why don't you just have Max ship it down with some of his regular delivery guys, or spend a little extra and have a regular motor carrier bring it down?"

"Oh no, honey. The seven pieces that he's talking about are too fragile for me to trust them to a regular shipping company. And if he has his guys do it they'll report back to everybody else about where they went. And they won't handle the pieces as carefully as they should because they don't know the value of them. I trust you to do it. I know you'll be careful. I'll line everything up."

I had some experiences with the truck drivers that worked for Max's company. They were the most competent, careful, and friendly roughnecks that I had ever run into. If I had to ship my Ming Vase and Faberge Egg collections to Florida, I would choose two of Max's drivers without a second thought. Of course, his drivers were also well paid. I totaled up the cost of fuel, their hourly rate at 24 hours a day, motel and food expanses, and arrived at a round trip figure of $6,500. I decided that Summer trusted me to save her thousands of dollars as well as to get her loot to Boca Raton in one piece.

As Christmas of 2002 approached I received frequent calls from a lonely and regretful Summer. One was at 11:00 P.M. on a Friday.

"Hi dear," she said with a sigh. "I don't know what I'm doing down here. I just got back from meeting a guy that my nail tech set me up with. What a loser. She said he was in the insurance business but she didn't say he was just an agent. He picked me up in a BMW at least but instead of asking what year it was I snuck a peak over at the odometer. Mark, it had like 85,000 miles on it!"

"BMWs last a long time," I pointed out.

"Yes, honey." she said condescendingly. "But that means that his car was at least four years old…maybe five! I mean, at dinner he held my chair for me and said and did all the right things but there were too many red flags. He said he was divorced and had a daughter so who knows how much he pays in child support or what his settlement arrangement was. I guess he owns a condo on a golf course but he could owe a lot on that still. I asked him a lot of questions and I admit that he was tall and good looking but the most I had him pulling down was $150,000 a year and how could he support his daughter *and* a new wife on that?"

"You're probably right," I encouraged, "That's just barely scraping by."

"Mark, you know what I mean." Now the lamentations began. "Look what I had. I should never have filed on Chuck. He was handsome. He was pulling down a sizable amount. He *adored* me, Mark, and I gave it up for what? For what? Some old man who can't see who I am…the role that I play in his life."

It had been three hours since dinner, so it was easy to keep it down as I listened.

"Mark, compared to what's out there Chuck was a catch and I blew it, I just blew it. I know he still loves me and would take me back in a minute."

Tears formed as I bit my tongue.

"But really, Mark, is that what I want? To go back to my old life? Do I want to go back and try to make it work when my heart's just not in it?"

I had heard about her ex-husband's gorgeous new girlfriend from a hairdresser who worked out at my studio. Whether Summer's heart signed on again or not, it sounded like her side of the bed back in the Pointes had already been claimed. I managed to hang up without mentioning anything to Summer. I resolved to lie low for a time and monitor my phone calls carefully to avoid her.

The next day I was driving in heavy traffic and I flipped open my ringing cell phone without checking first.

"Mark, the strangest thing just happened," Summer said.

You filled out a job application? I thought. "Tell me before I burst," I said.

"Max is supposed to fly down here this afternoon on his jet and I'm picking him up at the airport. A minute ago my phone rings and I can see that it's one of the lines from the mansion. So I answer it and I say *hi darling* and there's a long pause so I just say *hello?* Finally *she* comes on. Mark, it was Elizabeth and she says, *hello Summer, I wanted to let you know that his plane has just taken off and he should be down there with you in a few hours.* Mark, I didn't know what to say so I just said *thank you.* Do you think his wife is accepting us being together? I wonder if she'll give him a divorce. She said she would never be the one to file but maybe she's changed her mind."

I replied, "I think she just wanted to let you know that she wasn't buying any stories regarding his whereabouts for the next week or two."

"No, Mark. You're wrong. Elizabeth is starting to realize that we're going to be together no matter what and she's decided to give in as graciously as she can. After a while even the children will see that I'm *committed* to him and that I can *care* for him in his old age as well as they can! They'll see that two people can love each other in spite of a big age difference."

~~~~~~~~~~~~~~~~~~~~~~~~~~~~

When I was young I received a set of walkie-talkies for Christmas. They were bulky. They were heavy. In spite of having long, telescoping chrome antennae they only had a range of four or five houses and the reception was full of static under the best of conditions. They also used more power than an electric oven and my childhood bedroom was littered with dead 9-volt batteries. An older cousin was visiting one weekend and as the range on my favorite toy shrank to less than five feet, a dispute arose as to which of the two units had the weakest battery. After taking mine out, my cousin declared that a simple test with the tongue could be performed in seconds. If the battery was raised to the mouth and both tiny terminals were touched with the tongue at the same time, a faint bitterness meant that the battery was dead or dying. I tested my battery using this method. My battery was still good. The taste was not. It was bitter, sour and acidic all at the same time. Almost 40 years later I was experiencing the exact same taste in my mouth after Summer's declaration of love.

~~~~~~~~~~~~~~~~~~~~~~~~~~~

Max's arrival that afternoon kept Summer occupied until the first week in January. My cell phone rang furiously several times on a Monday morning while her number appeared—each time a message was left. That afternoon, on her fifth try of the day, I gave in and answered.

"Hi, Sweetie, I've been trying to reach you all day. Were you in a weak reception area? Never mind. What I needed to tell you is that they've got all of my furniture together on the loading dock and it needs to be picked up right away. I made arrangements with the truck rental people at a place not far from you. They took my credit card over the phone. All you have to do is show them a driver's license. I'm really looking forward to seeing you again, honey. You can stay at my place or on the yacht when you get here. Please, please be careful with everything. And be sure to ask if they found the last item. It's a pink chair and it's as expensive as any two of the other items."

My thoughts immediately went to the Internet. I wondered what words I had to punch in to find a clinic for the treatment of severe memory loss. Perhaps I had amnesia from a forgotten blow to the head. I did not remember agreeing to make the delivery, yet Summer sounded positive that the plans had been finalized. Clearly I needed a professional diagnosis before my condition worsened.

She continued, "Now Max has set everything up with Larry for tomorrow afternoon. You know where the Suburban Classics store is over in Troy, don't you? Larry will be there from one to five so you don't even need to call first. Let me give you the number of the truck rental right now so that you can confirm before you drive over. I am so looking forward to seeing you. Hurry down but drive carefully!"

I wrote down the number. My fingers grasped the pen as my mind fumbled around to recall the conversation I had missed. In a fog of self-doubt, I made a mental memo to call down to Fort Lauderdale to confirm that the spare bedroom at Doc's condo would be available. Upon replaying in my head the one-way conversation I just had with Summer, the name of Max's oldest son came up again. According to Summer, Larry was to meet his father's former driver/bodyguard, a man *loathed* by his mother, the other seven adult children, and twenty-five grandchildren. Upon my arrival, Larry would supervise the loading of $40,000 worth of furniture from Max's now-defunct store into a rented truck. The truck was bound for the South Florida condo of his father's mistress, an opportunist reviled by Larry's seven brothers and sisters as their godly mother suffered daily through the affair. I expected a warm reception.

53

Lawrence Lexington was in his early 50s and projected a confident, polished persona that would have aided his rise in any chosen field. Tall, handsome, and with a mane of salt and pepper hair that made him look distinguished, Larry was always dressed impeccably. His thousand-dollar suits left no doubt as to who was in charge in the executive offices of Suburban Classics, an upscale retailing chain purchased by his father's sprawling company in the 1980s.

Larry was the eldest of Max's eight offspring. Starting in his teens, he had been groomed for a top position in his father's burgeoning business—as befitted the first born. Good schools and the right MBA program qualified Larry for more than just an entry-level position in his father's company. As the heir apparent, Larry was given responsibilities—at one time or another—at every level of Max's soon-to-be chain of 50 retail stores. Purchasing, warehousing, display, shipping and finance were mastered quickly by the scion of the family business as he leapfrogged over the other managers. As Larry reached the upper echelon of the closely held corporation, he voiced his opinions and convictions ever more forcefully to his father. With his steadily growing insight about the inner workings of the statewide company, Larry increasingly reached out to touch the reins of the highly profitable enterprise. But with money steadily flowing in during weak economic times and gushing in torrents during good times, Max was not inclined to share the reins. Years away from thoughts of retirement, Max vetoed most of the changes and innovations presented by his son. Conflicts arose over advertising, the quality of the merchandise, and the recruitment of personnel. Arguments broke out about the course, direction, and public perception of a company whose name had become a household word for seven million people. Finally, Maxwell Lexington would tolerate the usurpment no longer. A venerable competing chain of three huge stores was purchased from the founding family, and the rebellious prince was banished to it to practice his modern marketing techniques in his own fiefdom. After several years, an uneasy truce began to form between Max and his firstborn. Fifteen years passed. The parent company under the father and a non-relative company president continued to flourish, making Maxwell Lexington a billionaire three times over. The business concept that proved unworkable for the founding family of Suburban Classics remained so for Larry and his youngest brother—in spite of millions spent in media advertising. At the lowest ebb, it made better business sense to dissolve the company and inflate the losses to mitigate the tax liabilities of the parent corporation. With reluctance, embarrassment, and little fanfare, the showrooms were gradually emptied and the employees laid off. Reordering stopped and the huge warehouses were emptied of their inventories.

I arrived in the rental truck promptly at one o'clock. Upon entering the small receiving door and climbing a flight of concrete steps, my eyes took a few moments to adjust to the dim light. I found a burly foreman and his wiry assistant with their feet up in the loading dock office. I stood in the doorway while they continued their conversation. I inched closer, staring down at the foreman until he coughed up a *can I help you?* After listening to my request for an audience with Larry, the foreman sent his assistant to search the cavernous complex and turned to engage me in a casual conversation.

"Pick-up?" he said.

I nodded and he smacked a fat green button on the wall.

"Back 'er in to number four."

A huge overhead door opened and daylight poured into the number four truckwell. I would have continued to follow the foreman's instructions—if a huge semi-trailer hadn't already been occupying well number four. I was beginning to understand why the company had floundered.

I hit the red button for number four and then a green button to the left of it. I had decided to forego any more instructions and back 'er up into number *three*.

Five minutes later, Larry came striding into the area in rolled-up shirtsleeves, a tie, and crisply-pressed pants. He had two additional helpers in tow and held a clipboard in his left hand. I braced myself for an opening tirade on the hurt and anguish I was causing his mother, but instead he extended his right hand and said, "Larry Lexington, I think we've met once before."

We had, and the man still oozed charisma. He also emitted the commanding presence that I remembered from two years prior.

Summer's latest plunder was fortunately grouped behind number three. Two items were boxed, two were "bubble wrapped," and two more were disassembled, with their various appendages piled high. Larry's helpers produced mountains of padded blankets and nylon webbing. The dock foreman sprang to life and in 15 minutes the three men had Summer's booty loaded and packed. During the process I tried to stay out of the way and make small talk with Larry until he was summoned to another area. A quick glance inside the truck assured me that the furniture could survive a rollover accident off of a Tennessee mountain road without a scratch. Still marveling at the class that Larry had exuded during the potentially awkward encounter, I smacked the green button for number three and drove the truck to my driveway. The next morning the temperature hovered at nine degrees as I began the trip to the Ohio border—and warmth.

After ten miles, my cell phone rang. It was Summer.

"Hi honey. Max says that Larry called and you got loaded up okay. He also said that the pink Louis Vuitton armchair never showed up and the warehouse manager is looking everywhere for it. If it shows up could you swing by again and get it?"

"I'm heading south to Ohio," I advised.

"Oh, I didn't realize that you were going to leave so early."

"It's Wednesday morning. It's 9 A.M. If you want me to drive 1500 miles to be there by Friday I need to get started," I reminded her.

"Oh, I'm sorry, Sweetie. Of course you do. It's just that one damn piece that I don't want to have to worry about. Say, can you wait and if they find it in the next half hour can you meet their driver on the road somewhere?"

The Unabomber has killed and maimed many innocent people and clearly deserves a fate worse than death. Summer had the gift of inciting people until they embrace another point of view. For a brief flicker of an instant, I experienced the psychotic anger that can drive someone to wreak such violence on a person. Visions of spending days and nights of my precious Florida vacation time idling in sub-zero temperatures at a Michigan truck stop clawed at me. I imagined Summer on one of the yacht's chaise lounges on her tummy, sunning her increasingly ample bottom while awaiting a pink armchair to place it in. I needed to put her in her place immediately!

"I would rather keep driving," I replied.

"Oh Sweetie, that's disappointing. Well, you know what? Mickey is looking for the chair and he wasn't sure if he was going to be able to locate it today anyway. Why don't you just go on. That way you'll be here on Friday and you can get some sun and eat dinner with us."

Apparently Ryder truck rental does not want their trucks tipping over on sharp turns—or speeding unnecessarily for any reason. The truck Summer had supplied me with had a governor. This meant that if the truck reached a speed that exceeded 70 miles an hour, the transmission would disengage and the truck would begin to slow. Seventy point one miles per hour quickly became 67 and then 64. Taking my foot off of the gas re-engaged the transmission and I could accelerate once again. With no cruise control available, maintaining a speed of 69 to 70 required a constant watching of the speedometer instead of the road. I abandoned that strategy after a moderate curve in the freeway caught me nudging the shoulder more than once. I managed to maintain a speed of 63 to 65, backing off slightly whenever the wind caused the sideview mirror to vibrate the driver's door. Nimble automobiles cut around me and passed like fighter jets around the Goodyear Blimp. Huge tractor trailers barreled down onto my rear bumper before pulling over to pass, rocking and bouncing my truck from lane to lane in the strong winds created by their wake.

Southern Ohio brought temperatures in the high 20s, Kentucky felt like the mid-30s, and northern Tennessee hit 40 degrees before nightfall but then began to drop. Checking back to the studio from the hills and valleys of Tennessee was a challenge. After goading my mechanically restrained ride up an impossibly long grade, I would check my phone for a signal. Anything over "one bar" meant a short window in which to call to my business. While January is normally a resolution-filled busy month in the fitness business, construction equipment had continued to block the roads and driveways that led to my studio. My manager Michelle assured me that business had flat-lined and I was wise to supplement my income with the truck-driving gig to sunny Florida. I thanked her and was punching in my attorney's phone number when the truck rolled slowly into a valley and my signal disappeared. I waited patiently until the road began to incline. My truck charged up the hill like a herd of turtles and several minutes later I had a signal. A rusty pick-up with one headlight, no muffler, and only two cylinders firing surged past me. The three good ol' boys in the front seat leered up at me and were showing me all 17 of their teeth when my cell phone sprang back to life. It was Summer.

"Hi, darling, are you in Florida yet?"

"Not yet. I'm only 750 miles away from Boca though."

"Oh honey, why is it taking so long? Max and I want you to join us for dinner by six. We've been eating early lately and then getting to bed early so that we can play tennis first thing in the morning."

"Summer, there's a couple of glaciers in Alaska that move faster than this truck." *And I would like to send you there to verify that I am correct.*

"Well, I sure appreciate you doing this, Sweetie. I've called up to Michigan once and so has Max and they still haven't located that armchair so it's a good thing that you left when you did."

I wondered how much Max appreciated me driving his furniture down. I had already learned that the more he appreciated something, the less it paid. If he just "appreciated" something, I could expect some meager compensation for my time and efforts. If Mr. Lexington "truly appreciated" a task or deed, there was an excellent chance I would break even, although there were no guarantees. But when Max said, "Maaark, I truly, *truly* appreciate this," it meant that every last one of his three billion George Washingtons was going to remain in his wallet, checkbook, or vault. It also meant that any expenses incurred were to be swallowed as the task was demoted to the status of a "favor."

~~~~~~~~~~~~~~~~~~~~~~~~~~~~

I stopped driving for the night at Tennessee's southern border. After checking out three motels, I selected one that had predominately ground floor rooms and requested a quiet one away from the din of the freeway. I backed the truck up to the window of the room as far as possible and opened the window a crack near the vehicle's tailpipe. A very light sleeper, I was determined not to have to explain to anyone that two brothers who called their sister "ma" had snuck off with $40,000 in dinettes and credenzas. A $15,000 teak cabinet was not a necessity for storing the equipment to make corn squeezins. If I was awakened by the starting of the rental truck, I was prepared to go outside at once and scold any miscreants.

Morning arrived without incident and I headed for the Georgia border. By the time I reached Atlanta the rising sun had nudged the temperature back up to 40. As the day progressed I relished a brief stop for breakfast in south Georgia. By noon I was five miles north of the Georgia/Florida border and the temperature was hovering at 55 degrees. I stopped for fuel and roasted pecans and had just re-entered the freeway when my cell phone rang. The caller I.D. showed up as Summer's cell phone number. I readied myself for an excited barrage of thank yous when she realized how close I was with her treasure.

"Hi, Sweetie. Guess what? They found the chair!"

"Hi, Summer, I am about to cross over the state border into Florida right now, but if you like, I can get off at the next exit and head back up north to get it," I jested.

"Is there still room for it on the truck?" she replied. "No. Forget that. It's too far for you to go back now," she said with a sigh. "I'll just have to find some other way to get it shipped down here. It's too bad, too, because that's the one piece I could have used at my condo right now. The other stuff is just going to have to go into storage. I've been looking to buy a bigger condo and then I'll have room for everything. So, you said you're at the Florida border. We're having lunch right now so I guess you'll miss that. It's noon. Do you think you'll be here by three?"

"Actually, no," I replied. "I have 350 miles to go. If I average 50 miles an hour I'll be pulling into your complex by seven o'clock."

"Oh, Mark. That's going to be too late. We like to eat dinner by six. Why are you going so slow? I know the truck is faster than that."

"I like to stop every three hours or so when my foot and back start to cramp up. I hobble around for a minute until the feeling starts coming back. I know that wastes time, but I'd hate to crash during a spasm and scratch up the cargo."

"Well…okay. I guess that will have to do." Summer sounded disappointed. I had a question for her. "Summer, I remember your entire condo complex as being totally fenced in."

"Oh, don't worry about that, honey. I left your name with the guard. He'll just wave you in. I left my unit unlocked. My car keys are on the kitchen counter. I'm sorry if I sound mad at you. I just thought that you'd be here sooner. Max has been pretty bitchy today and when you're around he behaves much better is all. He keeps asking me questions about Darren. He wants to know if I've heard from him or if he's trying to call me. Please don't say that you know anything if it comes up but I think that once you're here it won't."

"Perhaps you should confess if you're feeling guilty about it," I offered. "But don't do it on the boat unless you're wearing a life jacket."

"Guilty? Why should I feel guilty? I'm not the one who's flying back up to my wife every two weeks! *I* did the right thing. *I* got the divorce and now *he's* the one who refuses to commit! Oh…hang on…he's coming over here now. What is it, Sweetie?…it's Mark…Mark?…hang on…there's somebody here that wants to talk to you!"

"Hey buddy. This is Max. Lissen Maaark…I just wanted you to know that I truly, truly appreciate what you're doing for Summer. I truly do."

Two trulys, I thought, *three if you counted the last one. Shit.*

"Well, Maaark, don't rush on account of us. Summer and I have plenty to talk about until you get here. You have been such a good, good, friend to her. Don't think that I don't see it!"

I was sure Max's last observation had some double meaning attached, but I certainly did not care to delve into it with him. I took it at face value, thanked him, and hung up.

By one o'clock I was well into the state of Florida. Billboards promised me fresh orange juice at various exits. Although the sky had clouded up before I left Georgia and remained so, by one o'clock the temperature had crept up into the high 60s. Mercury Marquis' and Buick LeSabres, driven by geriatric Florida residents, began to replace the pick-up trucks as they caught and passed my plodding rental ride. I was only two hours from the turnpike that would allow me to cut across the middle of the state unimpeded to I-95. I cracked open a Diet Pepsi in celebration as I finally passed a LeSabre, one of the few cars the truck had ever overtaken. Looking down, I guessed the shriveled old lady behind the wheel to be 110, and her husband in the passenger seat at 111. I was mystified as to how she could see over the dash at all, and my eyes darted from the road to the Buick as I searched for signs of a periscope.

While my attention had been drawn to the occupants of the Buick, it had begun to grow darker. A gray cloud cover had turned nearly black and the first raindrops began to explode on the windshield. Initial raindrops were merely scouts for the main invasion, and 30 seconds later I was driving through sheets of water as my windshield wipers struggled to keep up. It felt as though I was driving underneath a huge lake when God sliced through the entire bottom with a celestial knife blade. As my truck barged through a near vertical wall of water, cars ahead slowed when the freeway began to flood. The shoulders beneath every overpass were spoken for by Lincolns, LeSabres and Marquis' as their geriatric owners took refuge. I pressed on as the wind rocked my truck from side to side. For the next hour the truck was blasted by one rain cell after another with only five-minute respites. During one such break I looked ahead to see a clean line separating black cloud from blue sky. I drove toward the break with great hope, finally bursting into glorious sunshine five miles before the exit for the turnpike. Like my first marriage, entering the turnpike was easy although I knew I'd pay dearly when it was time to get off. The temperature soared to a humid 78 as I drove east and south. The gas gauge dropped below one quarter, but I pushed on without stopping after five o'clock came and went. By six o'clock I was off of the turnpike and heading south on I-95, looking longingly at gas station signs but ever aware of my seven o'clock promise to Summer. Another call from her had advised me that hors d'oeuvres would be served on the yacht at 7:15 and that we would be joined by a special girlfriend of hers to ensure a foursome.

On Friday night at 7:05, with the needle of the truck's gas gauge a hair's breath above empty, I pulled up to the guard shack of Summer's complex. A skinny, uniformed guard stuck his head out the door. He looked to be in his early 20s. He didn't look Rastafarian, but he was.

"Yeah, mon. Who is you here for?"

"Summer Sevalas," I answered. "My name is on the list."

"Who *you* are, mon?" He inquired, checking over a list on a clipboard.

"Mark Steel. I was due in at seven. It's seven-oh-six."

A long pause ensued.

"Ahm sorry, mon. You are not on the list."

"It might be under her maiden name, Summer Lewis."

A long pause.

"Nooo, Ahm steel sorry, mon. Nothing like thaat."

"Look, I'm sure that my name is on there. If it's not, then somebody from the last shift screwed up. You can call him if you like. You can call your supervisor. You can call Miss Lewis, but I am supposed to be on the list."

Several minutes and three calls later, my Jamaican buddy leaned out again.

"Steel sorry, mon. No one knows about thees. Mees Lewis does not ahnswer. There are cars in baack of you. You must baack up now."

"This truck doesn't back up. You'll have to open the gate."

"Ess it broken then?"

"Yes, reverse is broken," I replied.

"Maybe we can poosh it then?"

"No, we're not going to poosh it," I assured him.

The guard began to look me over, as though wondering if this was the proper time to use brute force. He looked at the cars idling behind me as they waited to enter. His shoulders drooped, as though he were suddenly aware of the frailness of his own physique. He then made a command decision. Reaching just inside the doorway, he moved a switch. The gates began to swing open. I mustered a smile and thanked him while I dropped the shifter into drive.

By 7:30 I was in Summer's shower and by 7:36 I was out. At 7:40 Summer's Mercedes took me out through the gates guarded by the fierce Jamaican. My cell phone was ringing every five minutes, with Summer's cell number appearing each time. Eight minutes later I was negotiating the roundabout outside of the Boca Club's main entrance. The Mercedes got me past the guard house when I added a smile of acknowledgement and a friendly half-wave to security. A valet sprang to the car and gave me a voucher, whisking the vehicle away before the front door of the complex swung closed behind me. Resisting the temptation to negotiate the eighth mile of hallway at a trot, I settled for long strides—which allowed me to do some people watching. Voices from foreign tongues came in brief soundbites as Europeans mixed with Americans in the huge lobby. At 7:55 I sprang through the glass doors that separated the lobby from the marina. Thirty yachts of all sizes and shapes lie docked side by side with people and guests dining on the decks of every fourth one. Max's yacht floated in the last well—one of three boat wells installed at an angle to accommodate boats of unusual length. Like his old 82-foot yacht, the new one sported a black and white hull, setting it apart from the plain white hulls of most of the others. To my disappointment, the 105-footer had lost the killer-whale shape that had made his former boat look so powerful—even when it was sitting motionless and tied to the dock.

Lights glowed from the interior through every portal. As I boarded the gangplank, the amount of gold, chrome, and teak was overwhelming and I felt like a poor cow-herder from Somalia. The captain had been sent on errands and the first mate had once again inconsiderately taken the weekend off to recover from a round of chemotherapy. It was left up to Summer herself to greet me with hugs and air kisses and escort me to the rear deck, where Max sat across a table from Summer's friend Claudette. Claudette was tan, freckled, and fortyish. She wore a set of designer slacks that were meant to hide some plumpness below her waist. Her sequined tank top did not hide any of the plumpness that bulged out in a bounty of sunburned cleavage. Her huge breasts were corralled valiantly by a brassiere that made a huge indentation in the fat on her back, but I shook the hand she offered without mentioning this fact.

Max looked much younger than his age after a July facelift, but as I prepared to tell him so, Summer grabbed my wrist and led me across the deck and down below for a quick tour of the staterooms. I didn't protest because I had already complimented him a month earlier after arriving at his house to drive him *and* Mrs. Lexington to a Christmas fête. Held in a Detroit area museum complex called Greenfield Village, it attracted all manner of older, wealthy looking couples. The other chauffeurs and I were generally younger and poorer looking than our passengers. We lined up our Mercedes, Jaguars, BMWs and limos next to a long sidewalk that ringed the building. Every 20 minutes one of the cars would depart as its driver sought out a meal or a newspaper. Based upon past experiences, I knew that our six o'clock arrival may result in a nine or ten o'clock departure. I went Christmas shopping. Since Max and Elizabeth's children blamed me for everything from their father's affair to the assassination of JFK, I knew I wouldn't be exchanging with the family. I bought a gift for Natasha and one for my daughter. After some dinner I was back by 8:30. The event concluded at 10:30 and Max and Elizabeth appeared to be very civil toward one another. On the way home to the mansion Mrs. Lexington spoke to me for the first time in nearly a year. Her questions, though cursory, were pleasant—and made the return trip less awkward than the journey out.

The last time I had seen Max was one week after Greenfield Village. The Palace of Auburn Hills, an enclosed venue about 25 miles north of Detroit, was featuring Andrea Bocelli, a blind Italian tenor. I was again asked by Max to drive him and his wife, and I said yes out of curiosity more than loyalty or obligation. I was mystified as to why Mrs. Lexington would agree to go to a live performance of Max and Summer's favorite singer.

I soon had my explanation. We got off to a rocky start in the curving driveway of the mansion when Elizabeth began sniping at Max about the person that he would prefer to be going with that night. The 300-foot drive to the main road seemed to take longer than the opening remarks at a Statisticians Who Stutter support group—and I received no relief upon reaching Jefferson Avenue (although in front of the mansion it is named Lakeshore Drive). As the iron gates swung open and I eased the Mercedes out into traffic, Max began speaking in a loud stage whisper.

"Stop it, just stop it. How about if we just turn the car around right here?" he offered to Elizabeth.

What a splendid idea! I thought. *I'll just add one hour to last week's total and we'll call it a night!*

To my disappointment, Elizabeth did not call her husband's bluff. I drove on while the tension in the back seat built up and spilled over into the front until my palms began to sweat. As we approached the on-ramp to the freeway, the sniping began again. I had spent the past five minutes silently evaluating my future employment potential with Maxwell Lexington. I concluded that there was none. As the sniping resumed, I began a course of action that would either diffuse the situation or result in my being summarily dismissed. Both results held a great deal of appeal. I spoke up.

"Mr. Lexington, I can turn on the radio if you like, although I'd like to point out another option. If you or Mrs. Lexington desire, you can request different songs from Bocelli's last CD, and I will sing them to the best of my ability. I believe the words are included in a pamphlet that comes with the CD."

There was nothing coming now from the back seat but a deafening silence. The reaction could still go either way. I needed to clarify my statement.

"Of course, I sing like a wounded goose and my Italian is very poor. Could I get one of you to help me by reading one line at a time out loud?"

There was a short pause. My passengers were processing my strange request. Suddenly, Max and Elizabeth burst out laughing. All of the tension vaporized. The subject changed and we chatted like old times. When we arrived at The Palace there was a ten-dollar charge for parking. Max did not leap forward to contribute, so I paid it.

54

Instead of giving me a tour of the yacht, Summer busied herself in the galley. I wandered around down below for several minutes before returning topside. Claudette had both of her round, freckled cheeks stuffed full of shrimp from the last tray and was now lying on a chaise lounge like a beached manatee. She finally swallowed and began chattering at Max at 300 words a minute. My former employer stared at Claudette as if she was a radio and he was considering another station. Max looked up at me and a smile broke across his face as though the cavalry had arrived. He interrupted Claudette in mid-sentence.

"Maaark, c'mon and sit down," he said and pointed to a seat between himself and his vocal guest.

Claudette paused and looked up at me long enough to give me a welcoming smile. She had cocktail sauce on her front teeth. I smiled back and hesitated before I sat down, stopping to admire the view off the back of the yacht. The dark water of the bay distorted the light that fell on it from nearby yachts and condominium towers. Across the small bay, two well-lit mansions sprawled on either side, one of which was under construction. Max followed my gaze.

"Yes, yes, it's beautiful, isn't it, buddy?"

I nodded and moved a napkin full of shrimp tails to one side of the Corian topped table as I sat. Summer returned with another tray of peeled shrimp and two glasses of white wine. She bent to offer Claudette a sixth—judging by the empties that surrounded her—glass of wine.

Summer placed the tray on the tabletop, took the remaining glass for herself, and sat down next to Max. I was relieved to see Max was still passing on alcoholic beverages after nearly a year of sobriety. In a muted light of the yacht's massive aft deck, I stared at Summer as she curled up next to Max. It was my first uninterrupted look at her since my arrival. The hair was hers, as were the retouched eyes. The long regal nose was identical to the one that I remember being looked down from whenever I suggested that she find employment. The forehead was ripple free from a hundred botox injections, and the upper lip was puffier than ever from a hundred more injections of collagen. Nevertheless, Summer looked dramatically different than she had in the fall, and I could not ascertain why. I ruled out weight loss after I saw that her long, powerful legs filled out her designer slacks more forcefully than ever. Summer caught my stare and smiled smugly back at me.

The freckled lush to my left guzzled three-quarters of the wine in her fresh glass and decided to continue her diatribe.

"As I was saying, I've been well off and I've been poor. I've had material possessions and I've been without them. I have learned that all of this..." Claudette wafted a free hand around in the air, "isn't where happiness comes from. *Things* don't bring you contentment. Now don't get me wrong, I adore this boat and I can appreciate a nice car. But until one is in touch with one's own inner self and learns to let that self-awareness grow into an inner peace, one always searches for physical pleasures instead of spiritual ones."

I had been dividing my attention between the plate of cold shrimp and Summer's chin, but now began peeking sideways at the big breasted Dali Llama to my left. I waited for her to break out into peals of laughter and shout out, "Just kidding!" but she prattled on.

"What I really love about traveling is the opportunity to experience different cultures and the way that they view life."

I asked how she felt about yogurt cultures. Max and Summer smiled, but Claudette ignored me. She went on.

"I have traveled Europe with a four star chef and I have stayed in some of the finest hotels on the continent. But to be honest, my soul got the greatest amount of peace when we stayed literally in a grass hut on the beach in Borneo. We fell asleep in each other's arms and I slept deeper on a blanket than I ever did on a 500 thread count sheet. With the waves crashing down not 20 feet from where we slept, I felt as though I had been transported back to when we were first evolving. I realized that the only thing that mattered at that moment, in that place, was the moment itself and maybe somebody to share it with. We didn't need a house, we had a straw roof and walls. We didn't need a stereo or a radio, the waves made enough music. We didn't even need clothes. Our spirits provided warmth from within us!"

I looked over at Max and rolled my eyes just as he completed a roll of his own eyes. Even Summer was beginning to squirm. I silently hoped that Claudette's spirit was set to room temperature all night and that she kept her clothes on.

Max stood up. "Is everybody ready for dinner?"

Summer and I leaped to our feet. Neither of us extended a hand to Claudette, who rocked back and forth until she stood up on the third try. Max and Summer went below to change for dinner while I gave myself a tour of the helm station of the new yacht. When Max and Summer came back up, we all rejoined Claudette—only to find her staring up at a constellation—perhaps trying to determine which galaxy harbored her home planet. Max and Summer walked down the broad gangplank first and I motioned for Claudette to follow as an old habit surfaced. If Max's tipsy guest had pitched over and fallen in, I had already located the gaff hook I would use to haul her over to the dock. If that failed, I was confident that such a well-equipped yacht as this one would have a harpoon stowed somewhere.

The four of us retraced the route that I had taken half an hour earlier and went back into the huge complex. Max led the way with Summer as Claudette staggered along behind them. When Claudette began chattering to Max again, Summer began to drop back. Her tan pantsuit could not hide the extra pounds in her derriere and she glanced back and caught me staring. She dropped back further as Max picked up the pace in an attempt to rid himself of spirit woman. Summer leaned into my ear and spoke in a low voice.

"Claudette has had a rough time these past two years. She's still in debt from a rough divorce. She caught her husband in bed with a friend of hers and cannot seem to get over it."

"How long was she married?" I inquired.

"About one year," Summer replied.

"That must have seemed like forever to him. I've just met her and I'm already looking for a way to cheat on her."

"Sweetie," Summer implored, "try to be nice. She's really a spiritual person who's had a little too much wine. I think Max and his money make her feel uncomfortable."

"What does she do for a living?" I asked.

"She's a nail technician at the salon that I go to but she's going to cosmetology school to be a hairdresser."

"That will come in handy if someone from the spirit world needs their hair *and* nails done."

"Mark, please. Dinner will only last an hour. Try to be nice."

We came to a set of elevator doors that serviced The Tower, a collection of deluxe hotel rooms. The Tower was 27 floors in all, and was capped by a restaurant that offered an exquisite view of beaches, ocean, yachts, waterway, and mansions.

I deduced that the restaurant's location prompted its name: *27 Ocean Blue*. When we arrived at the top, we were confronted by one of three hostesses. She assured us all tables had been booked for days and that there was a two-hour wait with no guarantees. Max squinted at tuxedoed male personnel until he found one that had a name tag with the words *Assistant Manager*. He motioned the man over to him amid the hubbub of the packed dining room and put his arm around him to speak quietly into his ear. Three minutes later the same hostess seated us at a table on a raised platform overlooking the window tables. The waitress appeared so quickly that I began to suspect she had been hiding underneath our table.

Summer and Max sat across the table from me. Max looked as though he was in his mid-50s instead of 72. I made a mental note to begin researching plastic surgery options for myself soon to assuage my own aging phobias. But my attention kept returning to Summer. She had done something subtle to change her appearance dramatically. I stared at her during the entire appetizer, but received only smug smiles in return. She now looked like the actress Andie McDowell, and I could not determine why.

Seated to my left without any clue about anything was Claudette. She was now guzzling down a parade of martinis that our waitress kept bringing at a full gallop. She only nibbled at her own appetizer, but derived additional sustenance by eating half of Summer's and eventually Max's. I hurriedly finished my own smoked fish sampler before it caught Claudette's attention.

As I waited for my Oscar Bruso, Claudette began to recap her tour of Europe with the four star chef. I settled in for a miserable hour, but Claudette drew a blank after naming only two restaurants and a hotel that Max pointed out had been demolished. I seized the opportunity to observe how Max's last yacht had looked like a giant orca and then transitioned neatly into the feeding habits of killer whales. I began to delve into great detail about how senior pod members had learned to beach themselves in order to gulp down seal pups. With a yelp Claudette declared that the subject was repulsive, off limits, and that *she* was thinking of becoming a vegetarian! I assured our group that if this fine Florida restaurant were ever to offer seal pup on the menu, I would shun it as a gesture of apology to Claudette. Secretly, I felt relief in knowing that my entrée was probably safe from her. Claudette recommandeered the conversation by launching into a rambling dissertation about the benefits of a macrobiotic diet.

While I was eating, she somehow segued into suggesting some changes to Max regarding the running of his billion dollar retail empire. The loquacious lush continued to order martinis throughout dinner until the bartender ran out of olives. After dessert, Summer suggested that I drive Claudette home. I had been cringing at the thought of what favor would be asked for in return for my meal and sighed heavily when the chubby fountain of knowledge next to me agreed to be driven home. Her house keys were in her car, so it was determined that we would retrieve her car from the parking garage and then replace it—to be picked up the next day. At the valet window, Claudette handed in her ticket and I handed in the one for Summer's Mercedes. A platoon of valets dashed back and forth, retrieving Porsches, Cadillacs, Mercedes, Jaguars and BMWs with a Lexus and a Ferrari thrown in for variety. Four minutes later, Summer's Mercedes appeared in the line and, after tipping moderately, I pulled it off to one side. Eight minutes later, Claudette's car had not materialized. She began to inquire after nine minutes. She had a five-year-old Chevy Cavalier, it was red, and her voice grew loud after 12 minutes.

"I've watched people wait two minutes, just two ----in' minutes to get their *Jaguars* and drive off!" she said to no one in particular.

"I think they sent a second guy to look for it too," I offered.

"The last time I checked, there wasn't a ---damn caste system in this country. I might have borrowed that car for all they ----in' know because my Rolls Bentley is in the shop!" Her wrath was starting to direct itself my way. I went to the window and asked if I could help the valets look. Claudette stepped in front of me and pounded on the glass.

"Hey, I'm talkin' to you! I want my ----in' car now! It's been almost an hour and I want my ----in' car!"

It had only been about 16 minutes. Martinis are notoriously bad for enhancing one's ability to estimate time. I expected the glass pounding to draw security and management. Instead they chose to handle the raging lush with courtesy and aplomb. One concerned young manager stepped discreetly over from the front lobby.

"May I be of assistance?" he inquired.

"Do you know who I am?" Claudette yelled. "And do you have any idea who I just ----in' had dinner with? I just had dinner with

Max Luxerton and I've been waiting two hours for my car and if I call him you're gonna be workin' somewhere else!"

She was close enough on the name, but time was flying by so rapidly that I checked my cell phone's clock. It had been 17 minutes. The manager immediately put a third valet on the search party. The line of other people waiting was starting to grow long. Claudette wasn't through.

"Just because I don't drive a BM ----in' W doesn't make all of these others more important! It should be first come, most served!"

"You mean first come, first served," I gently corrected. As long as she was going to make a scene, I wanted her to get her policies straight. Claudette demanded that I call Max. I called Summer's cell, and to my surprise she answered. We had just gotten Max on the phone with the manager when the car showed up. As Claudette retrieved her keys, I got my phone back and said good night to Max. It had been 22 minutes but seemed like 22 days. The ten minute car ride to Claudette's apartment wasn't very serene either.

"What if I had a ----in' emergency to go to? What then?" She demanded.

I doubted that any surgeon performed liposuction at 10:30 on a Friday night but I did not point it out to my dramatic, drunken passenger. Claudette exited the Mercedes and plodded across the front lawn of her apartment house while I watched from the street. She inserted her lobby door key into the slot after only three tries and stumbled across the threshold. I returned to Summer's condo and was asleep by midnight.

My cell phone rang at 9 A.M. on Saturday. It was Summer, demanding that I join her and Max for breakfast back at the Boca Club's Cathedral restaurant. By the time I arrived, the official terminology for the 20-table spread would have been brunch.

The stress of the trip down to Boca Raton had caused my weight to slip just under 220 pounds. I was growing concerned about following in the frail footsteps of my 130th favorite female songstress of all-time, Karen Carpenter. After joining Max and Andie

McDowell/Summer Sevalas, I resolved to single-handedly capitalize the letter "g" in gluttony and get Max's full $20 worth.

The afternoon was divided between writing a chapter of my book at Summer's condo pool and swimming laps underwater.

Summer insisted that I join her and Max for dinner at a sumptuous French restaurant off of a large enclosed atrium. Without Claudette in attendance, the first topic was regarding where Summer would store her new cache of furniture and the rental costs as they related to the value of the items. The second topic involved the allocation of Max's two million dollar per month advertising budget for his chain of stores. His advertising department had been running out of misleading sales ideas to blanket the local newspapers and airwaves with. He was contemplating convening a summit of every available advertising medium and awarding a yearly contract to the bidders with the best ideas. His goal was to save additional millions in advertising agency fees as each medium spent a fortune vying for his business. The second option that he was pondering was whether to hire an established older female spokesperson to hawk his goods or a younger, attractive *Sports Illustrated* Swimsuit Model. Knowing that Sunday would be my last full day in Boca before heading to Ft. Lauderdale, I uncharacteristically spoke out and detailed yet a third marketing plan to the entrepreneur/billionaire.

My marketing plan went over about as well as an albino lifeguard and the remainder of the dinner turned quite frosty.

By noon Sunday the cloud cover had burned away over Boca and I was entrenched and writing once again by Summer's pool. An extremely tanned man of about 60, with a full head of gray hair, opened the gate and selected a lounge chair at one corner of the pool. For approximately 15 minutes he sat alone, reading and eyeing two other pool patrons. I had written another half page when the gate opened again and a taller, paler but handsome man purveyed the area before heading toward the first. He was perhaps 50.

"Sol, what's neeww?" he said in a New York accent.

"Herb, how are ya?" Sol replied.

"You wouldn't hear me complain at all if this wind stopped!" said Herb.

America is still considered to be one great melting pot of nationalities and I sometimes have trouble distinguishing whose ancestors came from where originally. In this case, though, I knew immediately that I was 40 feet away from two direct descendants of Moses.

The two men exchanged pleasantries and voiced opinions on the headlines in Sol's paper. After five minutes, both looked up as another man unlatched the wrought iron gate that encompassed the entire area. Curly haired and bearded, he was acknowledged by loud greetings of "David!" and "Missssster Bernstein!"

David squinted as he stepped from shadow to sunlight and claimed a chair next to the others with his towel and a cell phone. When he removed his shirt he sported some residual tan—presumably from *last* Sunday—but his physique in general said "accountant."

Two more men appeared at the gate and were summarily greeted and waved over to the group. "Herschel" was tall and silver haired, with a commanding voice that resonated in the poolhouse grotto and across the shallow end of the pool toward my chair. I guessed him at 70. When he pulled his shirt off, his tanned physique and wide shoulders hinted at a retired executive who faithfully swam dozens of laps every morning in the pool that separated us.

"Jerry" trailed a respectful step and a half behind Herschel. He was of medium height and looked to be about half the age of his companion. He was wearing dark sunglasses and a short brimmed baseball cap. The group had now increased in strength to six. Most wore shorts or thigh-length swimsuits, and all six wore sandals of one style or another.

Until now, the conversation had been sporadic and confined to one or two sentences at a time about the weather or the temperature of the pool or the in-ground Jacuzzi. There was some shifting of chairs to take advantage of the sun. More maneuvering was also necessary to provide a more suitable view of the bosomy woman and her tall female friend that had just entered the area.

David made the first statement that was directed at the entire group in general and in doing so raised his voice enough for me to eavesdrop without effort.

"I see where the Feds met and dropped the rate a quarter point again…I told you last week that it was coming and maybe twice more!"

Another spoke up. "The lady who bought the condo across the hall from me said she had just locked in for a refi at six percent. I told her to wait a month yet but she wouldn't listen."

Someone else offered, "The way the prices are jumping sometimes getting another appraisal is good anyway."

David again, "I paid 185 when I moved down here full time ten years ago and they said I was meshugganah. I got the three-bedroom corner unit and you know what the same thing on the floor below me went for last week? Try 485!"

A voice piped up, "You mean that widow on the fourth floor? I knew her to say *hi* to on the elevator. She has a son maybe 14 or 15. We were in the elevator once and by the time we got to the parking lot she asked me out. I met her for drinks at that spot in Mizner but I could tell right away what she was after. She's thinking that boy needs a fatha!"

"You seeing anyone else?"

"Naw, I think I'm just going to Internet date for awhile."

"Speaking of the Internet, I'm thinking of a business where people could register and then get regular updates for all of their insurance. They'd automatically get ten quotes *every toyme* they were up for renewal on anything!"

"Who'd pay for that?"

"The insurance *brow-kers*, that's who!"

"Speaking of that, this lady I met through my friend Andy got divorced from Heath Hazard and you know who he is. He underwrites all of the new construction from West Palm down to Lauderdale. Now I heard, but I can't verify, that her share was 50 or 60. Now, I'm 55 and she's 50 and I normally don't look at anything ovah 45 but in her case I'd make an exception!"

"Yeah, but now she's not gonna look at anything ovah 45 eitha!"

That got a big laugh. The conversation continued from money to women and then back to money again.

Somebody else weighed in, "I'll tell you what. I don't date anybody under 39, maybe 38 and I'll tell you why. At 34, 35 they're still thinking they're young enough to start a second family or at least have one more. But by 40, they're stahtin' to realoize that they're getting too old to have a kid that's gonna just be graduating high school by the time they're 60! By 40, they don't want to wait another 15 years to travel or eat at a nice restaurant without worrying!"

"Speaking of restaurants, I'm thinking of stahting a business where I hire somebody to go from one to another and talk to the manager about co-operative advertising…"

"…so the profile on the website says height proportionate to weight and you know what that always means. Anyway, it's Friday and I agree to meet her at that bar across from your condo. So she shows up and finds me and I sweah to Gawd she looks nothing like the pictcha she posted! I mean, I could see a resemblance…but to her daughta maybe. Then I realoize afta she sits down that the pictcha she put up is maybe ten years old! Maybe moah!"

"What did you do?"

"Well, I didn't feel too bad. I mean, she lied. After a couple minutes I just excused myself to the bathroom and found the waitress and paid her. Then I just walked out the side door!"

"Speaking of that, I'm thinking of stahting a business where you buy like a credit cahd. I get like 100 or 200 businesses to sign up and the cahd is good at any of them but you buy the cahd at like 25 percent off."

"That reminds me of the last lady I went out with. She asks to use my credit cahd because her car's in the shop and the rental car company won't take a check. So I get the bill and there's charges I don't recognize on there for a veterinary clinic and the local courthouse. I ask her right away and she says her dog was making a choking sound and she didn't have any cash on her. She says the court was about to issue a warrant for a traffic ticket that she didn't pay and she had no choice but not to worry 'cause she'd pay me right back! She didn't give me the card back either! I had to call the next day and cancel the thing! We went out a coupla times afta, but I knew she wasn't gonna pay me back and I just stopped callin' her or returning her calls."

"So what are ya' gonna do?"

"Oh, I'm just gonna Internet date for awhile."

"Naw, I mean about the money!"

"Oh, y' know, I coulda put a dispute on with the credit cahd company but then the cops would probably come haul her away. So I'm thinkin' it's just 300 bucks so forget about it."

"You know, you can probably write that off as a bad debt on your taxes."

"Yeah, you're right. I'll have my accountant look into that!"

I sat writing and listening to the group off and on until the sun began to wane at five o'clock. During that time, new members arrived and others left, but the number remained constant at six or seven. The subject matter was also a constant. It went from money to women and back to money again. The pitfalls of dating in South Florida were exposed ad nauseum until I wanted to don a necklace of garlic cloves in hopes of protecting myself.

Jerry remained the youngest of the group and as such had most of the dating advice directed his way. Jerry also had all of the prospective business deals directed his way and walked away that afternoon with a dozen offers of *possible* jobs. My head was swimming from the marathon session and I left after writing only two pages in five hours.

Sunday evening Summer called.

"Hi, honey. Sorry I'm calling so late about dinner but Max and I have been busy locating a storage space for all of my new stuff. I needed something that was climate controlled and let me tell you that unless I find a bigger condo I'm gonna be spending as much in storage fees as the stuff is worth! Also, remember my friend Tishelle the makeup artist that was having the health problems last year? Remember when I told you that she's had some *very* famous clients that she'll fly to meet on a movie set or wherever she's needed? Well, she called and was telling me that she's on the verge of a nervous breakdown because she can't work! Mark, she's got warts! She *cannot* get rid of them! They're all over her hands and she thinks that she gave them to a very famous actress who's now got them all over her *face*!"

I was sympathetic. "That's tragic. Are we going out to dinner tonight?"

"Oh, I'm sorry, Sweetie, Max says he's tired from driving all day. We went up to Palm Beach for a doctor's consult, too."

"On a Sunday?"

"The doctor is actually a plastic surgeon. He's one of the best, really he is. And if I can be frank with you I think that Max is a little mad at you. He mentioned that it would have been nice if you searched out a suitable storage unit instead of leaving it to us. He spoke to his boat captain and he thinks that he can round up some guys to unload the truck tomorrow. Are you going to be able to help?"

"No," I said. "I am outta here in the morning. My buddy Doc is expecting me down in Lauderdale. I was counting on you for a ride to the car rental."

"Oh, Sweetie, I know I promised but we've got so much to do with the truck and the furniture tomorrow!"

"Perhaps you'd like to pick up the truck at the car rental?" I inquired sweetly.

"Now don't be mean. I'll tell you what, I'll meet you in the morning at the condo and I'll reimburse you for your expenses. I wish you could help but if you say you can't I'll make sure that you get to the car rental. I'll be there by nine."

On Monday morning Max and Summer arrived at her condo at 10:30. Max was outwardly friendly but I sensed a thin layer of ice forming underneath. I brought out my gas and hotel receipts. Driving well under the speed limits and a stay at a Red Roof Inn resulted in a total of $376. Summer hesitated…and then wrote me a check for $500. Max showed some interest in the total of the receipts, but made no move whatsoever for any of his pockets. Picking up the truck and furniture had taken me five hours. The trip down had taken another 36. I calculated that the dinners had equaled out my chauffeur services for Summer's inebriated friend. My career in the interstate trucking business had netted me an impressive $3.02 per hour. Although my hourly rate worked out to less than half that of an inexperienced migrant farm worker, I thanked Summer for her generosity. Glowing, she suddenly felt compelled to share secrets with me.

"So," she said, "did you ever figure out why I looked different to you?"

I said that I had not.

"Well, remember that I was getting a double chin? I had a procedure in Palm Beach that's known as a "S" lift with lipo. See these two dots under my jaw? They're tiny little stitches where he went in with the wand and sucked fat out! Then he brought all the skin up around my jaw and stitched in front of my ears, see?" Summer drew her hair back from her ears and it quickly became apparent why I hadn't seen her in a ponytail during my visit. "I think it took ten years off and Max agrees, don't you, Sweetie?" Max nodded in assent. "Not that I looked 40 anyway. My friends said I looked more like 30."

I ran the numbers. If she looked 30 and took off ten with the "S" lift, that meant that she now looked 20. I could see that…if I rubbed my eyes with my fists for two minutes and then looked again quickly.

Of course, if Summer looked 20 then her 72-year-old lover still looked like a 72-year-old with a cleverly done facelift. At 45, I had been told that I only looked 44. I refrained from mentioning anything for fear of losing my ride to the car rental.

My long awaited ride was chilly—even with the climate control on Max's Mercedes set to vent. Summer spoke little and Max spoke less every time I mentioned the intersection that I needed to go to.

The outside temperature was well into the 70s when Max popped the rear deck lid and I unloaded my bags. Heading south to Fort Lauderdale in my shiny maroon Grand Prix, I was able to breathe a little easier with every mile that I put behind me.

I met Doc for lunch and he began to explain to me how the world worked as soon as we had ordered. The next day I wrote two pages while switching from his ocean front balcony to a lounge chair at the complex pool. The day after, I managed three. By week's end, I was at six per day and my manuscript now totaled more than 100 pages.

Doc grew tired of watching me write and we took a road trip across Alligator Alley to the west side of the state. My friend, always on the lookout for nightlife and a change of scenery, wanted to see if the city of Naples really did roll up its sidewalks at 8 P.M. We found, to my nomadic buddy's disappointment, that the rumor was essentially true. On the way back to his condo, Doc lamented repeatedly how the populace on the Gulf side acted like a bunch of 62-year-olds. When I pointed out that his actual age *was* 62, he began denying it vehemently until I asked to see his driver's license. A potentially embarrassing situation for my buddy was narrowly averted when my cell phone rang. It was a sighing Summer, asking if I was still in Florida. Max had flown back to Michigan—and she was lonely. It wasn't until I told her that I was heading back soon as well that she felt compelled to tell me how angry Max was. His ship's captain had found moving assistance—only to encounter a rental truck with a dead battery and no gas. I countered by stating that I could not warranty a used truck that belonged to someone else. I could not resist chiding the brunette golddigger by asking how I was to make a successful fuel run if the guard at her complex were to finally turn me away for good. She ignored my question. This was going to be about the heartache that plagued *her* today.

"I don't know why I ever moved down here," she complained. "I gave up everything for Max. My friends, my family, *everybody* I know lives up in Michigan. I have no one down here. *No one*."

"There's Claudette," I offered.

"She's dating some guy she met. Not that it's going well. He's already borrowed $500 off of her. She had to get an advance from her credit card. I met him and he *is* very good looking and he says that he loves her, but Mark, he doesn't even own a car! It just makes me think of the guy that I gave up for Max. Chuck was handsome, he was a great provider, he loved my son as his own, and I just *threw* it away! Meanwhile, I don't even have my settlement yet from the divorce. I have no idea how I'm supposed to pay for my condo. I'm going to call Max later. I miss him so much."

"Speaking of Max," I said, "I drove him around in December and I was wondering if you could ask him for my 200 bucks the next time that you see him."

She agreed. The next day I was sitting poolside, working on page 104, when my cell phone rang.

"Hi, Sweetie," Summer said with a sigh. "I talked to Max and his comment to me was that he thought that $200 for a ride to a concert was kind of high."

"It is. But you can tell him that I took *two* evenings off to drive him. The first was to a Christmas dinner at Greenfield Village. Two hundred is a bargain."

If Max had a Latin name it would have been Pennius Pinchimus. I often pictured his butler and the rest of his household staff around the kitchen table with scissors and the local paper, cutting coupons.

I left for Michigan in my rental car the next day. My intention was to sequester myself for the rest of the winter like a Trappist monk until my book was complete.

My sequestration may have sounded glamorous when I first came back, but the reality was that it was impractical. The personal training business remained strong and my presence was required at the studio more frequently than I had hoped for. Nevertheless, I had completed 250 handwritten pages by the end of February. My court case against the bumbling construction company that had nearly throttled my business continued to wend its way through the court system at a snail's pace. Motions, affidavits, pleadings and briefs were exchanged in torrents between my counsel and theirs. Accountants were consulted, losses were totaled, and witness lists were compiled. "Discovery" is the practice of reviewing all of the opposition's paperwork and records. It is the understanding of both parties that some of this paperwork may be used later at trial. By the end of discovery the only thing I was sure of was that my opponents had buried any paper trail of their wrongdoing. Their answers to my court filings painted a picture of a company that had done no wrong. To dig a trench, lay some concrete pipe, and restore the road should take at least a year and a half, they maintained. I disagreed at every opportunity. But they were steadfast. They had done no wrong. Businesses were hurt by their activities all of the time. They were amazed at my dissatisfaction with their work. My complaints were out of line. Later on, their defense would rest partially on the premise that I did not complain enough. I should have contacted them more often during the job…it was my own lack of persistence that caused me harm.

55

As the howling winds of winter began to subside near the end of March, another type of howling began to substitute for them. Summer's calls from Florida increased in frequency and intensity. She could not go on renting her condo forever. Before prices escalated even further, she must make a purchase. There were several for sale in the area that would meet her minimum standards of suitability, but the asking prices began at half a million. Her divorce settlement was not ample enough, she complained. Even a $500,000 condo would need updating and improvements. The better ocean views began at $600,000. Max did not care about her future. His life had become a constant quest for the best, she claimed, and she was the best thing that had ever happened to him. She was in a negative cash flow situation. After two years of faithfulness to Max—and only two or three other men—it was time for him to step up. In the next breath she spoke of the summer plans for the yacht. Martha's Vineyard, Chesapeake Bay, and Boston Harbor by Independence Day were on this year's agenda. The help would be a problem, of course. The captain had become sullen and distant after still another tongue-lashing by Max. The first mate was battling cancer yet again, and her treatments were interfering with her shipboard duties. They would both have to go. The former captain Boomer and his first mate Kaycee had approached Max on hands and knees, she claimed, and begged to get their old jobs back. Rotating the staff kept them humble.

During one of Summer's phone calls about her lack of cash flow, I had an unfortunate lapse of judgement. Perhaps I had been working too vigorously on the manuscript for my book. Producing 350 handwritten pages had apparently taken a toll on my thought processes. I had a part-time job 20 years ago as a guest relations engineer in a distilled and fermented beverage dispensary. Perhaps it had left me with damage to my brain's front temporal lobe. Regardless of the cause, I experienced a temporary malfunction of the filter between my brain and my mouth. I suggested to Summer that she find employment.

If a dozen male chimpanzees were being castrated simultaneously while two dozen female sopranos in the next room gave birth, Summer's reaction *could* be duplicated. She had never been so offended. I had no idea of how crazy her life was. Max expected her to be prepared at a moment's notice. Hair, nails, and bikini-line must be kept current. Tennis, cardio-walks, and massages to recover from both were essential to maintaining her weight, which had begun to climb. Areas needing liposuction must be identified after lengthy and honest sessions in front of her full-length mirror. Summer was nearing the final rounds in her quest for the championship belt of golddigging. Suggesting the distraction of employment was so ludicrous that it enraged her. She spewed some venom about simple-minded thinkers that always fail to grasp the big picture...and hung up on me.

~~~~~~~~~~~~~~~~~~~~~~~~~~~~

By late March my manuscript had accumulated 400 handwritten pages. I had become like a man possessed. I would stop only long enough to shower...and five times a day to eat, or to work out, or to check Ford Motor Company's stock price, or to chase Natasha around the house. I wanted to finish my manuscript by spring to allow at least six months to edit, typeset, photograph the cover and print. A December publication date was my goal, and I vowed to eliminate every outside distraction.

On a cold Monday morning I awoke with a new resolve. Ford Motor Company was up another 25 cents. I sat down to write. My cell phone rang. It was Summer.

"Hi, Sweetie, how aaaaare you? Listen, I'm at the Townsend and Max has just left for the office. I'd really like to see you but we just flew in yesterday on the jet and I don't have a car right now. If you come over I'll buy you breakfast and we can catch up. Then if you don't mind I could really use a ride to the Pointes. I'm staying at Connie's and she says that I can use her car. How soon can you be here?"

"Uh, I'm writing something right now," I hinted.

"Oh…are you still working on that silly book? I haven't seen you for months! You can take an hour off!"

Summer had absolutely no concept of time. Some people would propose that in this universe, for every positive there is a negative. It may be referred to as a yin and a yang, or even as Mother Theresa and my first wife.

I once had a neighbor. His name was Chris Huotari. The man was a human clock. A skilled machinist and a hot rod automobile enthusiast, Chris would spend hours in a large garage in the rear of his home sanding pieces of metal and welding steel suspension brackets to car frames. Chris performed these tasks and a thousand others in his "shop" sans wristwatch, clock, or even sundial. When I walked through the gate that separated our yards, I might find Chris inside or underneath his '56 Chevy—or painting his '37 Ford. In lieu of a traditional greeting, I would shout out, "Hey neighbor, what time is it?" The man never paused in his activity. His eyes would not leave his work. If he was wearing a welding helmet, he would *not* raise it up. But he would always reply, instantly and without hesitation. If it was seven minutes after 10 P.M., he would immediately tell me so with complete confidence. If the time was one minute to 12, Chris' response would reflect it precisely. I checked everywhere for timepieces to help me debunk his "gift." I would sneak up on the man before asking—after watching him for up to 15 minutes at a time. If his eyes were visible while I asked my question, I would stare at them intently. I was watching for any flicker of movement that might indicate a hidden watch or clock. I attempted the same tests of his amazing ability when Chris was in *my* "clockless" garage, and I never once saw him fail. In fact, I never received an answer that was more than one minute off…and soon grew to trust Chris more than my Pulsar.

An offshoot of my savant neighbor's time-telling ability was a skill in determining the actual price of any recently purchased object. Unfortunately, Chris was never able to convert either of these gifts into an income, despite some half-hearted attempts. Both his lottery and casino endeavors flopped, and Chris will retire at 65 as a machinist.

But if Chris Huotari was the yin, then Summer Sevalas was the yang. The word "hour" was just that…a word. To Summer, its meaning was vague and interchangeable…with other words like minute, moment, or the phrase "for a while."

If Summer was on the phone and claimed that she would "be there in a minute" it could very well be an hour, a day, a week, or a fortnight. Or, it might actually be a minute, in which case the impending activity that prompted her arrival must commence within four seconds or four hours, depending on whether she was talking on her cell phone. If Summer had lived at the time of Galileo, our solar system might have been mapped out quite differently, with the sun orbiting around *her*.

The Townsend was located in downtown Birmingham, Michigan. It combined impeccable service with a wide selection of sumptuous rooms and suites. Its staff was ultra-professional and discreet. When famous people were in town, they stayed at the Townsend. Madonna, President Bush (the first one) and Mike Tyson all enjoyed the amenities of the Townsend. The dining room was elegant, quiet, and replete with darkened corners where one could eat relatively unobserved. It was the ideal location for a rock star and his entourage to avoid an onslaught of paparazzi and groupies. It was also the ideal place for a billionaire to entertain his mistress and hide in plain sight—away from the prying eyes of his wife's friends.

Under ideal conditions, it was a 45-minute journey from my waterfront home to the center of Birmingham. By the time I found a metered parking spot and jogged to the hotel, 55 minutes of the "hour" that Summer had asked for would have disappeared. From that point on, her demands on my time might last for another hour if she were prepared to leave at once...or until the moon rose in the sky if errands awaited us. I had a self-imposed deadline in which to finish my book. Clients awaited me that evening at the fitness studio. Summer would have to be made to understand that my time was valuable and not available to be wasted as her chauffeur on her trivial wanderings. I would suggest a car service or a taxicab. I would be cordial, yet firm.

On my way to the Townsend I attempted to justify the time that would not be spent writing any more that day. Spending time with Summer would negate the need to watch various cable programs for weeks. First to leave the list would be *Ripley's Believe It or Not*. After an afternoon with Summer, nothing else produced by man or nature would surprise me. Gone also would be *The O'Reilly Factor*. After a barrage of opinions from Summer, there would be no more room for those of anyone else. The entire gamut of style and entertainment channels would lose their allure as well after listening to an afternoon of gossip from this ultimate fashionista.

Upon my arrival in the lobby of the Townsend I barely received a second look from the bellhop or the concierge. The time I had spent at home changing into clean jeans and running shoes had been well spent. I practically blended into the dark paneled surroundings and strode to the restaurant with the confidence of a man with fashion sense. There was a small dining area outside of the main room and to my complete shock Summer was already seated and waiting for me. She had made the entire trip down from the sixth floor in less than an hour, and I began to believe that perhaps a leopard *could* change its spots. As I approached, she leaped up to see me as though

I were returning from the Crusades. With a near squeal, she said, "Hi Sweetie!" and gave me two hugs and an air kiss. While I claimed my chair she reseated herself. Our waiter appeared immediately and I ordered a six-dollar glass of orange juice and twelve-dollar Eggs Benedict. Summer requested a ten-dollar bowl of fruit. She had a glow about her. Her hair was too orderly for that "just laid look" but she seemed happy…as if a decision had been made during the previous evening's activities. Although I have never claimed to be an expert at it, I had an unusually high degree of difficulty determining her mood that morning. It seemed teasing, as if she were preparing to gloat over a great victory. At the same time, an atmosphere of secrecy formed a bubble around our table, as though Summer possessed information of such great importance that it was oozing out through her pores. But even when I look back now at that mid-morning tête-à-tête, its main purpose was to taunt me with a secret that Summer was privy to and I was not. Summer began to chide me with the confidence of a woman of means and status.

"So, dear…I love your outfit. Did you purchase that shirt from K-mart?"

"Why no," I said defensively, "it was the last one on the clearance rack at Sam's Club, but I thought the brown stain at the bottom brought out the color of my eyes."

"Yes, it really suits you. But I'm getting angry with you. You haven't said a word about how I look. This top is Dolce and Gabbana and you wouldn't believe the thread count even if I told you." Summer stood up as she spoke, "and these slacks are Escada." She began to take a slow twirl as if she were at the end of a catwalk with a symphony playing in the background. "So what do you think? Have I gained or lost since you last saw me?" Then came a huge clue…which I missed. "I haven't worked out in over a month now. And after my sessions ran out, I haven't seen my trainer since before your last visit. So do you think I'm carrying it in the same places, or has it begun to shift around?" she said as she completed a second turn before sitting back down.

If personal trainers had existed during the Italian Renaissance, I would have been known from Rome to Sicily as Markalangelo. At one time Summer had been my canvas...she was the ceiling of my Sistine Chapel. I had transformed her from a plump but sexy housewife and socialite into a firm but still curvaceous temptress. Of course, I had not planned on my artwork being displayed so alluringly for the married billionaire that I was associated with. But for nearly a year, I was able to gaze with pride on my living piece of sculpture as her acquaintances began to consult with me in the hopes that I could achieve similar heights with them. Summer had supplied me with the perfect canvas. At 39, she had only been allowing her physique to slide for the past ten years. Employment as an entertainment engineer at a gentleman's club when in her 20s had left her with a tight, flawless physique that belied her motherhood status. She had been one of my most motivated and consistent proteges, doing whatever I asked of her in the gym and supplementing it with tennis and a change in diet when in the real world. But now, all of the distractions and pampering of her newfound profession as a mistress were beginning to take their toll. Warm Italian breads and seafood pasta swimming in creamy sauces were like a saltwater spray over the delicate oils across my canvas. Naively, my only thoughts were about how the vibrant pastels of her slacks failed to conceal the protruding pooch beneath the belt line. Nor could the floral pattern disguise the tushy that I had worked so diligently on narrowing. Her bosom seemed as generous as ever...perhaps even more that I remembered. And yet she seemed to be flaunting her shape, leading me to believe that what I had fought to create did not matter anymore. As an artisan, I was chagrined to find the paint beginning to peel off of the ceiling of my masterpiece. And I knew that my pièce de resistance was now the sole possession of the Medici, and that my commission was over. I could also see that the new owner had no intention of initiating any restorations, and that I was powerless to suggest any.

"For somebody who claims that she hasn't worked out for some time, I'd say that everything is right about where it belongs," I said.

Summer beamed, and then a salacious grin took the place of her toothy smile. She glanced at a couple seated to her right, and then at the empty table to her left. She was about to reveal something tantamount to the meaning of the Dead Sea Scrolls.

"And the Eggs Benedict for you, sir," the waiter said as he set down my plate. "And for you, miss…"

I could see it fade from her eyes. The desire to tell me was being suppressed. Like dying embers, the secret was going away…or at least her burning desire to reveal it was. I started in on my breakfast, and Summer dawdled with a strawberry.

"So honey, when do you think you'll be finished with this book?"

"I hope to begin editing around May first, and I might have it out by Christmas."

"If I can offer a word of advice, Sweetie, be very careful of what you say. It's not smart to offend people in high places. You know…people who know other people."

"It's just a story, Summer. It won't offend more than two or three hundred people. *The Da Vinci Code*, in contrast, has already offended millions."

"Well, just watch your back. I feel as though I'm constantly watching mine, and it's no fun let me tell you. Max's children have been anything but discreet. I can't go anywhere in the Pointes without feeling dozens of pairs of eyes watching me. They've spread around so many lies about our relationship that my friends up here simply can't keep track of them all anymore. I don't think that I told you this, but his eldest son Larry was down in Boca for a while and we crossed paths several times as I was either coming or going. He was quite cordial to me actually, although I realize that we only saw each other in the presence of his father. The last time, though, he seemed a lot more distant…or maybe it was disappointment, like he had been waiting for a deal to go through and it didn't. That was the last time that I saw him down there and when I asked Max why Larry cut his time short he said that he didn't know. I was kind of disappointed, too. I was looking for an opportunity to get him alone…maybe charm him a little bit. I would have told him how much I adored his father and asked him if he wanted Max to be happy for however many years he has left. I mean, Mark, the lights are out on Max's marriage. Max deserves to be with someone who's going to take care of him…somebody who's going to pamper him. I was hoping that if I could get Larry to come around then maybe the other kids would start to fall one by one. I'm not going away…not now. I was hoping that they might begin to accept me, certainly not at family functions but at least in private if we should run into each other. After all, they still have a mother…it's not like I'm trying to take her place in their hearts."

"That's good, because you're younger than half of his children." I reminded her.

"But Mark, age is just a chronological way of keeping track. It doesn't take into account a person's life experiences. I have had way more life experiences than those pampered brats. There were times where I didn't know where my next rent check was coming from. I didn't know if my son and I would be living in the street!"

"Summer, wouldn't your parents have taken you back in?"

"That's not the point. Max's kids will be taken care of for life, their trust funds kick in when they turn 35. And how do they say thanks to their father? Do they accept his wishes when he says that he wants to settle down with someone who brings him happiness? No. They take their quarter-million apiece every year and tell *him* how to run *his* life! They don't appreciate a thing that he's done for them! They feel entitled. And let me tell *you* that he deeply regrets not making them all earn it! And if they don't appreciate him then how are they ever going to appreciate me? What they don't realize Mark, is that I've already done them a favor. They should thank me. Because of what's happened they're all in therapy right now…and all of them really needed it!"

I had been listening while I raised my glass of orange juice to my lips. I was in mid sip when suddenly the ludicrousness of her last statement sank in. The glass itself caught most of the juice as I involuntarily sprayed. Unfortunately, a quarter of an ounce found its way to the pristine white tablecloth in a wide spray of droplets. I blushed—and laughed hard out loud simultaneously. Summer arched an eyebrow and then burst out laughing as well. We convulsed and rocked in our chairs for nearly a full minute. The couple at the table next to us were handed Academy Awards for "Best Attempt to Ignore Two Idiots." After we began to regain control of ourselves and wipe away the tears Summer observed, "That's funny, it came out much better when Max said it!" Once again our hoots reverberated throughout the small area. Our behavior prompted a concerned visit from our waiter, and we nodded our acceptance to his offer of a bill. As calm was again restored, Summer filled in their hotel room number and signed below it. Max had never before bought me a meal without buying himself one as well, and I regretted not ordering the filet mignon and eggs.

I was to hold several titles that day. Upon my arrival at the Townsend I was deigned as "Fashion Impaired." During breakfast my title evolved into "The Naïve One." By the end of breakfast, Summer once again bestowed upon me an old title that I was quite familiar with. For lack of any competition in the immediate vicinity, I had reclaimed the title of "Summer's Best Girlfriend and Confidant." The latter of these required patience and a wide repertoire of surprised and shocked looks, head shakes, grunts, plus other exclamations of dismay.

The *last* title necessitated a reliable car, a full tank of gas, and a roadmap of the area's shopping malls, hair salons, and coffee shops emblazoned into my brain. During Max's drinking days, my "chauffeur" title had been a relatively important one. Now, it was merely an efficient way for Summer to get from point "A" to point "Z" with many letters in between. I retrieved my Corvette and pulled it in front of the hotel's main entranceway. I popped the hatch when Summer materialized with the bellhop in tow and soon my cramped car was en route to Somerset Mall.

Located in a northern suburb of Detroit, Somerset is the favorite shopping destination of Grosse Pointers after the decline of most of the malls near their enclave. Somerset has North and South sections on either side of a major thoroughfare. The sections are connected by a huge span of an enclosed pedestrian bridge. Whenever I visit Somerset and use the bridge, I ponder how the developer met requirements imposed by the same city that once denied my former fitness studio a sign permit.

I believe that it was originally called Somerset because of the prices. Some are set too high. I had my first eight-dollar ice cream cone at Somerset. The stores are toney, scrupulously clean, and the help is polite, well groomed, energetic and knowledgeable. The anchor stores do not hire a sales assistant for their makeup or jewelry counters unless she was at least the first runner-up at a Miss America Pageant. If an item has just arrived from Europe, it can be found first at Somerset. Summer knew the layout of Somerset Mall better than that of her own closets. After she got out of my car, she broke into a run like a horse heading back to the barn. Once inside the main doors, her chest heaved as she took big savory gulps of the air within. I trotted to keep up with her in her natural habitat as she whizzed by store window displays exclaiming, "That's new…oh, that's new too!" Her platinum charge card flashed like the knife of a Samurai while clerks bowed and greeted her by name. Within an hour I was groaning under the weight of her packages and wondering where to rent a rooftop carrier for my car.

We made it back to the Pointes without popping the windows out of my jam-packed Corvette and screeched to a halt in front of her favorite coffee shop. She tasted and spat out samples like a sommelier until she found the perfect blend. From there it was several blocks more to a day spa for a touchup on her nails and eyebrows by two attendants working simultaneously. Finally, as evening began to manifest itself, we arrived at the house. After thanking me profusely, she allowed me to schlep her packages and luggage inside. Had I known it was going to be the last time that I was to ever see her in person, I would have lingered for another minute or so. Instead, I raced back to my studio—and half a dozen miffed clients.

~~~~~~~~~~~~~~~~~~~~~~~~~~~~

The remainder of spring was divided as evenly as possible between writing, the fitness studio, and my ongoing lawsuit with the construction company. On a good day I was able to add seven more pages to my rough draft. On a bad day…just one. Rarely did I forego writing at least one page per day. By July, the manuscript was finished. It was 535 handwritten pages. A printer estimated that I would be left with somewhere under 400 pages after typesetting. I got three estimates and sold some Ford stock to pay for the book's first print run.

~~~~~~~~~~~~~~~~~~~~~~~~~~~~

As far as I know, Summer got her "Fourth of July in Boston Harbor" wish. I say this because the only time that I spoke with her was when I called her to check facts while I wrote. I now knew the subject of my book had been broached between her and Max, because of the rapid tapering off of information from her. What had once been an outpouring of Summer's every hope, dream, and wish had now been reduced to a cursory, "I'm fine, and you?" or "A little tired today." It was only during the second phone call I made that Summer let her guard down enough to give me any flavor about what yachting with a billionaire on the Eastern Seaboard was like. She blurted out how Max was in a constant state of crankiness. He had been going through yacht captains like a wheat thresher. Summer might bid one captain and first mate good night—only to be greeted by two strangers in the morning. Max had an especially volatile relationship with Boomer who, in increments of weeks and months, had accumulated the most seniority. Boomer had been hired and fired by the fickle billionaire so many times that he never fully unpacked his seabags when a stint ensued.

The primary purpose of my calls was to corroborate the order in which many of the events of the previous three years had occurred. I confess to having an ulterior motive as well. I was also trying to prompt an admission from Summer that she had loosely planned the liaison with Max from the very beginning. If so, I had already deciphered the "why." Father figure, power broker, and a backdoor forced acceptance into the social hierarchy were three things Max represented to the adopted little girl that was still inside of Summer. But if the brunette beauty had been using her voluptuous body and wily charms to facilitate a grand master plan to ensnare a billionaire, she would not admit to it. Instead she began to select her words more carefully. By my fourth phone call, I had the creeping impression that her cell phone receiver was betwixt the ears of two people. I stopped calling.

56

The Central Intelligence Agency (CIA) was originally formed as the national Security Agency (NSA). While the FBI is entrusted with discovering, pursuing, and arresting criminals within the borders of the United States, the CIA has a completely different set of responsibilities. The U.S. government has long recognized it has many enemies outside of its borders that wish to harm us and our worldwide interests. During the Cold War, the nuclear program of the U.S.S.R. was greatly advanced by secrets and information stolen by K.G.B. spies that infiltrated the U.S. Government. Although the CIA has had many successes abroad that the American public never gets wind of, one of its most glaring failures of late had been thoroughly scrutinized. Prior to 9/11, the CIA had heard "chatter" from various sources. Terrorists planned on inserting multiple agents into the U.S. population for the purpose of carrying out an act that would cause the country great harm. One of the main criticisms of the CIA regarding the World Trade Center attack is that it should have forwarded this information, even if it was only in the rumor stage, to the FBI. At this point, the nationwide network of agents, profilers, and informants employed by this law enforcement branch could have been deployed or at least alerted. There is no guarantee that the FBI could have thwarted the attack without specifics about the terrorists' identities or plans. But the current saying, "you make your own luck," certainly applies and the CIA's closedmouthedness prevented the FBI from doing so.

I would like to enlighten the public as to how Maxwell Lexington uses taxpayers' money when he engages the FBI to do his bidding, but I would first like to return to the CIA—and how Max and Summer tried to duplicate one of its spy locating techniques.

On occasion, the CIA itself becomes infiltrated by an agent of a foreign government. The same is true of other branches of our government that deal with our secrets. The CIA knows this because they have agents inside these foreign governments that *tell* them when one of our government's secrets has been stolen. Without getting involved in the history of "moles" and "double agents," I would like to explain the basics of "disinformation." Since "moles," like their namesake, operate quietly and unobserved, by the time that the existence of one is realized, the damage is already done. Since a mole or any other spy is usually loathe to come forward for fear of execution for treason, other detection methods must be employed. If a mole is suspected, and the group of possible suspects can be narrowed down, a secret is *fabricated*. A different version of this secret is then fed to each suspect. If the mole is in fact in the group, then eventually one version of the secret will wind up in the hands of the foreign government. Our agent then forwards the recently arrived secret back to the CIA. The version that they receive is then checked against the version that was originally furnished to each suspect. When they have a match, they know who the mole is!

I do not know whether Max Lexington knows anything about the CIA and their methods. But I am positive that Summer does not. If pressed, she might even say that CIA stands for Clothed In Armani, but I cannot be sure. What I am now sure of, however, is that Summer began to feed me a steady diet of disinformation in late July of 2003.

The first phone call that I received from her began with a perfunctory hello. The entire tone was different. "Hey, how's my buddy Mark doing? You remember me?"

"One could never forget you," I replied.

"Are you still writing that book or did you finally give up?"

"Well, I'm not writing it anymore…because I'm finished."

"Now you don't have anything bad to say about me in it, do you?"

"Actually, it's about 70/30, with the 70 being all of the good stuff. I don't think people would want to read about somebody who is an angel 24 hours a day."

"I suppose I can see that. But what I really called about was to pick your brain. I have been looking at condos in high-rises in and around Boca. I've been looking at the ones with a view of the Intracoastal Waterway. I'd prefer something with a view of the ocean…actually I'd *prefer* something with a view of *both*…but they want an arm and a leg for those! Now, I've found a three-bedroom unit that I like…all brand new construction, for $460,000 but the agent says that if I act within two days they'll write it up for $445,000. Mark, I know for a fact that a similar unit in the same building that was just purchased three months ago has sold for $485,000!"

I began to do some math. With a respectable down payment and a reasonable interest rate, Summer's payment would be about $3000 a month. The information that she had given me many months ago was that she received a $2300 per month stipend from her ex-husband. I mentally added up association fees and utilities, then threw in the lease payment and insurance on her Mercedes. It was expensive to be Summer, and I could easily imagine her spending another $3000 a month after that. Red flags went up everywhere. I responded anyway. "Well, anything you buy in South Florida is bound to appreciate quickly."

She fed me some more. "I know. And Max has made some calls and says that he'll co-sign my loan and can get me a fixed rate of six percent or an adjustable of only four."

More red flags. A man worth three billion dollars, who wouldn't borrow money if he were suffocating and it was oxygen, was going to co-sign a loan for his mistress. Was the man who had more secret funds squirreled away than Saddam Hussein now claiming that he couldn't come up with four days of his income? I added up one and one repeatedly but kept arriving at four.

Summer fed me another question designed to determine whether or not I was buying into the "billionaire's mistress needs a condominium loan" routine.

"Mark, what I'm really worried about is the payments. They're going to be about $3000 a month plus incidentals. I have some money from the divorce, but what will I do when that runs out?"

I was being played. I was supposed to relay this information to someone, but I didn't know who. "You could just make the payments until you run low on money."

"Then what?"

"Then you sell it for a huge profit."

"But then where will I live?"

"You move to somewhere much cheaper and buy another place for cash."

"But what if I want to continue to live here?"

I had grown tired of my "Naïve One" role. I decided to speak of the unspeakable. "Well…you could always get a job."

Summer hung up soon after that.

I was never able to decide if that particular piece of disinformation was meant to be disseminated to her husband or to be written into my book somehow in true *Stop the Presses!* fashion. I *do* know that she owns that condo free and clear today—and that I have never been invited over to see it.

In August, the disinformation campaign began anew. I received her call on a Tuesday around mid-afternoon. Summer was doing her best to act tired and worried at the same moment. "Hiii, it's me. Long time no talk to."

"Hello Summer, did you close on your condo yet?"

She hedged and side-stepped before offering an explanation about various delays until she was able to procure new carpeting. I decided to make it easier for her to say what was on her mind. "You sound tired." I said, pointing out the obvious.

"I am. And I'm so worried too."

"How come?" I continued to bite.

"Mark," she said in a stage whisper, "I'm pregnant!"

"Whoa, congratulations! That's wonderful." I was tempted to add a little levity by asking her, *"Is it yours?"* but I refrained.

"No, Mark. It's *not* wonderful! I'm not ready to raise another child. I'm not settled in at my new place. I've been through an emotional wringer with Max. I'm just not up to it psychologically."

She sounded ready to entertain a personal question.

"Is it Max's?"

"Yes, yes, that's the one thing that I'm sure of. When I told him he flew down here right away and we had some testing done. One of them was a paternity test and it is definitely his."

"How far along are you?"

"I'm almost two months. But Mark, I made an appointment to get an abortion tomorrow at 11."

"That's a terrible idea." I was blunt even though I didn't believe that any such appointment existed.

"Why, Mark? Why? I don't have any right to bring another life into this world unless I'm prepared to love it and take care of it."

Summer spoke in hushed, gushy tones. If I had been on the Academy's nominating committee I would not have voted to put her name on the ballot. At this point I was sure that I was receiving a twofer. Summer was delivering two pieces of disinformation in one phone call. The first piece was undoubtedly about her inclination to have her pregnancy aborted. Summer craved acceptance into a family of her own flesh and blood. Since she was adopted and the names of her birth parents had proven maddenly elusive, her only other choice was to create her own relatives. Summer would have shopped at Wal-Mart before she terminated a Maxwell Lexington pregnancy. But this pregnancy meant more than a guaranteed family. It meant more than a chance to have a girl that she could pamper and dress and introduce to nail salons and cappuccino. This child would also mean financial security and the guarantee of an endless supply of the tasteful material things that gave her life meaning. Summer would be able to travel on a whim, and to join any club that struck her fancy.

Deep down, Summer suspected that she was the illegitimate offspring of uppercrust stock, but that the circumstances of her conception had denied the young ingenue her rightful place. Her ignominious upbringing in a farmhouse would now be avenged as soon as she could work out an arrangement with the obscenely wealthy father of her child. If Summer would be loathe to end the pregnancy, Max would be doubly so. His strict Catholic upbringing had ensured a lifetime of guilt long ago, and an absolutely forbidden abortion would only add to the burden that he carried with him daily.

A reaffirmation of his virility was at stake as well. Fathering an infant at 73 years would show the world that the aging lion was still a powerful force to be reckoned with. And what better justification to "carry on" with a woman 31 years his junior than procreation? The abortion threat looked, barked, and wagged its tail like a gambit. It had been whispered to me only to see who confronted them back with it.

I played my role. I spoke of the cadre of fine nannies that Summer would be able to afford this time around. I reminded her of the freedom that would normally be denied the average single mother…but not to her. If anything, I pitched, this newborn would give Summer the family and the financial security that she longed for. I used every word in my vocabulary that pertained to her "situation" other than the words *meal ticket*.

The second piece of disinformation lie in the progress to date of the gestation. Summer was not two months pregnant any more than I was (although in truth I was probably more cautious than her). By the time that I was privy to her "revelation" she had doubtless whispered it to her friends, ten obstetricians, every pair of ears belonging to anyone who groomed, massaged or fed her, and the doorman at her condo. I am very sure that if I had spoken to her neighbor's cat on the day after she told me, his response would have been "old news!"

By the time Summer broke her joyous news to me, she was in her eighth month. Perhaps she and Max were concerned I would insist on being Summer's Lamaze coach. Maybe they were worried I would want to review every medical file related to her prenatal care. In truth, I would *not* have requested the honor of cutting the umbilical cord—or to be allowed to videotape the blessed event. I would *not* have loaded up a posse of paparazzi into a limo and sped down the interstate to encamp outside of her condo building, either.

While I was approached by one excited Grosse Pointe gossip maven after another about the impending delivery, I was far more concerned with photographing the cover art for my book.

Whatever its original intention, Summer and Max's disinformation campaign fell short. My advice to Summer is that if she were ever to become a John LeCarre fan and desire a job at the CIA, she might want to leave the results of this particular foray into the intelligence field off her resume.

57

I NEEDED AN EDITOR. Two friends and a relative all took a crack at it. I furnished each with copies printed from my home computer. Eagerly, I awaited the return of each binder, ready to analyze and incorporate the sea of red ink I anticipated every page would prompt. The binders were finally turned in over a two-week period. I was grateful for every notation, but many pages had been left untouched. Since meeting Max and Summer, I had developed a credo: *If it is possible for a man to learn from his mistakes, I am one of the smartest men in the world.* As one of the world's smartest men, I knew that producing the final product could not be that easy. I knew that dozens of punctuation and spelling errors lurked in between the innocuous Greco-Roman characters on those pages. I needed a professional editor, and as the days flew by, the urgency grew. The editor would have to be highly educated and utterly anal. His or her life would have to be free of any distractions or obligations that might deter them from devoting their full time, energy, and attention to their assignment.

~~~~~~~~~~~~~~~~~~~~~~~~~~~~

Violet Snethcamp was not only a client at the studio, she was a retired schoolteacher. She filled her days with reading, tournament bridge, grandchildren, and charity work.

I explained to her that she would have to set these things aside for a time. My manuscript could take the place of any recommendations from her book club, and the ladies in her bridge group—most of them, anyway—would still be there next month. I assured Violet that while her grandchildren would not actually benefit from a month without her, they would appreciate her more when their regular relationship resumed. As for her charity work, I remained adamant in maintaining that the homeless simply would *not* consume much soup in the next month. To further tempt my prospective editor, I purchased a brand new red Bic pen, gift wrapped it, and presented it to her in an elaborate, if impromptu, ceremony. Finally, I gently hinted that nobody needs a 230-pound stalker marring their retirement years. To my delight, Violet agreed to peruse the first 50 pages—and filled them with red ink! She soon developed a routine that revolved around the remaining 450 pages, and I had a fully edited manuscript back on my desk in under a month.

A razor-sharp woman I had hired to set up the final text insisted on performing a final edit as well. By early October, the text and the cover art were on their way to the printer.

On December third, I rented a truck and picked up my first order. I sold ten at the fitness studio on that first night.

I knew that the major bookstores in the area were inundated daily with solicitations from first-time authors. To maintain a lofty goal of selling ten books a day, I knew that I would need more than one retail outlet and a website. I had lined up a sparkling, beautiful woman of Italian heritage named Rene to place them in coffee and gift shops. Orders began to flow in over the Internet. A Grosse Pointe real estate agent bought 14 as Christmas presents. Soon, I was selling *15* books per day. Within two weeks, Rene had convinced a dozen outlets to carry them on their shelves. But I still lacked a retail network in the five cities that comprised the Pointes.

I needed someone who knew the area intimately. I had to enlist the services of a long time Grosse Pointer who knew whether Ultima Hair Salon in the Farms would carry the book and why Basket Works in Grosse Pointe Park may not.

One of the most important requirements of a potential Grosse Pointe representative and wholesale distributor would be motivation. I wanted an individual who had strong feelings about the story that the book told...and wanted as many residents of the closely-knit enclave to read about it as possible.

After careful consideration, Jillian Campbell got the nod. She admitted to procuring and reading the book days after its publication, and seemed to have no qualms about the role I asked her to play in its distribution. While she knew of nearly every shoppe and possible retail outlet in the immediate area, most of the proprietors knew her only by her married name.

I was right, of course. Every second venue that Jillian approached agreed to accept a batch of books. Before I could say "Cheap Billionaire," six outlets were reordering almost daily. Within a week, the book's daily sales were at 50. Enthusiastically at first, Jillian re-supplied each store, and then dutifully drove back to my gym to surrender cash and checks. Max's other daughters began a vicious campaign of visiting each outlet and railing at their owners for carrying my book—until many acquiesced. Jillian soon hinted that she felt like a pack mule as she trudged through the January snows. But collectively, Rene, Jillian and myself began to expand our network to outlying cities, guided in part by my constant Internet orders. I placed a second and much larger order with the printer and girded myself for life as a delivery driver. As I was girding, it happened.

A woman left a message on the office answering machine. She claimed to represent an 800-strong chain of bookstores called *Barnes & Noble*. Always on the lookout for a hoax, I phoned back. The way that the woman's Executive Assistant answered the phone sounded legitimate. I held for a minute, listening to elevator music.

The woman came on and I introduced myself. She sounded even more legitimate than her assistant. Their bookstores in the Detroit area had received many inquiries. The managers were adamant about filling the demand. She wanted to know if I had applied to their headquarters as of yet, asking them to distribute my book. I replied that one of my PR people had sent a book and a cover letter to the New York office, but I had not heard anything back. The woman informed me that my request would eventually be reviewed in New York by a buyer—and that the usual protocol was for the buyer to make a decision as to whether an order for my book would be placed.

The woman then informed me that she was the buyer's boss. She had decided to skip the review process and place an order. In the meantime, I was to contact a local book distributor and begin the paperwork and contracts that would precede any orders. She asked for a copy of the book. I told her the I could not make it to the Fed Ex office for another eight minutes, but that she would have it before noon the next day. I thanked the woman, hung up the phone and steadied myself against a stack of book cartons in my living room. If this was a hoax, it was flawlessly executed. I would not chastise myself if the call turned out to be nothing more than a clever ruse.

In the meantime, I would operate under the assumption that my book had just been picked up by the Holy Grail of book chains. I had stumbled upon them…or rather they upon me, just as I was preparing for a year of delivering books in quantities of ten. I phoned the book distributor. I would still be delivering books…but by the hundreds. He faxed me an order for my entire remaining inventory. He told me that he not only distributed to Barnes & Noble but to Borders and Waldenbooks as well.

I had officially been in the publishing business for two months. My marketing plan was now one year ahead of schedule.

After my phone call from headquarters, I might have planned on a pleasant, relaxing year. I might have scheduled my weeks around driving the occasional truckload of books up to the distributor—and on checking my mailbox for checks. I might have planned on making up for all of the boating, camping, and vacations I had missed over the last four years. But I would have had to change my plans. As a mild recession ended, dozens of new clients began to pour into the studio. They were making money again and wanted to live long enough to spend it. Health and fitness once again became a greater priority than catching Osama and Saddam, and business hummed. At a time when I was trying to pare back my hours, I was forced to increase them.

Two weeks after my call from headquarters, my cell phone began to ring with unfamiliar numbers on the Caller ID. Bookstore managers began to call every other day to line up booksignings at their establishments. Nor had my original retail venues forgotten about me. A coffee shop called Cup-a-cinos on Kercheval—in the Pointes—and a restaurant named Perfetto Gelato—in a city to the north—hosted quaint little booksignings where complete strangers assured me that they enjoyed the book and then purchased more to send as gifts. A favorite restaurant called Crews Inn in the township of my residence insisted on selling the book behind the bar *and* hosting a signing as well. I reached a new level of Nirvana there as I discovered that I could stuff myself with swordfish and perch with my right hand—and sign books with my left.

Soon, the scraps of paper that I used to remind myself of an upcoming signing evolved into an appointment book. After months of calls, the appointment book had some weeks with more than half of the days spoken for.

Days after I had received my first website book order, I received my first e-mail from a reader. Although I was prepared for a scathing review, instead it was extremely laudatory. The next day brought another letter that was, for the most part, complimentary. The letter writer's only issue was that the book did not wrap up enough loose ends. After some time I began to notice a pattern. While most of the readers seemed to enjoy it, many wanted to chastise me for the inconclusive ending—some more vigorously than others. I had braced my editors and myself for a healthy portion of hate mail from readers who thought that they identified themselves or a loved one in the book. I was prepared to respond to every "…and may you burn in hell" letter to the best of my ability…and offer the writer a greater role in the sequel. Out of the hundreds of letters that I did receive, though, only a half dozen made any attempt to eternally damn me. I was disappointed, but my hopes rose when a woman who claimed to have attended college wrote more than a few lines. She claimed that I now had negative Karma. She jumped to the defense of her friend Summer. Her main point seemed to be that she had spotted a spelling error in the book. Amidst her ramblings, I counted four spelling errors. She also misspelled the name of her supposed friend, and further spoiled her diatribe with countless incomplete sentences. As politely as possible—and hoping to cultivate a pen pal—I wrote her back and corrected her errors. Sadly, I never heard from her again.

Perhaps the most intriguing of the communiqués that I received were from individuals who had read the book and either worked, had worked for, or claimed to know Max Lexington. I dismissed the two letters that accused Max outright of having one of his competitors murdered in the 1970s, but tried to answer the rest.

58

Before I delve into any specifics regarding information in some of the letters that I received and *was* able to verify, some background is necessary.

~~~~~~~~~~~~~~~~~~~~~~~~~~~~

During my own affiliation with Max, an extremely wealthy contemporary (and business partner in Max's fleet of private jets) ran afoul of the law. The contemporary had made his initial millions building and leasing out enormous real estate projects. His philanthropic pursuits led to his purchase of a world-renowned auction house. A profit boosting shortcut led to some tawdry accusations by the Federal Government. While Max's former partner remained silent, the accusations would not go away. Eventually, they became more than accusations. The billionaire was indicted by the Feds and relied on a phalanx of top flight attorneys to avoid the embarrassing consequences of the plea bargain that they offered. At the end of the trial, a jury found the billionaire guilty.

During the sentencing hearing, the convicted felon's legal eagles maintained that a man who had been responsible for so many good works in his lifetime should get a lighter sentence. A man whose largesse sent ripples of good fortune amongst those in need should receive only probation with no jail time, they begged. At 76 years of age, the man should pay a fine and return home to his grandchildren. The judge disagreed. The billionaire was ordered to prison for three years. The sentence hit Max close to home. They were close to the same age—each was a self-made man. They flew in the same social circles. They had once been partners. Max marveled and shook his head at the injustice of the outcome for weeks. I do not believe that he ever went to visit his friend in prison. He also privately resolved to be more cautious than ever before—insisting that paid underlings soil their hands while his own stayed clean.

~~~~~~~~~~~~~~~~~~~~~~~~~~~~~~

Most states in the U.S. levy sales taxes upon their residents. They tax automobiles, clothing, boats, sunglasses, and fence posts. In Michigan there is no tax on services or labor if you are getting your car repaired, your washing machine fixed or your lawn mowed. But there is a tax if you *buy* a new car, washing machine or lawn mower, and any grass seed or fertilizer is going to cost the consumer another six percent of the total bill. In Michigan, there is no sales tax on food bought in a grocery store but there is on food bought at a McDonalds. If you grow your own vegetables, and like to start from scratch, there is a sales tax on the seedlings and even on the seeds. If you own a home, you are taxed every year that you live in it—and pay extra to the government for anything that *keeps* it habitable like electricity, natural gas, water—both coming in and going out—and phone service. In Michigan, consumers pay a sales tax for every book they buy, but not for magazines, newspapers, and greeting cards. If a new car is purchased, a sales tax is rendered unto the state and, whether the car is resold to a neighbor or a stranger, another tax is paid before the transaction is official and duly recorded. If the owner of a car would like to drive it legally, he will cough up more fees on an annual basis for a license plate. The gasoline that is needed to make the car go is heavily taxed, and the brake pads that make the car stop are taxed. Unless it is necessary to journey over a toll road—that charges you to travel on concrete that was bought and paid for long ago—no overt fee to use roadways exist. Crossing bridges over certain bodies of water can be a source of government revenue, however, as is using some of the tunnels underneath.

This is in no way meant to infer that while some taxes may seem unfairly levied, the revenues derived from them are unnecessary. Gasoline and fuel taxes help to fund the concrete that we drive on. Property taxes are spent on protecting us from fire and criminals. These taxes educate our children and give them parks to play in. Sales taxes are parceled out by the state government to build and maintain roads, bridges, prisons for wily criminals like Martha Stewart, and our court system.

Federal income taxes keep the wheels of government spinning. This money pays the salaries of the federal employees that make new laws and policies. It pays the salaries of the employees that ensure the laws and policies are followed. Our huge military capability exists because American citizens and businesses pool together a percentage of their incomes to fund the men, women, and machines that keep our country safe from foreign threats. The CIA uses our tax dollars to furnish us with information about these potential foreign attacks.

The FBI has traditionally been charged with spending the money allotted to it by our government to provide security for our citizens within the borders of our country. The FBI employs agents who profile and catch serial killers that murder innocent people in one state and then travel to another to murder again. FBI agents are among the first on the scene of a bank robbery or kidnapping. The FBI employs accountants that follow the complex paper trails of people who steal, bilk, and cheat honest citizens out of billions of dollars every year. Special FBI agents protect our citizens from computerized predators that steal from U.S. citizens electronically from thousands of miles away. Clever agents prowl the Internet, searching for the child molesters and other sexual predators that try to lure our children out of their homes to clandestine meetings and worse.

Unfortunately, our precious tax money is sometimes wasted when a FBI agent is sent on a wild goose chase. If Maxwell Lexington feels wronged or insulted—he can call in chits through his attorneys and friends of friends. It is thus that he can use the same investigatory powers that the Federal Government has developed to protect its citizens from its enemies—to harass and intimidate his own.

As mentioned previously, a groundswell of demand prompted the Waldenbooks chain to order, stock, and sell my book. It was not long after the first copies went on display that I began to receive some surprising feedback from individual store managers. Accustomed to being approached by suburban moms seeking out the latest edition of *Harry Potter*, the managers were now being "interviewed" by a badge-flashing FBI agent. And the only book the agent was interested in was mine.

Of course, the interviews were the end result of Max, ranting and raving in his attorney's office, demanding that the book be "banned from all of the goddamn bookstores."

But the interviews had the opposite effect of the one desired by the belly-aching billionaire.

The presence of the FBI agents intrigued the managers, and they began to view the book as controversial—so they ordered more.

They also contacted the author as quickly as possible, scheduling book signings in their stores as rapidly as was feasible. For months, I would walk into a store at the allotted time to be greeted by a huge display of my books near the front door. In the future, I hope to contract out all of my PR work to Maxwell Lexington and his friends at the FBI.

If an individual has devoted a great deal of their life to accumulating wealth, it is their natural inclination to protect it from those who would seek to share it. Max's 11-million-dollar yacht was built and outfitted in Italy. As was common practice, however, it was registered under a corporate name in the Bahamas. Over the course of several years, Max saved hundreds of thousands in luxury taxes, sales taxes, and annual registration fees. Max never owned any of his 20-million-dollar private jets outright. Leasing corporations and seemingly fragmented partnerships owned the planes on paper and dreamt up one write-off after another—until the tax bill was zero. The depreciation of the planes resulted in the true owners owing less taxes to the Federal government, not more. Of course, the end result was always the same. Max could pick up his phone and have a private jet fueled—and its pilots ready—to whisk him away at 500 miles an hour to anywhere in the country within minutes. The captain and crew of his yacht were on call 24 hours a day to meet Max at any port that he dictated, and were expected to be prepared to accommodate guest parties of from two to fifty—depending on his whim.

Pilots and crewmembers may work at the beck and call of the rich man, but their paychecks originate from murky corporate bank accounts that deduct their entire salaries from governmental tax obligations. Oceanfront penthouses are listed as entertainment expenses whether anyone but the occasional mistress is entertained there or not. Automobiles with price tags that begin at $100,000 are driven by the wealthy man and his family and itemized on the corporate books as cars used for business purposes only.

It is important at this juncture to address the subject of "bartering." If a clever millionaire made his fortune by, for instance, leasing computers, he may seek to trade some of his companies' computers for something of value to him. If he were able to trade $120,000 worth of computers or related services for a $120,000 car, the advantages to both parties involved in the transaction are many. The seller of the computers would not have to declare a profit on their sale. The seller of the car may claim that he sold it at a loss, as the actual cost of the computers may have been only half of the car's retail value. Very wealthy Americans often smile when they hear about themselves being categorized in a 45 percent tax bracket. As soon as the federal employees who write the tax code close one loophole, two more are discovered by the clever CPAs that protect the wealth of the rich.

To a certain extent, Max Lexington paid and avoided paying taxes like any other wealthy man. A platoon of accountants and company controllers poured over tax laws to ensure that his privately held company was always in compliance. Millions of dollars in withholding taxes were forwarded to governmental treasuries every month as they were collected from Max's 4000 employees. Company checks for the personal expenses of Max and his family were never written to the same place in the exact same manner. This insured that each check would have its own separate category should an audit of the company's books occur. Miscellaneous accounts and funds were aggressively guarded by Max's trusted daughter Bertha, with whom any outsider needed to pass muster in order to speak to the founder and sole stockholder.

And outsiders clamored to speak to Max every day. Salesmen representing large manufacturers wished to expound on the benefits to Max of having their lines in his chain of 50 stores. Mutual fund managers hoped to personally tout their individual fund's impressive rate of return over one year, five years, and ten years in the hopes of being entrusted with a small portion of Max's billions. Real estate brokers howled at the gates with offers to sell retail chains, buildings, and vacant land. Advertising account executives begged for a five-minute block of time to espouse how their demographics were best suited to the customers that Max's company cultivated. Politicians sent representatives from their re-election committees to remind Max how pro-business their bosses were, and what attentive listeners they could be when Max had any concerns.

Local judges needed to run for office periodically as well. Lawn signs and newspaper ads cost their campaign committees money. In Michigan, the local communities provide facilities for District

Judges. The compensation of the positions averages $105,000 per year, with a liberal dose of vacation time, holiday pay, and time off for illness. Medical coverage for the judge and his loved ones is superb because no citizen wants a judge with a nagging brain tumor ruling on matters of local importance. The District Judges that I have encountered, while being very diverse in their work ethic, are not universally known for putting in a great deal of overtime. Their duties are far ranging and include drunken driving cases, traffic violations of all sorts, landlord/tenant decisions, barking dog and other local ordinance violations, and monetary disputes between parties involving less than $15,000.

On the criminal side, a local District Judge is responsible for deciding if an alleged violator of the law will go on to trial—and if that violator will be released on bail while awaiting trial. The District Judge is granted the authority to sentence a defendant—once found guilty of misdemeanors and minor felonies—to probation or a period of up to one year in the county jail. The Judge may also impose fines with no incarceration based on predetermined guidelines, and hold jail time like an ax over the head of a defendant to ensure prompt payment. District Judges are also given the power to approve search warrants—based on requests from local police departments—so that cars, homes, and businesses can be investigated or searched without the owner's consent to look for evidence of a crime. Inversely, District Judges have the power to toss out a piece of evidence if a policeman did not obtain it using the proper procedures. Every ten years or so, a District Judge will actually do the latter. A District Judge has the authority to enforce any law or ordinance enacted by an overzealous city council—no matter how unreasonable. Judges want to be re-elected…so they enforce with vigor.

In Michigan, a District Judge does not have the authority to sentence an individual to long prison terms (Circuit Court Judges do…they are employed by the County). They cannot award large dollar figures to plaintiffs in lengthy civil cases either. They do, however, have the power to make a small business owner's life miserable, or to allow an important person to plead a drunk driving charge into a careless driving one. District Judges are unable to promise anything to anyone who donates generously to their campaigns, but if one is to do business in their community, it may be wise to donate with gusto.

Influence peddling is a dirty term in any community, and the Pointes are no exception, but sometimes a driver can be on the very edge of losing their privilege to drive. Like my friend Lee, they may have a need for speed. Some people, by virtue of the fact that they drive 40,000 miles per year, may have a license in jeopardy simply because of the law of averages or their attentiveness to a cell phone instead of the rules of the road. But the law is meant to apply equally to everyone, and it does not recognize that this person's livelihood may depend on their ability to continue to drive. For special circumstances like these, a District Judge in the Pointes maintains a private practice as an attorney in a nearby community. If the errant driver's license is important enough to them, and surrendering it to the State of Michigan for a period of time is not an option, they may withdraw a large sum of cash from their bank account. The cash, along with a copy of the ticket, is then forwarded to the secretary of the attorney/judge. Beyond this point a court appearance on the part of the cited driver becomes unnecessary, and the cash will eventually be disbursed through the proper channels until the ticket goes away or is reduced to the point of a wrist-slap.

59

The Honorable Judge Richard Tomasinobeni, seated high up above his courtroom, surveyed his domain. He looked to his right at the line of people clutching their traffic tickets. He smiled inwardly. This was his courtroom, and they would wait. He looked out into the sea of concerned faces seated in front of him. He did not recognize most of them, but a few of them were familiar. In the back row was a landlord who was making his third visit due to a broken handrail. The man was from the old country—and defiant. Judge T. found it ironic that the same tenant who broke the handrail filed a complaint with the city inspector, but the law was the law. Two rows in front of the landlord was the woman who was afraid of her grown son. But if she could not find a way to keep him from driving her unlicensed automobile, then Judge T. would find a way to *fine* her until she did.

One row from the front sat the gym owner from down the street with his attorney. The guy had been here at least four or five times over some *parking dispute* with the city, for Chrissake! His attorney had unduly burdened this court with ridiculous briefs and motions that directed the Judge to do some research. This was the courtroom of Judge Richard Tomasinobeni, and *no one* would direct him to do anything! They could make four trips or forty—and they would discover the same thing each time. This Bench would uphold the law as it saw fit. Besides, he chortled to himself, he hadn't enjoyed researching laws that were written decades ago when he was just an attorney, so why should he do it now?

Judge T. had been shuffling some papers during his perusal, and now he looked down at the floor in front of his perch. A father and his teenage daughter stared up at him. They seemed sufficiently cowed by the trappings of justice around them. His clerk stared at them languidly, the boredom on her face apparent. The Judge's robe had been freshly cleaned before he donned it this morning and it felt soft. But did the landlord, or the gym owner, or these two in front of him care how much this spotless black robe mattered to the Judge? They did not. All they knew is that their lives had been put on hold until this man in the flowing robe decided when they could continue. God, he loved the power that this courtroom gave him. Judge T. wondered why it was even necessary these two appear before him today. The file was thin. Apparently the girl owned a dog that barked. But it was the father, as the owner of the home, that was responsible and would pay for whatever justice Judge T. decided to mete out. He wondered if either of them suspected, even in their wildest dreams, what the ruler of this courtroom was wearing underneath the fresh black robe? Judge T. rubbed his legs together slowly so as not to draw attention. He luxuriated for a moment in the way that the Christian Dior pantyhose felt when one leg caressed the other. The teenage girl probably already knew that feeling. He looked at the father. The man looked like he never would. He would never realize what he had missed out on his whole *life* before he died! The man was missing out on an entire world of sensuality that he didn't know existed! He rubbed his legs together even slower. Judge T. had stared at the ticket for long enough now. He needed to address this matter soon. The man's daughter probably looked up to him. She probably depended on him for everything. The father was well dressed. He gave her a regular allowance, there could be no doubt. Judge T. wondered how close they were. Maybe he could shake her up a little bit.

He began, "After careful review of this violation the court would like to ask the defendant at this time how he would like to plead. Bear in mind that if you plead not guilty you are entitled to a trial by jury..." The Judge went through the same spiel that he was forced to go through 20 times in the morning and as many times in the afternoon as it took to clear his docket. He already knew that the girl's father was going to plead guilty and that the Judge would then accept the plea and impose a $50 fine. The fun would come only after the Judge warned what the alternatives to the fine were.

The man plead guilty and the Judge imposed the 50 dollars. Then he began, "Now you two seem like nice people, and young lady I understand that the dog belongs to you, is that correct?" The girl nodded. "But your father is the owner of the property and is responsible for what happens there. So if your dog continues to bark, the city officer is going to come and issue you another violation."

Judge T. tried to smile benevolently as he said it. To the attorneys in the courtroom, it looked like he was starting to pass a kidney stone. The Judge went on. It was time to drop the hammer.

"Now, as I told you previously, this was a civil misdemeanor and as such I could have imposed a $250 fine and a sentence of 90 days in jail. But in spite of the dog belonging to you it is your father who receives the tickets and it is your father that could wind up in jail!"

God, Judge T. thought, *I just love saying the word jail. It always gets a rise out of them...even when they know how ridiculous it would be.*

"What are ya' in for? Murder, rape, robbery?..."

"Naw, my daughter's dog barks, but I was framed!"

Judge T.'s belly convulsed for an instant at his own wit. The brief movement reminded Judge T. of his secret as his skin rubbed against the waistband of the pantyhose. He touched his knees together. He hadn't always felt bold enough to wear them like this. When he had first taken the bench, he had been afraid to wear them at all. A political favor had gotten him narrowly elected, and a gaggle of female attorney bitches had seen through the politics and voted him not qualified. The nylons and everything else had stayed in the two bureau drawers for some time while he tried to master his new kingdom. His friend and mentor, the senior District Judge, had tried to help. He was able to smooth over enough of Richard's mistakes until he started to get the hang of it. The man, bless his gavel, still had to…but not nearly as often.

Gradually though, the nylons found their way out again. At first it was only under his pants, and not every day. Then, on one special day with a very light docket, the pants stayed locked up in his office. Judge T. felt so good and so free wearing only the pantyhose—he resolved never to mete out justice again while wearing conventional trousers. When things in the courtroom began to heat up and get too serious, His Honor only had to let his mind wander for an instant to the secret beneath the robes. His countenance could change from serious to serene in seconds—with no one ever the wiser.

He thought back wistfully to the afternoons that he had spent with Mistress Victoria. He smiled wickedly at the sharp rebuke he would receive from her if she knew about the nylons—and of his plans to use the *same* vibrating anal plug when he took the bench next week!

Next up was the gym owner and his attorney. This one had gall. He had requested a jury trial for a parking violation at his business. *The city wasn't going to back down either*, Judge T. thought with a sigh. His Honor detested jury trials. They ate up his afternoons and crowded his docket. The guy's attorney was dressed nice. She might live in Grosse Pointe, though. God, he hated those people. They would strut into his courtroom with their nice clothes and their fancy cars parked out in the lot. Sure, they had explanations for their violations—just like the poor people. But unlike the poor people they could afford to pay, even if they were as innocent as they professed to be.

For people who pretended to be as educated as they were well off, it took them a long time to learn a lesson. The only laws in this courtroom were the ones that produced revenue. The attorney was speaking again. If this went to a jury, His Honor could lose as much as two afternoons of Internet time and knew it. It felt good to network with others who shared his hobby, and after a tough morning Judge T. needed to feel good. It made his blood boil that this guy would have the audacity not to trust him. Judge T. made a notation. A couple of bench warrants ought to rattle his cage. Nothing said, "surprise" like opening the mail after a long day to find an arrest warrant! If his attorney bitched, the front office could cover. "Bureaucratic snafu" would be explanation enough. Maybe this guy's attorney was one of the bitches that voted him "not qualified" when he was just getting his feet wet. If she was and thought she'd get anywhere in *this* courtroom, she had bigger cajones than her client did. Of course, neither of them realized that Judge T. had been compensated quite handsomely for making the gym owner's life miserable.

His Honor took a deep breath while the guy's attorney babbled. He was getting upset. He crossed his legs at the shins. He felt better. He'd feel better still after the first of the year—when he'd start with the corset too. As his mind cleared, he wondered why the city had it in for this guy. Maybe the guy had just pissed off the wrong department head, but Judge T. didn't think so. It sounded like a higher power somewhere was angry. He had received the ticket *and* the cash envelope at the same time—for $5000; he'd do his part. He'd ensure that this ticket didn't go away. The attorney was still babbling. Too bad His Honor couldn't just take the guy aside and talk to him in private. He could explain how he was just wasting his time and money. Before a jury could rule, His Honor would just hand down a directed verdict. The guy would be found guilty before the trial started—but wouldn't have a clue until after it ended.

The attorney sounded ready to wind up her argument. His Honor looked down at his next case. It was an arraignment. The cops had grabbed some guy pouring roofing nails into the street. They claimed he had been doing it for six months. They said that people on six blocks had gotten hundreds of flat tires. They claimed that they staked out the area for weeks before arresting this poor guy. The Judge thought for a moment. People got flat tires all the time. Maybe it was just kids. Nobody got a flat the day they saw the defendant pouring. The cops cleaned it up too soon. Sounded like the poor guy was getting the shaft for some teenage vandals. Sounded like he wasn't guilty of anything more than littering. Judge T. resolved to bind the poor guy over for trial but set bail at $100. Sometimes these detectives thought that they were God's gift to the city. In a minute they'd find out who ruled this roost.

The gym owner's attorney stopped talking. That was good. The Honorable Judge Richard Tomasinobeni leaned over and ruled. "Motion denied!"

60

January of 2004 had not rung in well for Martin Fife, P.I. Divorced, bankrupt, and living in his brother's guestroom, Martin now spent the majority of his time investigating *The Movie Channel*. The phrase "having to look up to see bottom" fit, but was not descriptive enough. In a rare moment of communication, Martin informed his concerned younger brother that he "felt so low that he'd have to climb a ladder to suck off a dog."

On the positive side, now that Martin's aortas were full of stents, the pain in his chest had vanished. And somehow, his P.I. license had remained intact. It was one of the few assets that the bankruptcy court and his ex-wife's lawyer couldn't touch. With his health problems in a state of cease-fire, he had begun to ponder getting back into the field. Nevertheless, it was with some trepidation that he answered the phone on a Monday morning that first week of January. The number on the Caller I.D. was a familiar one, though not one that had appeared for quite some time.

"Martin speaking," he said with a wince.

"Did you recognize my cell number on your screen or do I have to reintroduce myself?"

"No, I know who this is," Martin responded.

"My wife heard on the gossip vine that you've fallen on some hard times lately."

"If you don't mind my saying so, the times wouldn't be as hard if you paid me that $75,000 from my last bill," Martin hinted.

"If we had settled up 18 months ago, one court or the other would have thrown it into the pot and it would still be gone. Is Benny out of the coma yet?"

"Yeah. Last time I heard from his attorney, he was back living with his mom and almost able to feed himself."

"How about your gambling problem? Have you been staying away from the casinos?"

Geez, Martin thought, *what don't you hear?* "Yeah, I got some help and I don't go near downtown anymore."

"Good, let's review where my money went two years ago. I hired you to ensure that my father's lady friend stayed away from him. Instead, she has borne him a child…which would be…my half brother, only 52 years younger. I paid you to secure several pieces of property…or at least to facilitate the demise of the businesses occupying some of them. Thirty thousand of it was in cash, which you supposedly divided between a district court Judge and a Mr. Beam that held a position with the city."

"I turned over every penny of that money!" Martin said defensively.

"Last time I checked, the fitness studio, the ice cream parlor, and the gas station were still in business."

"Look, sir," Martin jumped in. "Alvin managed to keep the road in front of all three of those places torn apart for a year and a half! He had his people write tickets to the fitness studio for parking violations and Judge T. did everything he could to get the owner arrested. I had no way of knowing that those construction crews ate so much ice cream and I couldn't stop 'em from keeping *that* guy in business. Your money got spent the way I said, they just managed to stay in business, is all." Martin paused, then asked. "This might be water over the dam, but what did you want that property for?"

"When my father used to reside on Lakeshore with my mother, he would often drive himself to the office in the morning. He liked to cut over to the freeway by passing through the city that those properties are located in. As we drove in together one time, I remember him commenting about how the entire corner was a gold mine. My intention was to buy up sufficient frontage for a 51st store. He used to like to tour every store when he was younger and a little less…ah…distracted, you know. I wanted him to have a reminder every morning, before he had time to dial up that bitch, of all that he had accomplished. I wanted him to see a part of his empire right after he left the gates of his mansion. Admittedly, I had still another motive. We used to have…ah…discussions about when I would be able to take over the reins of the business. He has a full-time company president, you know. The guy does a fine job, but I don't think that anyone will care about it after my father finally steps down like family. I had already commissioned the plans for this new store in case he went for the idea. I won't bring up what *that* cost me. My father has been a name in this state for many years now. He has built churches and medical facilities. I wanted him to start his day…or end it on the way home, with a brick and mortar visual, filled with people that depended on the paychecks that he signed."

Martin had never expected such an outpouring of words from this man…even less so such a thorough explanation. It was obvious that he was being taken into the man's confidence for a reason…and he was sure it would soon be forthcoming. Maybe if he chose his response carefully for a change, Martin's former client might help him dig himself out of his hole with a nice fat check. "I know what you're going through," Martin empathized, "I've had a few setbacks myself lately. 'Course, getting a big receivable cleared up might help get me back on track."

"I know that. And it brings me to the purpose of my phone call. I don't know whether or not you are aware of this, but that clown who used to drive my father around with his whore has written a book. In the front he claims he made the whole thing up, and in the back he says that he's going to write another one by this fall. He's peddling it at some of the local coffee shops and over the Internet, but I understand the locals are snapping it up pretty quick and having themselves a good laugh. It doesn't portray my father or the rest of my family in a very good light. I'm looking for some way to shut this asshole down before this garbage gets picked up by any of the major book chains. This filth started selling his piece of crap about a month ago and our attorneys said to screw it… ignore it, and it'll just fade away. Well, it doesn't look like that's happening and my sisters and I had a family meeting and I've been authorized to …ahh…take a stronger course of action. Are you able to work again?"

"Uh, yeah…sure," Martin responded.

"I'm not entirely sure that you are. But here's what I need. I need to know where this fool lives. I need to know what time he wakes up and what time he goes to bed. I need his work schedule and I want to know where he likes to go to eat…or shop…or visits his friends…if this asshole has any. What I'd really like to know is whether he perhaps sells or buys drugs…maybe stolen property…anything that I can get the police involved in, if it's real bad. Maybe he's a closet homo and we can get him to back down if we had some pictures. Check all of his records, he must have something in his background that we can embarrass or blackmail him with. There are two more things that I would like to touch upon before we end this conversation. The first, and the one I'm sure that you will be the happiest about, is your compensation. Tell me, do you still have the same checking account?"

"Uh, no…actually…I'm in between accounts right now," Martin replied.

"That was my assumption. Open an account this morning and phone me back with the number and the branch by noon. I will deposit $37,500 in cash into it by the end of business today. You can bill me for your usual daily rate beginning with today as well."

"What about the other $37,500? That will be the balance from last year after today's deposit. And what if I can't come up with anything we can use on the guy?"

"That was the last item that I wanted to address in our conversation. My father's law firm has already had someone do a cursory check on this filth peddler. They haven't come up with anything significant other than an ex-wife who hates him and one that does not. It would be the easiest for all concerned if you can dig up something useful during the course of the next several weeks. But let us say, for the purpose of argument, that you cannot. A year and a half ago when we were trying to discourage my father's... ahh...lady friend from being so persistent, you mentioned a...ahh...specialist?"

"You mean for a quick and permanent solution?"

"Yes."

"Yeah, I did. Actually, I can't contact the guy himself. I can only send a message to a mail drop. The guy who picks up the message was an officer years ago in the Army or Marines or something. He's supposed to have a whole crew of these specialists still workin' for him. They're really diversified, too. They do corporate work when somebody maybe wants to stop a merger or a hostile takeover. They do jobs for...um...importers of drugs when their customers or competitors aren't playing by the rules. They do high end husband/wife stuff too, like when hiring *them* would be a whole lot easier than a divorce."

"What is the normal fee?"

"It's $75,000, with 25 in cash as a down stroke. The balance is due 48 hours after the job is over, with no excuses. I heard about one guy who tried to negotiate down the balance after a job on his business partner. He got his wish. They waited 30 days and gave the guy a free job all right...except it was on himself."

"It would be worth an extra 25 from me and my father if you were to set this thing up."

"Oh, geez...25, huh. Well, you know I would have extra expenses too. I gotta get another I.D. to set up a mail drop of my own if these guys gotta reach me with questions. Then there *is* the factor that the solicitation of an act makes it the same as if you were gonna do it yourself. Then once it's done, it's just called conspiracy."

"Okay, I'll give you 50. When it's done, you'll have that, the balance of 37, and anything for your own investigation. You'll walk away with at least a hundred more than what I'm sending you today."

"Looks like we gotta deal."

"One more thing. It can't look like what it is. It cannot look like a suicide either. They do too much with forensics these days and I won't take that chance. This piece of crap has got to just disappear. I do not want whatever is left to be found. They will not know if he just took off or what."

"I think they're gonna want extra for that."

"How much extra?"

"I can't quote for them, but how about if I offer them another 25?"

61

One communiqué that warned how vengeful Max could be was from an outraged ex-employee of his retail empire. After many years of loyal service, the man felt underpaid. He put out feelers to test his value to Max's competitors. The man was welcomed with open arms at one of them and resigned from the company that employed him for so long. The man's wife worked for Max as well. But she was still happy there. She liked what she was doing. She had friends who worked there also and she enjoyed seeing them every day. She had a short ride to work and intended to work at Max's company until retirement. Max and his management, however, had other plans. When one sees everybody within one's sphere of influence as being divided into two groups: loyalists and traitors, there can be only one outcome for the wife of a traitor. The woman was summarily dismissed. The husband was the one who wrote me, and even the letters on my computer screen seemed smudged from his tears of frustration.

Still another letter reiterated the details of a newspaper article from some years ago. The article exposed an investment scheme that involved Max, a local hospital, and the Catholic Church. An investment broker came to Max with a deal that would require one million dollars from all three entities. To maximize the profits from their investment, the Church's tax-exempt status was going to be very useful. All three anted up the funds…and then the broker disappeared with the money. A major newspaper had the moxy to report on how one of its largest advertisers had been scammed.

Several days after reading the e-mail, I received a copy of the actual article. I was beginning to feel like the crypt-keeper for all of Max's secrets.

A former real estate agent from the Pointes wrote consistently. Her network of prior business associates still firmly intact, Pamela was quick to keep me apprised of current Lexington family comings and goings. Her acquaintances relayed accurate sightings of Max and his mistress back to her more rapidly than any Private Investigator could.

Max purchased a "turn key" residence in Turtle Creek Estates, an exclusive gated community 25 miles northwest of his lakefront mansion. One of his new neighbors reveled in e-mailing me information about whether the supplemental residence was occupied in any particular week. Max attempted to make the triangular relationship work between himself, his mistress, and his wife of 53 years.

An offer of $832 million for his retail empire from investment mogul Warren Buffet had been left standing for some time as Max tried to sort out his marital status.

Mrs. Lexington's wedding ring served as an accurate barometer of the couple's reconciliation efforts. As reported by nail technicians and cosmetologists, the presence of it on her finger indicated that the patient and determined grandmother was buying into promises made by her wandering husband. The absence of the ring meant that Max had moved out after yet another blowout.

A steady source of mind-boggling information about Mr. Lexington was forwarded to my website via e-mail from a contact that I nicknamed "Deep Throat." I bestowed the resurrected moniker on this particular individual because of the remarkable amount of confirmable insider information that was regularly delivered. Deep Throat maintained that they were a high level employee of Max's retail empire, and both the personal and professional information they supplied never failed to entertain and intrigue.

The first letter began by detailing an older incident that occurred on Detroit's northern border during Max's two-fisted drinking days. As the rapacious billionaire was driving along Eight Mile Road, his car stopped for a traffic light at Schaeffer Road. His keen eye spotted an attractive female "Freelance Entertainment Engineer." Influenced by many distilled beverages, Max spontaneously decided that some impromptu oral gratification would be in order. He rolled down his passenger window and signaled to the Engineer. After some cursory negotiations, she climbed into his car and they drove around the corner to a less public location. The Engineer commenced to uphold her end of the proposed transaction while Max closed his eyes and leaned back in his seat to prepare for the conclusion. Suddenly, they were interrupted by a pounding on the window— and a loud announcement. Two uniformed police officers stood on either side of the car and they were demanding that the occupants cease their activity at once and step out of the vehicle. Wide-eyed, Max complied, as did the Engineer. The officers began to realize who they had interrupted as their requests for identification were met by the man in the driver's seat. The Engineer, however, was a regular vendor at this particular intersection and was already well known to the officers. Besides the vendor's identity, the officers were also aware the "she" was not quite one yet. The Engineer was in a transitional phase at the time of the incident, and was frugally putting funds away for his gender reassignment surgery. Upon learning of this, one of the most heterosexual men in the state diverted the shock and embarrassment by adopting the only logical recourse available to a man of his age. He faked a heart attack. Clutching his chest, he was laid out by the officers on a grassy median while an ambulance was hastily summoned. By the time Max had been released from the hospital, enough phone calls had been made and enough favors had been called in by his attorneys to sweep the entire incident under the rug. Unfortunately, neither Deep Throat nor a confirming source was ever able to clarify if the Engineer successfully completed his transition to womanhood.

I found Deep Throat's description of Max's feelings about me and my first novel interesting, but not unexpected. He (or she) wrote that Max was unable to talk about me for more than 30 seconds without becoming "incoherent." The accuracy of the sale price of the exclusive Birmingham condominium the billionaire bought for his mistress (1.2 million) made me suspect that Deep Throat had attended the closing. I briefly considered applying as a doorman at the Willets in order to be able to greet Summer on a regular basis, but could not spare the time. With her Florida condo now paid for in full, my old friend was becoming a real estate mogul in her own right and I longed for the opportunity to congratulate her.

I was taken aback when I first read what Max had spent on the most well connected and thorough private investigator in the state. My first solid clue that other eyes were watching me occurred as I was changing the oil in my SUV. While some people garden as a hobby, I still like to work on my own vehicles. I knew immediately that the rectangular black box affixed to the undercarriage did not belong there. To my practiced eye, the GPS unit stood out like a sore thumb amid the components that belonged in the area.

A Global Positioning System sends signals to a satellite, which then relays the location to a website back on Earth. For a reasonable monthly fee, the customer can log onto the website via computer at any time of day or night. He can then track whatever vehicle the unit is affixed to—via a map that is displayed on his screen. For a period of time, I left the unit in place on my vehicle. If I felt like being followed to my regular destinations by a black Jeep that day, I drove my SUV. If I was not in the mood to be followed, or if I had somewhere more clandestine to go, I drove one of my other vehicles. I waited until one of my police buddies was able to tell me who owned the Jeep from the plate number I supplied before removing the GPS unit.

I realize I am not privy to all of the investigatory powers that the Federal government wields. I did not know that an Asset Forfeiture Division existed until a computer program flagged them as they went through the pages of my website. If the FBI ever concludes its investigation of me, I intend to request a copy of the original complaint.

My ongoing court case with the construction company at last began to come to a boil in the spring. Several court dates were assigned—some of them reserved for pre-trial motions—and some for the actual trial. The opposing council got wind of the book and had an underling purchase it. Strangely enough, the underling purchased the book off of the website—my shipping manager flagged the name and address for me.

I have been involved in court cases where the sitting judge rules on motions while depending on the direction of the wind and the shape of snowflakes for guidance. In my county, a notorious female Circuit Judge rants, raves, and pontificates from the bench while propositioning any male defense attorney that strikes her fancy. The attorneys at my fitness studio despised her inept, bullying, and volatile ways universally and requested mouthwash after saying her name. A dozen experienced attorneys were clients at the fitness studio and one by one they offered opinions about which judges were deemed fair and impartial and which ones had been on the bench too long. When I mentioned the judge my case had been assigned to was the Honorable James Biernat, their faces relaxed. *Don't worry*, they assured me, *he's fair, easy going, and well steeped in the law*. But my cynicism got the better of me and I braced for the worst. The defense attorney bombarded mine with one pretrial motion after another. I was pleasantly shocked, however, when the attorneys at my studio proved correct. Even when he ruled against me, the Judge's rulings seemed to be well reasoned and grounded in logic. I would be going to trial in the courtroom of an astute, well-balanced jurist. It looked like I would be getting a fair shake at last.

In a pre-emptive strike, my attorney introduced a motion to exclude the book from the trial. The judge agreed. He said he couldn't imagine eight jurors taking a week or two to read a book before proceedings could recommence. Defense counsel was furious.

In the late 1920s astronomers were puzzled. As the precision production of refractive lenses had improved over the past century, so had the quality of the telescope. Planets that had been mere glimmers in Man's past were now beginning to yield secrets of their moons, terrain, and even their very origins. A scientific community with an increasing thirst for knowledge and data about the beginnings of the universe would never be able to answer the questions that rose fast enough—but strove to keep pace nonetheless. Advances in mathematics and photographic processes aided these pioneers as well. By the late 1920s they were able to predict and plot orbits of the planets to a precise degree. Formulas that could be used to determine the amount of gravitational pull our sun had on the other planets—and thus their orbits—based on its mass (size) were widely accepted. During this time it was also discovered that all eight planets, from Mercury to Neptune, had a gravitational field of their own based on the mass of each. It was generally agreed upon that to qualify as a planet, a body would have to be spherical, or nearly perfectly round—versus elliptical or shaped haphazardly—like an errant asteroid journeying through our solar system. A substantial amount of mass would have been required to allow each planet to end up as a round ball as it cooled billions of years ago. The aforementioned advances in mathematics also allowed scientists to determine the amount of influence that certain planets have on *each other's* orbits as they followed their ancient paths around the sun. Not only is Earth's orbit not perfectly circular, it is influenced in varying proportions by the relatively miniscule gravity exuded by other planets as they approach our position.

The closest planet to our sun is Mercury, followed by Venus, Earth, and Mars. In the late 1920s Uranus and Neptune were acknowledged as being the two farthest planets from the sun. There was something amiss, however, with Neptune's orbit. Being much farther away from the sun than Earth, it naturally takes many more years than we do to complete a single orbit. This was to be expected—but it did not preclude astronomers from proudly predicting, with great precision, the exact path of its long journey. The puzzlement that they were experiencing in the late 1920s, however, was because at a certain point in its orbit, Neptune did not behave the way that it should have. It strayed ever so slightly from the path mapped out for it on charts and graphs. When peered at through a high-powered telescope on a particular date and at a particular time, Neptune was not exactly where it belonged. It was not taking a large detour, by any means. The variance in Neptune's path might be compared to a bird undertaking a long flight only to be distracted by a brief and unexpected gust of wind.

A scientist named Percival Lowell, whom as far as I know did not get beat up in school any more than the other boys, had a theory. He surmised that another unseen planet was causing Neptune to stray off of its predicted course. It was this theory that led him to discover the planet Pluto.

After a long day of questioning potential jurors, eight people were seated. The trial was set to begin. Then Neptune started acting strangely.

In a year and a half of pre-trial maneuverings, requests for information flew like flocks of pigeons between the offices of my attorney and those of the defense. Interrogatories, witness lists, answers to pleadings and contracts accumulated in file drawers—generating new paperwork that sprang out of the drawers every morning. My attorney had agreed to take the case on contingency, meaning that her firm did not get paid for her efforts until either a judgement was rendered or a settlement reached. Nevertheless, I was still responsible for mailing and filing costs and all expert witness fees. I was grilled for over eight hours by three defense attorneys. I was asked repeatedly how a business could possibly be harmed by a lack of customers. For my efforts, I received a bill for half of the fees charged by a court reporter to transcribe the sessions.

I wrote checks for many thousands of dollars, confident that vindication and reimbursement would come after a trial. Among the myriad of requests from defense counsel came one for my income tax returns for the previous five years. Although my view of the world is admittedly skewed at times, I strongly felt that a business that tries to shut my business down is an enemy. Defense counsel represented my enemy. I was not going to turn over my *personal* financial records to my enemy. They already had piles of my business records. That would have to suffice. I told my attorney so. She relayed the information to opposing counsel.

If they disagreed, we would have been delighted to get a ruling from the Judge. We never heard anything more about the matter.

Anything more, that is, until the jury was seated. Suddenly, last minute motions were being presented to my attorney faster than playing cards at a Blackjack table.

If the entire book was inadmissible, select portions must surely be admitted, howled one motion. Another motion to the court ranted at length about my calculated attempts to avoid producing critical documents pertaining to the case. Despite repeated tries by the defense to wrest copies of my personal tax returns from me, I had defied and ignored every request, the motion stated.

Like the astronomer Percival Lowell some 75 years ago, I began to look for outside influences. Opposing counsel was suddenly adamant that something on my personal tax returns was critical to his defense. I was less concerned about what that item was than about why he was so convinced. This was more than a fishing expedition. Defense counsel already had the fish lying in the bottom of the boat. He already had obtained my tax returns somehow…or they had been given to him! But defense counsel could not show the fish to anybody…because he had caught it illegally. The only way that he could ask me questions about the fish…or show it in court…would be if I produced the fish.

My attorney told me the defense hoped to show I received income from the studio in spite of their client's interference. I didn't think the IRS would tell me how Max had obtained my tax returns.

As an officer of the court whose ethics were supposedly beyond reproach, the defense counsel had not conspired to obtain the tax records himself. Whether his mere possession of them at the time constituted a felony, I could not be sure. I could be sure, however, of how the tax records had come into his possession. While a close examination of Max's palms would not reveal any dirt, I knew the order had filtered down through many protective layers of "flunkies."

More last-minute motions from the defense alluded to the discovery of "new" witnesses that would be used to refute any testimony that I could offer. The full impact of the results of Max's $210,000 investigation were coming to bear. Although I will never be mistaken for a cockroach, the odds do not favor me for canonization, either. One of the tactical rules of court is to never ask a witness a question unless one already knows the answer. After initially seating the jury, I felt as though my odds of winning at trial were one hundred to one in my favor. Because I had already turned down a mediation award, I would be liable for upwards of $40,000 in defense attorney fees—if the jury ruled against me. After several candid moments, I now felt as though my odds of prevailing were now only 50-50. A sure thing had now become a crapshoot. I instructed my attorney to settle for several thousand and keep it. I drove off to do a book signing that afternoon, poorer but wiser. Sometimes you are the windshield, and sometimes you are the bug.

62

THE CRAFTY OLD COLUMNIST first contacted me on my website in late February, after the book had been out for almost three months. The letter was short, friendly, and was even replete with a quick introduction. In fact, the introduction was the only thing in the e-mail that made me smile. The Crafty Old Columnist worked for the largest newspaper in the state and had done so—with brief forays into other journalistic pursuits—since around the time that I was learning to hold a pen. He began as a sports writer and I remembered reading his updates on Detroit's sports teams as my interest in baseball waxed and even occasionally after it waned. I smiled because to anyone who was both literate and a resident of the Michigan area for more than a few years, the man simply needed no introduction. I did not need to be reminded that his column still appeared thrice weekly on page one of the second section. I already knew about his evolution from sportswriter to sports columnist to a graft, corruption, and waste-exposing columnist with his thumb on the pulse of the city more often than not. I already knew about the Crafty Old Columnist's longtime crusade against Detroit's quasi-corrupt Mayor and the cadre of cronies that he surrounded himself with. Did the Crafty Columnist always present both sides of a story fairly and equally? Perhaps not. But the next question would be whether he did more good than harm over his long career. Did he save taxpayers and consumers millions, and perhaps billions, by looming in the background as a rabid watchdog over industrial tycoons and politicians? Were the greedy public servants that seemed to permeate Detroit's political scene kept in check not only by the fear of prosecution—but by exposure from the Crafty Columnist? And did the Columnist have the ability to laud and recognize the efforts of someone whose actions benefited taxpayers or the public in general? The answer to all four was a resounding yes, and therein lie my feelings of fear and trepidation. I had no way of divining in advance how the Columnist viewed my book. Had he already read it and decided to vilify me in front of one million readers? Or, had he read it, chuckled once or twice, and decided to give me a little pat on the back or mention it on a slow news day? My faith in the basic goodness of all humankind was shakier than a West Bank cease-fire at the time, and I printed out the friendly e-mail only to preserve the private phone number proffered at the end. *Even bad publicity is publicity*, I told myself—as a debate about whether to dial the number raged inside my head. Why should I care about what he thought? My skin had already grown thicker than the soles of a barefoot marathon runner. Should I ignore a seemingly sincere interview offer only because the man who extended it had castrated a few thousand others in a career than spanned a half-century? My brain told me to step up, call immediately, and treat the man like an old friend. My gut wanted to place the printout in a pile of credit card offers on my desk. After two days of deliberation, I decided to take action. I confronted my dilemma head on—while placating my gut instincts. I placed the printout in a pile of bills that were not due for three weeks.

I enjoyed two weeks of relative quiet with my head stuck deeply into the sand. But like a suicide bomber's knapsack, the e-mail could not remain unacknowledged indefinitely. I grew concerned that the longer I waited to address the situation, the greater my chances of a scathing review became. Finally, after two weeks, I called the phone number. To my great relief, I was connected only with an answering machine. I left a message in the hopes that I was only initiating a rollicking game of phone tag that may last until the

Crafty Columnist's inevitable retirement. Nearly two more weeks passed, and my apprehensions faded with each day. Then, like the annual migration of the golddiggers to North Palm Beach, the inevitable happened. The Crafty Old Columnist's phone number appeared on the Caller ID as my cell phone vibrated and shrilled to get my attention. A man without fear would have answered on the first ring. I caught it on the second. The C.O.C. was cordial enough, and unnecessarily reintroduced himself yet again. I told him that I had read his columns for years. He said his wife had handed him my book some time ago and that he was about halfway through it. I said I was flattered and thanked him for not burning it until he finished it. He had a few questions about it. He asked if we could meet the next morning for breakfast at an hour so wee that a Tibetan Monk would need a double-shot Starbucks before commencing his morning prayers—and roosters are still in full REM sleep. I cited a non-existent prior engagement and suggested a time that would offer a greater amount of brunch items to select from. I was going to suggest that I wear a yellow silk scarf to expedite the identification process, but did not want to begin by making the wrong impression.

At two minutes to ten, I pulled into a Big Boy restaurant on the outskirts of the Pointes and easily found the famous C.O.C. in a corner booth. I shook his hand and we exchanged some niceties while I slid into the seat across from him. When the waitress appeared, he ordered his eggs poached and his whole wheat toast unbuttered before I ordered breakfast menu items number two, six, and ten. I calculated that if the questions came in too fast or hard, I could delay answering by over-stuffing my mouth until the interview could be judged over. He broke the ice by alluding to a couple of books that he had written in years past and to a side job he once had with an obscure little magazine called *Sports Illustrated*! I stopped chewing long enough to ask him a couple of questions and he tried to further put me at ease by talking about his family and grandparental obligations. After I had relaxed a little more, he mentioned, almost as an aside, that he went to school years ago with the same Max

Lexington character that I had written about. I sidestepped by explaining how I had blundered into shelf space in the major bookstores. He brought up the character again by offering up an interesting fact about the man that an indisputable source had given to him. I hinted that I was aware that Max's retail chain spent millions with his newspaper. The C.O.C. reminded me that he was beholden to no one and had free rein from his editors to write about anything, regardless of who got their toes smashed. Citing a memory that was beginning to fail with age, the C.O.C. asked if I minded whether he took notes on our conversation on a pad that he had fortuitously brought. I did not buy into the failing memory excuse for even a nanosecond, and began to feel as though I was crossing thin ice on a pogo stick.

The C.O.C. began to encircle me with a cleverness born of ten thousand such encounters. Every innocuous, perfunctory question would be followed by a deeper, more layered one. His facial expressions told me that he was scoffing at my pat, practiced answers and wanted me to open up more about the reasons behind the words. He grilled me about my motives for writing the book as his pen hovered over the pad, ready to record words like *revenge* or *payback*. I offered nothing of the sort and poured a little syrup on menu item number six—as well as on my answers. Like an aging but still very cunning and powerful wolf, the C.O.C. stalked me in a big arc. He probed my defenses with little feints that might have seemed half-hearted, but were loaded with danger. With each feint I backed away, until after a while he decided that killing me would not be a sufficient challenge to his skills. He allowed me to change the subject and escape—our half-hour brunch turned into an hour and a half before the waitress finally brought the bill. His hand was a blur as he snatched it despite my protestations. I tried to recover some dignity by insisting on leaving the tip and did my best to calculate 40 percent of what I imagined the total to be. As we were leaving, he mentioned that he was going to write something up for placement in his Sunday morning column. I thanked him and went to the studio, trying to convince myself that no one sits down to read the Sunday paper anymore. Bits and pieces of our conversation continued to bubble up in my memory as I stayed busy with back-to-back book signings the rest of Friday and Saturday.

I lay in bed on Sunday morning, torn between putting on my slippers to face the day or grabbing the remote to just face CNN. Opting for the slippers, I crept out onto my driveway, half hoping that my deliveryman had quit. He was still employed, and the thick roll lie wrapped in plastic near the street. My x-ray vision was still malfunctioning and I knew that the newspaper would have to be carried back inside to be read. With more than a little trepidation I transported the package inside. I unwrapped the newspaper and skipped to section two where a teaser at the top of page one encouraged the reader to turn to see what the C.O.C. had written about my book on page three. The column was stretched across the entire top of the page. Before I began reading, I could not help but observe that the entire remainder of the page was devoted to the obituaries. *How apropo*, I mused. *After the C.O.C. is done reviewing my book it won't have far to go.*

Like a child watching a frightening movie, I began reading through eyes that were little more than slits. My wincing eased slightly when the C.O.C. did not fillet me in the first paragraph. Halfway through the column, he had still not recommended that anyone read the book, but neither did he ridicule the notion. By the end of the column there were no ringing endorsements of my 373-page tome. Low inventory concerns would remain something that need not be addressed the following day. On the other hand, I did not suffer the lambasting that was well within the C.O.C.'s power to administer. In fact, the general tone of the column was factual and decidedly neutral. I logged onto the secret counter for the website. Activity was normal for a Sunday morning at only ten hits—and I felt a little foolish at the Much Ado About Nothing. A casual check back at noon, however, revealed that at least 50 of the C.O.C.'s readers had wanted to know more. Several of these apparently did not reside near a bookstore—and had placed an order. By late evening I was very impressed by the C.O.C.'s ability to arouse curiosity in the public—I had recorded 250 visits in one day! But by Monday evening, even that record amount had been exceeded—with the final tally by midnight in the mid-300 range. On Tuesday morning the pace began to ebb slightly but the manager of the company that distributed the book e-mailed a very healthy order for more. I finished the delivery on Wednesday and my tiny shipping department had caught up with the flow of Internet orders by the end of the week.

63

The street that I live on is not very wide. Sure, two cars can pass each other quite comfortably, but if a car is parked on the street, some maneuvering is required. Fortunately, there is not much traffic on my street, so cars do not need to pass each other very often. I should explain that it dead ends as well—with only about 20 houses along either side. Technically, I live on a peninsula, with canals on three sides leading out to Anchor Bay in Lake St. Clair. In fact, dredging the canals created my 40-home-lot neighborhood back in the mid-1950s…the street and most of the houses sprang up soon after. Since all of the backyards boast of having a canal, the lots themselves are not very deep. At 80 feet they are not unusually wide. This means that not only is my dead end street narrow, it is not very long. A lot of retirees live on my street, and they do not seem to use it as much as the younger couples that still go to work, come home, and run errands. I seldom see any children on the street either…so I do not believe that any soccer moms reside there. During the cold months, many of the retirees turn into snowbirds and leave for warmer climes—which pares the already sparse traffic down even more. Thus, on a street that is lightly traveled and that no one can use to get to somewhere else, a late model white cargo van sticks out like a sore thumb…especially when it cruises slowly past my house at odd hours.

Most of the retirees have two cars parked in their garage, and it is only on rare occasions that a car is ever parked in the street. The retirees that remain in March are nosy old farts. If the new white van were to remain parked on the street, it would not be long before they found a reason to walk past with their little mop-like dogs and peer inside.

Coupled with the remoteness of my residence is its limited accessability. After exiting the freeway, my little neighborhood can only be reached by driving three miles due east…on yet another peninsula! The forbidding barbed wire fence of a heavily patrolled Air Force Base lines the left side of the road prior to arriving at my street. Vacant land, a nearly empty marina, and riverfront houses that crowd the roadway make up the passing scenery on the right side of the three-mile stretch. In early March, even the sailboaters traverse onto the peninsula but infrequently. There are no strip malls along the way. The only liquor store is one quarter of a mile *after* my street. The best restaurant in the area—Crews Inn—is a full mile *after* my street as one ventures even farther out onto the peninsula.

In short, there is not a single decent place to lurk along the entire route to my house—at least not without my noticing the lurker. And the odds that I will notice have been greatly enhanced as of late. It was already my habit to scrutinize the three-mile stretch to my street to identify in advance the sheriff's deputy that invested three years trying to trap me with his radar gun. But he had no success at finding a suitable spot to lurk, either, and my Corvette's radar detector reliably warned me of his position. After a while, the residents in my section of the Township grew tired of watching for the traffic cop too. We went to the polls and eviscerated the police budget. Now only one police car patrols my Township with any regularity—one patrolman for 28,000 people—and never ventures near my street. Knowing this, I derive some small measure of comfort from being the most heavily-armed citizen on my block.

By early March, my jumpiness had trebled. Even a wayward mail truck left me surmising whether the driver was lost or involved in something more sinister. So the white van that began to frequent my neck of the woods that first Monday in March stood out like an ostrich in chicken coop. I could tell immediately that the driver took his attempt at anonymity very seriously by the way that he tried to park behind drydocked boats and other fixtures. My paranoia ratcheted up a notch every time I saw my stalker—and two full notches when I saw him at night. The driver was either very short or slouched a lot to inhibit recognition. I doubted that the former was the case. Now that I no longer have a conventional form of employment, my schedule is very erratic. I may traverse the single road that leads to my street four times in one day…or not at all. I may drive the Corvette for two days in a row, or park it for a week and select one of the other three vehicles that are available to me.

By Tuesday afternoon, I was thoroughly convinced I had yet another P.I. keeping tabs on me, courtesy of my former employer. I had no idea at the time about the kind of danger I was in. Had I known how far wrong I was on the first part of my assumption, I would have fled to Detective Dan's house and hidden in the basement with his two cats until he and the 300 other Sheriff's Deputies in my county had everything sorted out.

The Borders Bookstore on Kercheval near the heart of Grosse Pointe Farms had sold out the first and second shipments of my book. A waiting list was developing and my next printing was not due in until Thursday. I had enough inventory to hold them over until then. I did not notice the white van on my way to the freeway, but when I finished my delivery and walked out to the parking lot behind the store, my tail was parked in the back lot. I did not acknowledge his presence. Instead, I continued up Kercheval to "The Hill." I was exactly on time for my meeting at Lucy's Tavern with a reader who had "startling new information about Max and his business dealings." Feeling even jumpier and more paranoid than usual, I waited out a Jaguar XK12 and parked on the street.

The meter had time, but I contributed another quarter anyway. I resisted the urge to dash to the front door with my hand in my coat pocket, wrapped around my gun. Instead, I reached the door with some decorum—catching the van out of the corner of my eye as it rounded the corner. If he knew I knew, he was *not* being very cautious…or he didn't care.

I had a turkey club and a disappointing meeting. The "startling information" would have been much more so had I not already known all about it. New warehouses are built everyday. I am quite sure that toxic soil from prior businesses on the sites can be found more often than people realize. While I was confident that the Department of Environmental Quality (DEQ) would have found the dirt's final resting place fascinating, I had no wish to get involved. I paid for the informant's lunch and thanked him anyway.

Farther down the street, Cavanaugh's Office Supply was down to their last two books. I still had ten, but decided to head for the studio and ask Jillian to drop some off after her workout. The early afternoon traffic was light and on two occasions I saw the white van in the distance behind me.

~~~~~~~~~~~~~~~~~~~~~~~~

Wednesday morning dawned cloudy and cold. I had an early morning obligation that, try as I might, could not be bumped back to a more reasonable hour. On my way to the freeway, I carefully perused every nook, cranny, and hidey-hole along the three-mile route. It had already occurred to me that whoever it was slouched down in that van's driver's seat could just as easily do his slouching in another make and model. Driving slower than usual, I peered into the only two cars along the route I did not recognize. They were empty. After my appointment ended, I followed the same procedure on the way home…and struck paydirt. Well onto the peninsula—only 300 yards from my street—is a strip of old wooden boat wells in a long, arcing line during a bend in the river. There is not much dry land between the boat wells and the road—little more than a gravel access road actually—but the end nearest my street fattens up a bit and affords *some* storage and parking. The Ford Taurus was black, new, and looked out of place between the old boat resting on its railroad ties and the transport trailer. It practically screamed out to be noticed as I passed—even louder when I saw the figure slouched down in the driver's seat. I had been correct…my stalker had access to more than one vehicle. But so did I.

I have added many feet to my fuse over the years so that the charge does not go off nearly as quickly as it used to. But the powder keg at the end of my fuse is just as large and packed with an even more powerful explosive than it had 20 years ago. The moment I spotted the black Taurus, my fuse lit. Back when the fuse was short, at least I knew how long it was. Now, it was more of a mystery. But I *did* know that I was growing weary of being followed and investigated. And I also knew that I needed to do something about that lit fuse before it reached the charge. I was not aware of a specific law in the Michigan Penal Code that covered the penalty for dismembering a Private Investigator, however, I was sure there was another law already covering it. I was also sure that a conviction would result in considerable jail time.

It is the custom of many big city police officers—when they are in dangerous situations—to have a drop weapon readily available. A drop weapon can be as complex as an unregistered handgun—or as simple as a wicked-looking knife. With a drop weapon at the ready, the law enforcement official need not be as concerned about whether the suspect expires due to an officer's faux pas (currently known as a "my bad"). A quick-thinking officer with access to a drop weapon can take action in order to avoid being fired, sued, and worse. Without witnesses or supervisory personnel present, the resourceful policeman may have time to plant the drop weapon on or around the suspect—thus bolstering his claim that the shooting was good because it was clearly in self-defense.

It was my intention to turn my looming confrontation with my stalker into a pushing match—or perhaps a streetfight—but not a homicide. I wanted to be afforded the same protection, however, that the big city policeman had if I pushed too hard. Once home, I selected an appropriate drop weapon and stuffed it into the pocket of my jacket. I exchanged my car keys for those of the SUV parked in my garage. I checked the clock. It was exactly 1:00 P.M. If the confrontation went very poorly in my disfavor, there were at least five hours of daylight left for someone to find my corpse before the seagulls picked at it all night. On my way out the door, I thought of Natasha. She was in Las Vegas with her sister and wasn't due back until Friday night. I sighed wistfully, wishing that my gun-toting girlfriend was somewhere in the vicinity. But she was not.

Natasha was thousands of miles away, pretending she barely understood the rules of blackjack until some poor sap fronted her $100 in chips. Then she would play until her winnings topped $500, at which point another casino would beckon and she would start over. I once suggested that she had found a new career—she just laughed and said, "I am just being stinker…don't need ma-nee." I thought about calling her on her cell phone, but didn't want to upset her rhythm.

Thinking about cell phones *did* give me an idea, however. My own cell phone had a built-in camera. I had become fairly adept at taking pictures while looking to all the world as though I was involved in an animated conversation. I wheeled my SUV into the muddy marina lot while blocking much of my face with my phone and my hand. The front bumper of the Taurus was facing the road, and I pulled directly into the slot beside it like a lost tourist calling for directions. I don't know if I startled him because I was too busy trying to line up my shot while looking straight ahead. I snapped off three quick pictures. When I closed the phone and looked down at my subject, I was the one who was surprised. Some people claim to never forget a face, and I forget less faces than most. I had not seen this face for nearly 20 years, but it was one I had spent almost three hours staring at.

He had sat across the table from me at Lee Pantely's wedding, and I vividly remembered speculating to myself about whether his eyes were real. His hair was light brown, short and flecked with gray—but his eyes were still so black that his pupils were undetectable. It did not end there. The eyes were still cold, emotionless, seldom moved—and never blinked. At the wedding, looking into those eyes had been like staring into a deep tunnel and only seeing a soulless representative of the Devil in Hell. And an inner warning told me that anyone who stepped into the tunnel would be transported quickly to the other end. The skin was ruddier than I remembered but still just as taut, and he had not shaved for at least a day. If he was surprised to see me up close so unexpectedly, he did not show it. Instead, he cocked his head slightly in a gesture of curiosity, although his face remained an impassive mask. From my four-wheel driven perch, I was able to see down into his car. The seats were empty save for a clear bottle of water. He was not holding the bottle of water, though. In fact, his right hand was moving away from it...slowly and inexorably heading toward the front opening of his unzipped jacket. He was going to reach for something without explaining what or why...and he was going to do it soon. It looked as though I might have about one second left to decide what he was going to pull out from behind the jacket. A badge, a cell phone, and even a cigarette were all on the list. But so was a gun. My own Beretta was tucked neatly into the holster under my arm. But the zipper of *my* jacket was up...and this guy's was not. I wasn't about to point a gun at a man holding a detective's badge, and the fact that he didn't speak gave me the ominous feeling that somewhere on my stalker was a piece of steel filled with small lead projectiles propelled by gunpowder. My decision came easily. I leaned away from the window and dropped the Explorer into reverse. If I heard his car start—or a gunshot—I would unzip my coat. Otherwise, it was my turn to slouch as I backed up to the road.

When Natasha finally decided that she had won enough money for that day, she called me. I told her everything, beginning with the white van. In a chiding, placating voice she said, *Don't vorry, Natasha come home end of week and beat up bully for you.* I thanked her for her concern.

Even with all of the windows closed and the furnace on, my dog—whose paranoia rivals my own—races from room to room growling whenever the yard is invaded by anything larger than a hummingbird. I spent the evening with the shades down, lighting at a minimum, and the dog on high alert.

On Thursday morning a quick check of the neighborhood did not reveal the presence of any unusual vehicles. A close scrutiny of the tell tales I left around the yard's perimeter led me to believe that no late night trespasses had been attempted.

I had not spoken with Lee Pantely in the seven years that had elapsed since assisting him in selling his Lincoln Mark VIII. After five minutes of catching up on the phone, I described the wedding guest with the creepy eyes—and mentioned that I had run into him. Lee was not very helpful when it came down to placing a name to the face, but he was good about putting Mary on the phone. After some reminiscing, some prompting, and Mary's patient checking of the invitation list, we were able to narrow down the name of my tablemate's date. It was she who had been the principal invitee and a longtime acquaintance of Mary's. While Mary and the friend had lost touch, the woman had dutifully signed the guest register in the lobby. On line 27, in extremely legible penmanship, were the names *Cynthia Kinney* and *Rico Pagan*. I thanked Mary profusely and promised to let less time elapse before calling again. My stalker had a name! I spent the next hour on the Internet trying to fill in more information after the name—until a book signing obligation forced me to sign off.

I began my sleuthing in earnest again upon my return, but was thwarted at every juncture for several more hours. While I never expected Mr. Pagan to be listed in bold type in the Super pages, I had hoped for a hint that may lead to a clue and perhaps eventually a trail that ended in a jackpot. But Rico—if that had been the wedding guest's real name—had not left a single trace of his existence...at least not on any public pages of the Internet. I spoke with Natasha when she called and told her of my frustration. As usual, her advice was to the point and without frills.

"Don't vorry about name. You see heem, you kick his ass. But you be done when Natasha come home so vee go out to restaurant."

I thanked her for her sympathy and explained that two trainers at the studio were down with the flu and I would be there on Friday night until nine.

On Friday morning I woke up with several bright ideas. The first was to tell my story to my detective buddy Dan. During a mental rehearsal, however, I kept having difficulty with the beginning...A man whose name may or may not be Rico Pagan may or may not be following me in two different vehicles that may or may not be his. I elected to postpone story hour with Dan and move on to my next idea. Going back to my computer, I eventually signed up on a website that promised its members complete military records on any serviceman...past or present. The database did not contain anything about a Rico Pagan...but *Ricardo* Pagan had an entry below his name. He had enlisted in the Marines in 1968. He was honorably discharged in 1972—as a Sergeant. *Wonderful, the man knows how to fire a gun.* Had I know what an understatement that thought was, I would have avoided the studio like it was a wedding chapel.

I signed off and while pondering my next tactic, thoughts of the fitness studio kept pushing themselves to the forefront. After the events of the past several days, my anxiety level was at a three-month high. Among the myriad of benefits that I received from my workouts, a significant one is that I will never have to go on Xanax. My only two concerns as I left my house early on Friday afternoon was the Taurus/van fleet and which CD I would pop into the player upon my arrival. Every possible observation spot on the peninsula was devoid of any suspicious vehicles and I relaxed and visualized my entire workout once on the freeway. When I got there the "joint was hoppin'." I got my own routine in and worked with clients nonstop until 8:45.

After the last client left, the sole remaining trainer there was a tall, classically beautiful blond named Jackie Scafone and she had a new hunk—whose first name was Scott—waiting for her at home. I teased her about a possible marriage to a man who, if he assumed her surname instead of vice versa, would be named Scott Scafone. I sensed that Jackie thought I was hysterical, even as she fought to suppress her laughter. Although I knew that she would have sat and listened to my witticisms all night—and hung on every word—I asked her if she wanted me to lock up so that she could leave early. She bolted out the door at a run, and I saw the glow of her taillights before I had set the studio's rechargeable phone back in its cradle. The studio dimmed considerably after I clicked off three banks of lights and some of the auxiliary lighting along the back wall. I turned off the sound system as I put on my jacket, grabbed my Beretta, and tucked it underneath. The studio was not far from the main road. I was just beginning to push open the glass front door when a car backfired and I tensed automatically as I ducked down several inches.

I had given the parking lot the once over from inside the darkened studio, but now took a long look around before I began to feel reassured. I resolved to vary my exit routine from the front door to the back—beginning the next day. While I normally backed my vehicle into its parking spot, it was a habit that exposed the driver's door to the main road. But I had pulled straight in that afternoon, cutting my journey from the front door to only eight steps. I locked the front door, and before taking the first step of the eight, recalled that I had not checked the mailbox during the chaos of the afternoon.

It was affixed to the outer brickwork two steps to my left. I turned slightly and as I did so, my peripheral vision caught a tall figure racing across Jefferson Avenue toward my position. My jacket was already unzipped this time, and a quarter second later my hand was wrapped around the handle of my .45, leaving me the luxury of a full half-second to make a go/no go decision.

64

THE WHITE FORD E-150 cargo van was just one of the 100,000 vehicles that would pass through this section of I-94 today. The van could still be on its way to one of a million destinations from here. It was registered to one Dennis Maxey. But if Mr. Maxey had been made aware that he owned a white 2002 Ford van with 32,157 miles on the odometer *and* a California license plate, he would have been stunned. The van was so nondescript that it could have been bound for any one of these million destinations for ten thousand different reasons. It may have been delivering documents from a main office in Chicago to a branch in or around Detroit, Lansing or Grand Rapids. It might have been transporting computers, or monitors, or simply a few cases of floppy disks. The van could have been carrying glassware or antiques or something of comparable delicacy—that demanded more of the driver's attention than a commercial carrier could promise. The van looked like the sort that a contractor or repairman would purchase to carry the tools of his trade—that is, of course, before the ladder carrier was mounted or the name of his company was stenciled onto the side. In fact, the last possibility would have been the closest to the truth.

A contractor *was* driving this van and the tools of his trade were wrapped up and enclosed in the back. The cargo area contained two AR15 assault rifles, three stainless steel barrels of varying lengths, 30-round magazines, telescopic sights—both conventional and night vision—and noise suppressors to silence it all. Their lethal presence was enhanced by an assortment of handguns, knives, ammunition and a small carton of C-4 explosive with its own accompaniment of wiring, igniters, and timers. Obscuring it all were tents, sleeping bags, backpacks, and enough other camping equipment to outfit a small hunting party—or even set up a booth at a flea market.

It had been a long ride from the mountains in Eastern California to this stretch of I-94 in Southwestern Michigan. It had also been a long time since Rico had hunted human quarry for money…six months and two days, to be exact. The hitchhiker in Arizona didn't count, even though Rico would have accepted any premise upon which to deliver a death sentence to his passenger. Amid all of the discipline and self-control that Rico still possessed in such abundance after these many years, he still allowed himself this one bad habit. He picked up hitchhikers on these road trips not because he craved companionship of any sort, but because he could randomly select a *Homo sapien* life form to snuff out indiscriminately—without any chance of apprehension.

The young man—still a teenager perhaps—had been a real talker… had Rico ever had the inclination to speak. He grew even gabbier after he spotted the cargo hold full of camping equipment, inferring that Rico might be interested in loaning some of it out. His fate already sealed, the thin, scruffy traveler then threw the first shovelful of dirt on his own grave. He hinted that if Rico were to advance him a small sum of money, he would not go to the police in Flagstaff to report a stranger in a white van with a handgun lying on the floor beneath the seat. Rico had picked up the aspiring blackmailer along I-40 in the late afternoon. Together, they reached the Scenic Overlook 50 miles outside of Flagstaff at dusk. With darkness swiftly approaching, no other travelers had seen fit to stop. In one smooth motion, Rico scooped up the handgun and signaled to the now wide-eyed extortionist that his ride had ended and he should step out of the van immediately.

Babbling apologies and promises, the young man complied. With tears forming, the skinny hustler obeyed Rico and walked over to the hip-high stone wall that served as a safety barrier between the Scenic Overlook and the rocky canyon below. A ray of hope peeked through his clouds of remorse when Rico set the gun back under the seat, closed the door and walked over to the wall to stand by his disheveled companion.

Until recently, a common explanation for an older woman's hospital stay was that "Grandma fell and broke her hip." But medical researchers now have far more information about the bone porosity and brittleness that beset the human skeleton as it ages—especially that of older females as their estrogen levels diminish. There is thus increasing speculation in the medical community that Grandma did *not* fall and break her hip. Instead, a growing percentage of geriatric care professionals now believe that Grandma's hip broke and *then* she fell.

In the cool twilight outside of Flagstaff, on the same Scenic Overlook that had awed so many weary travelers, there could be only one logical course of events. Moving in a blur, Rico reached out and clasped the young man's thin neck with his right hand, embedding his thumb into the windpipe. His open-palmed left moved an instant later with the same blinding, practiced speed. Neither a punch nor a slap, the palm connected in a flash with his victim's right cheek and jaw, snapping the shocked and choking traveler's head to the left...and beyond. The vertebrae—C2 and C3 specifically—both split apart simultaneously under the wrenching force. The cracking noise sounded like a small tree limb in an ice storm but was lost in the winds that swirled near the walls of the canyon. As the body went limp, Rico's right hand still gripped the neck while the powerful left grabbed and lifted loose pant material just below the knee. With a seemingly effortless heave, Rico thrust his former passenger up and over the stone wall—to begin his acceleration to the canyon floor 3,000 feet below.

Unlike Grandma's mishap, there was only one inevitable sequence of events in this instance. Rico broke the hitchhiker's neck, and after being thrown over the wall, he fell.

The hitchhiker's death was not entirely without purpose, however. Until then, Rico had not extinguished a human life for over six months and the craving to do so had grown strong. If Rico were impatient to satisfy his urgent need to kill a man, his professionalism and discretion could suffer. With the demise of the hitchhiker, this need had abated back down to a tolerable level and he could turn his focus to the task at hand—unrushed by inner demons. From the data report supplied by Lieutenant Spina, Rico knew that the neutralization of this quarry might require a little more recon work than the average job. The extra funds that the Lieutenant had required from the client were certainly justified.

A straightforward job, with the target's complete itinerary furnished, was $50,000. But disposal of the body necessitated an isolation kill—and an absolute absence of witnesses. It also cost the client an extra $25,000. With the quantum leaps in modern forensics and the stiffening of sentences for co-conspirators, it seemed as though every client of late wanted to insure that the body would not be found. Every one of the last ten, in fact, had paid the extra stipend for their problem to just disappear without a trace, thus hindering the onset of any murder investigation.

This job had some interesting challenges. The target was armed, but so were many of the ones that Rico had killed over the years. A rifle round delivered from 1000 yards away always cancelled out any handgun. A private investigator had noted in a report that the subject had "some work history related violence," whatever that meant. If anything, Rico would welcome some hand-to-hand if it came down to that…although he was still certain the outcome would be the same. The report also noted that the subject's behavior was irregular and erratic, that he avoided isolated areas at night, and his regular hours of employment could not be determined.

The avoidance of isolated areas at night could be a hindrance to a rapid resolution, but an extra day or two was already built into the figure that the Lieutenant quoted. And if the death of a witness could not be avoided, it would not be the first time that the completion of a job had involved some collateral damage. The report did furnish the subject's residential address and provided a work address that was deemed reliable.

The total quoted amount had taken into consideration all of the extra circumstances and travel expenses and the forwarding of $50,000 in cash as a deposit meant that the client had accepted the financial conditions.

The same Dennis Maxey who had no inkling about his ownership of the white van would have been doubly surprised had he known that it was loaded with firearms and explosives and parked behind a motel in Mount Clemens, Michigan at 10:00 A.M. Monday morning. Rico paid the clerk cash and flashed a driver's license to show that he was indeed Mr. Maxey. By 10:30 he had located the residence and was calculating the amount of exposure he would risk should he set up a stakeout in the proximity. By 10:40 some recon work revealed that the target lived on a peninsula and—by automobile at least—there was only one way off. Rico experimented with several observational positions, none of which he found to be even remotely suitable. There was only one route leading to the target's home, and the strips of land on either side were extremely exposed. On one side, three miles of the route was Selfridge Air Force, Army, Marine, and National Guard Base—complete with barbed wire fence, motion sensors and camera surveillance. Between the fence and the road, any land had been denuded of vegetation. On the other side, concealment opportunities were still inadequate. The terrain was predominately river and guardrail, punctuated by huge open plots of undeveloped land. Then, after a few residences, an underutilized marina followed the curve of the riverbank. It was the only piece of commercial property between the freeway and the target's residence. Every dock, boat trailer, and seagull was easily identifiable from the roadway by any passing car. Rico was going to have to earn every bit of the extra fee the Lieutenant had charged, but the truth was that this "urban hunting" had never been Rico's preferred type of job.

Rico spent the rest of Monday and all of Tuesday trying to learn more about the target's habits, only to conclude that they followed no set pattern. An attempt at surveillance work from the street that the target's house was on only resulted in a knock on the van's door after ten minutes from an elderly lady, asking if he was lost. A portion of Tuesday had been spent trailing the target as he ran errands in heavily populated areas. Rico hung back far enough to remain unobserved. Some recon work on Tuesday night roused a guard dog whenever Rico approached the property from the street. A canal behind the house was iced over and showed promise until Rico attempted to cross it. His weight caused the shifting ice to split, crack and reverberate between the steel seawalls in loud protests that sounded like gunshots. Spotlights came on in the back of three homes. A black Labrador named Buckwheat began barking furiously from the yard behind the targets and refused to re-enter the house despite the insistent calling of the blond homeowner. Rico quickly withdrew.

On Wednesday, Rico did not arrive at his observation post at the riverside marina until noon. While he had taken many precautions to remain inconspicuous, he had still felt the need to rent a car for a day or two using his false identification. He tucked the black Ford Taurus as far away from the road as the rocky bank of the river permitted. After only half an hour the target's ruby Corvette eased past Rico's post en route to his residence, catching Rico's full attention. He felt the weight of the silenced .22 in the holster beneath his left armpit, and briefly considered a takedown in broad daylight on the target's driveway. Quickly he remembered the elderly lady—and knew there were probably more—watching for any unusual movement down the deserted street. In addition, a takedown with the Ruger would involve getting the target's blood on the driveway—

thus instantly prompting a murder investigation. No... this job would have to be done at night, so that a cleansing of the immediate area could be performed if necessary. Rico settled back in to wait, satisfied that the rented vehicle had brought him two additional days of cover. Ten minutes later he removed his sunglasses to rub his eyes. His body had slowly begun to undergo changes over the past decade. His eyesight used to be fixed at 20/10 during his two tours of duty—and for many years afterward. A recent check showed that it was now only 20/20...but still a very good score for a man of 55. In Nam, when he was in country, he regularly went 48 hours without sleep—72 if he took catnaps—and still remained at 100 percent efficiency. Today, his level of alertness was feeling the effects of only a 36-hour period without sleep. The sunglasses still in his lap, Rico looked up as a red SUV pulled onto the narrow strip of land that served as the marina's parking lot. The driver's face was obscured by a baseball cap and the cell phone in his left hand. The SUV was right on top of the Taurus when Rico realized that the encounter was not by chance. The driver closed the cell phone to stare down at Rico as the early afternoon sun lit up his face. There was no time to re-don the sunglasses. It was the target of this job. He had switched vehicles and surprised Rico in a truck that he hadn't seen before. Rico saw a spark of recognition behind the target's eyes. For some vague reason, the target looked familiar to Rico as well. He looked too young to have been in one of Rico's units—maybe the guy had been part of the failed security team from one of Rico's past jobs.

Rico could not see either of the target's hands as he began a slow move to his own holster. For over 30 years now he had relied on stealth, planning, and surprise. He had none of those in his favor right now. The target might be holding a gun behind the door, waiting for a quick move, which Rico had no intention of making until the .22 was completely out of the custom holster. He would have to take the target out with a head shot, since he could only see that and the upper shoulders from his lower vantage point. For the second time in 15 seconds, the target of Rico's mission did the unexpected. Both the head and shoulders disappeared from Rico's line of sight. It was as though the guy had dropped something on the floor of his truck and ducked to the side to retrieve it. Rico used the instant to bring out the .22, exaggerating the motion slightly so that the noise suppressor cleared both the holster and his jacket without his eyes leaving the truck's window. For the third time in 16 seconds his quarry behaved erratically. Rico heard the click of the linkage and the idle kick down slightly before he actually saw the vehicle lurch into reverse and pull back and away. Rico did not like any of his three options. He could have transferred the handgun to his left hand and waited for the head to reappear, but he preferred to shoot with his right. Professional pride would not allow him to be placed in a situation where a miss was even a remote possibility. He could also exit his vehicle and await the head's reappearance, but he would immediately be exposed to counterfire and observation from not only the main road but the military base as well. Rico liked his last option least of all. The Taurus keys were in the ignition. Now that he had been made, he could chase down the SUV and deliver a head shot. But the superior weight of the SUV would put Rico at a disadvantage should the target decide that he was driving a battering ram. All of Rico's training had taught him to wait until he had the upper hand. The target reached the road with only two quick peeks in the rearview mirror. Rico glanced down at his own chest, wondering if the target had seen the butt of the semi-automatic sticking out of his jacket. Just as quickly, he ruled it out. Rico had tried it in front of a mirror from a dozen different angles years ago. No, this guy was just squirrelly and unpredictable. He would have to be taken at night. In a shower of mud and gravel, the target repointed his truck in the direction of his house and exited the zone. Rico started the Taurus and left the area for the remainder of the day to recalculate his strategy back in his motel room.

On Thursday Rico slept, exercised, and returned the rental car.

On Friday morning, Rico began his recon of the target's work address. The employees seemed to unlock and enter only through a front door facing the main road of Jefferson Avenue. There was a back door to a tiny parking lot that was walled in on three sides. None of the employees used the back lot, however, and Rico had to operate under the assumption that the target would not do so either.

Unlike the target's residential perimeter, the work address had an adequate location for setting up an observation post. A large restaurant directly across Jefferson that claimed to specialize in Cajun-style cooking had a huge parking lot in the rear. Fully half of the painted off areas had a suitable line of sight to the front door of the work address. In a brain filled with 53 years of killing scenarios and experiences, Rico's plan clicked quickly and easily into place. Tantamount to its success was the target's being at the work address after dark.

Methodically, Rico ran down the checklist: Opportunity, positioning, implementation, execution, disposal, and cleanup.

Opportunity was the only one that Rico had little control over. The target had already made him once…letting it happen again would reduce opportunity. It might take a day or a week, but if the address was still good, there would be a time when the target presented himself at night.

As far as positioning, Rico knew that he would have to remain fluid. If the restaurant was busy, the lot would be fuller and Rico could set up near the back. Even a noise-suppressed shot of 350 yards would be very routine with only the 20-inch barrel and a nightscope. An inhibiting factor would be the amount of SUVs parked in the line of sight…but Rico only needed an opening between them the width of a .223 caliber round.

Rico's weapon of choice would without doubt be one of the AR15s with the muzzle silencer. He would have preferred to fire out the back by simply leaving one of the doors ajar, but to do so would have meant parking the white van in a manner inconsistent with every other vehicle in the lot. Somehow, Rico had already drawn attention to his position at the marina—and he would not do so again. He would take his shot through the open passenger window from the driver's seat. This would also expedite repositioning the van if collateral interference blocked his line of sight.

Execution would have to be performed in a very specific area. It would necessitate dropping the target when he was between two parked vehicles...or between his vehicle and the building. Rico estimated that he would need a full two minutes to swoop down into the lot to begin the disposal process by tossing the body in through the back doors of his van. A chance discovery of the body would be greatly increased if it was lying in the middle of the parking lot. Lake Huron was only 50 miles to the north, and its deep waters should readily accept the weighted corpse.

Only if disposal went well would Rico address the last item. The garden hose coiled in front of the building looked long enough to reach to any part of the parking lot to hose away any bloodstains on the asphalt—provided the evening temperature stayed above freezing. There would be outlying areas of Detroit Metropolitan Airport that boasted of inexpensive long-term parking without TSA cameras installed everywhere. Eventually, the dead target's SUV would be found and speculation could begin in earnest from that point forward—the contractor would be long gone by then.

Rico began his vigil at one o'clock. At 1:30 a smirk played across his features as the target pulled into the parking lot across the street. The SUV headed front first into a slot near the glass doors, giving Rico only a three foot wide window in which to sight and get off a round from his current position. If the target waited until nightfall to exit, the small space would be more than enough.

By 6:30, the light in the business made everything visible through the large glass windows across the front of the building. Unless the target now exited the building with several people, he had missed the chance to return home alive. As Rico checked the sightings on the night scope, he watched the subject move about inside the business. While some of the people stood in front of, or moved past the windows without hesitation, Rico could see that the target never did. He always seemed to keep a piece of the exercise equipment between himself and the windows, as though he thought this simple habit could thwart the death that waited outside. *But death can show patience, too.* The dinner crowd began to troop into the parking lot of the restaurant with greater frequency, interrupting Rico's line of sight every minute or so. But Rico would only need a quarter of a second to send a 75-grain round hurtling on a direct path toward the building. Through the scope, Rico checked the hours posted on the door. The business closed at 9 P.M. If the target intended to wait until then and was the last to leave, his fate was sealed. Rico watched the target through the scope. If the target felt a measure of safety behind the upright steel posts of the exercise equipment, he was foolish. Rico had financial reasons for not taking the subject down where he stood, and the distortion of the older glass windows offered more protection than the equipment.

Rico had learned long ago to factor this distortion into his shot when a target presented an opportunity behind the windows of an older building. He had discovered that glass is actually a frozen liquid, and as such had a tendency to "flow" downwards over many years. The pattern to this flow was arbitrary, and could result in a slight refraction of an image behind the glass, like looking through a misground lens. Thus, the actual position of a target inside an older building could be misleading given the great distances from which Rico preferred to fire. His research material had stated that the thickness of the window glass in some structures of more than a century old could vary by as much as an inch from the top two inches to the bottom two. But Rico had combed the antique stores until he had accumulated enough panes to justify a trip to the remote area where he liked to "sight in" new equipment. He fired at targets behind the glass from 250 to 1000 yards until he had a "mean average" of the refraction variables in his mind. Right now, at 250 yards, the refraction rate of the 40-year-old glass that his scope and AR15 were directed at was negligible. With one squeeze of the trigger, the target was a dead man. But Rico waited.

He began to estimate the target's height—he measured and remeasured the target's stride. Rico imagined the target locking the door, turning to his right, and taking his last stride on earth. Rico picked out the four bricks on the outside wall that would be covered by the target's head after that initial two and a half-foot step. He sighted until the mortar where the four met was in clear relief in his cross hairs. And a head shot was the undisputed choice. The sooner the brain could be turned into a gelatinous mass by the high velocity round, the sooner all electrical activity would cease. The heart would stop pumping blood onto the asphalt. The hose would wash away most of the blood and brain matter from the wall and lot until only the most sophisticated investigator would think to perform a residual test in that area. By then, the body would be long disposed of beneath 90 feet of water.

That this process would be set in motion by a squeeze of the trigger was not entirely accurate. The trigger of this rifle did not need to be squeezed. The sensitivity of its mechanism had been modified to a dangerously light specification. Rico's trigger finger would only need to apply a hint of positive pressure to complete the first half of this job. The gun's modification was as close as Rico could come to killing with just a thought.

It was nearly 9:00 when the last customer left the business…the second to last witness. A blond woman left two minutes afterward…the last witness. Rico watched. Lights began to go out inside, row by row. Two freestanding lamps in the rear corners were extinguished by the now shadowy figure inside. Rico found the corners of the four bricks again with his right eye, and watched the shadow move around behind the windows with his left. It would not be a challenging shot, but sometimes Rico was compensated for just the kill…and sometimes for killing without a trace. The second half of the job would begin about 15 seconds after the target stepped outside and locked the door.

The passenger window of the van was halfway down. The top of the glass provided a good stable surface upon which to rest the tip of the gun barrel. There was no wind to rock the van. The shadow approached the door more consistently now. Rico's left eye caught a part of a shoulder. The shoulder was covered by a jacket. Phase one of the job would be over in seconds. There now. The target appeared in the doorway. He was reaching out to push on it. Rico's finger gently caressed the trigger.

Suddenly, Rico heard and felt the driver's door behind him open. The van's dome light bulb had long since been removed, but some additional light from the parking lot now dimly lit the floor of the van. Rico could not imagine why he had not shut the door properly. Quickly he spun around and reached out with his left arm to grasp the handle molded into the armrest. Something caught his eye— Rico froze. It was a hammerless, brushed-titanium pistol. It was being trained on him by a figure in a white ski jacket. The light from a tall orb in the parking lot was shining down from directly in back of the figure's head, leaving the face in shadow. The long blond hair suggested that the gun was being pointed by a woman, but the backlighting made her tresses appear to be surrounded by a halo. Suddenly the figure spoke, white teeth flashing.

"You mahst be Rico."

It *was* a woman. The words had no time to register, even if Rico were able to feel the emotion of surprise. His right leg already anchored, Rico withdrew his left arm and sent his left foot up in a well-aimed kick at the gun. But before it got there, a flash erupted out of the muzzle. A thousandth of a second later, a hollow point bullet slammed into Rico's nasal cavity and began eight different paths through his brain. His head snapped back and he fell onto the hard barrel of the AR15. Blood flowed out the front of his face until his heart stopped beating 20 seconds later. It was a shot that had been planned long before the kick had begun—in fact several hours ago as the Boeing 757 left the tarmac in Las Vegas. Opportunity, positioning, implementation, and execution. The woman in the ski jacket had run through the first four items of Rico's own checklist in just under three minutes. She slammed the door of the van.

After the coal black eyes had closed and the heart had ceased beating, the atmosphere in and around the van began to change. It was as though a clear bowl—100 feet in diameter—had been placed upside down and over the van, sealing it in.

The air inside the bowl felt as though oxygen had suddenly been pumped in—and every trace of humidity pumped out. It felt suddenly easier to breathe and somewhere, 2000 souls simultaneously let out a collective sigh. The woman in the white jacket did not pause to notice any of this effect, however, as she put her gun inside her pocket, wheeled around and ran. Forty strides took her to the front of the restaurant's parking lot, and a quick break in traffic allowed her to charge across the main road.

65

I IDENTIFIED THE running figure as Natasha and sheepishly removed my hand from my gun. I was about to form a question as to why she had parked across the street when she got close enough for me to see the excitement in her eyes. She ran toward me gracefully, like a cheetah at half-speed.

"Mock, Mock!" She was breathing harder from the adrenaline than the exertion. "Mock, plane land early. I decide surprise you here. When I in left turn lane, see vhite van across stritt. Go in lot. See vindow down and man with gun looking through scope at you."

I began to develop a sinking feeling.

"Natasha park behind van, open door quietly. He *vait* for you. I *know* ees Rico. Nobody around. I pull out gun. He cocky asshole, no lock door. I pull open and shoot heem!"

I looked across the street. The white van was easily discernable. I looked back at Natasha as she calmed her breathing. She said he had a gun. It was clearly self-defense. I needed to ask a question. I wasn't sure that there was any possible answer that I would find palatable. I steeled myself. "Where did you shoot him?" I almost cringed as I asked.

"I shoot son-av-beech between eyes."

"How many times?"

"Just vonce."

Based on Natasha's description of the entry wound's location, I thought that I would already know the answer to my next question. Perhaps I was just buying time while my thought processes caught up. "Was he moving or breathing when you left?"

"Oh, no Mock. The deeckhead bleed everyvhere. Beeg mess. He een hell now."

I recovered enough to make some decisions. I unlocked my SUV. I opened the front door of the studio and waved her inside. Working from a rapidly developing list in my head, I assigned two items to Natasha that needed to be located and loaded. I set about finding the rest myself. Four minutes later my SUV was loaded and Natasha and I eased across Jefferson Avenue into the restaurant parking lot. Natasha's car was where she had left it. A quick look around assured us that the white van had not drawn any undue attention. I approached the van cautiously from the rear, peeking through the back windows first. The back was half filled with canvas bundles. A still form bridged the gap between the two high-backed front seats. Slowly, I pulled on the handle for the right rear door while keeping my eyes fixed on the form in front. The door was unlocked and opened easily. The dome light stayed off and there was still no movement in front. I prodded the bundles with a fist—and climbed in—pulling the door closed from the inside.

Now I was at the point of no return so I moved quickly across the bundles to the front and found the man I had nearly confronted two days ago—as dead as Natasha had described him. He was wearing a thick black jacket and in the dim light the blood that had run down his nose, cheeks, and neck looked like dark ketchup. The keys were in the ignition. I took a deep breath and, gritting my teeth, gathered up the jacket material at each shoulder and pulled the torso up and into the back of the van. I repositioned myself rapidly in the back and grabbed the jacket again the same way. I dragged my lifeless tormentor completely into the back. I removed an intimidating-looking rifle and scope from the passenger compartment and laid it alongside Rico's body. When I rearranged some bundles to cover the body, I observed several long cases on the van's floor.

I scuttled between the seats, planted myself into the driver's seat, and started the van. I thought of asking Rico if I could drop him off somewhere, but decided to leave all of the "talking to the dead" to John Edwards. Rico had considerately left a full tank of gas and, carefully obeying all traffic laws, I led Natasha—who now drove my SUV—in an impromptu funeral procession to the nearest freeway. Forty-five minutes later we pulled into the long driveway that led to a former client's lakefront cottage. It was the first week in March, and I assumed that it would be vacant at 9:45 on a Friday night. It was—and every dwelling to the north and south appeared to be empty as well.

I backed the van over the frozen beach and retrieved a plastic tarp and four 25-pound steel weights that I had stored in a back room of the studio. It took nearly 15 minutes to bundle up the man who had planned to kill me with the tarp, weights, and some steel replacement cables from the machines at the studio. Lake Huron was still frozen along the shoreline, but I could see open water 200 yards out. I placed the large package on the ice and brought a ten-foot two-by-four out of my SUV. Rico's bundled corpse slid easily on the rough ice atop the smooth steel plates as I pushed it with the long piece of wood like a participant in a surreal shuffleboard tournament. With Rico leading the way, I pushed and scrambled for traction but made steady progress toward the open water. My bundle was about one foot from the water's edge when the ice cracked, split, and swallowed it with a splash.

Since no one showed up for Rico's funeral I did not feel compelled to say any words. Breathing heavily by now, I took my board and jogged carefully back to the white van. I led Natasha inland to the back of an old farmhouse with a "For Sale" sign on the front lawn. From my SUV, I took out a five-gallon gas can with over four gallons of gas in it. Two gallons would have soaked the front passenger compartment and seats thoroughly—four was definitely overkill. I laid the ten-foot board down and dribbled a trail of gasoline along its length, giving it a moment to soak in. Leaving the driver's door of the van open, I propped up one end of the board onto the gasoline-soaked driver's seat. I used a butane lighter to light the other end of the board like a long wooden fuse and backed up quickly as the flame raced up the board. Five seconds later I was sitting next to Natasha and she dropped the SUV into drive as the van ignited with an impressive roar. We were half a mile away down the country road when I saw a second fireball ignite in the sideview mirror as the van's gas tank erupted. From two miles away I could still see the glow of the second one and speculated as to whether our activities had awoken any of the distant neighbors in the remote area. By 10:20 P.M. we were on our way back to the studio.

Natasha kept her eyes on the road as we hurtled south on the freeway. I studied her for a moment. She did not seem shaken by what she had done earlier—or our disposal mission afterwards. I wondered if her stoicism was an act as she fought with her true emotions. Her fierce brown eyes yielded no clues. Her perfect jaw was neither clenched nor slack—a sign that she was thinking about something. Perhaps she was contemplating the finality of the taking of a human life. She might have concerns that an investigation of the remnants of the van would point in our direction at some juncture in the future. She might be wondering if simply blaring her horn might have distracted Rico long enough for her to call me and warn me to duck for cover. These situations probably required a unique kind of grief counseling, and I felt a growing sense of frustration at the lack of anyone I could turn to that could help Natasha through this. I did not know what kind of a shot Rico was, but judging by the ordnance that I had found and confiscated from beneath the bundles, Natasha had saved my life. I was experiencing a need to express my gratitude and assure her that I would help her to deal with any remorse she may feel during the ensuing days or weeks. Her beautiful but hard exterior might even now belie a woman who had been through a traumatic experience and was emotionally shaken to the core. My approach to opening up a dialogue would have to be gentle and show that I was receptive to her innermost thoughts and worries.

"How do you feel?" I asked her.

"Natasha hungry," she answered.

"Do you think that you'd be able to keep something down?"

She looked at me as though I had just announced that I was Mary Poppins.

"Natasha hungry two hour ago before shooting that preek. Now Sy Thai restaurant closed. Keetchen at Crews Inn closed. All is left is Travis Burger."

My inadequacies at discovering where she was emotionally with the evening were bubbling to the surface. After all, professional counselors had many years of schooling in psychology and human behavior—not to mention internships and other heavily supervised learning experiences—before they were turned loose to practice on real patients. Even then, sometimes the best ones failed to breach the walls that some patients had built around themselves.

I decided to try another tactic.

"Boy, whoever hired that guy must have been pretty mad at me."

"You theenk you know who pay Rico?"

"Yes, I do. And it is that person who is ultimately responsible for what you had to go through tonight."

"Mock, if you knew vhat asshole hire Rico then you should beat sheet out of heem or shoot hees ass too! Natasha gone five days. Come back and just vant to surprise you and go to restaurant." She turned to face me as she drove. "You always nice to Natasha. That Rico preek try to take you away from me. Try to make Natasha sad. Rico sent from hell to keel you. Natasha send heem back. *Nobody* take you away from Natasha. If they try, I keel them too!"

I decided that we had just experienced a real breakthrough session and to drop the entire matter for a while.

Visit Marksteelbooks.com to:

- Order autographed copies—shipping is free!

- Learn about book signing events—these are updated regularly

- Find a retailer near you

- Monitor the progress of the action-packed sequel!